ANGEL SOULS AND DEVIL HEARTS

CHRISTOPHER GOLDEN

ACE BOOKS, NEW YORK

THE BERKLEY PUBLISHING GROUP
Published by the Penguin Group
Penguin Group (USA) Inc.
375 Hudson Street, New York, New York 10014, USA
Penguin Group (Canada), 90 Eglinton Avenue East, Suite 700, Toronto, Ontario M4P 2Y3, Canada
(a division of Pearson Penguin Canada Inc.)
Penguin Books Ltd., 80 Strand, London WC2R 0RL, England
Penguin Group Ireland, 25 St. Stephen's Green, Dublin 2, Ireland (a division of Penguin Books Ltd.)
Penguin Group (Australia), 250 Camberwell Road, Camberwell, Victoria 3124, Australia
(a division of Pearson Australia Group Pty. Ltd.)
Penguin Books India Pvt. Ltd., 11 Community Centre, Panchsheel Park, New Delhi—110 017, India
Penguin Group (NZ), 67 Apollo Drive, Rosedale, North Shore 0632, New Zealand
(a division of Pearson New Zealand Ltd.)
Penguin Books (South Africa) (Pty.) Ltd., 24 Sturdee Avenue, Rosebank, Johannesburg 2196,
South Africa

Penguin Books Ltd., Registered Offices: 80 Strand, London WC2R 0RL, England

Excerpted material from Robert Service's poem "The March of the Dead" from *The Best of Robert
Service* copyright © 1907, 1909, 1912, 1916, 1921, 1949, 1950, 1951, 1952, 1953 by The Putnam
Publishing Group. Copyright © 1940 by Robert Service.

ANGEL SOULS AND DEVIL HEARTS

An Ace Book / published by arrangement with the author

PRINTING HISTORY
Berkley mass-market edition / July 1995
Ace mass-market edition / November 1998

Copyright © 1995 by Christopher Golden.
Cover art by Craig White.
Cover photo of "Post Stamp" © Madlen/Shutterstock.
Cover design by Diana Kolsky.

ISBN: 978-0-441-01946-5

ACE
Ace Books are published by The Berkley Publishing Group,
a division of Penguin Group (USA) Inc.,
375 Hudson Street, New York, New York 10014.
ACE and the "A" design are trademarks of Penguin Group (USA) Inc.

PRINTED IN THE UNITED STATES OF AMERICA

13   12   11   10   9   8   7   6   5   4

*Look for all
the Peter Octavian novels
from Ace Books*

OF SAINTS AND SHADOWS

ANGEL SOULS AND DEVIL HEARTS

OF MASQUES AND MARTYRS
(December 2010)

THE GATHERING DARK
(February 2011)

WAKING NIGHTMARES
(April 2011)

For my son, Nicholas James Cody Golden.
I now have a measure by which to judge myself:
his eyes.

Nothing will ever mean so much.

Acknowledgments

As always, thanks to my lovely wife, Connie, whose understanding truly baffles some people, and whose enthusiasm for the work often equals my own. Thanks, also, to . . .

Lori Perkins, who worked tirelessly to prepare me, emotionally and financially, for fatherhood.

Ginjer Buchanan, who *asked* for a sequel.

Everyone who read the first book, and still wanted to read this one.

And finally, of course, to my family and friends, who have continued to support and encourage me, often against their better judgment, and some of whom believed from the beginning.

"The world is full of other things. Some are friendly, some aren't."
—JONATHAN CARROLL, *Outside the Dog Museum*

"The hours go by like minutes, and the shadows come to stay."
—The Eagles, "Wasted Time"

"While the camp fire held out to burn, the vilest sinner might return."
—WILLIAM F. CODY, *The Life of Buffalo Bill*

PROLOGUE

The cruel war was over—oh, the triumph was so sweet!
  We watched the troops returning, through our tears;
There was triumph, triumph, triumph down the scarlet glit-
    tering street,
    And you scarce could hear the music for the cheers.
And you scarce could see the house-tops for the flags that
    flew between;
    The bells were pealing madly to the sky;
And everyone was shouting for the soldiers of the Queen,
    And the glory of an age was passing by.

And then there came a shadow, swift and sudden, dark and
    drear;
    The bells were silent, not an echo stirred.
The flags were drooping sullenly, the men forgot to cheer;
    We waited, and we never spoke a word.
The sky grew darker, darker, till from out the gloomy rack
    There came a voice that checked the heart with
      dread:
"Tear down, tear down your bunting now, and hang up sable
    black;
    They are coming—it's the Army of the Dead."
      —ROBERT SERVICE, "The March of the Dead"

*Humanity is jaded, that is true. At the dawn of the twenty-
first century, the capacity of human society to accept the ex-*

1

*traordinary, the incredible, the fantastic, has reached almost
infinite proportions. Less than five years ago, aided by a
nearly omniscient media, the world discovered the existence of
the Defiant Ones, known in the western lexicon as vampires.*

*Of course, humanity's initial reaction was fear, and rightly
so in many cases. But one of the Defiant Ones is a master
showman, a legend named Will Cody, known to millions
around the world as Buffalo Bill. Cody's natural rapport with
the media, and the CNN news reports and video footage
clearly showing the vampires as victims in the terrible conflict
that destroyed the city of Venice, turned things around.
Though these beings continue to refer to themselves as vampires, Cody has engendered within the world press the use of
the term "shadow." Once used by the Church to describe all
supernatural beings, the word is now the politically correct
referent for a vampire.*

*A United Nations probe guided by myself and the de facto
leader of the shadows, Meaghan Gallagher, exposed to the
public eye an ancient Roman Catholic conspiracy to destroy
the shadows, as well as Catholic control of other supernatural
elements through the use, incredibly, of magic. Rome, of
course, denied all charges, putting the blame on international
terrorists and a small sect within the church. But that was
mere fantasy. In the wake of the Pope's murder and the Venice Jihad, human governments and religions had no choice
but to ignore Vatican claims. The UN ordered its own investigation.*

*Vatican City shut its doors. Threats of force were empty,
and Rome knew that. Regardless of what might have been
suspected, the Roman Catholic Church was a monolithic figure, against which any open aggression would have been reviled the world over. Military solutions were, of course, ruled
out.*

*Still, the damage was done. The first to splinter, to nobody's
surprise, was the United States. Declaring themselves the
American Christian Church, the formerly Catholic U.S. clergy
avoided the use of the word "Catholic" altogether. Around*

the world, diplomatic ties were cut, Vatican ambassadors sent home. In time, Vatican City became an island unto itself, impregnable yet alone. By the time the smoke rose declaring a new Pope, few noticed. The church will have to build itself anew, drag itself kicking and screaming into the twenty-first century, or die an excommunicant dinosaur.

Religions that worshipped the shadows themselves sprang up around the world, many quite naturally based on blood rituals, many rising from the ashes of the worldwide network of volunteers who had given their lives for centuries in a fanatical worship of some of the darkest elements of vampiric society.

It was a PR nightmare.

Alexandra Nueva, one of the heroes of Venice, testified in Congress and before international governments, spearheading efforts to create a justice system to control errant shadows. Today, all shadows must obey the laws of the countries in which they declare primary residence. Many of them are excessively wealthy, but those that are not must make a living, and all must pay taxes and take responsibility for their actions.

What little analysis has been allowed by the shadows has shown that some of them are nearly indestructible, making it very difficult, and often nearly impossible, for human authorities to apprehend a shadow alone. Though loyalty to one another had prevented such things in the past, the necessity of living in the sunlit world of humanity requires that the law be enforced upon shadows by their own kind. The force charged with this mission is, of course, the Shadow Justice System. In the days before Venice, when the checks and balances of myth still held sway, a simple stake through the heart may have done the trick. Today, the more time that passes, the more invulnerable the vampires become, the more truth there is in the word "immortal."

Murder is not tolerated under any human legal system, but many shadows once survived through the murder of human beings. Fortunately that is no longer a necessity. As news of the shadows spreads, and more information becomes available about the effects of their bite, there seems to be no end to the number of new volunteers, new donors. Many seek the "gift" of death under the fang, to become shadows themselves, but apparently very few have received it. Of course, certain shadows were determined to live as they had in ages past, but in the new century, with satellite tracking and instant media, these rebels, criminals now, cannot avoid justice.

Those were the developments of the first year after Venice, and it is easy to see how much they have affected us already. In the four years since, shadow culture has adapted to its new strictures, woven itself into the fabric of human society, and moved from front-page news to the Lifestyles section. As they used to say, back when I was a very young man, they're all the rage.

Will Cody said to me that "humanity has slowed its vehicle down as if to observe a terrible car wreck, and now it's moving on." In truth, the squabbles are incessant on Capitol Hill and in the laboratories on every continent. Humanity has learned a new excitement, a new fascination. We've been wishing for centuries for such a revelation, and now that it has come true, we have thrown wide the door to the unknown with a sense of daring adventure born of fear and fear alone.

And the politics continue.

Lazarus shut the book from which he had been reading aloud, Allison Vigeant's *Jihad*, a first-hand account of the battle between Roman assassins and the vampires who had gathered that year for the Venice Carnival. The selection he'd read was the afterword, by Dr. George Marcopoulos, a human who had become the shadows' ambassador to the U.N. Lazarus thought Vigeant had scored quite a coup by including the ambassador's contribution. The Stranger, on the other hand, was less than impressed.

"No matter the uncertain tone of his words," the Stranger said, tapping the arm of his chair, "it is clear Marcopoulos believes we will continue to be integrated, that left to our own devices, we will blend into the world until one day we become as invisible as before. Also clear, however, is that he fears this will not happen, that the future will be far less, hmm, ordered.

"I would like to tell this man that his worst nightmares, his most unsettling fears *are* true. Though he whistles in the dark with his words of caution, he does not believe them. But the time for invisibility has passed, for better or for worse. No matter our name, we have returned to the sunlight at last. We'll never be able to hide in the shadows again. If chaos is our get, then so be it."

The Stranger had been speaking almost to himself, staring at nothing, but now he looked to where Lazarus stood in the door to the useless kitchen, awaiting a response.

"So now what?" Lazarus obliged. "Do we sit back and watch time go by?"

The Stranger stood and went to the window, where the hot Greek sun was finally beginning to sink back into the sea.

"Gallagher, Cody and Nueva," the Stranger said and shook his head. "Even Hannibal in his twisted way. Despite the burden that this . . . integration has laid upon their shoulders, they still find time to pursue Octavian's quest, to search for an answer to his final question. *Find out what we are*, Octavian instructed them before he went through the portal to Hell."

"He was beginning to suspect," Lazarus said as he joined the Stranger by the window.

"Oh, yes," the other said, the corners of his mouth turning up slightly. "He would never have made the final connection, though. Even with the assistance of every scientist in the world, there is no way our brother and sister shadows will ever discover their heritage on their own."

"You plan to tell them, then?"

"When they're ready, Lazarus. When they're ready."

"And what do we do in the meantime, my friend, now

that we have joined the world, now that our hunters hunt no longer?"

The smile disappeared from the Stranger's lips. The burning light died in his eyes, and another, colder light grew there.

"You are mistaken, Lazarus," the Stranger said. "The struggle of our people is far from over. And as quickly as the humans opened their arms to us, on the day our existence puts them in danger they will strike a match to the pyre of our kind.

"And believe me, that day is coming."

The Stranger turned and threw open the doors to the balcony. In the dying sunlight, he underwent a most fluid, graceful change, and took wing. Lazarus had been given instructions, but the Stranger kept his destination a mystery even to his one true friend. The words floated, a ghostly whisper in the air, and Lazarus could not brush them away.

They will strike a match to the pyre of our kind.

Lazarus knew that could mean only one thing.

Human and vampire would become hunters again.

CHAPTER ✦ ONE

Salzburg, Austria, European Union.
Monday, June 5, 2000, 3:27 P.M.:

"It's actually quite intimidating," Allison said. "I mean, the way it just sits up there, observing the city. Ominous, really."

"Oh, I don't know," Will answered. "I'm certain when it was built it was quite reassuring. A fortress of that size and strength must have allowed people to sleep much better at night."

They walked through Mirabell Gardens, in the city of Salzburg, Austria, hand in hand. Allison Vigeant, a reporter who had once used the name Tracey Sacco, and her lover, Will Cody, who'd been known by many names. She was a petite blond woman with hazel eyes, and he was a rugged-looking, bearded rogue. His brown hair had been cut short only days before, and he still felt slightly naked. He was a shadow, and she decidedly human and determined to stay that way. They were lovers, and this rendezvous in one of Europe's most romantic cities was their first real vacation in nearly a year.

Five years earlier, Allison had been conducting a CNN undercover investigation into what at first appeared to be nothing more than a particularly vicious cult. But the Defiant Ones had turned out to be much more than that. They were vampires.

7

Not the vampires of myth, to be sure, but the Defiant Ones, now simply called shadows, were the basis for that myth. Like humans, however, they were not all of one nature. Some were vicious and cruel, others kind and helpful, and many, oh so many, in between. One and all they gathered each year, with humans who had volunteered to feed their red hunger, in New Orleans, Rio, a small village in Germany, a rotating slate of a dozen or more cities around the world. Five years ago it had been Venice, and it was there that the vampires' ancient enemy, the Roman church, had attacked them in force. The lives of the Venetian people were forfeit, as was the city itself.

The vampires, or shadows as the world called them afterward, had been victorious, and Allison, with her cameraman Sandro Ricci, got it all on film. Yes, Allison had been present for the Venice Jihad, and if it had not been for her chance meeting with Will Cody, things might have gone quite differently in the months that followed. But she had met him, and Cody had changed her thinking completely regarding his kind, regarding shadows. And she was not alone. It had been her interview with Cody and Peter Octavian, coupled with footage of the vicious and darkly magical attacks by the clergy, that solidified the world's opinion of shadows.

They were victims, scapegoats, imperfect creatures, so much more than human, and yet so similar; deadly exaggerations of human nature, human interaction, all too easy for people to understand when presented correctly. And Allison was sure to present them correctly. The Venice Jihad changed the world, for humans and shadows both. And it changed Allison's world, bringing her international fame.

And fortune, of course, let's not forget that. Between her CNN salary and the royalties coming from her book, *Jihad*, she had plenty of disposable income these days.

After serving as anchorwoman for CNN for sixteen months, she returned to the field, reporting from six continents on legal, political and social issues affecting the shadows. The travel was a huge perk, and Will met her whenever and wherever he could. She had always been gravely serious, but now she had matured enough to lighten up, to have a good time.

On the other hand, she was pretty certain that Will had regressed. Allison imagined that the Will Cody she saw now was the exuberant, childish and magnanimous Will of his heyday, more than a century before, when he was known as "Buffalo Bill." He rarely got tired, and when he did he still hardly ever slept. Which was fortunate, because Will had dedicated himself to three jobs simultaneously. For Alexandra Nueva and Meaghan Gallagher, his blood-sister and her lover, he was searching for the vampire named Lazarus, and an answer to the mystery of their origin. For the shadows he was an international media spokesman, and for himself, finally, there was the show!

As a master showman in the late nineteenth and early twentieth centuries, Will had acted in plays and written books. He had created the "Wild West Show," a world-traveling exhibition of riding, shooting and dramatization which, though exaggerated to near mythic proportions, still informed the world's perception of the American West. He had been a pioneer in the development of the motion picture, bankrolling and appearing in one of the first feature films.

Well, the Wild West Show was back—Allison had covered it for CNN—and now Will had made her book, *Jihad*, into a film, producing and directing it himself. They had spent a month-and-a-half shooting it, and then another six weeks in London editing the monster, and now they were, for real, on vacation. Time to just enjoy each other.

Allison truly loved Will, a good and decent man by any estimation, although most of the world would not admit he even was a man. No matter, though, they were happy. She had become a sort of financial advisor to him, because though he never had trouble making money, he had a terrible time hanging on to it. They talked about getting married someday, but there were no laws as yet to govern such a union, and with Will's involvement in the SJS, the Shadow Justice System . . . they'd decided to wait. And if that time never came, well, Allison was happy.

Now, hand in hand, they walked through the beautiful Mirabell Gardens, deep breaths drawing in the scent of the flowers and the unseasonably nippy air. They marveled at the design of the garden and its colors, the architecture of the palace, Schloss Mirabell, home to the city's mayor. They chuckled over the statuary, especially the gnome-like creatures carved from stone, and sat by the fountain. They talked and laughed, kissed and held each other close.

And yet their eyes, like the eyes of every other visitor to Salzburg, were always drawn back to the Festung Hohensalzburg, the huge fortress overlooking the city from its southern edge, across the river.

"You're right, darlin'," Cody said finally, giving her a little squeeze. "The place is creepy. Still, it has a power and a . . . a majesty that is quite attractive."

"Okay, okay," she said, giving in. "Tomorrow morning, first thing, we'll go."

"Promise?"

"I promise. God, what a baby!"

"Why, madam," Cody said, lapsing into the cadence of the American West, "I do believe that was an insult."

"Believe whatever you want, Buffalo—"

"Don't say it!"

But she was off and running, with Cody in pursuit. As much as he was still trading off the nickname of his human life, with his books and the Wild West Show, that was for fun. In real life, he hated the name, and she knew it.

"You're in trouble now!" Will shouted after Allison as she headed for the gate and the road, Rainerstrasse, beyond.

Salzburg, Austria, European Union.
Monday, June 5, 2000, 7:26 P.M.:

Humanity had been surprised to find out how few shadows there actually were. When CNN had initially broken the news of their existence, most had an unrealistic reaction, honed from decades of first cold war, then terrorist paranoia—*"They're* among us, everywhere." In truth, Cody guessed that the shadows numbered in the mid-five figures somewhere. Not a lot of vampires to go around.

Still, most major cities had a few, and so it was not surprising that he and Allison ran into a shadow on the street outside their hotel that evening.

"Will Cody, right?" the shadow asked.

"That I am, sir. And you are?"

"John Courage, Mr. Cody, and pleased to meet you."

"John Courage?" Allison smiled. "As in, 'give me a pint of Courage'?"

"Yes, ma'am. That's right," Courage said, returning the smile with his own, self-deprecating version, then turning his attention back to Cody. "But that particular brew was named after *me*, not the other way around. And aren't I modest?"

They laughed politely, good-naturedly.

"I live here in Salzburg, now," Courage told them. "I'm a musician. Twice a week I play sax at the Urbanikeller, the jazz club."

Even though he shouldn't have been, Cody was surprised. They were really doing it, he thought. Shadows were actually merging with human society. Will smiled at the boy, who might well have been hundreds of years older than he was.

"What time's your show tonight?"

"Ten P.M."

"We'll be there," Allison said, reading Cody's intentions.

"I'm flattered, Ms. Vigeant," John Courage said sincerely.

"You know me?" she asked.

"Shouldn't I?" Courage replied, and raised an eyebrow. "Say, if you two are headed to dinner, I have a wonderful tip. Try the Peterskeller, off Kapitelplatz by St. Peter's Cemetery."

"It's that good?" Allison asked, knowing any meal was really for her rather than for Cody, and thinking how courteous it was for this shadow even to mention dining, since his kind needed such sustenance not at all.

"It's incredible!" Courage said. "I'm told the food is wonderful, but the atmosphere is . . . It's the oldest restaurant in the country, about twelve centuries old, and local legend says it's where Mephistopheles met up with Faust."

"Sounds great," Allison said, and meant it.

"Say, John," Cody began, "why don't you come to dinner with us?"

Courage looked surprised and pleased by the offer.

"Really I'd love to, but I've got a lot to do before tonight's set. Please do come by the club, though. It would be an honor, really."

Will looked at Allison, who nodded.

"We'll be there," he confirmed.

Courage continued on his way, and Allison and Will left their hotel, the Goldener Hirsch, behind. They walked along Getreidergasse, window-shopping the whole way, chattering about the wonders of the Old City, as that part of Salzburg was called. They had arrived late the night before, and that day had explored the right bank of the Salzach River, the Makartplatz, Mirabell Gardens and the shops along the winding cobblestones of Linzer Gasse. Tonight, though, they wanted to stroll, not explore. On their map, they found the location of Peterskeller, the restaurant John Courage had suggested, and now they turned their feet in that direction.

In Residenzplatz, they passed the archbishop's palace and the Salzburg Cathedral with little more than an appreciative glance. Music played somewhere in the background, Mozart, to be sure—the city was, after all, the composer's birthplace. The carillon bells of the Glockenspiel sounded out the harmony of 8 P.M. just as they reached Peterskeller, but all of that was for tomorrow, for the day. Now that Cody could experience both, he set the daylight hours aside for the trivia of life. Nighttime was for actual living.

The restaurant was as wonderful as Courage had described it. Will and Allison had a chuckle over the shadow's name, and she threatened to call him "Bud Weiser" next time they met. Arm in arm, the couple passed through a courtyard with vaults cut right out of the mountainside, then ate in a brick cellar with extraordinary chandeliers. Allison was delighted with the flavor of the dumplings she had ordered, and she even convinced Will to try some of her cheese soup.

Later, as they made their way to the Urbanikeller to catch John Courage's ten o'clock set, Allison's eyes returned to the fortress, which towered still above their heads, above the city. She had been constantly aware of the huge castle, which could be seen from nearly any point in the city, ever present, ever vigilant.

"Even at night," she said to Will as they reached the club. "Even at night it watches."

"Maybe it's standing guard," Will suggested, grabbing her hand and squeezing as he opened the door to the place.

"Maybe," she answered.

But that's not how it feels.

Salzburg, Austria, European Union.
Tuesday, June 6, 2000, 11:42 A.M.:

Will and Allison sat down for a late breakfast in the hotel restaurant, though it was a lot closer to lunch. John Courage had played two sets the night before, and he was good enough that they stayed through the second. Between

sets, Courage joined them for a drink, and they both found
him refreshingly offbeat, even for a shadow. His self-deprecating humor was equally balanced by an often caustic wit,
and he seemed to know everything there was to know
about his adopted city. They returned quite late, and Allison slept in the next morning. Cody had found himself a
bit tired as well.

After brunch, the couple wasted no time making their
way to the base of the *festung*, the fortress of Hohensalzburg. There was a small tram that carried visitors to the
top, but after one too many pancakes, Allison insisted they
walk. Halfway up, she regretted it, but there was no going
back. Through the trees, as they made their way up the
incredible incline, they could see the sides of the fortress.
The sheer wall of the structure met almost precisely with
the edge of the cliff; taken together, they formed a several-
hundred-foot drop.

It was times like this when Allison felt her humanity
most. Though she worked out regularly, she had to rest a
couple of times on the walk up, and Will stood patiently by,
understanding but not sharing her discomfort. As they finally approached the massive gates, they got their first real
idea of the size of the place. Inside the fortress, yet still
walking up an incline, they found alleys and paths that
were almost streets, an open courtyard and a warren of
hallways and rooms which must have housed the many
soldiers stationed there over the centuries. Medieval art
and arms were on display in several rooms, but Will and
Allison found they had a common interest in the structure
itself.

Battlements and watchtowers loomed above the city, offering clear views of the Alps. Cannon bastions peppered
the walls, and the wind, even on a warm summer day,
whickered through them with cold, grasping breath. The
foundation of the fortress was begun in 1077, and the different areas of the castle completed over five centuries. It
was this feat, this achievement, existing in the structure

itself, that impressed them. Allison's creepy feelings about the fortress were gone, replaced with an emotion somewhat akin to awe. Even Will, who had been around much longer than she, was astonished by the immensity, the strength of the place.

"How much of this are we not getting to see?" Allison said, pulling on an iron grate which blocked their progress down a particular hall.

Will looked down at his feet, wondering whether there were rooms beneath them. Certainly the locked iron door kept them from exploring certain sections, maybe huge areas of the castle. It could be unsafe beyond that gate, he thought. Then again, the people who arranged these things weren't used to shadow tourists.

"Let's find out," he said, and reached for the lock.

Salzburg, Austria, European Union.
Tuesday, June 6, 2000, 2:07 P.M.:

Matt and Tammy Monahan had left their baby son home for the first time. Even though he was with Tammy's mom, they were still worried. Nevertheless, they were determined to enjoy themselves. Along for the ride were Tammy's brother, George Esper, and Jack Rice, a family friend. The group split up soon after entering the fortress, Matt and Tammy wandering off to see the art on display and Jack and George finding their way up to a windswept watchtower.

"Watchtower," George said. "Like Dylan."

He started to hum the song and strum air guitar, but George wasn't your usual air guitarist. He actually played.

"The Hendrix version is better," Jack said with certainty. "Dylan sucks."

"Bullshit" was George's only reply. He'd grown used to such statements from Jack, but he'd never been able to figure out if the guy was serious, or just busting his balls.

The two of them glanced furtively around and saw that

they were alone, save for a decidedly non-American couple several feet away. George pulled out a joint and lit it, taking a long puff before passing it to Jack.

"It would really suck if we got bagged up here," Jack said. "I mean, what's the local law?"

"Don't know," George said. "Just be cool. Don't attract attention."

They didn't.

"Hey, you know what I almost forgot?" Jack said. "Norm's got this rock collection thing going, pieces of stuff. The Berlin Wall, the Pyramids. He wanted me to get a piece of something, and this thing is fuckin' old."

George helped him look around, noticing that the stone walls and battlements, especially near the edge, were supplemented here and there with modern concrete. Chunks of the cement had fallen to the ground, and it was a simple task to find a big one.

"How 'bout this?" he asked.

"No, man," Jack said, as he continued his search. "It's gotta be somethin' from the oldest part, none of this cement shit."

Their search took them to an open doorway off to the left, and the floor within. Its surface was rough stone and dolomite chunks, and Jack knew they'd found what they were looking for. Now they just had to work a piece loose. He took a drag off the joint and handed it back to George, then kicked at several large pieces of rock that jutted slightly from the floor. After a few tries, he found a chunk a couple of inches wide that moved.

With his heel, Jack kicked the thing again and again, and it moved more and more. But it didn't come out. Apparently it was bigger than it looked. He had to stop for a couple of minutes as the couple on the watchtower came closer to them and then finally left. George tried kicking a bit, and then Jack took over again, going farther into the hall to lean against the wall and kick.

It happened on the fourth swing of his foot. One minute

Jack's back was firmly against the wall, and the next, as George watched, he disappeared through it.

"Jack! What the hell . . . ?" George moved toward the wall, but not too close. One of Jack's hands came back through, and George noticed for the first time that the wall had changed. Its color was almost silver, and its surface too flat, rippling like a pool of water where the hand broke through. George didn't want to have anything to do with this weird shit, but he and Jack went way back. George grabbed Jack's hand, scrabbling for a hold on the rough, stone floor. Bracing his feet, and holding that hand with both of his own, George pulled.

Jack moved forward, just barely, then stopped. To George it seemed as though the silver pool in the wall, whatever it was, *and I don't want to fucking think about that right now*, were jelly, or quicksand. Some kind of suction held Jack—wherever he was. And then, beyond that reflective surface, in which George could see his own face, beyond the quicksilver sand that held Jack in place, something tugged.

George was jerked roughly forward. He almost let go of his friend's hand as his boots slid over the stone, but instead his grip tightened. No way was he letting go. George slid farther, closer to the opening, and then noticed something that saved him from being pulled in right behind Jack. The opening in the wall was only so big, and on either side of it, the wall was still solid stone. Or at least it looked solid.

In an instant, George's feet were up, gripping Jack's hand and being pulled along, his ass cut and scraped by stone as he lifted his legs and planted his boots on either side of the opening. The muscles in his neck and back, in his arms and shoulders, strained for a few seconds, and then the opposing force, the one pulling Jack in, let up. It still wasn't easy, pulling him out of there, and George wasn't about to let go in case his tug-of-war opponent was giving him a false rest, but with a grunting effort, he did it.

Slowly, once his head and upper torso had emerged, Jack crawled out of the wall, over the struggling form of his friend, and lay still on the stone by his side. They both rose, slowly, panting, moving away from the wall. George looked up.

"My God, Jack, what the hell—" And then George stopped. Because the man he'd pulled out of the wall wasn't Jack at all.

Sure, he looked like Jack. Same killer baby blues, dirty blond hair and beard. Same clothes, same smile. But this was an older Jack, a haggard, hard-looking man with something lurking in the shadows of his face that Jack had never had.

"What's wrong with you?" George asked him.

"Not a blessed thing," not-Jack said in a voice that George had never heard before, a voice that scared him.

"In fact," he said as he moved around to put George between himself and the wall, "I've never felt better in my life. I feel *perfect.*"

Matt and Tammy came around the corner.

"What are you guys doing . . . ," Matt began, but he shut up when Jack turned to look at them.

Tammy saw it before any of them, even Jack, and she screamed. A huge hand shot out of the hole in the wall, clutching George like a child's doll, talons impaling his face, stomach and side. Tammy's was the only scream as her brother disappeared through the hole in an instant. Matt stared, mouth open wide, and Jack just smiled.

"Jack!" Matt finally said. *"Jack*! Do something!"

Matt ran to the wall, but by the time he reached it, it was only stone again, and he pounded his fists against it. When he turned, Jack was standing out on the watchtower with Tammy in his arms. She was sobbing loudly with her eyes closed. But Jack was staring directly at him, and as Matt started to move into the open, Tammy's crying began again. Jack lifted her, with incredible strength, and hurled her, wailing, out over the edge of the tower. From there, it was a straight drop to the trees five hundred feet below, and Tammy screamed all the way down.

Matt was on Jack in a moment, the two scrabbling on the stone floor of the tower. Matt was on top, and his hands locked around Jack's throat, choking him, but Jack stopped fighting back. Instead, he touched the bare skin of Matt's arm with one hand and the stone floor with the other hand and mumbled one word through his choking gasps.

Matt Monahan turned to stone, a statue, made from the same rock as the fortress itself, almost growing out of it. It was simple for not-Jack to pry himself loose from the statue's grip, breaking several stone fingers in the process. The statue looked quite alone. And somehow, too new.

"Well, this is an old castle," not-Jack said in his not-Jack voice. "And you, boy, have got to *look* old."

A hard roundhouse kick and the statue's head, a head which had once belonged to Matt Monahan, flew into the air and tumbled down the mountainside to join the corpse of his wife, broken and twisted at the bottom of the cliff, an offering to the fortress itself.

Above, the laughter began.

Salzburg, Austria, European Union.
Tuesday, June 6, 2000, 2:16 P.M.:

Just below the watchtower, in a crumbling hallway with large, open windows, an area off-limits for visitors to Festung Hohensalzburg, Allison Vigeant and Will Cody heard the screaming begin. As Cody searched for the fastest way out and up, Allison gasped and called for him to come back to the window. Only seconds had passed, but Tammy Monahan's body had already fallen too far for Will to rescue her, whatever form he took.

"Stay here," Will said to her, and Allison winced.

"I'll find my way up and meet you topside," she said. Will bit his lip.

"Please," he asked. "Stay here?"

"Five minutes," she said, and looked at her watch.

In seconds, a large raven flapped out of that window and took to the sky, circling above the fortress, the only bird in the sky. As he dipped among the wind currents at that height, Will Cody watched as the man who had been Jack Rice turned Matt Monahan to stone, then smashed the head from the statue's neck and sent it flying over the edge.

Sorcery, Cody thought, and the very idea chilled him, ruffling his feathers. For as far as he knew, the one book that held the secrets to such magic, *The Gospel of Shadows*, was safe in Meaghan Gallagher's possession. But this was magic, just the same.

The sorcerer moved away from the watchtower, back toward the main section of the castle, where dozens of tourists milled about the courtyard, ducking into hallways and rooms. He raised his arms to begin a spell, and Cody dove toward him, determined to stop whatever the magician had in mind. But as he flew, straight toward the man in T-shirt and blue jeans, a ripple ran through reality, an illusion taking hold, and the man changed. His clothes became black, blond hair turned white-gray, and his words picked up in rhythm, a new spell.

He turned.

It was Liam Mulkerrin.

Cody turned toward the sky, veering up and away before Mulkerrin could notice him, his mind in temporary shock.

No! he thought. *He's dead. I saw him die, and Peter with him.*

But he knew that was untrue. He had not seen Mulkerrin die, but pass through into the realm of the real shadows, the demons that had done the sorcerer-priest's bidding. And Cody's friend, Peter Octavian, had carried him there, apparently sacrificing his life.

But if Mulkerrin was alive?

He did a slow circle, keeping behind the sorcerer, and when he looked again, Cody saw the spirits rising.

From out of the stone beneath the frightened tourists'

feet, from the walls around them, ghostly apparitions oozed in wet clouds the color of parchment yellowed with age. They were dark things, yes, but not demons, not the shadows of hell. As they overtook men, women and children, each fell in turn, the apparitions disappearing within them. When the people rose again, seconds later, new intelligence burned in their eyes.

Will Cody looked closer, using other senses, senses born of all that was inhuman within him, to focus his vision. And he saw. The apparitions were just that—ghosts. The spirits of those soldiers, warriors who had served the prince-archbishops of Salzburg and had been stationed in the fortress, whose souls must have returned there, to the place of their greatest duty, after their deaths. Regardless of everything he knew to be true, Will Cody had never believed in ghosts. And yet here they were; Mulkerrin had called them to his service, and with the humans in the fortress as physical hosts for the spirits, the sorcerer now had a small force of slave warriors.

The question, Cody realized, was how he had done it. Mulkerrin had not had this ability before, or he would certainly have used it. Now he worked such magic with no visible effort? Wherever he had been, Cody thought, as he glided on raven's wings, he'd been busy.

And what of Octavian? Where did that leave *him*?

Cody made one final circuit, soaring higher, away from the castle, and prepared to return to the time-worn window where he'd left Allison.

Allison! What if the spirits were all over the castle and not just around Mulkerrin? He dove now, hurtling down toward that window, but just before he passed out of sight of the courtyard, he saw something out of place, something not an attacking apparition or a fleeing human, something subtle—

It can't be!

But he knew it was. Allison had ventured upstairs, not bothering to wait the five minutes, her reporter's instincts forcing her to break her word. She stood in the shadows of a doorway, and even now, as Cody crested the courtyard walls once again, she emerged into the light, to get a better look at what was happening.

Already, a dark and heavy cloud, the only true remains of a centuries-old soldier, drifted toward her as if it knew it had all the time in the world. After all, where could she run? And Allison, for all that she could see chaos had taken over, had not yet discovered the source of this anarchy. She had not yet seen Mulkerrin.

Where could she run? The question was moot; she wasn't running.

The raven, Will Cody, sped on, past the floating thing. He was larger than any raven the world had ever seen, and even now he changed, becoming something else, something completely new in the world. His talons grew larger, their sharp ends turning soft, strong. Before she truly knew what was happening, Cody had picked up Allison at the arms and carried her over the side, five hundred feet above the city.

Mulkerrin turned, hearing a woman scream, but did not see them disappearing over the side. Instead, he assumed some human had been so overwhelmed with the terrors he had raised, that she had thrown herself over the edge. He had taken over the mind and body of Jack Rice, who was, for all intents and purposes, dead. And yet, clad in illusion, it was Liam Mulkerrin's head that was thrown back, his mouth open wide, ringing with laughter. A maniacal gleam shone in the former priest's eyes as he surveyed his work, and he laughed again as he thought of the woman who had jumped to her death rather than serve him.

"Ah," he said and laughed, wiping tears from his eyes. "There's no place like home. There's no place like home."

He could barely catch his breath from laughing.

"No place like home."

CHAPTER ✦ TWO

Boston, Massachusetts, United States of America.
Tuesday, June 6, 2000, 7:45 A.M.:

The sun rose slowly over Boston, its heat marching inexorably forward, like the tide rolling in. It was the fifth day of the worst heat wave in a decade—over one hundred degrees by noon, and not less than eighty at night. Fortunately, there was air-conditioning in the Back Bay brownstone shared by Meaghan Gallagher and Alexandra Nueva. Though their shadow physiology was quite adaptable, and they certainly did not sweat much, or often, still the week had taken its toll. Even with the a/c on full blast, they were tired and slightly cranky.

"Come on, sweetheart, get your ass in gear," Alexandra said, and dragged Meaghan feet first out of bed.

"Noooo," Meaghan howled, pillow held over her head even as she slammed to the floor from the height of the mattress. "Ouch."

"Meaghan Rae Gallagher," Alex said, scolding, "we have got a video-conference with the shadow ambassador and the secretary-general of the United Nations in forty-five minutes. *You. Must. Get. Up!*"

Alex grabbed Meaghan under her armpits, pillow falling to the ground, and lifted her easily to her feet. At first Meaghan played dead, but then she whipped her face around to meet Alex's gaze, and spit her words like venom.

23

"Bitch! You couldn't let me sleep fifteen more minutes?"

"You don't have fifteen minutes," Alex snapped back, getting mad now. "And besides, you're dead. You don't need to sleep!"

A smile crept over Meaghan's face, as her feet finally took her own weight. She pulled Alex to her, pressing herself against the other woman. Meaghan's full breasts against her own reminded Alex that they were both naked. Meaghan's tongue snaked out, licking the ridge of Alexandra's chin, then her neck, and finally finding her lips. As their mouths met, Meaghan slipped a hand between Alex's thighs and began to stroke her there. Alexandra purred against her lover.

Meaghan turned her around, and began to lower her to the bed. Alex looked up into Meaghan's face, to share her pleasure, but was puzzled by the mischievous smile she saw there.

And then Meaghan dropped her, and Alex flopped onto the bed, already starting to laugh.

"Dead, am I?" Meaghan said, then she lifted an eyebrow, picked up her towel from a chair by the bed and headed for the shower.

"Well," Alex said, rising once again, her hand reaching down to rub where Meaghan's had been only moments before. "Maybe 'dead' was a poor word choice."

"Hey," Meaghan said, rushing to the bathroom as Alex followed, closing the distance between them, "I thought you said we didn't have fifteen minutes to spare."

"Not for sleep!" Alex said, kicking at the door Meaghan had locked behind her. It flew open, and Alex saw that rather than running the shower, Meaghan had begun to fill the big Jacuzzi tub they had installed. She was sitting on the edge of the tub, both hands on her left breast.

The hell with the office, Alex thought, *we'll take the vid-conference right here in the apartment.*

"Don't worry, sweetheart," Meaghan said. "I never start something I don't intend to finish."

Then there were no more words. Alex went to Meaghan, their kiss deep and full of truth and love, pushed her back into the tub and joined her there. They made love with purpose and without hurry.

Before the Jihad, before the world changed, their love would have seemed incredible. In the new world order, it was merely extraordinary. Meaghan: auburn hair and truly green eyes, her body subconsciously made near perfect by the shape-shifting ability all shadows shared. She had only become a shadow five years before, and yet she was one of the most powerful, both physically and politically. Before the Jihad, she had been a young, attractive professional woman, orphaned as a child and bored with her life.

Peter Octavian had taken her away from all that, made her a shadow and brought her into a war that changed everything, for her, for the world. And he died for it.

Alexandra: black hair and brown eyes, skin as dark and soft as sable. Tall and elegant, her heart made hard as diamonds by life in Karl Von Reinman's coven, she had also been a lover of Peter Octavian's. Later, she wanted to kill him. But the war had changed her as well; the loss of her lover, Shi-er Zhi Sheng, had threatened to shatter that diamond heart. Instead, Meaghan was there, and Alex felt alive again for the first time since Von Reinman had discovered her, a runaway slave not long off the trading ships, and brought her to the life of the vampire.

They were open about their relationship. They were lovers, plain and simple. They claimed neither homosexual nor heterosexual origin. Such terminology was useless to shadows, because of course if one of them had wanted a penis, they most assuredly could have managed such a minor change in form. Still, gay and lesbian groups around the world, still fighting against discrimination and injustice, claimed Meaghan and Alex as their own. While the discrimination went on, very few dared to be critical of the two vampire women. And if their status could help the plight of those fighting prejudice, the lovers would not deny them that. When Will Cody cast the film version of Allison Vigeant's book, *Jihad*, every woman in Hollywood vied for the roles of Meaghan Gallagher and Alexandra Nueva.

They were running late, but after their bath, Alex and Meaghan dried each other off, enjoying the afterglow of their lovemaking and the sensations of the soft cotton. The conference had been planned to discuss the hottest topic of the day: whether world government could, or should, put some controls on the passing of vampirism from one being to another. Within the boundaries of this subject fell many other, seemingly smaller topics such as marriage, integration, adoption, hiring practices . . . but what it boiled down to was, how much could the world really trust them?

Alex herded Meaghan into the bedroom, and they dressed hurriedly. If they were going to do this thing from home, the least they could do was look presentable. Meaghan was buttoning her shirt while Alex stepped into a floral-print summer dress.

"Button me up," she said, and turned her back to Meaghan.

As Meaghan reached out to do so, Alexandra went rigid, fell to her knees, then backward into Meaghan's arms. Her eyes were wide, dilated, and she twitched, a single tear rolling down her cheek.

"Alex!" Meaghan knelt by her. "What is it, honey? What's wrong?"

Alex's head was in her lap. Meaghan looked into her lover's eyes and saw no recognition there. Wherever Alex had gone, she was far away. Meaghan slapped her face, trying to bring her back. She knew what was happening. Alexandra's mind was linked to those of each of Karl Von Reinman's vampiric children. But as far as Meaghan knew, only two of Von Reinman's brood still lived: Rolf Sechs and . . .

"Cody!" Alex yelled from within her catatonia, confirming Meaghan's suspicions but frightening her as well. She had never guessed that anything could force Cody to communicate in this way. Years past, he had shut down the mind-link he shared with his blood-brothers and -sisters, as part of an ongoing feud. But now, his mind had opened again.

All vampires related by blood could converse, mentally, with words and pictures. In times of trauma, such linkages were overwhelming for the recipient as well as the sender. Whatever was happening to Cody, he obviously had no time for subtlety.

Meaghan could only hold Alexandra's head, stroke her hair and wait for the linking to end. As she waited, she wondered if she would ever experience such an intimate communication. Peter Octavian had been her blood-father, and had passed the gift to no one else. Now he was dead, or gone, and unless she passed the gift on, she would never be able to communicate the way Cody and Alex now did.

"Oh, shit," Alex said, choking and coming awake, and then Meaghan saw something she'd never expected to see.

Alexandra Nueva was crying. Tears streamed down her face as she gritted her teeth, babbling angrily to herself.

"How can we . . . got to kill that son of a . . . *Fuck*!"

"Cody," Meaghan said, bringing Alex truly around, "is he . . . ?"

Alex looked up, her face ugly with rage but her eyes betraying a softness, a trace of fear that frightened Meaghan even as she kissed the tears from her lover's cheek. Meaghan smelled apples, their shampoo.

"Cody's fine," Alex growled, her upper lip drawn back in a scowl. "For now, Cody's fine. But we've got to act fast or we're all going to be dead."

Alexandra got to her feet, grabbed the blue jeans that lay on the bed and began to step into them.

"What the . . . ," Meaghan began, but Alex whirled on her, the warrior that she had become in Von Reinman's coven evident in her every move.

"I vowed that we wouldn't go through this again, Meg!" she snapped. "We've lost so much already, but I swear . . ."

Then she stopped, realizing that Meaghan did not know what she knew, had not been privy to the mental images, the message from Cody. Alex hated to have to tell her.

"He's back, Meaghan," Alexandra said, her teeth clenched. "Mulkerrin's back, and it looks like he's much more powerful than before."

"Back?" George Marcopoulos said, incredulous. "How could he be back? What does that mean, back?"

"What the hell do you think it means?" Alexandra shouted.

They had been fifteen minutes late calling in for the video-conference, and found that everyone else had been late as well. Things were just beginning.

"But he's dead," added Rafael Nieto, the UN secretary-general. "You both saw him die, along with Peter Octavian."

The thirty-five-inch screen on the wall of their apartment was split four ways, and each quarter of the screen held a face. Marcopoulos, the Boston doctor whom the shadows had chosen as their ambassador to the United Nations (Who better than a human, they'd thought, and though some member nations criticized his lack of political experience, he'd done an exceptional job thus far) was in the top left quarter, and Nieto in the top right. The bottom left corner held the face of Julie Graham, the United States secretary of state, and the bottom right showed the frowning countenance of Hannibal, once upon a time among the most feared of shadows.

Diplomacy and the will to survive had made Hannibal see the light, so to speak, and now Hannibal was the chief marshal of the SJS, the Shadow Justice System. Alexandra's blood-brother, the mute Rolf Sechs, was his deputy chief, and though the shadows had no true government, they all recognized Meaghan and Alex as the top of the hierarchy. The older ones, the elder vampires who would naturally have taken that spot, were less than interested.

At least for the moment.

"That is what you said," Secretary Graham chimed in. "The report is firm on this, that you saw Mulkerrin die."

"Actually," Hannibal finally spoke up, "that was mainly for the benefit of your, um, human sensibilities."

"Meaning what, exactly?" Graham asked. She was a hothead, never mindful of her words, even when speaking to beings who could destroy her in an instant. Typical American politician.

"Meaning," Meaghan said, and all four faces on the screen came to attention, "quite simply, that we lied."

"You lied?" Now even Rafael Nieto was upset.

"Well, not lied exactly," Alex added, her natural belligerence making her placating tone sound more sarcastic than anything else. "Even though you'd been forced to accept our existence by the media and, of course, our physical presence, we didn't think you'd believe what really happened."

Of all the shadows, only Alexandra truly understood how much power they held in the world. The old doctor, Marcopoulos, who'd refused the gift of immortality more times than Alex could count, was probably the only human who understood. After all, acting together, the shadows would be virtually unstoppable.

"You've seen all the videotapes," Marcopoulos began, cutting off any further protest by the others. "Those portals Mulkerrin used to bring the other shadows, the demonic things, into our world? Well, that's where he and Octavian went. Peter carried the sorcerer through the largest of those portals, and into whatever was on the other side. We had to assume they were dead because of what we believe was on the other side of those portals."

"And what, Ambassador, is that?" Nieto said, calmer now.

They were all silent, until Meaghan finally spoke up.

"Hell, sir. We believe that Hell itself is beyond those portals."

The uproar was incredible, with the American secretary of state uttering several expletives ill befitting her station. When the furor died down, it was Hannibal who spoke, showing restraint that was, to Meaghan and Alex at least, nothing short of remarkable.

"Ms. Graham, Mr. Nieto, please understand that we do not wish to imply, even for a moment, that the 'Hell' of Christian teachings exists as it has been depicted in myth. Nor that the place to which we refer exists beneath the surface of the Earth. Rather, the 'Hell' we are discussing exists simultaneously in space with our own world, half a step to the right of what we would call reality. But make no mistake, it is very real in its way, and is the basis for all of the myths of that place of fire and suffering."

"But, is it supernatural?" Graham asked.

"Of course it is!" Alexandra barked. "Haven't you seen the monsters it has spawned? The magic which exists there? Anything science has yet to define is supernatural."

"Never mind this," George Marcopoulos cut in. "We're wasting time. What we've got is this: Mulkerrin is back, all communications to Salzburg are out. According to Secretary Graham, satellite recon is blacked out in that area. Obviously, wherever he's been, he's much more powerful than before. So, what are we going to do about it?"

"Thank you, George. Now, Rafe," Alexandra said and smiled, ruffling the UNSG's feathers with her familiarity and enjoying every moment of it, "what do you say we scramble a joint UN/SJS force and surround Salzburg, hum?"

"What about it, Julie?" Nieto asked the American secretary. "Will your boy jump in with the rest of us?"

"You know he will," Graham answered. "We're in, all right, but only under UN auspices."

"SJS will take command," Hannibal said curtly.

"I think not," Nieto snapped.

"Hannibal," Meaghan said softly, and they were quiet once more. "You *will* cooperate with the UN on this, but you'll only take orders from Rafael's appointed commander. Is that clear?"

"Quite."

"Good. Now let's stop fucking around and take this bastard down hard and for good."

Alexandra smiled to herself. She was usually the one playing hardball, just naturally a bitch, but she loved to watch Meaghan take command. Mostly because, as smart as she was, Meaghan was almost never aware of it. She had yet to truly notice how much deference she was given, how much power she had, and she only shook her head whenever Alex pointed it out to her. Alex loved her for her innocence, but she knew that Meaghan's power would someday make her a target as well. International governments wouldn't touch her, for fear of shadow retribution, but the elders had already begun to question her right to lead. Eventually, it would become dangerous for Meaghan to retain even an ounce of her humanity.

They were preparing to disconnect the vid-conference when George spoke up. They all paid attention, for not only was he the shadows' ambassador, he had been Peter Octavian's best friend.

"Meaghan?" He paused, not sure how to continue. "If Mulkerrin made it back, what about Peter?"

"I don't know, George. I'm afraid to hope."

"Don't be," Alexandra said to her, to all of them, resolved to the battle ahead. "Hope is all we have."

Salzburg, Austria, European Union.
Tuesday, June 6, 2000, 2:33 P.M.:

When Cody put Allison down among the trees, and reverted to his true form, he saw that she was in a state of
near shock.

"Allison," he snapped at her, and her eyes went wide in
reply. "We've got to go!"

She paid little attention as Cody dragged her along, taking a shortcut behind buildings onto Hofstallgasse and then
pounding the pavement toward their hotel. Only when they
were almost there did she seem to come out of her daze,
and even then she didn't speak. Rather, she picked up her
pace so they were running full tilt toward the hotel. When
they came bursting into the lobby, every head turned to
take them in, arrogant scowls on so many faces. They realized then that the city was unaware of the danger, the evil,
looming over them within the walls of the Festung Hohensalzburg.

Cody understood how foolish they must have appeared,
but that was his last concern. Once again with Allison in
tow, he bolted for their room, not bothering to wait for an
elevator, bounding instead up three flights of stairs, then
stopping to wait for Allison, who was quite out of breath.
On the fifth floor, they walked briskly down the hallway to
their room.

Allison picked up the phone immediately and began to
dial an outside line.

"Shit!" she said, pounded the receiver down, then picked
it up and dialed again.

"Come on," she growled, hanging up again and punch-
ing "0" for the hotel operator.

"Why can't I get an outside line?" she said, and as Will
Cody watched, the color ran out of Allison's face.

"A coincidence, maybe?" she said, looking at Will.

"What is?"

"The phones are working in the city, but as of about ten

minutes ago, nobody can get an outside line. Nobody! I'm sure you realize this, but we need a little goddamn help here."

"Don't worry," Cody said, sitting down next to her on the bed.

"Don't worry? Are you kidding me? The phones aren't out all by themselves, we both know that. This guy was supposed to be dead and instead he's back and stronger than before, and now we're all alone here, the two of us against him and whatever those things were in the fortress, and of course, whatever other assistance he manages to raise. Don't worry? I'm terrified! And what about all these people? The nice people of this city? They're going to die."

She paused for a breath, a decision lighting her eyes.

"We've got to tell them," Allison said, and then she was up and headed for the door.

Cody caught her by the arm and spun her, effortlessly, to face him. His face was grave, his eyes frightened, but his voice was calm and pleasant as ever.

"Allison, sweetheart, wake up now and pay attention. First up, we *are* going to tell people, but the first person we'll tell is the mayor, and let him and his people worry about evacuating. We've got other concerns. Second, as far as help goes, you can believe it's on the way. I've already been in touch with Alexandra, and they'll be—"

"How? I was with you the—"

"In my head, remember. We're of the same blood-father. Everything we just lived through, she was there with me. She knows what's happening and I'm sure that she and Meaghan are already scrambling help for us. No, we can't take this bastard on alone, but we can start making preparations for when the cavalry does arrive."

Allison looked at the floor for a second, took a couple of deep breaths, then picked up the phone again.

"This is Allison Vigeant from CNN News," she told the hotel operator. "Get me the mayor, please, this is an emergency."

Cody smiled then. This was the woman he'd fallen in love with in Venice. She was back in action. And to think he'd been certain she and Sandro Ricci, the cameraman who'd worked with her in Venice, would end up together. Will Cody thought he was pretty perceptive when it came to people, but he had to admit he'd called that one wrong. Though he'd seemed like a nice guy, and was certainly brave, Sandro had turned out to be an arrogant pipsqueak. When Cody saw her again, in Rome, three weeks after the Jihad, Allison, who'd been pointing a gun at Will's head the first time they met, had made her attraction to him no secret.

It was amazing, really. He'd spent his human life as two people, one man torn between two callings. One, William F. Cody, had been a buffalo hunter, an army scout, a scoundrel who gambled and drank and stole beer shipments with Wild Bill Hickok. The other, "Buffalo Bill," was an entertainer and the star of thousands of dime novels with barely an ounce of truth in them. One scalped Chief Yellow Hand in memory of an idiot named Custer, while the other was known around the world, even among the American tribes, as a kind, fair, generous man who was good with everyone's money but his own.

Two people, one man. When Karl Von Reinman had brought him to the life of shadows, as Cody October, Will had at once been excited and repulsed. He couldn't be changed. From the beginning, though he'd never really needed it, he continued to carry a gun. He rebelled against his coven, sought a life of adventure, and was reviled for it. Over time, his two natures merged, and by the time of the Venice Jihad, he had become nearly as much of a hero in his heart as he had been made by time and legend.

He remembered what it was like to be human, to be afraid. And his relationship with Allison helped to keep both things close to him, the fear and the heroism. She helped him be what he was without trying to fulfill the expectations of others, hard enough as a human, and harder still once the world found out he was alive, and a vampire. He was happy to license the revival of Buffalo Bill's Wild West Show, but he wouldn't perform. His serious commentary was in the film industry, and there he would be known as Will Cody.

Whatever shadows were, whatever William F. Cody had become, Allison reminded him, and he became a reminder to his own kind, that vampires had human hearts. *Never let it be said that we have no souls*, Meaghan Gallagher had said to him once. Words to live by, even if you lived forever.

"No!" Allison shouted at the mayor of Salzburg over the phone. "You don't understand . . . Yes, I am with Colonel Cody right now, and the threat is real. That is why your communications are malfunctioning. Believe me, troops are on the way, you must evacuate."

She was silent for a moment, and even across the room, Cody could hear every word the mayor said in reply. There was no way he was going to take any action based on her word alone, even if "Colonel" Cody backed her up. He just couldn't take such a risk.

"Can you afford the risk if you don't evacuate?" Allison said, getting angry now.

And then the earthquake began.

The hotel shook to its foundations, windows shattered and the floor beneath the bed began to buckle. Cody moved barely fast enough to knock Allison away from the bed and onto the marble bathroom threshold. Above them, the ceiling was about to cave in, and Cody saw it just in time. He covered Allison with his own body as it gave way.

The quake lasted seventeen seconds. When it was over, Cody's back had been torn open by a falling beam, which even now he held up, away from Allison, with his body. As soon as the ground stopped shaking, he used his strength to turn slowly, sending the beam sliding into the hole that had opened in the center of the room. For the moment, their spot half-in, half-out of the bathroom seemed safe enough.

Even as he checked Allison for injuries, and found none, Cody's back was healing. By the time Allison had the presence of mind to look him over, the only evidence of any wound was his torn and bloody shirt. He looked around for a fresh one, and saw that most of their belongings had fallen down to the floors below. Aftershocks could come at any time, Cody knew, so he didn't waste a second worrying about clothing. He made do with an old Allman Brothers Band concert T-shirt that he'd worn to bed the night before. His tan-colored light cotton jacket was hung on the bathroom door, and he grabbed that as well.

The one other thing he was able to salvage, from behind a heating grate in the wall, was his holstered Beretta— nine-millimeter, semi-automatic, loaded with hollow points, fifteen in the clip and one in the chamber. He was a better rifle shot, but rifles were a tad conspicuous on most days. He slid into both holster and jacket, and turned to find Allison observing the entire transformation with raised eyebrows.

"I've never understood why you feel the need to carry that," she said.

"Call it a security blanket," he answered. "I'll never shoot as well as my old friend Annie Oakley, but then, I'm still around, aren't I?"

She looked as if she were going to say something, and then must have realized it was not the time.

"Well, I'm certain the mayor will get with the program now, so what's our next move?" Allison asked.

"You mean after we get out of here?"

"Yeah."

"Let's talk about it after we get out of here."

They smiled together, and then Cody walked to the edge of the hole, stepping gingerly. He wouldn't have any trouble getting back up if he fell, but it *would* be inconvenient.

What he saw when he looked down was unexpected.

Where he had assumed that their bed and most of their furniture had collapsed into the room below, in truth a chain reaction had taken place, with the weight of each floor collapsing the next until they had all fallen in. And at the bottom . . . At the bottom there was only darkness. Cody struggled to concentrate, to focus his vision, and then realized what he was seeing. A huge fissure had opened up right beneath the hotel, tearing its foundation wide enough that much of its bulk had fallen into that hole. But then, how deep was the hole if most of the debris had disappeared into it?

"Allison," he said, "look out the window and tell me what you see."

"Cracks," she answered. "A lot of cracks, why?"

They shared a look then, which was nearly as effective as telepathy. It had been obvious from the first tremor that Mulkerrin's power had caused the earthquake. They didn't know how, but they were certain it was him. Therefore, they could no longer put any limit on his abilities, not until they learned those limits for themselves. In the meantime, they had to get out of the hotel, perhaps out of the city proper, before another quake hit. They had both realized that there would very likely be another.

The first problem to be surmounted was that between them and the door was approximately twelve feet of open space, its edges crumbling, and a fall of sixty or seventy feet, minimum, waiting below. The easiest way to go was out the window and onto the ledge which ran around the building on each of its three topmost floors. Once there, it was a simple task, as long as the next quake took its time, to make their way along the ledge to the next room.

Cody smashed the remaining glass away from the shattered window frame and helped Allison through. The couple who'd been staying in the next room had either not been in the room or had already fled the hotel. The stairs, on the way down, were cracked and crumbling, and when they reached the lobby, they joined a large group trying to

get a look into the hole without falling. As was true in any
disaster, it would be some time before the police could
clear the gawkers away.

Cody could see the bottom of the hole now, and all of
the debris and furniture strewn there. In fact, he could see
Allison's suitcase sticking out of the pile. The top of the
junkheap was about thirty feet down. Cody thought of
coming back for Allison's case later. But first . . .

"Okay, people," Allison said, in English, to the crowd.
"We don't know when there will be another . . . an after-
shock, and this is about the worst place to be if and when
that comes. Why don't we all get into the street and wait
for help to arrive?"

She received a dirty look from the hotel manager, who
was now surrounded by people chattering at him about
their losses. Several people were apparently injured, but it
didn't seem as though anyone had been killed, at least not
any guests of the hotel. In any case, people were beginning
to file out now, and she and Cody turned to follow.

"Ma che diavolo succede?" a voice exclaimed behind
them.

Neither Cody nor Allison understood more than a few
words in Italian, but they got the idea. Back at the hole, an
older, white-haired man was peering into the depths, and
as they watched, he backed off slightly, as if frightened.

Before they had reached the edge, Allison knew what
they would find, and she was sure that Cody knew it too.
But to see it was horror. The hole was now only ten feet
deep, blocked after that point by a shimmering pool, a
silver mirror that rippled with each stone that fell from the
crumbling floor to touch its surface.

"Out!" Cody yelled. "All of you get out of here, now!
Get out of the city, as far away as you can. Go!"

The manager approached, determined to put a stop to
Cody's raving.

"Sir," he began, his English flawless, "I'm afraid if you
do not lower your—"

Cody rounded on him, changing, his face growing fierce, feral, eyes burning red and canines lengthening to almost absurd proportions. His voice was a bass growl, from deep inside him.

"Let me make something perfectly clear! Hell is breaking loose! If you want to live, leave. NOW!"

The manager was gone. Cody whirled back toward the giant fissure, awaiting the emergence of whatever was beyond that portal, his blood boiling, hunger rising within him along with anger and frustration.

"No." A hand grabbed his arm, and he turned with a snarl only to see Allison looking at him sternly, no fear in her face.

But she should fear, he thought sadly, when the hunger comes on. Normally he was in complete control, but when his temper flared the hunger became nearly overwhelming. Bloodlust.

"I'm hungry," he growled.

"Come on, Will! We'll deal with hungry in a minute. For now, let's get out of here. We've got to figure out the extent of what's happening, otherwise the cavalry may be useless. Let's go."

Into the street they ran, only to find that the people from the hotel had simply gathered there.

"Away," Allison yelled at them. "You have no idea what's coming. Run, damn you! Have you forgotten Venice so quickly?"

That got to them. The whole world had seen the videotape of Venice, and now as they looked into fissures in the street, and saw the silver pools glistening there under the sun, they remembered where they had seen such things before, and terror took them. In the rush to escape whatever would drag itself through, several people were shoved, knocked or simply slipped into the pits. It was too late to help them, and Allison finally reached the harsh realization that the others would have to fend for themselves as well.

Many of them would not make it. First priority, though, was Will.

Allison drew him close, amid the rising tide of panic that swept across the street and through the city, and forced him to take some of her blood. He argued that she would need all her strength, but she insisted he take a little, to tide him over until they could find a volunteer, or if necessary, an unknowing donor. She felt a sharp pain and a weird arousal which had become very familiar to her, and she smelled lilacs, as always. She never understood that, the lilacs, but the smell was there. When she had pushed his head away, she finally voiced her questions.

"This isn't a meeting place for shadows! Why is Mulkerrin doing this?"

"He wants to rule, that's my guess."

Cody and Allison turned to see John Courage standing quietly by. Allison noticed for the first time how handsome the shadow was, with his perfect smile, close-cropped brown hair and blue eyes.

"We'd better be getting out of here, don't you think?" Courage spoke again, and Allison let out a breath she hadn't realized she'd been holding.

"Leaving!" she said. "What a *good* idea!"

"Where to, John?" Cody asked him, deferring to the other shadow's knowledge of the area. "We'll talk about theories later."

"I think I know where we'll be safe for now," Courage said. "And I know where we might find some reinforcements as well. Unfortunately, it looks like we may have to fight our way out."

They turned to see soldiers coming toward them down the street, soldiers wearing armor at least four centuries old, swords drawn high above them. The screaming began as people were cut down in the street, and behind them something huge was rising from the fissure within the hotel. Cody realized that the soldiers were tourists from the fortress, possessed by the ghosts of dead warriors.

"Holy shit!" Allison gasped.

"Damnation!" Cody shouted.

"An excellent choice of words, both of you," Courage said with a smirk, already beginning to change into something else. "Obviously you share a certain eloquence . . ."

Allison reached inside Will's jacket and pulled his Beretta from its holster, aimed it at the oncoming soldiers and squeezed off a round. She addressed Courage without looking at him.

"Shut up and fight, wiseguy."

CHAPTER ✦ THREE

Washington, D.C., United States of America.
Tuesday, June 6, 2000, 9:36 A.M.:

The President of the United States spoke urgently into
the videophone on his cherrywood desk while Julie Graham paced across the large Oriental rug. Julie liked the
President, thought of him as a stand-up kind of guy, but
she was worried about his temper.

Henry Russo had won the presidency primarily because
of his stern view regarding the trade imbalance with Germany, but a large part of his popularity came from his
wary, vigilant acceptance of the shadows. Russo was a serious man. In fact, he had little or no sense of humor about
him. The President spent his days dealing harshly with cor-
ruption and slackers, trying to clean up Washington, so that
even if he failed to visibly accomplish anything, his succes-
sor would have a much easier time changing the world. To
some, Henry Russo was the best thing that had happened
to Washington in a long time; to others, he was the Inquisi-
tion all over again. Either way he was a rarity, a President
who, as he often said in private, didn't "give a flying fuck"
about his image.

Julie Graham thought it was a miracle Russo had been
elected at all.

They made a poor team, really, a gravely serious President with a temper and little patience, and his closest con-

fidante, the first female secretary of state, whose own temper was notoriously short. Henry Russo knew he'd never be reelected, and he had resolved to accomplish what he could in the time alotted.

Regarding the German trade imbalance, he and Julie were in almost constant contact with all of Europe's leaders, including Erich Strauss, the president of Austria. Henry didn't like the man, but liking him wasn't a part of the job.

"Erich, listen to me," Henry said. "The emergency resolution has passed. Britain, France, Germany, the U.S.—we *are* coming. Just cooperate with the UN on this, will you? You need our help!"

"*Ja*," Strauss said with a sneer. "I have seen the kind of help you offer, Henry. I don't want any. Even if this problem exists—"

"Communications are out, satellites are out and now you've had an earthquake!" Julie interrupted, stepping behind the President so Strauss could see them both on his own screen. "Is this all coincidence, Erich?"

Henry and Julie both watched the President's screen as Strauss fidgeted in his chair. Julie knew the man had seen footage of the Venice Jihad, and he couldn't accept that such tragedy might be occurring in his own country. But she also knew that quite soon, he wouldn't have a choice.

"What of the shadows?" Strauss asked. "I don't want them tearing my country apart, Julie. Henry. I think I'd better do this myself."

Henry Russo and Julie Graham exchanged doubtful glances, each silently questioning Strauss's grasp of reality.

"As far as the SJS is concerned," Julie said, "they've agreed to act as just another part of the UN security force on this one. There will be no raping and pillaging of your nation by shadows; that's what the SJS was set up to *prevent*."

Even while Julie was talking, she could see Henry's face

reddening. Time was wasting, and the President could not
bear to waste time.

"Erich," Henry snapped. "You are, of course, free to
send all the troops you want into Salzburg, but our *suggestion* is that you attempt to evacuate what citizens you can
and surround the city. Rafael Nieto has assured us that UN
security forces will begin to arrive within the hour to assist
you in that."

"I said I don't want—" Erich Strauss began.

"Jeeezus Christ!" Henry snapped, and Julie dug her fingers into his shoulder as soon as the words were out. Too
late.

"Listen here, Erich: it doesn't matter worth a damn what
you want. Rafael Nieto is secretary general of the UN, and
the Security Council has passed an emergency resolution
to go in there and pull that bastard out like a rotten tooth.
Now, you can cooperate, or get your boys out of the way,
but one way or another, you're not going to take on that
crazy son of a bitch by yourself. Got it?"

"I really don't appreciate . . . ," Strauss began, but Julie wouldn't let him go on. She forcibly slid the President's
chair from behind his desk and leaned over to look closely
into the videophone, giving the Austrian president a clear
view of her face.

"Erich, Henry's lost his temper, and we both apologize.
But he does have a point. Don't be parochial about this; it
isn't just an Austrian matter, it's a UN matter. As a member nation, you must respond to that. You have my word
that the shadow troops will behave themselves, and that
the rest of the security force will do its best to keep the
damage at a minimum. But let's face it, you've already had
an earthquake in Salzburg. The city is going to take some
heavy hits."

Silence, uncomfortable enough on a phone, was made
even worse by being able to see the person with whom you
were speaking. As Henry Russo pulled his chair back up to
his desk, appropriately ashamed of his behavior, he and

Julie watched as the face of Erich Strauss finally registered the pain in his heart.

"You're right, of course, I just . . . I don't want Salzburg to become a war zone. I was born there, you know. My . . . my mother is there."

All the fire went out of Henry Russo. He didn't like Erich Strauss, but "like" had nothing to do with it.

"Erich, I'm sorry," Henry said. "I didn't mean to, well, I didn't know. Of course we'll all proceed with caution, and you should get in there as soon as possible, but you do realize . . ."

The President of the United States wished he'd kept his mouth shut, as his Austrian counterpart turned his face away from the videophone. Then the screen went dark as the video portion of the signal was turned off from the other end. Only the audio remained.

"Of course I do," Erich's voice said. "I've already said good-bye to the city in my heart. I only hope my mother fares better."

Then the connection was severed.

In the oval office of the White House, the President and secretary of state of the United States of America looked at each other with a terrible mixture of anger, fear and sadness. As homey as Henry Russo had tried to make the office when he was first elected, at that moment it felt colder and more heartless than ever.

Henry touched an intercom button on his phone and asked his aide to get George Marcopoulos on the line. Then he turned back to Julie, his only true "friend" in politics.

"This is going to be a nightmare," he said, remembering the tapes of Venice.

"Henry," Julie said, letting out a breath and shaking her head, "there'll be no waking up from this one."

London, England, European Union.
Tuesday, June 6, 2000, 3:01 P.M.:

His trench coat was not nearly enough to keep him dry,
as Hannibal trudged along London's Baker Street in the
pouring rain. He passed the address where a fictional
detective had once made his home, and gave a broad, exaggerated smile to those humans he encountered. Its effect
was exactly as he desired, clearing the sidewalk in front of
him. A smile from Hannibal was sometimes more unsettling than a scowl.

Hannibal had discovered that, contrary to popular opinion, it didn't always rain in London. Just most of the time.
Hannibal smiled again, and passersby gave him a wide
berth. He was amused to find that the locals were more
frightened than the tourists. Still, London had had more
than its share of the weird and terrible over the centuries.
The British had grown smart enough to fear, where Americans were still dumb with fascination.

The rain fell in a blanketing torrent which turned the
already black-and-white streets of London into a misty gray
wasteland, a classic film, but out of focus. It could be a
truly enjoyable city, especially if one was familiar with the
ins and outs of its nightlife, but the days were horrible. On
the other hand, the gray rain meant no sun, and no sun
meant Hannibal didn't have to think about it for once,
about Venice and the change, and how his entire unlife was
filled to bursting with lies and deception. He'd never had a
problem with deception in the past, when he had been the
engineer of such acts, but now that he *had* to lie, was
forced to live a deception . . . He despised it.

A life of peace.

Hannibal had lived for centuries, first as a leader among
men, then as a lonely, rebellious vampire, and finally, as
time went on, as the leader of one of the most powerful
covens of the Defiant Ones, helping to establish the tradi-
tions of his kind. He had been instrumental in building a

corps of volunteers, humans who offered themselves once a year as blood sacrifices to Hannibal's kind. He had organized an international array of agents who answered only to him, who spied on whomever he wished them to, who kept him informed on every aspect of his people's evolution. He had been respected . . . feared . . .

Worshipped.

But no more. No, the actions of the clergyman, Mulkerrin, and the foolishness of Will Cody and Peter Octavian, had revealed the existence of vampires to the entire world —a world programmed by fictional representations of his kind as evil, vile, villainous creatures who must, at all costs, be destroyed. Humanity had been placated by soothing words, tales of the church's attempts at genocide, and the efforts by certain members of the shadow community to be accepted into human society.

Only Hannibal didn't want to be accepted.

Hannibal wanted to kill.

To feast, to drink the blood of *unwilling* human hosts— this was the destiny of his kind, the Defiant Ones. They were parasites who lived off the body of humanity, and Hannibal reveled in that knowledge. Evil, vile, villainous— this was an image he embraced, and a life he missed. But no, the children of his one-time adversary, the late Karl Von Reinman, now ascribed to a different philosophy, one which allowed a merging of two societies, shadow and human. But Hannibal knew such a merging was impossible.

Shadows and humans were natural enemies, predator and prey. They might toy with peace, but it could not last. The nature of shadows was to kill, to feed, to take without permission, without warning and without mercy, whatever was needed. And that way of life was not gone, only held in abeyance. For now, those shadows who, like Hannibal, lusted for the old ways, must hide themselves among the sheep, falsely advocating peace, or die. Hannibal himself had found the perfect hiding place, for in his position as chief marshal of the SJS, it was his job to hunt and often destroy those shadows who reverted to the old ways.

"Rebels" and "criminals" they were called. Hannibal called them brothers. While he was forced to destroy some, many others had been saved, organized, hidden away until the day Hannibal called them forward.

For the peace could not last. He would not allow it. Unified, the shadows would destroy their human counterparts. And if unity did not come naturally to them, especially to the children of Von Reinman, well then Hannibal would force it upon them.

Soon.

Now his plan had a new wrinkle. Mulkerrin had returned. Father Liam Mulkerrin, the last of a line of powerful sorcerers, a sect within the Roman Catholic Church, who had used magic to control all supernatural creatures, all shadows, except Hannibal's people. The church came to call the vampires "Defiant Ones," and sought to subjugate them for centuries, attempting genocide several times. The last attempt had been in Venice, the Jihad, when Mulkerrin had opened doors into hell from which emerged the true shadows, demon-things born of brimstone and death.

Though the Jihad revealed the existence of the shadows to the world, it also held a glimpse of the future for Hannibal. For the first time, he had seen the true potential in the unity of his people. Mulkerrin and his demons had been defeated, the sorcerer himself carried into Hell on the back of the shadows' self-appointed savior, the arrogant whelp Peter Octavian. And the Church had been brought to its knees.

Somehow, Mulkerrin had returned. Once again, Von Reinman's blood-children were at the center of things. And Hannibal had been ordered, *ordered*, by Meaghan Gallagher—herself not even the spawn of Von Reinman but of Octavian—to obey the United Nations commander, Jimenez. Well, that remained to be seen. Hannibal wanted

Mulkerrin destroyed once and for all, a goal he shared with all other shadows, and humans as well.

But if Mulkerrin's presence could be used as the means to an end?

"Watch your step, ya bloody git!!" came the gruff voice of a burly Englishman, just as Hannibal collided with him, knocking the big man back on his ass.

In seconds the man had regained his feet and pulled Hannibal up by the collar of his coat.

"Lissen 'ere, you fancy bast—"

No change had come upon Hannibal; he had not even bared fangs, but the man somehow sensed that something terrible was there and that he'd stepped in it. He smoothed the lapels on Hannibal's coat, then began to back away, slowly at first, and then in a light jog. He was lost to the misty, rain-shrouded street in seconds, devoured.

The collision had done Hannibal some good, though. He had spent far too much time in the past five years brooding, lost in his thoughts. The big man had just jolted him from that reverie, and now he found himself just a block from his office, the headquarters of the SJS.

He took the steps two at a time, not to hurry, simply to get there. A shorter stride was uncomfortable for him, unnatural. The door was closed, but a light shone through the opaque windows at either side of the entrance. Inside, Hannibal quickly doffed his trench coat and shook the rain from his long white hair. The receptionist, a human named Marie, who was obsessed with vampires, nearly came to attention when he entered. She was as fascinated as she was frightened, and he smiled at her as she got up to make him a cup of tea. Thirsty for blood though he might be, he was never above a good cup of tea. And this Marie was attractive. Eventually, he would have her in all the ways they both imagined, and some she would never have dreamed.

Hannibal heard a file drawer sliding shut in the other room, and then the approach of his deputy chief, Rolf

Sechs. The shadow was large, as burly as the man Hannibal
had knocked down, and yet almost gentle, if such could be
believed of any vampire. And silent. He had light brown
hair and crystal blue eyes, and his kindly features belied his
size and strength.

Mute, Rolf communicated with his face and hands, and
when necessary with a voice-pad which vocalized his writing. Intelligent, loyal and a fierce warrior, he would have
been the logical choice for deputy chief if he had wanted
the job. Hannibal knew better. Rolf had no interest in the
SJS. He had been asked to take his present position by
Meaghan Gallagher, the de facto leader of the world's
shadows. Rolf was also a blood-son of Karl Von Reinman,
and Gallagher had given him the job to keep an eye on
Hannibal.

"You have taken the appropriate measures, I presume,"
Hannibal said, but did not wait for a reply. "We leave for
Salzburg in one hour. Be certain the entire unit is pre-
pared."

Rolf simply nodded. Hannibal was comfortable with the
knowledge that whatever happened, when he finally made
his move, Rolf would have to be destroyed.

The mute German watched as Hannibal carried a cup of
tea into his office and shut the door. When he was gone,
Rolf flirted silently with Marie. Though he felt no special
attachment to her, they had been lovers for more than a
year, and she often told him about things she shouldn't
have, things she'd heard Hannibal saying in the office. Rolf
knew far more than Hannibal imagined, and was preparing
for their eventual confrontation. Hannibal would have
killed Marie if he'd known.

Rolf knew that thought thrilled her.

Boston, Massachusetts, United States of America.
Tuesday, June 6, 2000, 11:39 A.M.:

As far as Meaghan Gallagher was concerned, it was a
stroke of luck that George Marcopoulos was still in Boston. He and his wife Valerie, who had been ill, did still live
in town, but George spent so much of his time running
back and forth to New York and Washington that it was
unusual to find him at home. If Valerie's recovery were less
than complete, George would most likely have to retire as
shadow ambassador. The thought disturbed Meaghan, for
she could think of no other acceptable human candidates.

Bitch, she thought to herself. *How can you be so selfish
and cold?*

She ought to be thinking about Valerie, she knew, and
about George's feelings. Though she was loathe to admit it,
since her death Meaghan had become increasingly insensi-
tive to the frailty of humankind. She imagined it was a trait
of all shadows, and perhaps a natural one. As she became
less and less human, her new chemistry distanced her more
and more from her origins, so that she could hunt without
feeling for her prey.

She would not allow it. Peter Octavian had overcome
that same encroaching numbness, and he was her blood-
father after all.

Now, as Alexandra made preparations for their departure and eventual rendezvous with Hannibal at the Austrian border, Meaghan stepped out of the "T" station at
Government Center and began to walk toward Fanueil
Hall. Though she could have flown and simply landed in
the middle of Quincy Market, it had become etiquette for
her kind not to do so. Such a display instilled fear and awe,
and attracted a lot of unwanted attention. Though melo-
dramatic by nature, she had determined that her people
must refrain from such showboating, even if to do so made
life more difficult.

The city block between Government Center and Boston

Harbor was called Quincy Market, a group of buildings filled with shopping and food and, outdoors, merchants' carts filled with everything from Harvard University T-shirts to fresh-squeezed lemonade. Visitors and locals alike tended to refer to the marketplace as Fanueil Hall, the name of a colonial era meeting house at the front of Quincy Market. George Marcopoulos had never confused the two. Though they were going to have lunch inside Quincy Market, he met Meaghan where he always did, outside Faneuil Hall.

Meaghan loved George Marcopoulos like a father—her own had died when she was quite young—and he returned the affection.

"Hello, darling," he said, and bent slightly to kiss her cheek as she hugged him. George was an old man, or so he constantly told himself, and he knew that people began to shrink with age. But Meaghan had once been significantly shorter than him. He had not shrunk that much, he knew. She had grown. It was just one more in an endless series of fascinating discoveries he and the world were making about the shadows.

But as usual, he kept it to himself. Let the rest of them find out on their own, and not badger his loved ones.

"Mr. Ambassador," Meaghan answered, with a smile that reached her eyes. "How are you today?"

"Worried," he answered, his own smile disappearing. "But let's discuss it over lunch."

George offered Meaghan his arm and she took it. They walked, linked in that manner, across the cobblestones of Quincy Market, examining the wares of the merchant carts. The noonday sun beat down on them, though the ocean breeze made it bearable, and Meaghan squinted against the glare. They passed a vendor selling flowers, and their myriad scents joined into one, overpowering bouquet. Powerful smells also wafted out of other establishments, including the hypnotically sweet, commanding smell of chocolate chip cookies from the Boston Chipyard. Finally they reached Cityside, a café which boasted the "best burger in Boston." Although red meat was definitely not in his diet, and Valerie would scream if she knew, George was dying for a cheeseburger . . . and damn the fat content!

"How's Alexandra?" he asked as they waited to be seated.

"Like the rest of us, scared. But the funny thing is that she's mainly scared for Will. It wasn't so many years ago that she wanted Will Cody dead, but now she's even more worried about him than I am. I never figured her for the mother hen type, but there it is."

"And how are things between you?" he asked, sincerely.

"Wonderful," Meaghan answered, and meant it. She was glad George was so comfortable when it came to her relationship with Alex. Most people his age wouldn't have been.

But then, the whole world had changed, and George had been through the changes firsthand. He had been forced to accept a lot of things in light of which her relationship with Alex appeared as normal as she and Alex knew it to be. Life went on, love went on, and George had a kind heart. They would miss him when he died. Meaghan, Alex and Cody had all offered him the gift of life, the Revenant Transformation, more than once, separately and together. He had always refused. They had offered to save Valerie's life, and she had reacted with fear and disgust, being not as open-minded as her husband. She would rather take her chances with the doctors. And George would join her when his time came.

But for now, he lived, and he was their greatest friend among humans.

When they had finally been seated and their orders taken, Meaghan asked him what, other than the obvious, he was worried about.

"We're clueless here," he began, quietly and calmly, so as not to draw the attention of the loud crowd seated around them. "We don't know where Mulkerrin's been or how he came back. We have no idea where his apparently new abilities come from, or what their limitations are. Peter's status is unknown. We don't know what's gone on inside Salzburg in the hours since the earthquake, or what's happened to Cody and Allison Vigeant."

"You can rest assured," she interrupted, "that if anything had happened to Cody, Alexandra would know of it."

"Well, that's something at least," George said, and was thoughtful for a moment before continuing. "The UN is afraid of you, all of you, I mean. But strangely enough, mostly of you. Because of the power you hold over your people, and because of the book."

"I won't . . . I can't give up the book."

"I know that." He looked at her sternly, a reminder of who he was. "I'm not suggesting that you do. The safest place for *The Gospel of Shadows* is with you and Alex, away from any government, especially America's, away from the less, shall we say civilized, of your kind, like Hannibal. In the wrong hands . . . Well, I don't have to tell you this, but they're also afraid because, while they know you're not really vampires, at least not the mythical kind, they don't have a clue as to what you really are."

"Neither do we!" She raised her voice, gaining her unwanted attention from the other diners, some of whom easily recognized her. She was a celebrity after all. "Neither do we," she said again, quietly.

"They didn't believe you before," George replied, "and now that they know we lied to them about the end of the Jihad, about Mulkerrin, they *really* don't believe you. They want to do research, to study—"

"Out of the question, unless they have shadow scientists," she said, stopping him. "We've been over this. I don't want them trying some synthetic replication of the process; you know where that could lead. I also don't want them developing weapons against us."

Meaghan reached across and held George's hand, tight. Their eyes met.

"The only thing keeping the world at peace right now is their fear of the unknown, their fear of us. The more they know about us, the less frightened they become. This new order is a tenuous thing."

"And Mulkerrin may be enough to bring it down," he said. "Listen, I'll continue to stall, and I think the truth of your words will hold them off a while, but we've got to find out everything there is to know about your people . . ."

His voice trailed off, but Meaghan heard the phrase he'd left unsaid.

Before they do.

"Peace is a dangerous place," Meaghan said, her mind far away now.

"A mine field," George agreed.

International Airspace.
Tuesday, June 6, 2000, 12:15 P.M., EST:

High above the Atlantic, a military transport jet carried Roberto Jimenez toward Germany. He'd been visiting relatives in New York City when the call came through. There wasn't a person in the world he hated more than the UN secretary general, Rafael Nieto. His boss. He'd never met a more arrogant, aggravating man. And yet, Jimenez respected his boss. He knew the job, did it well, and earned the attention of the world.

At forty-four, hair white at the temples and streaked through the otherwise dark, close-cut fur of his head and mustache, Jimenez was still young to have been made commander of the UN Security Forces. Still, they didn't want him out there, fighting. But that was the condition upon which he'd taken the job. He'd trained with nearly every elite fighting force allied with his homeland, Spain. He was not going to give orders from safety. He couldn't, no matter how badly they wanted to protect him; the thought sickened him.

And they did want to protect him. The job had gotten

that much more important in the three years since '97, when NATO and the UN had finally merged. The two organizations had been stepping all over each other's toes for years, but after the whole Bosnia debacle, there was no putting off the merger. NATO had begun to play diplomacy games, and the UN had moved more and more into the area of military intervention. Technology and time had made the Earth like a small town, and there wasn't room in town for both of them. The new balance of power made Roberto Jimenez one of the two or three most powerful military men in the world. Maybe *the* most powerful.

But he didn't let it go to his head.

Now the transport brought him at top speed toward a rendezvous in Munich with the UNSF troops gathering to take the hot spot. By dawn, they'd be invading Salzburg on his orders. For the moment, though, he was arguing with his boss on the phone. The duties of the UN secretary general had grown in the past five years, as more and more of the world's protection was heaped on his shoulders. The man was not one to mince words.

"I don't give a goddamn whether you like it or not," Nieto snapped, and the viewscreen was good enough that Jimenez could see a vein pulse on his superior's forehead.

"Listen, Rafe," Jimenez reasoned, "you know and I know that Hannibal has his own agenda. I don't know what the SJS is up to, or even if the whole group is under his control, but their presence will compromise this mission."

Nieto heaved a sigh, calming himself down.

"Berto," he said, "I know you don't trust him. I don't. Even the shadows don't. But chances are, you're going to need him. His people know a lot more about this shit than we do! He's agreed to follow your orders. Besides, Gallagher and Nueva will be there to keep him in line."

Roberto Jimenez listened, but wasn't buying any of it. He feared the shadows, and didn't trust any of them, even the "good" ones.

"Who's going to keep them in line?" he asked, sarcastically.

A cloud fell over UNSG Nieto's face.

"Just do your job."

The connection was broken, leaving Jimenez with the thrumming of the jet for company. He unzipped his jacket and reached inside to pull a sharp object from under his arm, where it had been hidden in a leather sheath. It was a crucifix, made of silver, whose base tapered down to a razor point. A dagger. A friend of his, a lieutenant in the Italian army, had found it in the ruins of Venice after the Jihad, and given it to Roberto as a gift.

And for protection.

Jimenez stroked the blade for a moment before replacing it inside his jacket, then zipping up. It made him feel a little better to have that weapon, and symbol, nestled against his body.

It bothered him that Nieto referred to the shadows as people. They weren't. They were exactly what they were called—shadows. Shadows of human beings.

And shadows were fickle things.

Roberto Jimenez didn't trust any of them.

CHAPTER ✦ FOUR

Salzburg, Austria, European Union.
Tuesday, June 6, 2000, 3:14 P.M.:

It was amazingly quiet.

Everything human had fled this particular street except Allison Vigeant, and she stood between John Courage and Will Cody, Beretta in hand. They couldn't even hear screaming in the distance. No sirens, no vehicles. For a moment, the only sound was the chilly summer wind whipping down Getreidergasse.

In front of them, were humans whose souls had been torn out and replaced with the supernatural will of the ghosts of centuries-dead soldiers, their tourist clothing replaced by perfectly preserved, clanking armor, stolen from the museum at the Fortress Hohensalzburg. Behind them was a demon, eleven feet tall, with lobster-like pincers for hands and eyes all over its man-shaped body. Only the enormous, sharply glimmering horn on its forehead was without eyes. And certainly there were more demons where it had came from.

"We've got to get out of here," John Courage said aloud, and the silence was broken.

Noise came shrieking back into life: sirens started up in the distance, and the rumbling of trucks could be heard nearby. People were screaming as the demons emerged all over the city and the evacuation began in earnest. A large group of people ran screaming across the street several blocks behind them, and then something large and black charged after them.

In front of them, armor began clanking anew, as the dead soldiers rushed forward.

Behind them, a roar, as the demon lumbered ahead.

"Unless you want to leave Allison here, just how do you propose doing that?" Cody answered, acid in his voice.

"Only one way," Allison said, answering both their questions as she squared her feet the way Cody had taught her, aimed the Beretta, and shot the nearest soldier in the eye.

"Allison, they're tourists," Cody reminded her, right hand nervously tugging his beard.

"Get with it, Will. We've got no clue what's really happened to them. What Mulkerrin's done. Besides, it's them or us. That's a no-brainer."

She squeezed off another round, then pawed Cody's jacket for backup clips. There weren't any. And there were a lot of soldiers, moving in slowly, but inexorable as the tide.

"John," Cody said. "Can you burn?"

"Of course I can, but—" He wasn't allowed to finish.

"Take the demon." He flashed a look at Allison. "I'll take these guys; you cover me. We've got to get an escape route."

Behind the demon was a side street from which some civilians still appeared, screaming and shouting but afraid to turn back, fleeing instead to the east, away from them. That side street led to Franz-Joseph-Kai, and the Salzach River beyond. At least from there, Cody figured, they'd have space to figure out their next move. He transformed, in a heartbeat, from William F. Cody into a tiger, a form he'd first seen taken by Meaghan Gallagher. Then he sprang, launching himself into the armored, possessed creatures that hunted him. Shots rang out, as Allison fired her weapon. Bullets glanced off armor near him, one lodging in his flesh, stinging for a moment.

He tore into them, their armor no match for strength that could smash their ribs, tear the limbs from their bodies. Claws raked skulls and fangs bit deep. Allison would run out of bullets quickly, and then she'd be defenseless. Cody was not going to let anything happen to her. Swords bit deep into his flesh, and he knew he was lucky they were only steel. The sheer numbers of the soldiers, many with no protection—there were only so many suits of armor—began to overwhelm him, and he turned to mist to escape the press of their flesh.

John Courage lived up to his name, his flesh flowing like liquid, forming itself into the body of a huge hawk. His wings spread wide, and he dove to avoid the scrabbling arms of the many-eyed demon as it rushed toward them. Talons raked the thing's groin and thighs, eyes popped, spurting an acid ejaculate which soaked John's wings, and his scream was that of the bird. He changed fast, fire enveloping the demon, immolating it. Flames licked at the creature's body, and it let out another roar, using its hands to smash at the flames, slapping its burning, charring flesh in a feeble attempt to douse the flames. Eyes burst all over its form, the sound like popcorn popping, and the thing threw itself to the street, rolling around to kill the fire.

Allison watched as Cody fought the possessed ones off, then turned to mist as they overwhelmed him. One of the few armored attackers still intact rushed toward her, sword raised. She brought the Beretta up to meet him, trying her best to stay calm, her breathing steady. She fired, and the bullet struck the ghost-man in the shoulder, just under the armor plate. The soldier's arm spasmed, dropping the sword as he held the arm close to his body. Allison squeezed the trigger again, and nothing happened.

The gun was empty, useless. She dropped it.

With no time for hesitation, Allison ran toward the once human thing, rather than away. She had been trained to fight, to protect herself, in the years since the Venice Jihad. Now she used those newly honed skills. Four steps brought her left foot down on the sword before the possessed one could use his right hand to raise it. She grabbed his helmet as her knee came up and smashed, crunching bones, into his face. The spirit within this man obviously felt his pain, for it shrieked a hellish noise, then fell to its side on the street.

Allison picked up the sword. She kicked away an arm raised to protect the fallen man, and lifted the blade above her head. As it whickered through the air toward the man's bare neck, she saw in his upturned face, in his dark eyes, a trace of the humanity that had once resided there. Then the sword fell. It was not a clean cut, but it would do, for the neck had broken.

She knew it was an act of mercy.

Allison turned to face the mob again, but Cody had destroyed most of them. She could see the spirits leaving the corpses piled around him, and out of the corner of her eye, for she did not want to look close, the ghostly form rising from the body of the man she had killed. She knew the soldiers themselves had not been evil, but what was left of them was easily manipulated by Mulkerrin's sorcery. The floating forms were gone from the street in an instant, and the way was nearly clear.

Behind her, in his own form, John Courage struggled with the charred and smoldering demon, who had only a handful of eyes left on his body. Courage was sinking his hand into the demon's flesh and tearing, searching for something vital. Allison turned to watch just in time to see him raise his hand to strike, but when the blow fell, it was not his hand at all. John Courage's entire arm had changed, but not in shape. It had changed its substance.

John's arm was made of stone.

Blows rained down on the demon, until it was almost whimpering in its defiance. It struggled and clawed at Courage, but could not shake him off. It had proven unusually resistant to fire, and now Courage raised his stone arm, and it changed again, to fresh wood, its bark slightly green. The wooden fist was lengthening, sharpening, until it resembled nothing so much as a newly carved stake.

"Cody," Courage heard Allison call behind him. He knew that he had their unwanted attention, but it could not be helped. He thrust his arm into the creature's belly, the sharp wood passing nearly through the thing, then wrenched around inside before pulling out and thrusting again. On the third thrust, he found something, his hand piercing it. The wood had the desired reaction, as the beast screamed.

The creature shuddered and expelled a fetid breath, and John Courage looked up. From inside the hotel came another demon, this one snake-like of a kind he had seen only once before. It slithered in a lumbering fashion. It had no eyes but a sense of smell that led it slowly toward Allison, the human. Far down the street, other things moved and people ran in the streets. In the darkened corners, even smaller things scuttled, the size of human children. They were the scavengers, dark jackals, waiting for their larger counterparts to do the serious damage first. But in packs, they were just as dangerous.

It was getting worse; they had to get out. Courage turned toward Allison and Cody, and saw Cody finishing off the last of the soldiers as Allison stared at him. Cody, apparently, had not heard her shout, had not seen Courage's latest transformations. All the better for now.

John Courage walked toward her, and Allison turned to shout to Cody that it was time to go, while the getting was good. Then she saw them: more soldiers, former human beings who had been overcome by Mulkerrin's ghostly slaves, pushed from their bodies to make way for new tenants. Allison realized what had happened. For every human host Cody killed, the spirits simply found a new one.

They were fighting a losing battle, no matter what.

"Will, come on. We've got to get out of here." He ignored her, finishing off what he thought was the last of them. "Look behind you!"

Cody did, and they rushed him from all sides, all corners, and toward Allison as well. Courage was next to her, knocking several of her attackers away, one with enough force to snap its neck. She saw Cody buried beneath a mound of the creatures, who had jumped him all at once, bringing him down. Then fire blossomed at the bottom of the pile, kindling under dry logs, and the whole group was in flames, their clothing burning out of control and their skin beginning to give off a greasy smell and a crackling noise.

"Allison, pay attention!" Courage said, then yanked her aside.

She looked up to see that the ghost had fled the body of the man whose neck he had broken, and was moving toward her. It would not approach Courage directly, and his arm burst into flame as he tried to wave it off.

"Why does it want me?" she asked.

"It doesn't care, it needs a host to stay alive, to stay here, in our world. You'll do as well as any human."

Finally, the thing apparently decided there would be easier targets, and fled the scene, even as Courage was lifting another of the soldiers and tossing him away.

In our world. Allison heard the words again. Not *on, in.* Not even on Earth, but *in our world.*

"What do you mean by . . . ?" she started, but there wasn't time.

"We've got to get you out of here, or you'll be one of them," he said, and then he was dragging her away, north toward the side street the demon had blocked.

She turned to see the huge snake-like thing, at least thirty feet long and three feet thick, sliding to block their way, and screamed.

"Will!"

She realized he was in trouble too. She looked at Courage out of the corner of her eye.

"What about Will?" she demanded.

"He'll have to fend for himself! He should be fine, but

we've got to get you out of here! Once we're gone, he won't have to fight, he can run."

"I'm not going anywhere without him," Allison said, trying to stand her ground.

"I'm sorry, but you are," Courage answered, then threw her over his shoulder and shot into the side street just in time to escape the serpent, which even now coiled back to slither toward the overwhelmed Will Cody.

Will was fighting hard, but he was getting very tired. Changing from flame to mist to a tiger to himself and then back to flame again, the battle a constant, combined with the serpent he saw sliding toward him now, had begun to take a toll on his body, and his psyche. He was glad that Allison and Courage had gone. He knew of the danger to her, and he stood a better chance of getting out if he didn't have to worry about her. All he had to do now was change to something with wings, or to mist, and fly out of there.

A sword entered through his back and out his stomach, and he vomited blood, hunching over. He turned fast, his movement pulling the sword from its owner's grasp, then reached around behind him to pull the blade from his body.

"That . . . fucking . . . *hurt*!" he said, swinging the blade down into the shoulder of his attacker, a woman. The sword sank deep into the body, cracking through the collarbone and splintering ribs. He turned to face the rest, his wounds healing, but not as quickly as they should. Human hands driven by ghostly minds grabbed him from all around, and he felt a burning, searing pain that made him scream.

He clamped his mouth shut, willing the scream, the pain, away, even as he felt his arms yanked to his sides by the mob that surrounded him. He wanted to strike out, to burn them, to fly away, but he could not gather his thoughts, his concentration, enough for the change. The pain overwhelmed him, covering his entire body now, and despite his greatest efforts, he did scream again.

"Yeeaaarggghhhh!"

Then the hands were gone, the mob was gone, though the pain remained. His mind aflame, he fell to the pavement with a clank. Opening his eyes, he saw the chains. Silver chains, wrapped around his entire body. And then he heard the voice.

"Well." The voice floated on the breeze. *"If it isn't our old friend, Buffalo Bill."*

Cody recognized the voice.

It belonged to Liam Mulkerrin.

Boston, Massachusetts, United States of America.
Tuesday, June 6, 2000, 1:31 P.M.:

Meaghan was pretty ambivalent about being the boss. Here she was, one of the youngest shadows on Earth, certainly with less experience in their culture than the creatures she surrounded herself with. She didn't really rate, at a surface glance, the kind of attention she received. She was nervous and frightened sometimes, when Alex was sleeping and couldn't comfort her. She was insecure because not long ago she'd been human, a young woman with a so-so job and no steady relationship, who had no family and whose only real friend had been murdered. Not much of a résumé.

But other times, she knew all the reasons why she was the leader, and agreed with them. Other times she was confident in her strength and ability, and the rightness of her position. She had been strong enough as a human to walk among the walking dead, to befriend them, to take Peter Octavian as her lover. She had chosen to become one of them, to help them fight a centuries-old battle to the death. She had helped ease the pain of the reconciliation between Peter and his blood-brothers and -sisters. She had shown them the way out of their self-imposed limits, shown them that their shape-shifting abilities could be used for far more than even Peter had imagined, that they didn't have to limit themselves to bats, wolves and mist, forms imposed by Rome's brainwashing.

She was young, but she was strong. And good. And for those among them that had a difficult time remembering what it was like to believe in one's own, innate goodness, she was an example to be emulated. Her innocence was a beacon to them. To others, for the moment in the minority, that beacon became a target, and Meaghan knew she would be defending herself very soon. She also knew that chief among her detractors was Hannibal, and that keeping him in line would require more effort than she had believed.

That threat, she knew, would have to be eliminated. And if that required that Hannibal be eliminated, so be it.

Though voices screamed in the back of her mind at such a thought, Meaghan Gallagher resisted their input, their logic, which wondered if what she was doing were so much different from the culling of the herd practiced by the Church for centuries. She insisted to herself that it was different, that she was doing it, not for her own good, or any evil purpose, but for the good of her own kind, for humanity, and for the world, which could not stand a war between humans and shadows. The smoldering remains of Venice, the hundreds of bodies, proved that.

But still, Meaghan was a woman full of doubts and insecurities, and so she was glad to have the distraction of a common enemy. Though Mulkerrin's return frightened her almost more than anything else, it also gave her one problem upon which to concentrate her thoughts, and a time in which she did not have to concern herself with long-term questions. Only immediate solutions mattered. She was also glad to be returning home to Alexandra Nueva, whom she loved more than life, more than what little was left of her humanity, more than the goodness in that elusive thing she persisted in thinking of as her soul.

And Alexandra's kiss, her touch, her voice, served to soothe Meaghan's doubts, to quiet the storm in her soul.

Alex gave her the first part of an answer to their forever question: the nature of their kind. Meaghan knew they had the capacity for atrocity, horror and great evil, but Alexandra, who had lived such terrible acts, been a hunter of humans and reveled in it, was now a constant reminder that the shadows also had the capacity for love, for kindness, for great good. Like humanity's, the shadow soul contained an extraordinary duality of spirit, but magnified a thousandfold.

But the question remained.

Meaghan shook such thoughts from her head as she rushed along the sidewalk toward her Back Bay home. Alex would be waiting, she knew, packed and ready to scramble off to Otis Air Force Base. They'd be in Germany in less than seven hours. By then it would be nearly 3 A.M. in Salzburg, and hell would be in full swing.

She rounded the corner by their brownstone, and there was Alexandra, sitting on the steps with their bags packed, like a child with whom no one will play. The image didn't last long, though, as she looked up at Meaghan and smiled that beautiful smile of hers. Whatever they faced, they would do it together. Always.

"Hello, sweetie," Meaghan called to her as she approached.

Alex stood up and handed Meaghan her bag, then gave her a firm kiss, nuzzling for a moment. When she pulled back, she sighed, knowing there was work to be done.

"Time to go, sugar," Alex said, and shouldered the strap of her own bag.

They locked hands, and Alexandra raised her free one to call over the inconspicuous government sedan that waited at the corner to rush them to Otis. The car was there in a moment, and the clean-cut, quiet type who stepped out of it was wearing sunglasses and did not smile. These two factors had always seemed to Meaghan a prerequisite for working in government security. CIA, FBI, OSP, NSA—

the letters didn't matter. They all looked the same, as if they were all grown in the same laboratory somewhere.

Brrr. A chilling thought.

Their bags were in the trunk, and Alex had already climbed in. Meaghan had one foot in the door when a hand landed on her shoulder, strong enough to stop her.

"Wait," a cold, familiar voice said.

In the space between heartbeats, Meaghan turned, pulling the hand from her shoulder and toward her, prepared to strike its owner with a ferocity born when she died. Then she saw the face of the being who had accosted her, and could not have been more surprised. She knew she'd recognized that voice.

"Where the fuck have you been?" Alexandra spat the words as she got out of the car behind Meaghan, just as their driver finally freed his sidearm from its holster. For a distracted moment, Meaghan pitied humans their loss of superiority. They would never again be the strongest or the fastest, the best at anything. But the thought was passing. There were far more important issues at hand.

"Yes," Meaghan said with barely suppressed anger and frustration. "Where exactly *have* you been, Lazarus?"

The smile of greeting had left the ancient shadow's lined face as soon as Alex spoke. Only grim resolution remained.

"I would like to say I expected a more, shall we say, cordial reunion. But I did not, and so, shall not. Why don't we go inside?"

Meaghan and Alex looked at each other, both still quite angry. Meaghan spoke only because Alexandra had even less control of her temper.

"You may not realize this, but we have far more important things to worry about right now than you. If you'd wanted to talk to us, you should have shown up when we still wanted to talk to you."

With that, she turned and began to usher Alex back into the sedan. The driver still stood at attention, wary and stupidly unafraid, his ego denying his own uselessness.

But Lazarus was not through.

"Cody is Mulkerrin's prisoner," he said.

And now they were prepared to listen.

Meaghan and Alexandra had first met the vampire known only as Lazarus the night before the Venice Jihad. He had fought at their sides, in the sunlight. Octavian had just revealed Rome's treachery to them, revealed that they could exist in the sun without fear of death. But it was new to them, and painful, and many were afraid even to try. Lazarus, on the other hand, did not seem at all pained by daytime battle, or surprised by their newly expanded shapeshifting abilities. In fact, they were forced to surmise that he'd been aware of them from the start. Lazarus had participated in the battle only until the tide had turned irrevocably in their favor, and then he had departed.

Peter Octavian had known Lazarus was different, had suspected something of the truth, and Lazarus had hinted that he was on the right track. But then Peter was gone. Meaghan and Alexandra had made the same connections, but later, as Will Cody searched the world for Lazarus and found nothing.

Centuries upon centuries earlier, when the church realized it would be impossible to destroy all of the so-called Defiant Ones, the shadows who refused to bow to Roman Catholic rule, sorcerous clergymen trapped as many as they could. Using dark and hurtful magic, those sorcerers tampered with the minds of the vampires they captured, ingraining within them certain . . . weaknesses. These shadow creatures had complete control over their own molecules. With the church's influence, they now believed that they could not enter holy ground, could not bear the touch of silver or blessed water, could not change their shape into any but supposedly "unclean" animals or mist, and most importantly, could not bear the touch of the light of day. Of these all, only silver's poison had a grain of truth.

Lies all, but so effectively woven into the minds of these Defiant Ones that they infected those others with whom they came in contact after their release, as well as each successive generation. Lies that would cause the vampires own minds, own powers, to destroy them.

Psychosomatic suicide.

The Church believed that these controls would enable them to control the shadows from afar. And for a time, it had worked. And then came Peter Octavian. He had overcome the pain of sunlight, though other such triumphs eluded him. Peter had abandoned the life of hunter, and instead spent his time in the service of humans, investigating their losses and broken hearts and crimes. It was a subject of great fascination for him. Eventually, this vocation led him in pursuit of a book, a book stolen from the bowels of the Vatican: *The Gospel of Shadows*. It detailed all of the atrocities perpetrated by the Church on their kind, as well as the many magical spells used to control other creatures of darkness, from beyond what they referred to as "the veil."

In the end, Peter had carried the church sorcerer, Liam Mulkerrin, to the other side of that veil, leaving *The Gospel of Shadows* behind in his people's safekeeping. Meaghan and Alexandra had kept it from the world's governments, even from the United Nations, and fear prevented any of those powers from attempting to take it.

And what of Lazarus?

Within the pages of *The Gospel of Shadows*, a tainted pope spoke of five Defiant Ones who had been captured but whose minds were impossible to tamper with. They were to be executed, but then in a terrible battle they escaped.

"You're one of the five," Meaghan said now, as they settled onto the sofa in the living room of the brownstone she shared with Alexandra. Alex took a chair.

"Pardon me?" Lazarus said, eyebrow arched.

"You are one of the five who were never brainwashed,"

she elaborated, knowing it was unnecessary. "Peter figured it out before he . . . died, and Alex and I did, not much later than that."

The room was silent, and the smile returned to Lazarus's lips. He looked at Meaghan, then to Alexandra, who stared at him in return with open hostility.

"Proceed," he said.

"Cody searched the world for you," Alex finally said. "We know you are one of the five. What we want to know is, who are the others? Where are they? Where were you in hiding? And how do you know about Mulkerrin's return?"

Alex paused, her tough exterior momentarily revealing the concern beneath. "And what makes you say Cody has been captured?" she asked.

Lazarus smiled now, wide and friendly, almost like an excited child.

"Well done!" he said, and for a half second, Meaghan thought he would applaud.

"Actually, there were four of us, not five. Mary was killed during the escape. Martha is in Salzburg now, preparing to help however she can. Who is the other? Good question. I tend to think of him as "the Stranger," and for now, that should be good enough for you. We were in Greece when Cody came looking, and we knew where he was all along. He could not have found me because I didn't want to be found. You three were doing quite all right on your own. As to how I know about Mulkerrin's return and Cody's capture, I cannot, or rather I will not, say. Know only that I wish to remedy both situations as expediently as do both of you. Which is why I am here, after all."

Lazarus could see the questions ready to erupt from the lovers, and so he continued.

"Cody is, as far as we know, all right. I expect he is captive in the Hohensalzburg fortress at the south end of the city."

"Well, what the hell are we waiting for?" Meaghan finally asked. All other questions could be put aside, but Mulkerrin must be destroyed and, if possible, Cody freed.

Lazarus stood, ran his hand through his shoulder-length brown hair and stepped away from the sofa. Meaghan watched him. His prominent nose gave his face an aquiline aspect, and the wrinkles of his olive-complexioned face and his brown eyes were quite expressive. She realized that he didn't look exactly the same as he had during their previous meeting. He was different in subtle ways: the shape of his nose, the point of his chin, even the color of his hair.

Was this by choice, or did great age such as Lazarus had endured wear away the memory of oneself? Did such ancient shadows become just that, shadows of their former selves? How different, then, did he look from his true countenance? How long must one live to forget his or her appearance? Disturbing questions all. She had asked what they had waited for, and yet she was aware that time, for Lazarus, would be different than it was even for them.

And yet, Alexandra was not quite so understanding.

"While we suffer your silence," she snarled at Lazarus, "my blood-brother awaits his death. Speak your mind, Lazarus, or we go, now."

Alexandra looked at Meaghan then, and although it was clear who was the leader among them, Meaghan knew that this time, her lover would accept no argument, no instruction, no suggestion. Once, Alexandra had wanted her blood-brother, Will Cody, dead. Now he and Rolf Sechs were her only family, and she would not lose them.

Lazarus walked toward the restored masonry fireplace, and rested a hand on the mantel as he examined the room. Art surrounded him: what appeared to be a genuine Monet next to a framed, toilet-paper sketch by Andy Warhol. And yet it was here, by his right hand, where lay the one piece of art that mattered. Lazarus knew that the two women, each once a lover to Peter Octavian, had taken it and perhaps these others, from his abandoned apartment after the

Jihad. The sculpture was a perfect likeness, a bust of Octavian himself, ponytail and lopsided smile intact.

"This," Lazarus said sternly as he lifted the sculpture and turned it to them. "This is our weapon. Mulkerrin has returned from Hell, where Peter Octavian took him, far more powerful than before. He has achieved such a feat without even the so-called *Gospel of Shadows* to guide him. It makes one wonder, does it not? For if Mulkerrin has gathered such power to him, what might Octavian have accomplished beyond the veil? What powers has Hell given to him?"

Silence.

CHAPTER ✦ FIVE

Allison Vigeant was being pulled, dragged really, across Makartsteg, a narrow bridge spanning the Salzach River. John Courage was trying not to be rough, but he would hear no argument. Not that he could have heard her over the screaming. Allison imagined that they must look like a swarm of insects from above, so many people clogged the bridge and the streets around it. Several times she had almost been separated from John, but he roughly shoved people out of the way if he had to.

Allison took an elbow in the chest then, and bent over to catch her breath while the rush of people flowed around and past her, as if she were a rock in the rapids. Then Courage was pulling insistently on her arm, and she was moving again, one hand clutched to her breasts. They reached the north side of the river, and headed east along its bank, but then she stopped again, even as the tide of panicked humanity started to thin out.

"Damn it, John," she said, her anger turning into a panic for her lover, "we can't just leave him back there!"

He wanted to ignore her, but could not.

"Look!" he said, sweeping his arm wide, forcing her to take in the hell that had sprung up around them. Back across the bridge, demons of all sizes roamed free, though

74

she didn't see Mulkerrin's possessed soldiers anywhere. A splash made her look downriver, and Allison saw something impossibly huge, incredibly black, sliding up toward them. For the first time she noticed that the bridge they had crossed was the only one standing, that the other three in this part of town had been torn apart by the earthquake and that this thing was thrashing at their pilings, bringing even their remains down into the water. The bridge was still packed with people, and whatever was in the water would soon bring them all tumbling down.

"We've got to help them," Allison said quietly, but she knew the reality of their situation. The police and army were already coming in, starting to evacuate people. A small force of soldiers ran by them even now and stood at the river's edge, shooting at the black thing which splashed water up at them. No, Allison knew that she and Courage, and Will, of course, would have to find other ways to help. Mulkerrin had to be destroyed if any of these people were to survive.

Courage had a grip on her arm which never faltered, and he'd been pulling, hurrying her along. But now it was Allison who picked up the pace. They had not run into a single demon on the north side yet, among the frantic crowds, but she knew that was nothing more than luck.

"Where are we going?" she finally thought to ask.

"It's close," he said, "and I think we'll be safe there for a while."

Allison kept her mouth shut after that, concentrating on getting wherever this safe place was. They were rushing toward the plaza where Elisabethkai, the street they were on, met Linzer Gasse and several other narrow roads. The city which had seemed so vibrant to her before, smelling of chocolate and filled with the music of Mozart, was now a maze of danger. Blue skies which had reflected off cobblestones and golden domes had become black clouds hovering above shattered homes, churches and fountains. The stench of sulphur filled Allison's nostrils.

They heard screams ahead, and a woman ran into the plaza, floral dress torn down the back, blood smeared and running down her calves. Dozens of other maddened civilians scattered as she shrieked like a lunatic, stumbling into their midst. She tripped, nearly tumbling over crumbled masonry, and then stopped short at a huge fissure that separated her from the river side of the plaza. The woman was young and attractive, and terrified, her blond hair sweeping back as she spun to face her pursuers. Three small but ravenous-looking demons rushed toward her on all fours, the dark jackals stopping just short of her and snapping at her feet like wild dogs. More were behind them, and the scene became a near riot as people pushed one another aside in their attempts to get away.

Courage seemed about to move, to help, but it was too late. Even the jackals weren't fast enough, as an enormous head with skin like steel poked out of the crack in the ground, and a great length of tongue lashed out, wrapped around the woman and dragged her into the creature's gaping maw. Many of the city's people would survive this nightmare, but those with them in the square were doomed. Allison had never felt so helpless.

"Damned beast!" Courage said, sincerely, obviously stunned.

Then the jackals turned toward them, and there was no time for conversation. Even though the things could not leap across the ravine in the middle of the street, their shrieking bark caught the attention of the demon inside the fissure, and the thing was rising a bit farther from the hole, its eyes on Allison and John.

After Venice, Allison Vigeant thought she had seen it all, but today she was learning how arrogant that assumption had been. The creature began to slide out of its hole, dragging itself by three-clawed hands, a dragon seemingly made of metal. Allison had to tear her eyes away to look at John Courage, and her mouth hung open. Not long before, she had seen him use his vampiric shapeshifting abilities in ways Cody had never suggested, taking forms she had never imagined them able to assume. Now he was doing it again. John grimaced in pain as huge wings sprang from his back.

"Let's go," he said, then grabbed her around the waist with both his arms—and they were flying. The dragon gave a terrible hiss and shot its tongue after them, but they were already out of range.

It was a moment before Allison realized that rather than flying away, they were simply going up. Up and up and up. Hundreds of feet in the air they flew, compounding her terror, and she hugged John tight and closed her eyes. When she opened them, she was staring straight at the fortress, the spring from which Liam Mulkerrin's evil now overran the city. And she thought of Will.

"Oh, God. Will." And finally the tears came.

"He's alive," Courage said, and she looked up at him, not understanding.

"How can you . . ."

"Trust me."

"Where are we going?"

"Actually, we're here," he said, and she looked away from the fortress and at the top of a cliff, so close at hand. In a moment, their feet touched ground and they were standing by a small, apparently ancient structure which looked as if a castle turret had sprouted from the hillside. Above them, forest stretched away as far as Allison could see, and below, the trees dropped off to nothing except the street far below and the river beyond.

"Let's go," John said, and started off a few paces before he realized Allison wasn't following.

"You bastard," she said, terrible knowledge dawning on her. Courage only tilted his head and raised an eyebrow in question.

"You asshole!" Allison said now, with more conviction. "You could have done that Icarus angel imitation back in front of my hotel, and Will Cody would be here, safe with us. What the hell's the matter with you, John? Why did you let that happen?"

Courage bit his lip, and for all the toughness of his appearance, the military-style hair, the square jaw, he looked vulnerable at that moment. His whole manner, his voice, his eyes were penitent.

"I don't have a good excuse," he said sadly. "You're right, I could have flown with you and we all could have escaped. But I wasn't thinking about escape then, Allison. It happened so fast, all I was thinking about was battle. Retreat is foreign to me. I'm not used to having humans around, not used to being . . ."

"Vulnerable," she finished for him, and it was not a question. John nodded.

"I'm sorry," he said, meeting her gaze finally.

"We're not done yet," she told him. "I was in Venice, my lover is a vampire, but I've never seen a vampire do some of the things I've seen you do today. And I have no idea how you could know whether Will is alive or dead. What's going on?"

The sadness disappeared from John Courage's face, replaced by a barrier of determination, a fierce secrecy.

"I've had a lot of practice," he said, but there was no sarcasm in his voice. "I've been around awhile. All shadows have the same abilities, but they must learn to utilize them. In fact, the vampires you know are much more powerful than even they are aware."

"So how old are you, and who are you really?" she asked.

"That," John said and let out a breath, "that you'll know soon enough. It's why I was in Salzburg in the first place, why I found you and Cody. But the answers to those questions must be found to be believed. If I simply told you, you'd never buy it."

Allison nodded, satisfied that, for the moment at least, that's all she was getting from him. They walked at a good clip, ducking low branches along their rough path. She scanned around them, expecting at any moment to see giant demonic things lumbering toward them through the trees, or those small, vicious jackals snapping toward them up the path. Nothing happened except that they continued to move uphill, and Allison began to believe that she could feel a difference up here. As if, for the moment, they had escaped.

"You knew there wouldn't be any demons up here," she said.

"Call it a hunch."

They slowed and Allison looked up the path. Ominous walls stood to the right, towering twenty-five or so feet above the path. As far as she could tell, there were no windows.

"What is it?" she asked.

"You didn't come up here with Will?" John smiled at her finally. "Shame on you. Bad tourists! It's a monastery. Capuchin monks, in cloister, as far as the locals know."

They drew up toward huge double doors of wood and iron, and as John went forward to ring a bell hung next to them, Allison watched him closely, frowning, thinking. He backed off to wait, and looked toward her again.

"Before you ask, it was a monastery once. The older brothers died over time, and the younger ones we shipped to other locations."

"We?"

"A couple of my friends and I. We own this place, now. Of course, not on paper."

A bolt slid noisily back on the other side of the doors, the left swung open slowly, and a short, portly but not unattractive woman stood there with a cross look on her face, like an angry mother.

"Next time, take your time, why don't you?" she said, then turned to Allison with a friendly smile, the crankiness gone from her face. "And you are?"

"Allison Vigeant," John said, "Martha. Martha, Allison."

They stepped into a great courtyard, around which the stone building stood, almost a fortress in itself. In the center, an enormous fountain lay dormant. Two slender young men appeared in a doorway on their right, came quickly forward and bowed their heads to John Courage. They were twins, and quite handsome as far as Allison was concerned, but how many vampires weren't? Of course, Martha was a vampire as well, though certainly the least attractive Allison had seen. She had long since realized that with the control they could wield over their forms, the shadows honed their appearance, both consciously and unconsciously, throughout their existence. She wondered why Martha did not practice that particular art.

"Allison, these are the sons of Lazarus: Jared and Isaac," Martha said, and each man bowed as his name was said.

Lazarus! Her mind raced.

"You're full of surprises," she said, turning on Courage. He smiled at her, obviously enjoying the mystery.

"Come on, now. You're a reporter. You'll figure it out."

Martha bolted the door behind them, then joined John and Allison as they went inside the monastery. Behind them, Isaac and Jared took up positions on either side of the great door. Once inside, they sat at a long wooden table in a completely bare room, and Allison wondered whether Courage had removed anything, or simply not added anything after the monks had gone. She shook her head and brought herself back to the business at hand.

"Why aren't there any demons up here?" she asked.

"Thin air?" Courage chuckled.

"Would you stop fucking around! The man I love may be dead, an incredibly powerful lunatic has apparently come back to life, demons are wrecking the city below us and ghosts are taking over the bodies of tourists. People are dying down there, John. Now what are you going to do about it?"

Courage wasn't smiling anymore.

"I'm sorry," he said. "You're right."

"He was trying to make you feel better by distracting you," Martha said, earning an angry glance from John.

"Distracted is the last thing I need to be," she hissed. "Now, can we please get on with it? What's going on?"

Courage sat up straight.

"There aren't any demons up here because we're protected," he said.

"By what?"

"Magic."

"Whose?"

Courage looked away.

"Mine," he said, and Allison forgot to be angry.

"Cody is fine," he continued. "I would know if he wasn't. We can only assume he is Mulkerrin's prisoner or he would have tracked us here by now. Here's what's going on. The UN and SJS have sent troops to Munich. They're amassing there now, and will begin to move on Salzburg tonight so that they can enter the city in the morning."

"Alex and Meaghan with them?" Allison asked, hopeful.

"No. They're otherwise occupied."

"How in hell do you know all this?"

"That's not important."

"So what do we do until they get here, just hang out while people are dying down below?" Allison shivered at the thought.

"Well, that depends on you," Courage said, smiling again.

He liked to smile, Allison thought, and realized that Cody shared that trait. It wasn't something she'd ever considered before.

"How's that?"

"We need reinforcements. With the power Mulkerrin has now—and I'm embarrassed to say I don't know his new limits—the humans won't be able to do a thing. The SJS doesn't have any shadows old enough to have the power, the ability, to destroy Mulkerrin. And that's if they can keep from killing each other, with the crazy politics involved. Ten miles south of here, there's a mountain called Untersberg. Inside that mountain are our reinforcements, old shadows. With them we'd have a chance. What we need to do is wake them up and bring them back."

"And how do we do that?"

"That's the catch," John said. "We need some blood from a willing, living human female."

"How much is 'some'?" Allison asked quietly.

"You'll live."

I don't want to die.

"How important is this?"

"Victory depends on it."

"Well, then, I think you know my answer," Allison nodded her head. "Just one thing. You won't tell me who you are or how you know all these things, but it's obvious to me that you know a lot of things without being told them. I think you knew Mulkerrin was coming back, or at least suspected. You know Cody's okay, right now.

"What I want to know is, will he get out of this alive?"

Courage looked sad for the first time, and suddenly Allison was terrified to hear his answer. She had to fight to avoid running from the room, hands over her ears.

"I wish I knew," John said, and though it was better than the answer she had expected, for some reason Allison was not relieved.

Boston, Massachusetts, United States of America.
Tuesday, June 6, 2000, 1:45 P.M.:

In their bedroom, Meaghan Gallagher and Alex Nueva held each other tight. Their embrace lasted minutes, as they inhaled the familiar smells of their life together: fresh cut flowers and light perfumes, Italian cooking and fresh-baked brownies. When their eyes opened, they pressed their foreheads together, eyes meeting, and smiled nervous smiles to hide their anxiety. They had changed into jeans and sneakers, Meaghan with a cotton dress shirt, and Alex with the Batman tank top Meg had given her the previous Christmas. They loved their place, their life together, and they didn't know if they would ever return.

In the next room, Lazarus began to weave the spell they would need to travel. Finally, Alexandra let her lover go and then held her at arm's length, searching her eyes.

"I hate this, Mcaghan," she said quietly, almost whispering. "I hate being afraid. I thought fear was something I'd overcome. I've been afraid for others, in Venice, and now for Cody in Salzburg, but I forgot what it's like to fear for myself. I wasn't afraid to go to Salzburg, no matter what Mulkerrin has become, but this . . ."

She waved her hand toward the closed door, beyond which they could hear the voice of Lazarus rise and fall in an eerie cadence. The lights in the room began to dim, flickered for a moment, and then came back on full force, one of the bulbs exploding beneath its shade. Alex jumped.

"Alex, honey, listen," Meaghan said, holding her lover's hand tight. "You all fell for the myth of the vampire. We shadows are not creatures of myth, we're flesh and blood. Even if we're not really human anymore, we still have that humanity in us. Even if we're that much stronger, it's impossible to deny our fundamental nature. No matter how much wc nccd the blood, at our core most of us know that it's wrong to kill humans. We do what we must to live, but we can't deny the humanity that's still part of us. At our core, we can still feel fear, and sorrow. And love. Sweetheart, these things are not our weakness, they are our strength, our tether to all the things we hope for the future."

Alex nodded; she knew Meaghan was right. That knowledge had been hard won, but now, in her heart, she did know.

From the other room, Lazarus called for them. It was time. They embraced again, their lips joining in a desperate kiss.

"Meg," Alex broke off, breathless, "what do you think we'll find?"

Meaghan was thoughtful a moment, then kissed Alex on the forehead and grabbed her leather jacket from the bed.

"I'm afraid to think about it," she said, taking Alex by the elbow and opening their bedroom door.

Meaghan and Alex had known Matt and Ellen Tillinger for three years. They were a fortysomething couple who lived in a brownstone diagonally across the street, and they were the only close, human friends the shadow women had made who were not already involved in vampire politics. They weren't blood cultists, they didn't worship vampires, they weren't mindless volunteers. They were friends.

The four neighbors exchanged nervous hugs and kisses, as Lazarus chanted silently above the open *Gospel of Shadows*. Alex hadn't told Matt what was going on over the phone, but the Tillingers had a good idea why they were there.

"What's going on?" Ellen asked, concern creasing her brow.

"We don't have time to beat around the bush, you guys," Meaghan said, her hands clasped together. "So you'll forgive us if we just sort of dump this on you. We're going away for a while; I don't know how long but probably not more than a few days. We don't know if we'll be able to get any sustenance where we're going . . ." She let her words trail off.

"You need blood?" Matt asked, and as Meaghan nodded, he shook his head nervously. "Look, we're friends, you know. I mean, we love you guys and we'll do anything you need us to do, but you don't want my blood."

Matt had HIV.

"It's okay, Matt," Alex said, soothing. "In fact, we had a doctor friend of ours confirm this last week, and we've been meaning to tell you. We can't be infected. Shadows can't get, carry or pass on HIV. We've always said it, but we've finally confirmed it, and since that's been the number one fear among potential donors, we've got to get a press release out about it as soon as we get back."

"I wish I had your blood," he quipped, and then fell silent.

"If that's so," Ellen said, "then of course we'll help. I know you wouldn't ask if you didn't have to. What should we do?"

"Just give me a hug," Meaghan said to her, and Ellen did.

Matt went to Alex in much the same way, then snickered and told thcm he felt awkward, "like we're playing strip poker or something." They all smiled, understanding. It was an intimacy friends rarely shared, and far more profound than simply seeing one another naked.

"Thanks for trusting us," Meaghan said when it was over, then looked at Matt. "You know about the Revenant Transformation. When we get back, Alex and I will tell you all about what it means to be one of us. I know you were being a wiseguy, but if you do want our blood, it's yours. Your life would never be the same, but you'd be alive.

"Think about it," she said, and then she and Alex walked them back to the door, kissed them good-bye, and shut it.

Lazarus looked up from the book, and Meaghan thought that, for a moment, even he looked afraid.

"They don't know you," Meaghan said. "I didn't feel I could ask . . ."

"Not to worry," he assured her. "I satisfied my, hm, cravings before I arrived. And now . . ." He slammed the book shut and stood up.

"The bus is leaving," Lazarus announced. "Shall we?"

As he stretched out his arm, bowing as if to say *After you*, that arm disappeared completely. Meaghan was startled, but Alexandra understood immediately. It was just what she'd expected. The closer they got to Lazarus, the more they could see of the portal, nearly invisible when looked at from the side. Its reflective surface made Meaghan shiver as she thought about Peter, and Lazarus seemed to read her mind.

"If I've read this right," he said, holding up *The Gospel of Shadows*, "this passage should be much less painful for us than it was for Peter and the sorcerer."

"Let's hope . . . Did you say 'us'?" Alex raised an eyebrow.

Lazarus nodded.

"The Stranger has said that if we can't find Octavian and bring him back, we have little chance of defeating Mulkerrin. In that light, I think I'll be more use to you than I will be in Salzburg. Not, of course, that I want to do this . . . but then I'm sure a little milk run to Hell wasn't on your agenda either."

Hell. He'd said it, and now Meaghan's own fear rose up to enfold her, whispering in her ear. She'd comforted Alex as well as she could, but that was what lovers were for. She could not let on how nervous she was, especially about finding Peter. Lazarus had told them that time passed much more quickly *there.* Peter had been gone five years, but what did that mean for him? If they could even find him, if he were still alive, what shape might he be in? What state of mind? Mulkerrin had been evil, and his time in Hell had obviously nurtured him, but Peter, shadow or no, had been the essence of good. A hero. Oh, shit, she didn't want to think about it.

"You're bringing the book, right?" Alexandra said, cutting off Meaghan's thoughts.

"Of course," Lazarus said. "How else will we get back?"

"Guard it with your life," Alex said, "or we won't get back."

Finally, the two of them looked at Meaghan. The youngest shadow in the room, and yet they both acknowledged her as the leader of this little expedition. She expected it from Alex; it had been that way since Venice. But Lazarus had seemed haughty, almost omniscient at times. Why would he . . . and then she realized that he must be just as frightened as they were, that he had no real, clear idea of what they might find through that portal, what it would feel like, look like, smell like. No matter what they'd faced before, the concept of Hell was buried so deep within them, the fear of it so pervasive . . .

"Fuck it," Meaghan snapped, slipping into her jacket. "We're outta here."

She stepped through the portal, and the others followed.

Salzburg, Austria, European Union.
Tuesday, June 6, 2000, 4:45 P.M.:

They were flying again, but there was no way that Allison was going to get used to it. Courage had spread his wings and, holding her tight, fallen off the side of the cliff. For the count of three they had fallen toward the river, then leveled off, gliding, the wind whipping them in the face, the smell of fires, started by the earthquake, heavy in the damp air. John was trying to save his strength. There was no way he was going to be able to fly all the way to Mount Untersberg with her in his arms, but it would take far too long to try to fight their way out of the city. And so, for the moment at least, they flew.

They stayed, for the most part, above the river, where they had an excellent view of the surrounding area. At first, Allison had felt sick from the flying, and then from the sights below. Parts of the city and the countryside were in flames, and some of the demons were so huge they could be seen much more clearly than the houses and buildings. Twice, she saw things off in the distance, gliding on the air as they were, and her heart pounded in her chest as she imagined them being attacked in mid-flight, Courage forced to drop her or die himself. But mercifully, neither creature even noticed them floating above.

As they moved along the river, the number of shadows—no, scratch that, they don't deserve to be called anything but demons—diminished greatly. What she guessed was a couple of miles from the monastery, they finally made a rough landing beside a bridge marked "Hellbrunner," which was intact. There were cars everywhere, moving away from the city proper, and she was pleased to realize that word had finally gotten out. Action was being taken. Police and military vehicles screamed by, on their way to help evacuate those they could. To the southeast, there were homes and shops, but to the southwest nothing but countryside.

"Still a long way to go," she said, "what do we do now?"

"We do what we must," Courage answered. "We hitch-hike."

"Get out!"

"No kidding," he laughed, and stuck out his thumb.

Allison watched as the cars moved past them. Some of the drivers' faces were panic-stricken, others annoyed. It was easy to tell which of them knew why they were being evacuated and which did not. Allison figured nobody would stop, or if someone did, it would be one of those who had no clue as to what was going on. A few of the passersby actually noticed them, and a couple had enough perception to realize that John was a shadow. Those cars sped up as they moved away.

An old Volkswagen rumbled toward them, and Allison watched the driver's eyes take them in, narrow as if in disgust at their transience, and then open wide upon realizing Courage's nature. The car bumped onto the shoulder and shut off, and the driver stepped out looking angry, but motioning to his passenger to stay in the car.

"You!" the man barked in German, a language Allison understood fairly well but could not speak. "Why do you go away from the city, why do you not help the people there?"

Allison was stunned. The man was either very brave or very stupid. Not that John would hurt him, or at least she didn't think he would, but this man didn't know that. John Courage was a vampire, after all. But he just wrinkled his brows in a question, then tilted his head in further inquiry, and finally laughed his little laugh, that Allison had begun to appreciate. She trusted John. She hoped that was the right choice.

"Why do you not help your own people?" John asked the man. "Why do *you* go away from the city?"

The man's face burned red, with anger or embarrassment, Allison could not tell. He sputtered unintelligibly, then muttered under his breath, but before he could finally think of some response, John cut him off.

"We are heading away from the city to find reinforcements. We need more of my kind if we are to destroy the sorcerer, to save what we can of your city, your nation."

The man looked doubtful.

"And," John continued, "we need a ride."

The man looked completely bewildered, and Allison knew she had to step in.

"We need to reach Mount Untersberg," she said in English, hoping he would get at least part of it. "It's our only hope. Do you know it?"

"Of course I know it," the man said in flawless English, his pride hurt by the question.

Allison shouldn't have been surprised. Many people in Austria and Germany who spoke English never let on that they do. She had always figured they thought Americans had it too easy as it was. Now she looked at the man, her face, she hoped, expressing all of the desperation that she felt.

"Fine," the man said. "I'll take you. My brother will be thrilled."

Just then the Volkswagen's passenger hopped out, beaming with pleasure, and rushed over to fall prostrate at John's feet. He started babbling something about honor and sacrifice, calling John his "bloodlord," and Courage finally hauled the man to his feet, his face the only question the car's driver needed.

"He's a cultist," the man said. "He thinks you're a god or

something. If you need blood, he's your man. In the mean-time, let's get out of here."

Very soon, they were creeping slowly along Alpenstrasse with hundreds of other evacuees. The driver's brother was not only a cultist, but a volunteer, and Allison began to realize how plentiful they'd become. John didn't take the blood the man offered, and Allison hoped that he'd made a wise choice, worried that before long he would need all the strength he could muster. The mountains rose up in the distance, and Allison wondered what might be left of the beautiful city when they returned.

And whether the man she loved would still be alive.

CHAPTER ✦ SIX

In the depths of the fortress, Will Cody began, quite painfully, to come around. He lay on the stone floor, and felt the cold of the hundreds of feet of solid stone that made up the foundation of the ancient structure. His eyelids fluttered halfway open as he glanced about the room, able to see well enough in the near-complete darkness. What surprised him most was that he still lived. Almost as surprising, however, was his pain.

Will had felt all kinds of pain, both in his human life and after. He'd suffered a broken heart, a broken spirit, broken limbs and broken promises. He'd been stabbed, shot, kicked and beaten, and eventually he'd died of old age and exhaustion, and that broken spirit as well. Karl Von Reinman's intervention had given him another life, but that first death had hurt him body and soul.

This pain was like that, only worse. It was despair over what might have happened to Allison, and it was the far-too-slow knitting of the gaping hole in his belly, where his innards had spilled out and were even now being replaced. The regrowth hurt even more than the wound. Still, he used his hands to sit up, and dragged himself backward until he found the support of a wall to lean against. He carefully avoided looking down at his gut, and concentrated on his other pain instead.

Allison.

Where was she? He'd seen Courage slipping down a side street with her, and fought that much harder to buy them time, expecting to follow. But then Mulkerrin had come . . . Still, he had to believe that Allison was okay or he'd go crazy in here. And somehow, it was not hard to have faith in Courage. There seemed more to that shadow than met the eye, and he certainly had mastered his abilities.

Yeah. Allison was okay.

Just keep telling yourself that, Will.

He held a hand across his stomach and was slightly disconcerted at the feeling. Under his palm, he could feel the wounds healing, the flesh growing back. Disembowelment was something he did not plan to experience again. And yet how could he protect himself when he was barely strong enough to move? Certainly he was too weak to make the change into mist, at least for the moment.

That was how vampires could be killed. If you were strong enough, fast enough, to stay alive, to batter away at a shadow over and over, to wound him and make him bleed, eventually, you could kill him, scattering the pieces far enough away that he'd never be able to draw them back together. Of course, if a vampire's mind were still clouded by the tampering of the Roman Church, it was even easier.

Will looked around for an escape, but found none. There were no windows, only a large iron door on the wall opposite him. Once he felt a bit stronger, he might be able to shapeshift, healing himself in the process. Then perhaps he could try the strength of that door. And if that didn't work, he would have to wait a bit longer, until he could make the change to mist. One way or another, he had to get out.

Cody was not used to being a captive. In fact, he had never been anyone's prisoner, unless he counted his business enslavement to that bastard Harry Tammen.

And at the thought of that, the memories flooded back.

Memories of Major North giving him his infamous nickname, of Ned Buntline making him a dime-novel hero, of his parents in Iowa and the death of his brother Sam, of his best boyhood friend, his dog Turk. He remembered herding cattle, scouting for Custer and the all-black tenth cavalry. He spoke the sign language of the Sioux (which he still could do), drank with Bill Hickok and fathered beautiful children. The death of his son Kit, his first standing ovation onstage in New York, scalping Yellow Hand, the murders of Wild Bill and Sitting Bull, the triumph of the Wild West Show, traveling around the world—a star. His affection for Annie Oakley, his love for his wife Lulu, and his mistress Katherine, and his daughter Irma and so many others.

All dead and gone, the way he often thought he should have gone, on to whatever there was past this plane. But he couldn't.

Harry Tammen had used Will's own irresponsibility against him, leveraging the Wild West Show until he owned the whole thing. Will was a prisoner. Even when Will "died," Tammen thought he owned Buffalo Bill, hook, line and corpse. Years later, when Tammen died, Cody was there. The look on Tammen's face made it all worthwhile. But at first, after Cody's supposed death, things only got worse. His wife, Louisa Cody, took Tammen's damned money and agreed to bury her husband, against his final wishes, where it would benefit Tammen's pocketbook. His country, which he had faithfully served, took back his Congressional Medal of Honor because he hadn't been a soldier when he performed the deeds for which he was given the award.

Betrayals abounded. And all those who refused to betray Cody, who truly loved him, died. If not before him, then later, while he was forced to continue the charade of his death, they all died. Since the truth of the shadows had come out, since the world had discovered he was still alive, supposed relatives had been attempting to contact him every day. For five years, he had refused to see them. He loved Allison, he had Meaghan and Alexandra, even Rolf and George Marcopoulos. He had gotten back into show business, made a movie, and gotten the rights to the Wild West Show back. He didn't need these long lost family members.

But now, with his guts lying in a pile in the middle of a cold, stone room, with a man who spelled almost certain death for him lurking somewhere about, with him captive once again and perhaps feeling a little sorry for himself, he realized that he'd made a terrible mistake. He should have embraced them all, poseurs or no. Possessions could be owned. In the modern world, even words could be owned. But emotions had to be freely given. He'd been afraid to really have a life again, to let those emotions free from the prison of his heart, because he could not forget the pain of the string of tragedies in his life as "Buffalo Bill."

How he hated that name. It signified every painful moment of his life. But now he knew that to truly live he had to risk tragedy again. Knowing his loved ones would die, he must still allow himself to care for them.

Perhaps being a prisoner again had, in a way, liberated him.

But enough of that—Will was getting out of there. He had to find Allison; they had to destroy Mulkerrin. He had a life out there, one that was just beginning, and he wouldn't let the evil bastard take that away from him the way Tammen took away the show, his old life.

Never again.

Colonel William F. Cody stood, clutching his stomach but already feeling much better. He coughed harshly, then spat several times, wads of blood and phlegm hitting the floor. He realized how much blood he had lost, and how hungry he was, and he felt badly for the tourists whose bodies had been possessed. They would have to sate his hunger.

But first he would have to get out of this room. He stumbled over to the door, propping himself against the wall with one arm. He pulled . . . and it opened.

But his moment of freedom was fleeting, for as he stumbled to his hands and knees in the next room, he knew he was not alone. All around him the ghost warriors rattled to attention. He could smell the demon-beasts in the room as well, and looked up to see two huge, snarling creatures chained to either side of a seat, hewn from the stone wall and positioned as if it were a throne. Upon it, he sat, looking just as he always had, and dressed all in black.

"Well, I was beginning to wonder if you'd actually died in there. More fool me. My Lord, Colonel, but you're a mess. And to think we're just getting started."

Cody tried to will himself to mist, to float out of this nightmare as if it were a fever dream. He felt the change coming, slowly, slowly.

Too slow.

Mulkerrin had stepped down from his throne, a strange green light playing about his open right palm. The armored creatures grabbed Cody and held him, their fingers digging into his flesh and destroying his concentration. He could not think straight enough to make the change, though his eyes were closed tight.

"Open them," Mulkerrin said.

And he did; he wanted the evil to see he was not afraid.

So he watched while the sorcerer's right hand was enveloped in green flame; he clenched his teeth when the once-priest touched that flame to his chest; he screamed as that hand plunged inside him and grabbed hold of his beating, blood-hungry heart and ripped it from his body; he fell to the ground, eyes open, staring, fading, as Mulkerrin knelt beside him and showed him his own heart, licked it, then opened his mouth and tore into it with his teeth.

Mulkerrin kissed Will Cody's forehead, lips smeared with the vampire's own blood.

"Delicious," he whispered, and then his laughter boomed, echoing through the fortress.

And somewhere, Cody's mind drifted, dreaming.

Of vengeance.

Munich, Germany, European Union.
Wednesday, June 7, 2000, 12:02 A.M.:

It was raining when Roberto Jimenez arrived in Munich, and his mood left him hard-pressed to remember a single sunny day spent in Germany. Castillians were a proud and emotional people, and though it had frequently jeopardized his career, Roberto had long since tired of hiding those emotions. Now, as he marched down the hallway of the air-base offices, his second, Gloria Rodriguez, at his side and his personal guard only two steps behind, he was one cranky son of a bitch.

Never one for ceremony, he opened the conference room door himself and stomped in. Immediately, the commanders of the six nations involved in this op stood in a gesture of respect. Toward the back of the room, a large, silent figure rose as well, yet next to him, sprawled on the room's one comfortable chair, another figure did not.

Roberto would not call him a man, and yet he was in such a mood as to allow himself to be annoyed by the creature's disrespect. He would have dearly loved to dismiss the SJS chief marshal, but even though he wasn't certain the shadows would be needed for this operation, he knew he didn't want them working against him. Not to mention, of course, that he had his orders. So, rather than reward his impudence, Roberto simply ignored Chief Marshal Hannibal completely.

"Commanders," he said, addressing the room, "please be seated."

They sat. Out of the corner of his eye, Roberto saw the SJS deputy marshal give his chief a disdainful glance. *Hmm*, Roberto thought, *dissension among the ranks*. Also

interesting that the deputy marshal was the only subordinate, besides his own second, Rodriguez, attending the
meeting.

"Commander Gruber, a report on our current status
please."

Hans Gruber barked a single word in German, and the
table upon which they leaned became an enormous video
console. The picture that appeared there was a satellite
view of Earth. In its center, a large portion of the picture
was completely black.

"This is Land Salzburg," Gruber said in English. "The
dark area is approximately three square miles, the focus of
which is Fortress Hohensalzburg."

Gruber stood and began to walk around the table, pointing at various locations for emphasis.

"This would seem to coincide with reports from the
shadow leader, Meaghan Gallagher—"

The SJS chief marshal coughed.

"We cannot confirm Mulkerrin's presence here," Gruber
said. "However, Austrian authorities have reported sighting monstrous creatures as much as four miles from the
fortress, especially in the river and air."

The room was buzzing.

"The evacuation is under way, with those troops and
police within the city doing their best to get people out,
and those outside surrounding the city upon your orders.
Within, fires rage out of control and many buildings have
collapsed due to the earlier earthquake."

"According to reports from Geneva," interrupted the
French commander, Jeanette Surro, "that earthquake
never happened."

"How's that?" Roberto said, raising a brow.

"Well," Gruber nodded, "though we have plenty of physical evidence that the quake indeed took place, it created
no measurable seismic activity."

"How can that be?" Philip Locke, the British commander asked. "That's impossible."

"Apparently not," Jimenez said, then turned to the American commander, Elissa Thomas.

"Commander Thomas, you're awfully quiet today. What's on your mind?"

Thomas had been leaning back in her chair, eyes slitted, taking it all in with one finger tapping her lips and her chin in her hand. She continued that motion for a moment as she scanned the room, lingering on the SJS reps and finally resting on Jimenez.

"I'll tell you what's on my mind, Commander Jimenez," she said and sat up. "First, I want to know where the Austrian commander is, and why the German commander is speaking for them."

She nodded toward Gruber.

"Second, I want to know why Gallagher and Nueva are not here, since they know Mulkerrin's methods and alerted us as to his involvement in this. And finally, I want to know what we've heard about Colonel Cody."

Roberto was about to reply when a snicker from the back of the room distracted him. He was close to losing his cool, but Commander Thomas did it for him.

"Is there something you find amusing, Chief Marshal Hannibal?" Thomas snapped at the shadow who still looked quite comfortable in his corner. She had returned her attention to Jimenez, not really expecting an answer, when Hannibal stood and placed his open palms on the table in front of him, leaning forward.

"It's that whole 'Colonel' thing, if you must know," he said, unpleasantly. "Cody was never a colonel of anything, and I would think you military types would be insulted by his continued use of that title. Also your implication that Gallagher and Nueva are even needed is insulting to myself and my deputy, Rolf Sechs."

He motioned a hand to indicate Rolf.

"We had as much exposure to Mulkerrin and his methods as they, perhaps more. Not to mention the fact that I am far older than either of those upstarts, and far more skilled in matters of war. Surely you all know my record."

Hannibal smiled, and sat back down.

"You're not trying to imply—" Commander Locke began.

"I have never found a need for implication, Commander," Hannibal interrupted, dismissing the Brit.

"You have not answered Commander Thomas's question, Chief Marshal," Roberto said calmly, reasserting control of the room.

"No," Hannibal agreed. "I have not."

Rolf Sechs leaned forward, his size a distraction in itself, and slammed his hand on the table. Even Hannibal jumped. The deputy marshal reached inside his jacket and withdrew a black plastic strip, in the shape of a small calculator but much thinner, and a pen. He scribbled on the black strip, and as he did so, a computer-generated voice rose from it. Technology had made his muteness less of a problem than ever.

"The chief . . . marshal's . . . evasiveness aside," Rolf wrote, "we are . . . unaware . . . of the reason for Gallagher and . . . Nueva's absence. They have . . . for the moment . . . disappeared. Colonel Cody . . . and I are blood . . . brothers. As such we share a . . . mental rapport. Several minutes . . . ago that . . . rapport was broken."

Roberto Jimenez was certain he was not the only person in the room to notice the way Hannibal's face lit up at this information, before being overcome by his usual mask once again. Clearly he considered it very good news. Jimenez did not.

"Does that mean he's dead?" Roberto asked, and Rolf scribbled in reply.

"I have felt the . . . death of a family . . . member before," the computer voice said. "This was quite . . . different. But, Commander . . . most certainly not a . . . good thing."

"Thank you, Deputy Marshal," Commander Thomas said, smiling at Rolf.

It was clear to Roberto that Elissa Thomas actually liked the big shadow. Though he hated the creatures, he had to admit to himself a grudging admiration for the mute, especially in light of his feelings toward Hannibal: disgust, mistrust, revulsion, hostility. Just to name a few. But Rolf Sechs seemed different, was different. Though he didn't want to, Roberto automatically trusted the man.

Not a man, he reminded himself, *a thing.*

"Yes," he finally said, no longer hiding his hostility toward Hannibal, "thank you for stepping up to fulfill your chief marshal's duties. Hopefully, it will not be a constant necessity."

"As for your other question, Commander Thomas," Commander Gruber began, "my speaking for Commander Friedrich was requested by the Austrian president, not forced upon them by my own country, if that was your implication."

"Curiousity only, Hans," Commander Thomas said, smoothing ruffled feathers.

"Friedrich is engaged in a relief and containment effort like nothing he has ever experienced. He is prepared to follow whatever plan we decide to implement," Gruber added.

"To the plan, then," Roberto said. "Deputy Commander Rodriguez will outline for you what we will refer to henceforth as 'Operation: Jericho.' Our job is to see that the walls come tumbling down."

Gloria Rodriguez had been silent until now. She stood and began to walk around the table, as Gruber had done, referring to the satellite image on the table.

"First let me say that during Operation: Jericho, using satellite and aerial recon, German and Austrian forces will be hunting and eliminating what we'll call 'strays.' These will be the so-called monsters who run free. According to records from Venice, this should be a relatively simple task, which will be performed gradually until we have destroyed or contained them all. Priority, however, is preventing any more of them from appearing, or, uh, coming through from wherever it is they come from."

Hannibal snickered again.

"Commander Thomas will join her forces with Austrian troops at the airport, here—that's about two miles west of the fortress—and then move east to Rainberg, half a mile from it. Commander Gruber's troops will rendezvous at Lehener Park, where the Ducks are being defended right now. This will enable—"

"Ducks?" Hannibal asked, and Rodriguez was surprised he showed any interest at all.

"Ducks, Chief Marshal, are what we call our land-and-water attack vehicles."

Hannibal grunted.

"The Ducks will proceed upriver, destroying whatever they find in the water, and come ashore on the southern bank at Mozart's Plaza, here. This will be the largest force and the most difficult section of the city. At that time, Austrian and German forces will move south from Itzling and Hallwang to take the old city north of the river. Eventually, if possible, they will move to help the rest of us at the fortress.

"Commander Locke's forces will meet with the Austrians at Hellbrunn Castle here in the south, then proceed north to eventually take up position at the stadium, here, just east of the fortress. Commander Surro's troops will meet up with Commander Locke there, after they have swept from the hospital in Heuberg, here, southwest to the river, and made the crossing. From there, both groups will take Nonnberg Abbey, on the mountainside, and will therefore be the closest to the fortress at that time.

"Chief Marshal Hannibal's SJS forces will be split evenly among six groups. Thirty-six each with Commanders Locke, Surro, Gruber and Thomas, thirty-six with my Spanish paratroopers, making the sky drop into the fortress, and thirty-six with a much smaller group, made up of soldiers hand-picked and led by Commander Jimenez. Chief Marshal Hannibal and Deputy Marshall Sechs are also needed for this special force, which will, in effect, walk right up to this bastard's door and break it in."

Hannibal's face showed no surprise, only resolution.

"If you think I will give up command of the SJS—"

"Nobody is asking you to," Roberto interrupted. "You can maintain constant contact with them, but each force needs the knowledge and skills of your kind to—"

"My 'kind,' " Hannibal said and stopped him. "I don't believe I like the sound of that."

Roberto's eyes narrowed.

"I'm sorry," he said. "Your *people* are needed everywhere, to best assist with this operation. And I need both of you with me because our job is, quite simply, to take out the sorcerer himself, to kill Mulkerrin."

Rolf's voice-pad was still on the table, and now he picked up his pen again.

"Easier said than done," he wrote.

Munich, Germany, European Union.
Wednesday, June 7, 2000, 12:59 A.M.:

"I'm telling you, 'Berto, he's got something going, and whatever it is, it's going to be a danger to this operation!"

Roberto looked up from his desk, where he'd been keying in a coded message to UN Secretary General Nieto, and gave his second, Gloria Rodriguez, the once over. She was not angry, or afraid, only frustrated that she couldn't figure out what it was Hannibal had in mind. He could tell it was making her nuts by the way she was pacing, and the manner in which her eyes moved, never stopping to rest on anything long enough to focus, as if she were literally, visually, looking for the answer in that very room.

"He's dangerous," Roberto Jimenez agreed, "and he's certainly been scheming something, but we have no way of knowing it will interfere with this operation. Certainly it's in his best interests just as it is in ours to get rid of Mulkerrin once and for all."

Roberto could almost hear Gloria's mind racing. She was not a beautiful woman. Tough, yes, and in perfect shape. Those qualities, and her intelligence and personality, made her attractive. Her face was pretty enough, dark hair and eyes, but she would never be beautiful. Eye of the beholder, Roberto thought.

"You didn't see Sechs," Gloria said. She had already told him about the gesture Rolf Sechs, the deputy marshal of the Shadow Justice System, had made when she had made brief eye contact with him. Rolf had caught her attention, lifted a finger to his eye and bowed his head, almost imperceptibly, toward Hannibal. It was a clear message, an intentional warning: *watch him.*

"Look, Glory, I want you to understand something." Roberto keyed off his hand-held PC scrambler and slipped it inside his jacket pocket. "Whether our friend Rolf was signaling you or had an itch, we would still watch Hannibal more closely than we have ever watched anyone, even the enemy. I despise the creature, and would feel much safer, much more confident about the potential success of this op, if he were not around."

"But we have our orders," she said, finishing for him.

"Yes, we have our orders. But nobody said we shouldn't be careful."

Gloria looked at him, and Roberto felt her attention, like a physical thing, return to the reality of the room, to him. Her mind focused for the moment on him, and he liked that. He knew he shouldn't, but he did. Glory smiled at him, and Roberto couldn't help but return that smile.

"Don't worry, *bonita*," he said, "we'll keep him reined in."

She went to him, then, and he held her in his arms, giving her small kisses on her head and cheek and neck and rubbing her back. There was nothing sexual in it, for the

moment, but Roberto knew that would come later. Their
relationship had been building up to it for more than a
year, and each day, as his feelings for her grew, so did his
longing.

Gloria broke their embrace and looked up at Roberto,
touching his face with her hand. She loved his eyes, the
gray stripes in his cropped, silky hair. Part of her so wanted
to just let go and rely on his plans for controlling Hannibal,
but she couldn't. She was just as able as he, just as canny
and intuitive, his equal in all but raw force and combat
skill, and even with that she was catching up every day—
thanks most especially to his personal training. No, she
couldn't just leave the question of Hannibal to her superior
officer. One mind might miss something that two would
not, and they could not afford such an error.

"What do you have in mind?" she asked in a low voice,
understanding his reluctance to discuss the matter. Still,
when he looked at her, she knew he realized everything
she'd just thought, and agreed with her.

"Well," he began, and his tone brought them both back
to business, "in a sense we've already started. Hannibal will
be with us during this op, and Rolf will be there. If anything happens, I'll dismiss Hannibal and hand Rolf his
command. Beyond that, I've got a number of operatives on
both of them at all times."

Gloria nodded slowly, but her mind was off again, a mile
a minute, searching for extra precautions.

"His kind disgust me," Roberto said suddenly, the ferocity of the statement distracting Gloria from her thoughts.
"I don't want to be anywhere near their kind, but we need
them now, their abilities. And as long as we need them, I'm
going to be as near to them as is necessary to see this
operation through. You've read the file on this Mulkerrin."

Gloria nodded, then patted the holster at her hip, inside
of which her H-K auto nestled snugly, heavier than usual,
pregnant with the weight of sixty silver rounds. According
to the file, the silver worked wonders on Mulkerrin's "crea-

tures," the real shadows. But it also hurt, at least temporarily, the pseudo-shadows, the vampires. They couldn't supply that ammunition to their entire force—only she and Roberto carried it—but they'd see that the silver went to good use.

"I've read it," she said. "It seems we know more about Mulkerrin than we do about Hannibal. I would hate to think we're better prepared to take on this mad sorcerer than a soldier on our own side."

"He's no soldier!" Roberto snapped. "And you'd be hard-pressed to convince me that he's on our side, or that any of the shadows are for that matter. The SJS is looking more and more like a smoke screen, like a survival tactic, every day. I can't believe we're letting them become even more organized, more dangerous, than before, and we only have personal histories on a couple of dozen out of thousands. Hell, there could be thousands we don't even know about.

"Aw, shit," he said and shook his head. "I can't be worrying about this now. We've got to get rid of Mulkerrin first, before his blackness taints everything. Then we'll worry about Hannibal and his clan."

"Better the devil you know . . ." Gloria shook her head, sighing. "Takes on a whole new meaning, doesn't it?"

Munich, Germany, European Union.
Wednesday, June 7, 2000, 1:01 A.M.:

Rolf knew he'd taken a chance in gesturing to Rodriguez. If Hannibal had seen him . . . but he hadn't, and that was important. Hannibal had to continue thinking Rolf was no more than an inconvenience. It wouldn't do to tip his hand too early. Rolf had guaranteed Meaghan and Alexandra that he would be ready when Hannibal made his move, and that he would take the elder shadow down.

This way, the humans were also on the alert. Not that he'd needed to warn them. From what he could tell, they'd been plenty suspicious of Hannibal already, but he'd wanted to be certain. And there was no way Rodriguez had misunderstood his meaning; in fact, she had nodded in return and almost given him away. But Hannibal was too distracted by the smug game he was playing to notice anything.

Several shadows had been added to each platoon since Rolf had drawn up their duty rosters, yet each time he walked through the barracks, he did not see a single face he did not recognize. He knew that these extra bodies were the outlaws that Hannibal had enlisted rather than killed, rebellious shadows who wanted nothing more than to kill humans. He knew that they would make their move at some point during this operation, and to that end he had taken into his confidence a number of his own soldiers, those he could trust, to neutralize Hannibal's plans as soon as something unusual took place. If they tried anything, Rolf himself would kill Hannibal. It was the only way. And despite the elder's much greater age, Rolf felt that his own evolution had become so rapid that he was at least a match for the old hunter.

And yet, he hoped that Hannibal had enough sense to wait until Mulkerrin was dead, to assist in the extermination of one threat before presenting another. Unfortunately, Rolf didn't have much faith in that scenario. More likely, Hannibal intended to use Mulkerrin's atrocities as a springboard for his own, and come back to take the sorcerer on later. Rolf knew such a strategy would not work in the long run, and he wondered how Hannibal could believe in it. For one brief moment, Rolf had believed that shadows could live in peace among humans, could become a society of their own and merge with the world, in the light of day.

His faith had been fleeting.

Now he steeled himself for battle again, fighting the poisons that threatened to destroy his kind from outside, and in.

And what if I'm alone now? he asked himself, then shook it off, not daring to address such questions. He had not felt his brother Will Cody, die, but he did know what it was he *had* felt: pain; extraordinary pain for one of their kind, and then nothing at all. Cody's mind had been shut to him before, a trick few of the shadows could perform, but Rolf didn't think this was a trick. Whatever had happened to sever Cody's psychic bonds with his family, it had not been by the old showman's own choice. Rolf had once shared his family's hatred of Cody for reasons he had never been too clear on, though he knew his brothers and sisters had been completely certain of their motives. But in Venice, he and Cody had stood side by side, fought together for their people, for their lives, and Rolf had been proud to stand with him.

Heaven help Mulkerrin if Will Cody were dead. Meaghan and Alex were closer to him as friends, but Rolf shared a warrior's bond with Cody, a thing of pride and honor.

And what of Alexandra and Meaghan, his sister and her lover, both his friends? What had become of them? They had been planning to reach Munich today, and yet George Marcopoulos and Julie Graham had sent a joint communiqué saying that they had disappeared from their home just before they were to leave for the airport, apparently intercepted by another shadow. Rolf could not begin to guess who this shadow was, or what business could take Alexandra and Meaghan away from something as dire as Mulkerrin's return.

But of course, that's not what had happened. Rolf knew that they had not simply gone off on some other adventure, because when he reached out with his mind, to attempt to locate Alexandra, she too was gone. Not dead, for he would have felt such a tragedy, but simply gone.

All of this confusion wore away at his confidence, at his resolution, but he pushed it back. There was Mulkerrin to deal with, more powerful now than when Peter Octavian had been victorious over him in Venice, and this time they didn't have Peter to rely on. And Hannibal . . .

Rolf rose from where he'd been sitting, staring out the window at the gray dusk falling over Munich. Very shortly it would be time to muster the forces of Operation: Jericho. Before then, he would see if he couldn't learn a bit more of what Hannibal had in mind.

Before he was halfway to the door, someone knocked. He opened it to find the American commander, Elissa Thomas, alone in the hall.

He stood for a moment, unsure how to respond to her visit.

"May I come in?" she finally said, and he gestured for her to enter.

"I think we need to talk," she said as she passed him, and the lilt in her voice, the pride in her step and the sweet, sweet smell of her convinced Rolf that Hannibal could wait a few minutes. He didn't bother to remind her that he was unable, really, to talk. She knew that, of course. And there were, after all, other forms of communication.

Rolf closed the door and turned to find Commander Thomas leaning against the bare desk. His eyes flitted involuntarily to the single bed in the corner of the Spartan quarters he'd been given, then back to her. The commander had not missed the glance, and her lips turned up at the edges. Without the power of speech, Rolf had learned early how to interpret facial expressions, and there could be no mistaking the woman's intent.

He was surprised, even a little suspicious, but he was also excited. He had been attracted to Elissa Thomas the moment he laid eyes on her, and he respected her strength of will, her boldness and the courage in evidence within the personal records the SJS had on all UNSF commanders. He wondered if there were an ulterior motive, hoped there were not, and walked to her across the room.

Rolf motioned with his large hands, shrugging his shoulders, asking why she had come. Commander Thomas tossed her hair to one side like a schoolgirl, and Rolf felt his erection growing. An intelligent woman confident enough to allow her sexuality through. Yes, he wanted this woman.

"Rolf," she began, and he liked to hear her say his name, "let me lay it on the line here. I have no reason to trust you, but I do. I see in you a courage and cunning that I can respect and admire. And, of course, other things."

She reached up and put a hand on his neck, and the warmth of it made him even harder.

"Later, I'd like to talk to you about, shall we say, a strategic alliance. But for now . . ."

And her other hand moved forward and rested on the enormous bulge that had grown under his pants. Rolf closed his eyes a moment, a light breath escaping his mouth, warm on her cheek as she went to kiss him. Their lips met, and now Rolf's hands came up and held her face, enveloped it, and he pulled her to him and kissed her deep. Their tongues intertwined and then he broke off, leaving her breathless. His tongue flicked out and traced her lips, engraving a promise there of what he would do when he reached lower.

Rolf picked her up and carried her to the small bed, where he undressed her slowly, kissing, nibbling and licking at each newly bared region of her body. He caressed her so softly, gently, that she could hardly believe it was this great, powerful man who touched her. He rolled her nipples between his fingers as he lay her back and spread her legs with one strong hand. She didn't feel the urge to speak, because he, simply, could not. It wasn't just his tongue, but his lips and teeth, the stubble of his chin—he took control of her in a way no one had before.

As she approached her orgasm, building to something she knew would wrack her body with convulsions, just as she took that final breath . . . he stopped. He looked up at her in that moment that she thought she would suffocate, that she would never be released from the frozen muscles of her body, and he grinned at her, a naughty child, knowing what he'd done.

He had barely entered her when Elissa bucked up against him, pulling him deep into her. Then her legs were around his back, her fingernails raking his shoulders as she urged him on, her orgasm rocking her entire body with convulsions. She bit her lip and it bled, and somewhere in the back of her brain she wondered why he had not bitten her, but she couldn't hold any thought for long.

After he shuddered into an orgasm of his own, she wondered again why he hadn't taken her blood, but found she didn't care. She became suddenly aware of the muscles in her face, as he lay his head on her breast and snuggled close to her, and realized that she shared that grin of his.

And they slept.

CHAPTER ✦ SEVEN

Somewhere Between.
Thirty-Seven Seconds After Departure:

Lazarus had said that passing through the portal would hurt them less than it had Peter. As the three of them emerged on hands and knees, all retching and shivering, or perhaps convulsing, Meaghan and Alexandra were unaware that they shared a thought. If it had been this bad for them, exactly how bad *had* it been for Peter?

"Lions and tigers and bears, oh my," Alexandra said, weakly, and Meaghan attempted a soft chuckle to reward the effort, but couldn't manage it.

Lazarus didn't even try; he only moaned as he slowly worked himself, trial and error, to his feet. Meaghan was standing first, if only because her muscles ached more lying down. She thought that they might have experienced a weird sort of birth, and she wondered if babies experienced that kind of trauma. She reached out and pulled Alex to her feet, letting Lazarus take care of himself. He was, after all, supposedly older and stronger than either of them.

They had emerged in a dark alleyway, which was nothing like what they had expected, though if they had discussed it aloud they would both have realized that they had not really expected anything. Alex and Meaghan walked in silence to where the alley opened onto the main street, and Lazarus was right behind them.

"Lazarus," Meaghan said. "Where are we?"

It was, of course, Hell. But not the Hell they had expected. The street upon which they now stood was lined with old stone buildings, a crumbling inner city that resembled so many they had known, and yet was none of them. There was something about the architecture that was at once familiar, and yet accented with so many unfamiliar details and almost nonsensical geometry as to make them completely certain they were no longer "home." And it seemed that everything—buildings, street and sky—was gray.

Indeed, they had passed through to somewhere else, but not necessarily to the elsewhere they'd intended. And as Lazarus took his time responding to Meaghan's question, she realized what his answer would be before he could voice it.

"You don't know, do you? You don't know. Oh, well, that's just fucking wonderful."

"What now?" Alexandra asked.

Meaghan thought her lover sounded quite courageous, but she herself was nearing a panic. If Lazarus didn't know . . . Uh-uh. She wasn't going to let that happen.

"Lazarus," she said, back in command, "look through the book and try to find out where we went wrong, and how to get us out of here and on our way again. Alex and I will head opposite ways up the street, only a block, to get our bearings and perhaps a clue as to what this place is."

There was no discussion. Alexandra began to drift off down the street in one direction, and Meaghan in the other. The one thing that struck Meaghan as most chilling, the fact that threatened to undermine her new resolve, was the complete and unrelenting silence. This was a city, though not one they were familiar with, and yet it had no loud vehicles, no construction, no people. It was deserted. Up ahead in the distance, above the row of buildings that were like brownstones but not, the city's skyline shot up into towering glass-and-metal structures. Meaghan thought, not for the first time, that the word "skyscrapers" was incredibly appropriate.

But these were like no skyscrapers she had ever seen, and their weird geometry—harsh, cutting angles—confirmed for her that they were nowhere on Earth. There were lights in those distant towers, the same way there were streetlights burning just above her now, and yet Meaghan was suddenly sure that those signs of life were false. She knew, intuitively, that those buildings were as empty as the streets around them.

"Meaghan!" Alexandra called from behind.

Meaghan turned to see Alex waving for her to come back. Obviously she'd found something, and Meaghan hoped it was an answer, rather than more questions. She walked back past Lazarus, and as she got closer to Alex, she began to notice the destruction. She had to step around a huge crevice which had torn open the ground. To her left, charred embers were all that remained of two adjacent homes. To her right, all of the windows in one building were shattered, the lack of glass in the street suggesting an external force as the cause. Several others had their heavy wooden doors torn out, frames shattered, brick and stone smashed, steps crushed under incredible weight.

Fifty feet from Alexandra, with no wind at all, Meaghan could smell it. Filling her nose and activating an all too human gag reflex—it wasn't the smell of death, but of what comes after, the rotting. She came to a halt two yards away from her lover, but Meaghan didn't need Alex to point the way. Her nose brought her around to the sight of the crumbled remains of an entire building, most of which had collapsed into a huge crevice much like the one in the street. Other than the remains of the foundation wall and what had fallen outside that wall, the building was gone, into the crevice. But the crevice was apparently not a bottomless pit, because it wasn't empty now.

The bodies were not piled, they were packed, tight, with no discernible relationship or continuity. The dead, many burned, maimed and disemboweled, were all ages and races and both sexes. Some clothed, some naked, their stink was the only thing they shared besides death. Intertwined like dozens of lovers locked frozen in the midst of an orgy, the dead were, without question, human. And yet Meaghan could again detect an essential difference. Perhaps it was the heightened senses she had as a shadow, or mere logic in the face of their alien surroundings.

"My blood!" Alexandra said finally, and Meaghan realized they had both been holding their breath.

"We don't know where we are," Meaghan said and shook her head, "and now we have no idea how this happened. What did this?"

"More importantly," Alex said, grabbing Meaghan's hand, "is it coming back?"

"Let's get back and see if Lazarus has some answers."

They turned to go, but Meaghan caught sudden movement out of the corner of her eye, and as she turned, she noticed that the street was no longer silent. Staring out over the sea of dead once again, she was prepared to think she had imagined the movement, though the new sound, a sort of distant chuffing, like a powerful pump, remained. And then the movement came again, a ripple, a wave sending arms and legs flailing and blood spattering, as something huge moved under the dead. With the drying scab ripped from the top of the mass grave, a new, more powerful wave of odor rolled over them, and this time Meaghan did gag.

And then the cesspool erupted in a fountain of gore and decaying flesh, spraying sixty feet into the air. Meaghan and Alex were spattered by the initial burst and then showered in gobs of humanity, body parts raining down and slapping the ground around them. In front of them, rising up through the falling dead, was a behemoth unlike anything either of them had seen, even during the Venice Jihad.

At the same time, however, both Meaghan and Alexandra knew immediately that this creature was a sibling to those from Venice, a shadow-demon from the Hell Mulkerrin had dredged once too often. It's long snout was huge, the eyes on either side a dozen feet apart. It's hundreds of bared teeth were long and sharp as sabers, covered with gore, flesh hanging in strings from its black lips. The nostrils of the snout were flaring, blood spraying in a fine mist, and it occurred to Meaghan that the things were like the blowholes of a whale, and that the remains of the dead the creature had consumed had been blasted out of those nostrils with explosive power.

And thinking of that power, she had to wonder how much of the creature was still underground, to supply the energy for such a burst. It's green-scaled flesh was still coming and they had yet to see limbs. It's head seemed snake-like, or more accurately, sharklike, as it continued to rise from the hole. Then, heavy under its own weight, it flopped forward, its jaws clacking together only yards from where they stood. At the edges of the hole, they now saw relatively small, lizardlike talons appear and begin to claw at the remains of the building's stone foundation, pulling forward.

Watching in fascination, Meaghan's attention was finally brought back to their safety as Alex grabbed her arm.

"Meaghan!" she said, obviously not for the first time. "Do we fight, or get out of here?"

Meaghan looked at her lover, saw the concern in her eyes, the questions there, held for later. She knew them, for they were the same questions in her own mind. She looked at the huge shadow, then back to Alex.

"Screw that," she said, "we're out of here. If it catches us, then we fight."

Lazarus was running up behind them now, the *Gospel* clutched in his hands. As they turned to flee from the creature, they nearly ran him down.

"Run!" Meaghan shouted at him.

"What?" Lazarus looked as if he'd been goosed, his eyebrows lifting as his mouth fell open.

"Run!" Meaghan said again, and this time Lazarus did turn his steps back the way he'd come, but not without a frown of great displeasure. Meaghan knew it was difficult for him, who had probably not run from anything since his human death.

But, she thought, *wisdom being the better part of valor, he can go to . . .*

"So," she said as they ran, "where are we anyway?"

"Well," Lazarus said, slowing down now and looking over his shoulder, "we're not in Hell if that's what you're wondering.

"It's stopped," he added, coming to a complete halt and turning back the way they'd come.

Meaghan and Alex also stopped, and now they watched from several blocks away as the huge creature settled itself back into the mass grave that had become its home. As far away from it as they were, they could still hear the chuffing noise, which meant the monster was sucking the flesh and bones of the dead into its mouth, but this time there was no explosion from its nostrils. Soon, the thing was out of sight and the hole itself was merely a gap in the block of buildings.

"So if we're not in Hell . . . ?" Alexandra said, making a conscious choice for all of them to put off discussion of the demon until they were gone from this place.

"Where are we?" Lazarus mused aloud, holding up *The Gospel of Shadows* to emphasize his words. "A good question, but the answer isn't in here . . . Or maybe it is."

"How do you mean?" Meaghan asked, but she could see in Lazarus's eyes that his mind was drifting someplace else. She repeated the question, and finally he faced her.

"I have a theory," he said, spreading his arms to encompass everything around them. "The Stranger has told me many times that there are worlds other than our own, but I thought he meant this 'Hell,' and whatever passes for

Heaven, if anything does. We know that Hell exists because that's where these creatures come from, and it's discussed in the book. But what if there are other planes as well, planes not mentioned in the *Gospel*?"

Alex and Meaghan exchanged glances, and Meaghan was amused to see the way her lover's brows arched in obvious doubt.

"Just a minute," Alexandra interrupted. "Are you trying to say that we're in some kind of alternate world, like a parallel dimension or some such thing? I mean, give me a fucking—"

"Don't jump to conclusions, Alex," Meaghan broke in. "Lazarus may be on to something here."

Lazarus was surprised at her defense, but appreciated it.

"Don't forget, Miss Nueva," he said, "you are, after all, a vampire."

Meaghan's mind was racing, and she paced in time to its rhythm, chewing on her right index knuckle in a way that Alex had always found endearing.

"Okay," she said and stopped pacing. "Are either of you familiar with the theories of Stephen Hawking?"

Both nodded then began to speak, but Meaghan cut them off.

"No, just listen. Hawking postulated that the existence of black holes, which he has proven, themselves prove the existence of parallel universes because some matter which passes into the hole does not emerge. It has to go somewhere. Now, if Hell is one of these parallels, then the portal that we used to travel here, and those Mulkerrin was able to create, have got to be . . . what? Gray holes? Somehow they allow matter to pass in both directions but do not have the vacuum effect of a black hole."

"Do you know how crazy this sounds?!" Alex yelled, frustrated and already tired.

Meaghan flinched.

"Honey," she said. "There's no need to yell like that."

"No need to . . . ?" Alex was dumbfounded. "This is

not like a domestic squabble or something, Meg. How can you be so calm?"

"You're not," Meaghan smiled. "I have to be."

Alex was sorry, and the two embraced a moment as Lazarus spoke.

"The only problem," he said, "is that if all of this is true, we still don't know exactly where we are, what happened here, or how to get out."

They were all quiet then, and in the silence finally heard the noises in the buildings all around them. Lazarus spun quickly and saw a thin, bony face disappear from behind a window. He started for the house, thinking there were people there after all, but Meaghan stopped him.

"I saw some too," she said. "In fact, I think they're all around us now, but they're not what you think."

"How can you know what I think?"

" 'Cause it's exactly what I would have thought, if I hadn't seen that." She pointed down the street toward the city skyline, and in the shadows of buildings, small, bony wolflike creatures scampered, with faces like those from the windows around them. A pair of huge, fat, hairy bipeds, one with tusks pushing out from its face, emerged from the distant darkness.

"He's been here," Meaghan whispered, and then louder: "Mulkerrin had to have been here!"

"We were waylaid here en route to our destination," Lazarus started in, "and so was he. Now it becomes clear. Mulkerrin isn't just after vampires now, he just wants to conquer, to destroy."

"So this is a sneak preview of what happens if we don't stop him?" Alexandra asked. "So what are you waiting for, Lazarus? Get us out of here."

Though he still didn't like to flee any more than he wanted to let these females fight for him, Lazarus knew what their responsibilities were. As the skeletal demon-wolves moved in for the attack, their gargantuan brothers slowly falling in behind, he opened the book to the spell that had gotten them where they were. He hoped the same spell would allow them to complete their trip. He didn't bother to tell them he had no idea if it would.

Unlike most younger shadows, Lazarus prayed. The Stranger had assured him that someone was listening. And at that moment, Lazarus made a conscious decision to believe him.

The first of the demon-wolves reached Alex and Meaghan, but they didn't have a chance. The vampire women were much more powerful, and shattered the creatures' bony frames with ease. But the huge, brown, ape-like shadows approached now, so slowly, and the tusked one in the lead became uglier as it moved closer. Its black lips pulled back from blacker gums in a roar through strong, sharp, clenching teeth. Alex clamped her hands over her ears.

"Come on, Laz," Meaghan shouted, "how 'bout it?"

And then the portal was there.

"Go," he shouted, standing with the book in his hand, and in seconds Meaghan and Alexandra were through the passage, magical or scientific, and the two great beasts roared their displeasure.

Lazarus turned to go, clutching the *Gospel* to his chest and leaping for the portal. In midair, his legs were snagged, crunching painfully in the huge hands of the tusked creature, whose anger had added speed to its attack. Lazarus fell face-first toward the ground, his hands flying out to break his fall and *The Gospel of Shadows* tumbling into the air . . . through the portal.

Furious, Lazarus turned on the creature, its mate not three steps behind, and ignoring the pain in his crushed legs, forced them to burst into flame in the creature's hands. Matted with disgusting hair as it was, the creature's body caught the fire, and it spread rapidly over its form. The creature howled in distress and began to beat at its burning arms and chest, only succeeding in spreading the flames. As it crawled to the portal, the last sight Lazarus had was of the demon's mate arriving to help, and having the flames leap from one to the other instead.

As the cold womb of pain presented by passage through the worlds enveloped him, Lazarus had to wonder about those creatures. Other than vampires, he'd never seen shadows with mates before, never seen them care for one another. Had they, then, been an example of the native life forms of that universe that became demonic half-breeds the way Lazarus and his kindred had been?

As he was belched out onto hot, hard stone, at the feet of Meaghan Gallagher and Alexandra Nueva, Lazarus felt momentarily sorry for the creatures and wished he could take back the flames. And then his companions were at his side, helping him up even as his legs finished their self-healing. He breathed a sigh of relief as he scanned the cavern in which they now stood.

They were on a rocky shelf, which was slashed out of the wall behind them. Though apparently made of stone, the wall and shelf were black, charred by terrible flames, and their feet kicked up a fine powderlike soot while flakes and bubbles crunched under them. Flames burned from cracks in the walls, and burning ash fell in a light shower from somewhere high above, whirled into eddies by wind currents that buffeted them with heat as well. The wall behind them curved around, and in the distance they could barely make out the shimmering flames from the opposite wall. They could see hundreds of feet above, and no ceiling, so that all three assumed they were in a hole of some kind. And far, far below, the fire burned.

"It's a wonder our portal didn't open above that," he said, looking down at the red glow of the pit beneath them. "It reminds me of a stovepipe. Though strangely it does look somewhat like what I'd expected."

"We were just talking about that," Meaghan said. "Maybe part of the spell controls the point of egress?"

Lazarus thought about that, the spell. *The spell*! What the hell happened to . . .

"The book!" he snapped at them, noticing that neither held it. "What happened to the book?"

Meaghan and Alex looked quite alarmed.

"What do you mean?" Alex hissed. "You had the damn book!"

"I was attacked," he mumbled. "It flew from my hands and through the portal. I thought it would . . ."

They all looked down, around their feet, realizing the futility of the act even as they performed it, and then out over the abyss.

"Do you think?" Alexandra said, but Meaghan shook her head as they looked down into nothing.

"No. I think we would have seen it come through and go over."

"So then what?"

Meaghan didn't have an answer, but Lazarus turned to face the black wall where the portal had been.

"Lost," he said. "Lost somewhere between that devastated world and this place."

"Great!" Alex snapped.

"Now how do we get back?" Meaghan said to no one.

"We find Peter, of course," Alexandra said, stepping to the edge. "If he's still alive, maybe he can get us out. If not, we'll die here with his bones."

Meaghan looked at Lazarus, and he shook his head.

"We have little choice," he said, then turned to Alex. "But we have no idea how to find him. For starters, do we go up or down?"

Alexandra laughed then, a sick, angry, frustrated, frightened laugh that scared Meaghan in a way.

"Don't be stupid," she said. "This place even looks like the Hell of myth, at least for me. If there's anything to be found here, we *won't* find it by going up."

"I don't know if we ought to fly through that," Lazarus said, pointing at the cinder and ash tumbling down the center of the pit.

"We don't have to," Meaghan broke in, standing at the

edge of the shelf, pointing along the wall. "There's a kind of ledge over here that seems to wind down and around."

Hell.
One Hour, Four Minutes, Twenty Seconds After
Departure:

Meaghan estimated that they'd been descending for at least half an hour when she fell. It was getting hotter, and Lazarus had left his light jacket behind. They knew that it must be far hotter even than it felt, for temperatures that would force humans unconscious were just enough to make shadows break a sweat. It was very uncomfortable. Not to mention how filthy they were, covered in the black soot that seemed to blanket everything.

They had yet to see a single of Hell's shadows, but agreed that it would only be a matter of time. Still, they found themselves alone. They had given up conversation and conjecture almost completely, setting their minds to the task at hand, when Meaghan stepped forward, over stone that Alexandra had just crossed, and fell away into nothing. The ledge did not crumble beneath her feet; rather, it simply fell, in one block section, away from the wall and hurtled down toward the inferno she imagined waited below.

She heard both Alexandra and Lazarus cry her name, but Meaghan was not terribly concerned. Though the heat made it slightly more difficult, it was a simple task to shift her shape into that of a bat, and rise on the hot breeze she now realized was flowing up from the huge hole in the ground that they had been circling. Soaring back up to where the others stood, looking down after her, Meaghan knew that the ledge went all the way around, spiraling down to lead them eventually to the point she would have found faster if she'd simply kept falling.

They could fly. How stupid of them to be moving so carefully, so delicately. Lazarus was concerned about the embers falling in the center of the stovepipe, but they didn't have a lot of time, and this was time wasted. They could survive a flaming shower if they had to. Certainly there were risks, as they never knew when they were going to run into the demon-creatures who called that plane home, but—

And then she knew she'd jumped the gun. Winged monsters appeared above and below her, as if she were a diver who'd fallen into a pool of sharks. They circled, leather wings barely moving, long, pterodactyl-like beaks snapping in the air, making a terrible noise, like doors slamming over and over again. And there were at least a dozen of the flying creatures.

"Meaghan!" She heard Alexandra calling her name even over the snapping of the creatures' beaks and the high-pitched, roaring call that now went out, like nails on a blackboard.

Meaghan feinted in one direction, then turned toward Alex's voice and dove. One of the creatures was right behind her, it's snapping beak ready to swallow her nearly whole. Ahead, she saw sanctuary! Alex and Lazarus had somehow found a cave or tunnel leading off the ledge they'd been following, hopefully leading far away from the stovepipe. Now that these guardians, or whatever they were, had discovered them, they would not be safe in the open.

But she wasn't going to make it, was she? She thought she could feel the heat from the thing's nostrils on her back, and knew that at any moment that beak would clamp down on her, destroying her bat form . . . unless she wasn't in bat form! And what was that Lazarus was screaming at her from the hole in the wall? Yes!

"Mist!" he screamed.

And Meaghan angled away from the hole in which her friends hid, the flying demon right behind her, and others on its tail. She flew straight at the soot-covered walls, and then she changed. The demon's beak snapped down on the spot she had occupied a second before, and the moment of confusion, in which it realized it held nothing in its throat, was enough. It was too late for the thing to turn away, and the flying demon slammed into the wall, sending a puff of charcoal smoke into the air, bones splintering, black blood spurting. And then it tumbled down into the pit, and as Meaghan floated over to the cave mouth, Alexandra and Lazarus watched the thing fall. It took so long that Meaghan was with them, watching, when the thing was finally out of sight.

And then the demons were flying, up and away, shrieking as they went . . . and the flames came. Fire rocketed up through the center of the stovepipe, scorching everything in its path, the walls charred even further as the furnace blasted for several seconds. Meaghan felt her face blistering and heard Alexandra crying out, and then it was over and the flames subsided.

"That sucked," Alex said with a sniffle, but as Meaghan looked at her lover, her burnt flesh was already healing itself. In fact, she could feel her own flesh healing as well. Lazarus, who'd been farther back, was barely singed.

"A good thing we weren't on that ledge just now," Lazarus said. "I don't want to guess whether we'd survive something like that."

Meaghan slumped against the wall of the tunnel, which is what it was after all. Her mind raced and she frowned, looking at Lazarus.

"What is it?" he asked.

"Well," Meaghan began, "does it seem to either of you that we're not really thinking very clearly? I mean, since we got here? We could have flown from the beginning, especially with time of the essence, but we were deterred by that flaming . . . avalanche or whatever it was in the center there. And I ought to have turned to mist immediately when I saw those creatures, but it took much longer than normal for me to think of it."

"You're right," Alex said, wincing as the last of her blisters cracked and healed. "But what can we do about it? We can't exactly leave here."

"The only thing we can do," Lazarus said, "is watch each other very carefully for signs of muddled thinking. Otherwise, none of us will ever get out of here."

"So, I guess we're going down this tunnel," Alex said. " 'Course we have no idea what we'll meet down there."

"We've been lucky so far," Meaghan said grimly. "But look at it this way, we can't stay in the stovepipe, and anything we meet in here has to be a lot smaller than those pterodactyl things."

They looked at each other, and then all three of them were smiling, chuckling, and shaking off the dangers they'd just avoided. Alex gave Meaghan a kiss, then helped her up, and they turned to join Lazarus as he started into the tunnel.

"I hope this thing isn't just a smaller chimney," Lazarus said, and they stopped smiling.

And that's when the screaming started.

All three of them turned around to face the tunnel mouth, and outside, in the stovepipe, they could see the screamers, falling, arms and legs flailing, trailing fire from their burnt and broken flesh. The chorus of wails came from dozens of beings, some apparently human, men, women and children, and countless other sentient but alien races, tumbling through the air down into the pit of flame far below.

When Alexandra could not stand to look anymore and turned away, she saw Meaghan with her back against the wall, eyes closed, hands covering her ears. Bloody tears were wet on her cheeks, and Alex went to her and held her tight, kissing the tears away.

"We're really here," Meaghan whispered. "This is really it, isn't it, Alex?"

"Yes, honey, we're really here." Alex hugged her even harder. "But once we find Peter, we get to leave. Don't worry, we'll get out of here."

"Well," Meaghan said, breaking off their embrace, "what are we waiting for? Lazarus, you watch our backs; I'll take point."

"No," Alex said. "If you can mind-link, you may be our only chance of finding Peter and getting out of here. You're in the middle; I'll take point."

And without another word, they proceeded into the tunnel that way, Alexandra first, then Meaghan and, finally, Lazarus. Meaghan was pleased. She'd thought they would have to rely on their vampiric senses to "see" in the darkness, but there were open flames burning through cracks in the tunnel's stone walls. The tunnel itself was warm, but not nearly as warm as she'd imagined it would be, considering. In fact, it was cooler than the cavern they'd come from. Still, though it was barely perceptible, the tunnel sloped down and to the right. Several times they came to a fork or intersection where other tunnels ran into theirs, and each time Meaghan made the decision, led by an unidentifiable feeling, a sense of "right."

They heard no sound but that of their own rustling movement, their snippets of murmured conversation and the slap of Lazarus's shoes on the stone. Meaghan and Alex both wore sneakers, and their footfalls sounded much quieter in the flickering dark, but in that silence, they too were audible.

Alexandra stopped suddenly, leaning against the wall and bringing one hand up to stroke through her black hair. Meaghan thought how funny they all looked, covered in grime, but she wasn't laughing.

"What is it, honey?" she asked Alex.

"Haven't you guys noticed it yet?" Alexandra said, surprised. "The tunnel has gotten smaller."

Lazarus looked around, eyes narrowed, and realized that Alexandra was right. The tunnel had been shrinking gradually as they moved. In fact, he had even begun to stoop slightly because of the encroaching ceiling, and had barely noticed it. Meaghan leaned against the wall next to Alex, holding her lover's hand to her lips and kissing it in that way that meant nothing and everything, requiring a complete response, and none at all. She felt Alex's fingers tighten in her own, that squeeze the only affirmation her heart needed.

"There's something else we missed, or at least I did," Meaghan said. "The incline is getting steeper."

"So we started in a tunnel," Lazarus said, "but we may end up in a well."

"I don't like the sound of that," Meaghan said, then pushed off from the wall. "Let's go."

They began walking again, and Meaghan took the lead over Alex's protests. Immediately, they realized it had gotten darker. With their senses, it was not an issue, but it was strange. Also, the size and slope of the tunnel was changing more rapidly now, so that they all had to bend to avoid hitting their heads, and shift their weight to avoid falling forward.

"You know what's strange?" Alex said after they'd been moving along that way for several minutes. "The only demons we've seen were those prehistoric-looking things, and nothing like the creatures Mulkerrin brought through during the Venice Jihad. I mean, if there are any intelligent demons, anybody running the place, don't you think they'd know we were here by now? Isn't anybody in charge? It's just too quiet. Doesn't it seem the least bit—"

A cry of pain, or rage, perhaps of both, but definitely human, called to them from the depths of the tunnel. The time for talk was over then, and they hunched over even further and headed down the tunnel as quickly as they could.

And then something had hold of Meaghan's ankle, and she was falling forward, arms stretched out, face slamming hard into the sharply angled stone floor, cheekbone cracking, breath knocked out of her. It happened fast, as she instinctively pulled hard on her foot, the momentum of her fall helping to free her ankle. She heard a surprised gasp from Alexandra behind her, and attempted to turn and look, but halfway around she was pummeled by the weight of Lazarus landing atop her in the small, confined space of the tunnel. They struggled, tangled together by their limbs and momentary panic. Freed, finally, they managed to turn themselves around.

"Oh, shit! What the fuck is—" Meaghan crawled forward and grabbed Alexandra's arms, pulling, just as her lover began to scream.

"Get'emoffme! Meg! Get'emoffme!"

Alex was up to her neck in a hole lined with human bodies, corpses in a living death, whose arms and legs trapped her there, tore at her pants and the already bare flesh of her upper body, whose heads leaned out and fastened lips and teeth to her. Meaghan had nearly stepped right over the hole, a single hand snagging her, but she pulled free. Alex had not been so lucky, had stepped right in the narrow pit of writhing bodies just as Meaghan fell forward. Finally, Lazarus had stumbled over Alex, kicking her in the back even as she was pulled down and he plowed into Meaghan's fallen form.

Now Meaghan stared in horror, and Lazarus said nothing but moved up next to her in the cramped space to grab Alex's left hand with both of his own so that Meaghan could pull on the right.

"It's okay, honey," Meaghan started, "we're getting you out! We're getting them off."

Meaghan closed her eyes as they pulled, hard, and she thought the popping she heard might have been one of Alex's shoulders coming out of the socket. When her eyes opened again, Alex was still screaming but her head had sunk deeper into the hole.

"No!" Meaghan snarled. *"Alex!"*

But Alex wasn't listening.

"Alex!" she screamed again, and this time Alex looked up, away from what was happening below, as claws tore

chunks of skin from her immortal flesh, as jaws gobbled down bloody scraps of her flesh.

Meaghan saw that it was a throat, the gullet of Hell, pulling her lover down for digestion.

"Change!" she yelled. "Alex, change to mist, you've got to do it now!"

"I . . . uff . . . I caann't," Alexandra sobbed, then giggled, the madness of the pain creeping over her.

"*Do it!*" Meaghan screamed. "Change!"

And Alex began to transform, mist swirling in the throat cut out of stone. But the dead creatures there would not stop, and their mouths and nostrils opened, heads craning as far out from their woven mingling as possible as they *inhaled* Alexandra, breathed in as much of the mist as they could.

Meaghan was nearly sick, about to scream to Alex again, and then one of the faces in the hole caught her eye. It was looking at her as it sucked in the essence of her lover. Its eyes locked on hers and its grin widened. Meaghan looked around at the other faces and saw that many of them, some not human-looking at all, also stared at her, also grinned. And then she knew Alexandra had been right. Their presence in Hell had been no secret, and whatever knew they were there was truly evil, and intelligent.

And before she could try to help any further, Alex changed again, to fire this time, and Meaghan wanted to cheer but could only watch and hope. She and Lazarus had to back away slightly, as the throat seemed to widen and hands reached out and groped around its stone edges for them. She wished for *The Gospel of Shadows*, for any power it might have held, but knew that wishes were only that.

A twinge of triumph swept through Meaghan as the flesh of the throat, the arms and bellies, breasts and legs, penises and buttocks, faces and eyes, especially eyes, began to blacken and blister under the fire that was Alexandra Nueva. The eyes that had been staring at Meaghan burst, spurting some black, malodorous liquid, but the faces kept on grinning. With a scream of fury, Meaghan began to crawl forward, but Lazarus held her back.

The dead mouths were sucking in the flame as easily as they had the mist. Even as lips charred to the teeth, the flames disappeared through the open mouths of the damned creatures. Meaghan broke Lazarus's hold and rushed forward, upward on her knees. She lay on the stone and reached down into the burning gullet and began smashing faces, breaking skulls, shattering bones.

And then they had her, and were pulling her down, headfirst, into the throat of Hell. She could feel Lazarus pulling from behind, and she thought she felt the bones in her left ankle break in his grip. Claws tore at her face and throat; teeth took a bite from her cheek. She opened her eyes even as a burnt, skeletal hand reached out to pluck them from her skull—and then Alex was there, face-to-face with her, blocking the attack of that hand. Her face was covered in blood, her beautiful chocolate skin shredded to the bone from the lips down. Hanging upside down as she was, Meaghan could see that Alex's left breast had been torn away with her left arm. Below that, she was just gone.

Gone.

Hanging gore was all that remained there, but still, Alexandra thrashed her upper body, her right arm broken but flailing at the voracious damned around her. Her efforts were a distraction to the creatures of the throat, and their hold on Meaghan loosened, only for a moment, but long enough for Lazarus's pulling on the other end to make a difference. Meaghan's head, shoulders and arms, all that had been pulled into the hole, popped out, and then she was being dragged on the stone. She had one, final glimpse of Alexandra, love and pain in her eyes, and tears on her cheeks, and then nothing.

Meaghan sat up, backing away, and she could feel her broken ankle, the tears in the flesh of her face, neck and arms, all healing, even as she heard the sounds of what remained of her lover being consumed. She backed into Lazarus, who had saved her, but neither had been able to save Alex. Their strength was meaningless, she thought. How could they have thought to survive such a journey? Mulkerrin's creatures had been mindless, but here, in Hell, it was different. She had seen those eyes, the cruelty there.

Hell was aware, and it knew them.

Meaghan turned her head from the sight of the burnt hands grasping at the air around the open throat, scratching at the stone for the food that had escaped. She fell into Lazarus's arms, and he held her uncomfortably, as she wept in a manner all too human. She knew he could not find words to comfort her, and she was glad. She did not want to be comforted.

"Alex," she sobbed. "Oh, my God."

Meaghan had purposely not addressed God since becoming a vampire during the Jihad five years before. She'd been confused, uncertain, no matter what she told her own kind. But now she knew.

She'd seen it up close, and now Meaghan Gallagher knew that, no matter what she was, she was not evil.

"Dear God," she sobbed, her heart crying, her chest exploding, "We need you . . . We all need you."

Lazarus held her hand tight as he led her farther down into the tunnel, and soon the only sounds were of her weeping. First her parents, then her lover and best friend, Janet Harris, then Peter Octavian, and now Alexandra—everyone Meaghan Gallagher loved, died. She could not help but think that she was just one more tortured soul, suffering, in Hell.

CHAPTER ✦ EIGHT

Washington, D.C., United States of America.
Tuesday, June 6, 2000, 8:14 P.M.:

"Where the fuck did they go, George?"

Henry Russo was not fooling around. George Marco-poulos sat in the study of his Washington, D.C., home and argued with the President of the United States. In addition to the two men, both U.S. Secretary of State Julie Graham and United Nations Secretary General Rafael Nieto were attending the video conference.

George wasn't in the mood.

"Listen, Henry, you can play hardball all you want, but I'm in the dark just as much as you. The difference is, I care what happened to them, not just why they aren't on their way to Austria. Give me a break, will you? These are my friends!"

"That's what has me worried, George," Julie Graham said grimly.

"And just what the hell is that supposed to mean?" George snapped.

"What it means," the President resumed, "is that we think you know what happened to Nueva and Gallagher, and we want to know if it poses a threat to us and to Operation: Jericho!"

"If it poses . . . Are you out of your fucking mind?"

George lost it completely. "Don't you know who you're talking about here? These two women—"

"Vampires," Graham said, stabbing.

"Vampires, yes!" George roared. "Women first, human beings whether you believe it or not. They are your greatest allies among their kind. Without them, the entire world might have suffered in the wake of the Venice Jihad. They are almost solely responsible for the peace you have today, and you dare imply—"

"What peace?" Rafael Nieto finally spoke up, and the mere fact of his calm was enough to defuse George's rage for a moment.

"Yes, yes, Austria," George said and nodded, understanding Nieto's implication. "But the shadows have nothing to do with that. Mulkerrin is their sworn enemy. They have vowed to destroy him, with or without *your* help."

George gave a *hmph* to let them know exactly what he thought of their insane suspicions. Why, the very idea! And did they think he was stupid? A man of his age and reputation, his closeness to the shadows—well, he ought to know, oughtn't he?

But of course, he ought to know where Meaghan and Alex had gotten to as well. And now this news of Cody's capture.

"And where does Rome fit into all this?" George asked. "Is anybody actually listening to the Vatican these days? If the Pope has got you guys all introspective, it's because he wants you to forget that Mulkerrin was a priest once, not to mention all the Vatican busboys who ended up corpses in Venice."

"The Pope," Rafael Nieto said patiently, "has not contacted anyone. In fact, I'd guess right about now he's hiding under his desk. Now, if we could get back to our subject, a moment ago you referred to the Shadow Justice System. That, dear Doctor, is exactly where all of this sudden mistrust is rooted. My Field Commander, Roberto Jimenez, is on record regarding his feelings toward shadows in general, and now his suspicions relating to the SJS chief marshal."

Hannibal, George thought. *So that's what this is about.*

"Now I understand," he said and nodded. "You suspect Hannibal is up to no good, and you fear that Nueva and Gallagher's disappearance bodes ill, perhaps indicates some conspiracy?"

He chuckled, and watched all three faces on his view-screen frown at the act. *The hell with them*, he thought. *They could indulge an old man.*

"If Meaghan and Alex's disappearance is cause for alarm, it is because of some harm which may have befallen them," George said sharply, nostrils flared. "Not, certainly, because they have planned some insane insurrection at a time when their worst enemy walks the earth again. Talk about stupid! I'll let you in on a little secret."

Ah, he had their attention. Did he ever!

"Hannibal is a liar, a killer, and an incredibly intelligent creature with a network of operatives all his own. He is as vicious as the legends portray his kind to be, the antithesis of everything Meaghan and her team stand for."

"But," the President sputtered, "what were you thinking when—"

"We know Hannibal too well," George said, though he was really speaking for the shadows, for he'd never actually met Hannibal. "The creature wanted the SJS job so that he would be above suspicion, and therefore, above punishment for his own misdeeds. He has pretended to be above reproach so that humanity will not demand his destruction. The position was intended to be, in a way, a prison for him. A way for us to keep an eye on him."

"But how can you—" Julie Graham began.

"Rolf Sechs, the deputy chief?" George continued. "He and Cody and Nueva shared the same blood-father, as they say. He is one of them, and he is also Hannibal's watchdog. Don't worry, my friends. If Hannibal gets out of hand, Rolf will simply kill him, or die trying, and then you've got the rest of the SJS to keep the beast in check. Now, can we discuss what's truly important here, like destroying Mulkerrin before his madness spreads any further, and perhaps what's being done to find Meaghan and Alexandra?"

George Marcopoulos looked at his viewscreen and saw three of the most powerful individuals in the world looking back at him like cowed schoolchildren. *Good*! he thought. They were acting like fools, and here he was, nothing but an old sawbones, telling them what to do. A sudden memory nearly forced a smile onto his face, but he stifled the urge before they could see it. Still, the memory came, of younger days, laughing with his kids in front of the television set.

Damnit, Jim, he thought, *I'm a doctor not a diplomat.*

Who would have guessed?

St. Leonhard, Austria, European Union.
Tuesday, June 6, 2000, 6:23 P.M.:

They had ridden in near complete silence as the miles ticked away on the odometer. The only thing Allison Vigeant and John Courage had learned about their driver was his name: Kurt Wagner. Beyond that, the man was silent. He seemed both frightened and fascinated by being in the same car as Courage, and it occurred to Allison that humans had become quite adept at picking the shadows out of the herd, which was ironic because the vampires had hidden among them for so many years. On the other hand, much to Wagner's chagrin, his brother, the volunteer, had babbled continuously, until Courage finally ordered him to be silent, which he was.

Now, though, they had pulled to a stop in Saint Leonhard, at the foot of Mount Untersberg, with the Alps rising all around them and a cable car hanging in the air on the mountainside. This, apparently, was their destination, though Allison had held off asking the many questions sprinting across her mind. She was not comfortable with the Wagner brothers there.

As they got out of the car, with barely a few syllables to spare for the men, Courage set off toward the cable car at a brisk pace. Wagner's tires turned up stones pulling away. Allison looked up toward the mountain.

Shit!

The cable car was not moving. Assuming they needed the car to get where they were going, and John's direction certainly hinted that they did, they had finally run into a major obstacle. She followed him quickly and arrived at the car's enclosed terminal several paces behind him. The door had shut, but even as she opened it, Allison could hear Courage yelling.

". . . you're dealing with!" he roared. "Do you have any idea what's going on in Salzburg? If you don't get this thing up and going, a lot more people will die!"

Two men, obviously the operators of the car, were on the receiving end of this tirade, and they looked completely overwhelmed, but not necessarily cooperative. Courage leaned forward, his eyes narrowing, and bared his fangs, hissing at them. His nose elongated slightly and his ears began to point.

The cable car was operational in seconds, and on its way down to them.

"What happened?" Allison whispered to him as the hum of the descending car filled the terminal.

"They've been shut down since the quake," John whispered back, "expecting aftershocks."

"You could have gone on without me," she said.

"No," he answered, a hand on her shoulder. "I need you for this, remember? And I have to conserve my strength for the battle; it would have been a huge drain to try to fly you up there."

She nodded, and the car arrived. As they got in, John turned to snarl at the operators again.

"When we're out, shut her down again," he said. "We won't be back this way."

Then the doors were closing, they were moving up the mountainside, and reporter that she was, Allison couldn't hold the questions back any longer.

"Why won't we be back this way?" she asked.

But Courage took it the wrong way. His face fell, disappointed, and it was a moment before Allison understood. Her question had been motivated by innocent curiosity, but in it he had heard suspicion, and now that she thought of it, she had reason to be suspicious. After all, if she needed the cable car to ascend, she couldn't conceive of a form of descent that would not require the car . . . unless she weren't coming back. It was an awkward moment between them, but John seemed finally to decide to ignore the less palatable implications of her question.

"There is only one way in, but there are many ways out," he said.

"In where?"

"Inside the mountain."

Allison raised an eyebrow, then looked out the window of the rising cable car, at the peak high above. When she turned back to John, he read the question in her eyes.

"You wouldn't believe me if I told you," he said, and she laughed.

"Give me a break, John! My boyfriend is Buffalo Bill! Man, get a grip, would you?"

Courage smiled and shook his head, but Allison felt a tightening in her chest as she thought of Will, trapped in that fortress. She shook it off, for the moment. They'd get him out. For now, her curiosity was getting the better of her.

"Well?" she asked.

John Courage joined her at the front of the cable car, looked up at the peak and put a hand on the glass.

"Inside that mountain," he said softly, "is a king."

•   •   •

It was only seven or eight minutes before they reached the top, and the view all around them was breathtaking. They were in high Alpine terrain, but the cold was not what Allison had imagined it would be. Still, it was early summer, and she didn't want to think about being up on that mountain in January. From the cable car terminal, they hiked up the mountain to the top of a steep, danger-ous-looking trail. To Allison's surprise, there were still tourists on the mountain, as well as two employees who seemed quietly annoyed at having to baby-sit them. The employees didn't bat an eye as she and Courage crested the hill.

"Their friends at the bottom must have radioed up not to bother us," John said. "That's good. Still, now that the car's running again, it's going to be almost impossible for them to keep these people up here."

"I'm sure they'll be happy to be rid of them," Allison said, noting that the squabbling of the tourists was already getting results.

They started down the path, Allison stumbling from time to time, and came across a number of dead birds along their way.

"Ravens," Courage told her. "According to the legend, the king sleeps in the heart of the mountain with one hun-dred of his most loyal soldiers, and when Europe needs him most and the ravens no longer fly at the summit he will return. Magic works strangely at times," he said sadly, "but I didn't expect it to kill the poor guys."

Allison thought about the implications of those words, the suggestion that Courage at least knew a heck of a lot about magic and how this king had come to be under the mountain in the first place, and perhaps Courage had even been the one to put him there, to cast the spell about the ravens, whose death he now regretted.

Agh! There was so much she didn't know, but she was certain he wasn't about to tell her. They made their way along the face of the mountain, and their path grew more rough and narrow as they went, until finally it petered out altogether. Still, they went on, picking their way along a windblown ledge for a few minutes, with John holding Allison's elbow to keep her confidence up, until they came upon a crevice in the mountainside. The ledge they were on continued on the other side, but they weren't going that far.

"Fifth floor," Courage joked, "cosmetics, lingerie, young miss. Going down!"

Allison wasn't laughing.

"You're kidding, right? You've got me climbing along a mountainside and now you want me to crawl into a crack in the ground?"

"What did you expect?" Courage asked sincerely. "An escalator?"

"Well, maybe a ladder at least," she said weakly, looking upon the fissure with dread.

"For vampires?" he laughed. "Well, I'll go you one better."

John's hands slid under her arms and lifted her from the ground. Allison shrieked and struggled until she saw that the ground was no longer under her. She berated him as he lowered her into the hole in the ground, afraid he would drop her, certain he would drop her. And when he was kneeling at the edge of the crack, his arms extended as far inside as possible, and while Allison was yelling "Don't let go! Don't let go," that's just what he did.

"Now, don't move a muscle," he ordered as she dropped mere inches, her feet landing on a rocky shelf in the darkness of the hole.

"You son of a bitch," she snapped, angry and embarrassed. "You scared the daylights out of me."

When John had lowered himself down, they began to work their way along a stone path that sloped gently into the mountain. In minutes, Allison felt blind, and the darkness had become total.

"I can't see a blessed thing," she said, scared though his hand held hers tightly.

"Are you sure you want to?" he asked, and Allison nodded.

John's hand suddenly burst into flames, a torch of flesh, throwing flickering illumination around the cavern they'd found themselves in, and down into the blackness to their right. It looked like a nasty drop, and Allison realized why Courage had wanted her in the dark. Luckily heights were one thing she'd never had a problem with, and she did have him there to watch out for her should anything go wrong.

She noticed that up ahead a pile of huge stones lay in their path, effectively putting an end to the shelf they were walking on. She wondered what John would do about that, but he didn't even seem to slow down as he neared the rocks.

Even with the light from John's flaming hand, it was dark. Ghostly shapes flickered on the stone walls inside the crevice, and the world fell away into nothing only feet away.

Allison was afraid.

It was a difficult realization for her. After everything she'd been through in her life, she'd promised herself over and over that she'd never be afraid again. It was a promise she never kept. As a child, her parents had beaten her badly, for punishment rather than recreation, but it was still terrible abuse. Her mother had once broken her nose; blood had shot from her nostrils, and the old woman had actually hit her harder, as if that would stop the bleeding. She only thanked God that they hadn't been pedophiles, or she might have killed herself one of the many times she considered it.

The authorities had taken her away from them. She was an only child, and then she'd been set adrift in the foster care system, some of whose chosen parental replacements were no better than her originals. But finally she had found a home with Rory and Carole Vigeant. When she'd gone undercover for CNN, in an elaborate ruse that included the very public termination of her job, she had used names from her past. Terry and Shaughnessy had been the last names of two foster families that she had particularly liked, so she became Terri Shaughnessy. Later, when she was working her way into the circle of volunteers, people who willingly gave up their blood and their lives to the Defiant Ones, she had been Tracey Sacco—her birth name, which she hated.

The Defiant Ones—what a joke. She had originally thought they were some kind of death cult, and they turned out to be vampires. Some were as evil as legend claimed. Others, unfortunate victims of an ancient, insane church conspiracy. She had watched a woman she knew be ravaged by Hannibal, who had raped her, held her captive, and was now a "respected" member of the shadow community. Then, later, she had met Will Cody, Peter Octavian and the rest, watched them fight for their lives, and fallen in love with Will.

And now she was following another vampire, one she barely knew, into the bowels of the Alps, where supposedly a hundred powerful vampires slept, and she would have to give her blood willingly to one of them in order to wake them up, to loose them upon an unsuspecting world. In order to do that, she had to put all of her faith in a man who wouldn't even tell her his real name . . . but then, she'd never been terribly forthcoming with her own. But what frightened her the most was that not far away, her lover's life, and thousands, perhaps millions, more, depended on their success.

Trust me, he says. As if she had a choice.

"There are two ways to do this," John said as they stopped short at the stone blockade across their path. "Hard and fast, or easy but slow. And we can't be wasting time. Step back a few yards, Allison, and lean against the wall. I'm afraid it's going to be dark in here for a minute or so. Whatever you do, don't move."

She didn't argue as John's flaming hand returned to normal. He took a deep breath, and she thought for the first time about the strain such a sustained combination of forms might cause . . . and then she couldn't hear him breathing anymore. In fact, though she wasn't about to move forward in the dark to test her theory, she didn't think he was even there, in front of her, anymore.

"John?" she called, and sure enough, there was no answer. It didn't occur to her that there were many forms he could take in which he couldn't answer. What did occur to her was that she did not hear rocks being moved, thrown over the side, stones grinding out of the way. The nothingness, which stretched out, away from the wall for several yards and then fell away into nothing, began to coalesce into something tangible. The lack of substance, the knowledge that there was nothing in front of her, and so much mountain above her, began to make Allison feel claustrophobic. And worse, she became disoriented, her center of gravity moving forward, her equilibrium unbalanced as if she actually wanted to go to the edge of the ledge, and past it, as if that were, somehow, right.

Once before she'd felt something like it, standing on one of the observation decks of the Empire State Building in New York City. But it had been a beautiful sunny day then, and she'd been with the Vigeants, her adoptive parents. Her body had felt strange, "funny," she'd said, but she hadn't been afraid then, hadn't been alone in the dark.

"John? John!" she yelled, slamming her back against the wall, bending over slightly to counter the magnetic draw the edge, the danger of it, held for her body. Could he possibly have brought her down here only to leave her?

No. That's idiotic. What purpose would it serve? And besides, she knew he was good, could sense it in him.

But then where was he?

Her eyes searched around her, frantically trying to pierce the darkness, trying to force her brain to access some hidden reserve, to *see* . . .

And then there came a roar, loud but muffled, as if it were beyond the stone barricade, and a terrible crashing, scraping, plowing sound as something shattered that barricade, tearing it down, sending stones ricocheting off the opposite wall, over the cavern, only to knock and skitter their way down into . . . whatever was down there. Allison automatically flung her arms up to protect herself, and was glad she did when several small stone shards hit her and a good-size chunk of rock slammed into her shoulder, throwing her to the ground.

At first she sucked on her right hand, which was bleeding, but then she gave up and rubbed vigorously at her left shoulder where she'd been hit. She sensed it, sensed him, for she knew it was John, standing over her. But it wasn't him really, at that moment. Whatever stood there, it was huge, and its breath was heaving, panting, and it wasn't at all comfortable on two feet. A gorilla? she wondered. No, more likely a bear. But when his left hand burst into flame, finally illuminating their path once again, he was just John Courage again, and she understood what he'd done.

The path they wanted was not along the ledge, beyond the barricade, but behind it, where the rocks had been piled up against the wall. He must have turned to mist and found his way through the rocks, only to transform again inside, taking a shape with the size and strength to drive through the barrier. A whole lot faster than trying to dig from outside. She wondered for a minute why there was such a good-size opening at all. Why take the chance, she wondered, when only vampires were inside? But then she remembered why she was there. Blood from a willing, human female. They needed to be sure their sacrificial lamb could get inside.

John was quiet now, and he looked exhausted, which didn't really surprise Allison. They made their way into this new tunnel, which went forward half a dozen feet, then turned a corner and down a crumbling, rocky slope for another dozen, after which it came to an end at a huge wooden door. The door was strapped together with iron, but it had no handle or knocker as far as Allison could tell. Somewhere, she heard a trickling sound, like a brook running, and she thought of melting snow from high up on the mountain.

John pounded on the door, but there was no response. Once again, he held up a fist and slammed it against the door, again and again, but still they heard nothing but their own mutterings and the echo of his "knock." Courage kept it up, knocking every minute or so, louder each time, though it seemed impossible.

And then they heard it, a rustling of movement behind the door, light footfalls on stone and then, finally, a voice, low and ominous, in a language Allison didn't think she'd ever heard before. Even so, she knew what its question must have been. John Courage replied in that same language, though it didn't seem to her that his reply included his own name, and certainly not hers.

And then another sound joined the others: that of a bolt being drawn back, large and rusted. The wood of the door seemed to have swollen tight with moisture, though Allison thought it quite dry at that moment, and though it scraped both floor and ceiling, the figure behind drew it open without any trouble.

And the tip of a long sword rested on John Courage's throat.

The holder of the sword was dressed all in a sort of linen, with a scabbard hung from his leather belt. On his feet he had leather shoes, which Allison immediately recognized as having been handmade, and probably not in this century, or the last. Over the linen pants he had wound some cloth around his legs, for what reason she could not guess.

He was not an attractive man. Though obviously clean, he had a scraggly beard and wild hair which, when combined with his thin lips and wide, flat nose gave him a bestial appearance.

Not to mention that sword.

John Courage spoke again in that language, which sounded familiar to her, fluid like Italian or Spanish, yet guttural as well. He spoke in calming, friendly tones, but the holder of the sword barked something in return, and Allison was discouraged.

"Can't you disarm him?" she hissed, and the warrior's eyes flicked to her for the first time, examining her as if he were window-shopping at the butcher's.

"Unnecessary" was Courage's only reply.

If you say so, she thought, but didn't speak again, because she didn't like the way the man with the sword looked at her. He barked something else and shook his head, and John continued to speak in that soothing voice. And then the voice changed suddenly, became deeper, older. Though she couldn't see him clearly from behind, Allison could tell that John was changing. His head seemed longer, his body thinner; his hair hung, now, long down his back, and she could see even from behind that he had a light edge of beard. His skin had darkened significantly, to almost an olive color. In short, though she couldn't see his face, she knew that John Courage looked nothing like the shadow she had come to know.

The sword fell clanging to the stone floor inside that door, and a moment later, its wielder was also there, prostrate on his knees, eyes downcast, hands together as if pleading for forgiveness, which was obviously what he *was* doing. When John leaned forward to urge the man to stand, Allison caught a good glimpse of his face in the firelight he himself generated, but his features had returned to those she knew.

Clearly, John had been here before, and had worn a different face, one the guard, for she was sure that was what he was, had not only seen before, but respected, even feared.

Allison wasn't sure she liked that idea.

The warrior turned now, and led them through a stone

tunnel and to a set of stairs, which eventually opened into a large cavern. The stairs went down and down, with John's fire lighting the way, and before long Allison realized that there were two more of the warriors behind her, following them.

"What language was that?" she asked John.

"Frankish."

"Uh-hmm," she said and nodded. "They seem to know you."

"Oh, they don't know me much better than you do," he said.

"Which is not at all," she said archly. "Never mind that I haven't yet prostrated myself before you."

John was quiet for a while, so Allison voiced the question currently on her mind.

"Why won't you tell me your real name?"

John stopped, turned and looked at her, studying her a moment. Allison was defiant, unintimidated, but not petulant. She needed to know what the hell was going on. The guards around them stood still, waiting for John to continue. He smiled at her kindly, without any trace of menace, and she felt somewhat more comfortable.

"You thought you had a story with Venice," he said. "Wait till you get to the bottom of this one."

Then he chuckled and turned away, and they continued down the stairs for a good five minutes more. Finally, the stairs ended at the floor of the cavern, stretched out far before them. Allison thought she could see still forms on the ground around them, but her eyes would not focus much past the circle of light thrown by John's flaming fist.

"Here we are," he said to her.

"Here?" she asked. "How 'bout some light?"

Courage said something quickly to their companions, and the one who had confronted them pointed ahead to the right. John walked forward, leaving Allison in the dark, but she was nervous about doing anything that might set off their guards, so she waited for him to give the word. He didn't. But she could still see him as he moved to the wall of the cavern. As he moved farther from her, but closer to the wall, she saw a huge iron chain hitched by a single link to an iron spike that had been hammered into the wall. John said something, and the two who had been following Allison rushed to him and, pulling the chain from the spike, played out two dozen rusty feet of slack that had been coiled on the stone floor.

Above them, Allison heard a creaking and rattling as a huge weight descended. It drew her attention but also made her suddenly aware again of the sound of running water, which had disappeared for a while but now was back, and louder than before. Courage, with his light, came closer to her, and they both craned their necks to see whatever was rattling its way down to them. As it came lower, Allison began to make out a huge circle of iron, more than twenty feet in diameter, and through its center the elaborate network of chains that held it aloft. In seconds it hung six feet above the floor, and John walked over and stood under it.

And Allison finally realized what it was: a chandelier.

John turned in a circle, his fiery touch reaching out to the huge candles melted onto the iron. Allison wondered how long it had been since those candles had been lit, but she didn't need to worry about whether they would still burn. Moments later, the two guards were hoisting the chandelier once again toward the ceiling of the cavern, and Allison looked around, nearly overwhelmed by what the light had revealed.

She thought back to what John had told her, to his vague words: *The king sleeps in the heart of the mountain with one hundred of his most loyal soldiers, and when Europe needs him most, and the ravens no longer fly at the summit, he will return.*

She had been able to pass off the dead ravens; after all, they might have been some sign of Mulkerrin's return, his influence. But now, in the heart of the mountain, Allison

Vigeant was looking at one hundred sleeping soldiers in linen and leather, covered in furs, with swords at their sides. Far to her left, an underground stream ran through the cavern, above her the candles burned on, and across the huge room, opposite the stairs they had walked down, was what might have been an altar. On top of it was a bed carved of stone, and upon that bed lay the creature of legend. Even in that repose, he looked like a king.

"Come," John said, taking her by the hand and leading her across the room. They moved carefully around the dead-looking forms of the soldiers, and the three who had escorted them followed behind and kneeled at the base of the stone upon which their leader lay. But she and John continued up those steps, and in a moment, she was looking down upon his face.

His eyes were closed, but there were bags under them and his face was deeply lined. His long hair and equally long beard and bushy mustache were a reddish brown, streaked with gray. His nose was aquiline, his cheekbones high and proud, and his skin was the white of ivory, as had been the skin of the sleeping men behind Allison. He was dressed very much like his soldiers, save for the blue cloak that was wrapped about him, the silk edges of his tunic, and the pure gold belt and scabbard he wore. His crown sat next to his head on the stone bed. It was gold, encrusted with jewels, and had a cross on top. Only when John Courage touched her arm was Allison able to tear her gaze away. The man was fascinating to look at.

"Are you sure you want to do this?" John asked, and she thought that was a pretty stupid question. She'd come all this way, and the life of the man she loved, not to mention so many others, hung in the balance.

She raised a sarcastic eyebrow, a comment he'd become used to in the short time they'd known each other, and no other reply was necessary. The blood of a willing human female was needed. As far as she could tell, she was the only female at the party, not to mention the only human!

John reached behind him, and one of the soldiers kneeling there stood to hand up his sword. He took Allison's hand and lay the sword in her palm, and then before she had time to think about it, he drew the blade across her flesh. She flinched, wanting to pull her hand away, but his strength held her there as her eyes began to water.

"Mother of God!" she hissed, but that was all, as she bit her lip. John curled her hand into a fist and kissed her knuckles before handing the sword back to its owner. He nodded his approval of her strength, of her determination, and yet Allison could see the sympathy he felt for her pain.

"Let it drip on his lips," John said, and she turned, held her hand above the old king's face and bled.

His lips parted slightly, and Courage told her it was enough. Allison stepped back as the king's eyes opened, and he smiled. His tongue slid out and cleaned his mouth of her blood, and she couldn't help but shiver. She watched as John Courage helped him sit up, and then stand. They exchanged greetings in a language she recognized—Latin —but again she could not understand. The old king had known John immediately, not needing the shapechange that his soldier had, and to Allison's incredible surprise, attempted to kneel before him. But Courage wouldn't have it, looking around at Allison with an almost annoyed glance, muttering something to the king.

Finally, the old warrior's eyes rested on her, and then he smiled benevolently and took the few steps toward her. One hand on the pommel of the sword hanging at his side, he made a deep, regal bow and then looked at John Courage for assistance.

"Your Majesty," John said in English, "it is my pleasure to present Allison Vigeant."

"Allison," he said, finally turning his attention back to her. "I'd like you to meet Carolus Magnus, whom some have called the father of Europe. Better known to you, of course, as Charlemagne."

And behind them, an army began to rise.

CHAPTER ✦ NINE

Salzburg, Austria, European Union.
Wednesday, June 7, 2000, 5:01 A.M.:

Hannibal was many things, but foolish was not among them. He was perfectly aware that every ranking officer, and probably most of their subordinates, involved with Operation: Jericho suspected him of duplicity. When they separated, he had earned several suspicious and even fearful glances, and certainly every member of Commander Jimenez's strike team had been prepped for his possible betrayal.

No, Hannibal was no fool, but he suspected those around him, human and vampire alike, were fools indeed. Did they actually believe he would side with Mulkerrin? Such a concept was ridiculous. However, Mulkerrin's presence did provide Hannibal's own plans with a perfect diversion. If the sorcerer managed to defeat the forces arrayed against him, *then* Hannibal would step in and finish the job. In the meantime, he would use the opportunity to set his plans in motion. Hannibal was crafting a new future for the world, and though some might disagree with him, he vowed to become the savior of his people. One day, they would revere his name.

For the moment, Hannibal sat calmly in the back of a troop carrier, along with his deputy, Rolf Sechs, six other shadows, and a crowd of human soldiers including UNSF

Commander Roberto Jimenez. Jimenez was making inquiries and delivering orders over a complicated communications system that each member of the United Nations security force carried in the collar of his or her uniform. Even the agents and marshals of the Shadow Justice System had been given uniforms with these collarcomms for Operation: Jericho. Though unadorned, the uniforms of each unit were different colors, all dark variants on green, blue and brown. The shadows wore gray, and the rest of Jimenez's strike team wore black.

The collarcomms interested Hannibal only in that he was privy to every conversation among the UN commanders. Each unit's leader, in this case each commander, had two channels, one on either side of the head. The left side was for general communication within the commander's own unit, the right for communication with the other commanders and with Jimenez himself. Some of the seconds, including Rolf, had both channels as well, but Hannibal was not concerned. Rolf could listen, but not speak. And Hannibal had a third channel, which he could switch to whenever he wished by depressing a button on his collar, and which cut off communication to all SJS agents who were not on his handpicked team.

"All units have reported arriving at preliminary rendezvous, Chief Marshal," Roberto Jimenez said. "We are the last to reach our position. Everything proceeds on schedule."

These were the first words the UNSF commander had spoken to him, or any of the shadows, since they had departed Munich. He had not even spoken to Rolf, whom Hannibal thought Jimenez might actually trust.

"I have ears, Commander," Hannibal said, having indeed listened quite closely as the other commanders made their reports to Jimenez. "We are not *that* different."

Hannibal turned to Rolf then.

"And so thus far, Commander Thomas is safe and

sound. An admirable woman, don't you think?" he asked his subordinate.

Rolf glared at Hannibal, but did not bother pulling the voice-pad from his belt. Roberto Jimenez raised his eyebrows but said nothing, and the other soldiers on the strike team, shadows included, were intelligent enough to look only at their feet.

Hannibal chuckled to himself as Rolf looked away. Did the fool really think he was not spied upon? Did he truly expect Hannibal to miss something as monumental as the coupling of the American commander and the deputy marshal of the Shadow Justice System? Ah, well, sex will do that, Hannibal thought. He mourned once again Rolf's unflagging loyalty to his dead mentor's clan, to Gallagher, Nueva and Cody. The mute would have been an asset, no question, to Hannibal's plans, especially considering his new involvement with Commander Thomas.

The lingering smirk on Hannibal's face finally drove Rolf to reply. He took out his voice-pad and wrote: "None of us is safe while Mulkerrin lives."

Hannibal only nodded, with a slight shrug and an innocent look on his face. Oh, Rolf certainly knew something was up. In fact, Hannibal took a particular pleasure in confusing his deputy. For instance, he had allowed Rolf to handpick the six shadows who would accompany Jimenez's strike team. Rolf could then be certain Hannibal's accomplices would not be among them, or so he thought. Hannibal had enjoyed the surprise on Rolf's face when he had not argued the choices, and in his frustration, Rolf had changed the lineup several times, finally giving up when Hannibal still did not respond.

The truck rolled along the *bundestrasse*, Route 155 according to the signs, and out the back they were able to see the traffic leaving the city, the broken-down vehicles, and . . . *Ah, there we are*, Hannibal thought, *a stray*! As the truck carrying the strike team passed, Austrian soldiers emptied automatic weapons into the still moving body of a demon-creature who had strayed too far from the city. There would be many who wandered away from Salzburg without being killed, Hannibal knew, and he made a mental note to try and round those up when all of this was over. It was likely they could be put to good use.

The strike team did not stop to help the Austrian troops, who may or may not have succeeded. Hannibal looked over at Jimenez, but his face was a mask of meditation, as were those of the rest of the soldiers. Only Hannibal seemed above the grave atmosphere in the truck, and he knew his levity was unappreciated. He glanced at Rolf and saw that, though also serious, the mute was concentrating on something other than Operation: Jericho. He was staring at Hannibal with open suspicion and dislike, even hate.

Excellent. Hannibal hated phonies.

The truck slowed down and took a right turn. Hannibal saw the sign for Rudolf-Biebl-Strasse, and snickered at the street name.

"All units," Jimenez touched his right collarbone, "move to secondary positions immediately. Rodriguez, lock in holding pattern above Jericho. Austrian emergency personnel will be behind you so, do not, I repeat, do not stop to assist civilians. Sweep the streets, flamethrowers up front. Destroy all hostiles. Move out."

Hannibal closed his eyes, knowing that Rolf would be certain to notice and not caring if he did. He listened carefully as each commander detailed his or her unit's move from preliminary to secondary position.

Commander Thomas's unit had encountered fourteen demons of varying sizes on her short trek to Rainberg. There had been no concentrated resistance whatsoever, as the demons seemed to be roaming about with no direction. Commander Gruber's troops had met with an extraordinarily large water-based shadow in the river, and two of the Ducks had been capsized, several men killed. Still, they made it to Mozart's Plaza with nearly their entire complement, thanks in large part to the efforts of the SJS soldiers with them.

Commander Locke's unit had met almost no resistance on their march from Hellbrun Castle to the stadium. In fact, there had been little by way of destruction, either from demons or from the earthquake, and the area had been the fastest and easiest to evacuate. Commander Surro's troops had had slightly more trouble, but were lucky to find the bridge intact when it came time for them to cross the Salzach. The two units had combined and scaled the mountainside, encountering a huge number of shadows and setting fire to a large portion of the woods below Nonnberg Abbey, where Maria Von Trapp was said to have been a novice. When Locke brought this up, Surro merely scowled at him over her collarcomm. Nevertheless, and again with the help of the shadows, their secondary position was attained.

In all, though the total number of troops including the paratroopers had been nearly twenty-five hundred, only thirty-seven soldiers had been lost, twelve of them Austrians who had been killed during earlier evacuations. It had been much too easy.

"It's a mousetrap," Hannibal suddenly said aloud, and this time the strike force did look at him, some with open hostility. Rolf looked ready to pounce if he made a move.

"What?" Jimenez snapped.

"It's a mousetrap, Commander." And now Hannibal smiled, for though this was not a part of his plan, it would certainly be a joy to watch.

"Mulkerrin is the cheese, you see," he said seriously, lecturing. "He's there, all right, waiting for you. The real thing. But the closer you get, the greater your danger of having your back broken."

"There are thousands of us!" Jimenez said.

"Ah, true," Hannibal said, "but his reinforcements are endless. He can demolish your troops even if you're a million miles away, in safety, but to stem the tide of his creatures, you've got to kill *him*."

"We've destroyed all the creatures we've found."

"Ah, yes, but now reverse the analogy," Hannibal said. "For every rodent you kill, there are usually a dozen more lurking about, in their holes, waiting for you to turn your back."

Jimenez just looked at Hannibal for a minute, and the vampire knew that the commander was trying to decide what to believe. Hannibal watched as he looked over at Rolf, obviously seeking a second opinion. When the mute simply nodded, Jimenez swore loudly, even as he thumbed his collarcomm.

"Do it!" he ordered. "Move in, fry anything that gets in your way, and watch your asses. It's possible we've been flanked. Rodriguez, when the front door goes down, your people hit the silk."

There was one thing Hannibal admired about Jimenez, though he was loath to admit it. The human had a no-bullshit attitude and didn't rely on moronic military jargon, code words and the like. He was all soldier, and showed not a trace of the officer he'd become. He played by his own rules. It was a shame the commander hated shadows so much, or Hannibal might have made him one.

On the other hand, Hannibal realized, that could still be amusing.

As the huge attack force began to converge on the fortress and the strike force abandoned their vehicle to walk the last half mile—knowing that being inside the truck would be a liability—around them, before them and especially behind them, portals that had been opened during the earthquake now spewed forth hundreds of demonic creatures. New portals began to open in the side of the fortress wall itself, demon-creatures leaping from within to tumble down the slopes out of control, savaging whatever soldiers were in their way when they finally regained their footing.

And while Jimenez barked orders into his collarcomm, Hannibal began to change. By the time Jimenez turned to seek his help, all he saw was Rolf Sechs diving through a cloud of mist, trying to grab at it as it drifted away.

Hell.
Twenty-Four Days, One Hour, Sixteen Seconds After Departure:

Meaghan Gallagher knew very little about her current situation, but there were two things of which she was certain. She and Lazarus were in Hell, which for the first time in her life she really thought of with a capital H, and her one, true love, Alexandra Nueva, was dead.

It was not a simple bit of knowledge, but rather one she had come to understand over days, weeks. Her first love, Janet Harris, had been killed by the sorcerer Liam Mulkerrin. They were now in search of her second, Peter Octavian, whom, though she had never been certain of his death, she had never expected to see again. She felt nothing regarding a possible reunion with Peter, except a slight glimmer of hope that they would somehow escape this place in time to prevent Mulkerrin from turning Earth into a world overrun by monsters, a world like that darkened plane they had passed through on their way to Hell.

First Janet, then Peter, and now Alex, whom she'd loved most, and best. Alexandra had been an angry woman at first, and a vicious one, but their initial coupling had led quickly to Alex remembering her humanity, regretting many of her actions, and allowing love and kindness back into her world. Meaghan had fallen in love with her easily after that. It had been Alex who'd engineered Meaghan's leadership of the shadows, not anything of her own doing. It had been Alex who had brainstormed the Shadow Justice System. It had been Alex who pushed Cody back into the limelight, forced him to become everything he was capable of.

Alexandra Nueva had been the rhyme and reason behind so much of the new existence for their people, and behind Meaghan Gallagher's entire existence. And now she was dead. Of course, at first Meaghan had argued with Lazarus. She knew that there were very few things from which shadows would not recover. But Lazarus brought her again and again back to the moment when she had seen the horrible, burning faces in that hole sucking Alex's flames in through their mouths and nostrils, flames that were Alex herself, body and soul. She had been consumed by dozens of different creatures, split apart and digested in so many pieces. Only now, after countless days, could Meaghan really admit the truth.

Her lover was dead. The hours of begging Lazarus to return to that spot, to attempt to revive Alex—that was all over. After it had happened, they had continued down the ever-steeper, ever-narrower tunnel, until it had indeed become a hole. As mist, then, they had floated down that well, finding nothing for hours, perhaps more than a day. Once in a while, tired of keeping the one form, or perhaps too comfortable in it, they would shapeshift into bats so that they could rest, tiny claws stuck to the rock walls of the hole.

Twice they had floated on past "throats" similar to that which had consumed Alexandra—killed her—but they were mist and passed so quickly the hands and mouths could not touch them. In the end, the hole began to widen, and turn so that eventually it became a tunnel again, and when it did, they changed into their human forms and took turns sleeping, something neither had *had* to do in a long time. Lazarus's patience grew ever shorter in dealing with her outbursts concerning Alex, and he became more and more concerned with the barrenness they'd found thus far in Hell. Their prospects of finding Peter and escaping with him seemed to grow more dim with each passing hour.

As the days had passed, Meaghan lost her faith in Lazarus. Once he had seemed so powerful to her, so filled with knowledge. She had respected that, feared him in a way. No more. Though she was certain there were many things about their plight that he kept from her, she knew there was also much he had been unprepared for, unaware of, and she didn't look to him for answers anymore.

Now, as they made their way through the tunnel, after weeks of traveling, Meaghan found it quite strange that she had no need of sustenance, and apparently neither did her companion. Had she gone so long without blood in her own world, she would have been a ravenous lunatic by now. Perhaps, she considered, though they felt each moment pass, though their bodies told them when another day had ended, perhaps the bloodthirst was still governed, through some tenuous connection, by the far slower passage of time in their own world.

Suddenly Meaghan was sure this was the truth. Which would mean that, though weeks had gone by in Hell, less than a day had passed on the other side. Why, the battle had barely begun! Though she knew her certainty might be somewhat premature, Meaghan was excited. She and Lazarus would now be able to tell time in their own world based upon the bloodthirst. Their suffering would be their clock.

She was about to tell him when the tunnel began to widen drastically, and she saw that they were coming into a cavern ahead. Unlike the stovepipe where they had first arrived, and the tunnel in which Alex had met her end, the solid rock path they had been following had very little light. There had been few of the fiery cracks in its walls, but luckily there had been enough for their vampiric vision.

The cavern they entered now had plenty of light. Flames licked the walls of the enormous, empty space. At the opposite end, the cavern opened onto the edge of a flaming pit at the bottom of a stovepipe. It might have been the pit they'd appeared in originally, or it might not—Meaghan could not say. At the edge of the pit stood a naked man, or something like a man. They approached with caution, yet before they had taken half a dozen steps in his direction, the man turned and motioned for them to come closer.

"Take a look," he said, motioning to the pit. "It's really quite fascinating."

And they did. In the pit, atop huge stones red with fire, bodies writhed in ecstasy and torment. Like those they had seen tumbling through the stovepipe so long ago, some looked human while others were not even vaguely humanoid. It was impossible to tell how many different beings were in the pit. Meaghan refused to consider the implications, to wonder how these creatures had gotten to Hell and what their crimes had been. She would not bow to the Judeo-Christian myths she had been taught as a girl.

"That would be wise," the man said, and she flinched.

He had read her mind! This could not be one of the damned, whatever they were, she thought. This was a true demon, not like the shadows they had battled before, not like those creatures who had been enslaved by Mulkerrin's magic.

"Everything you see is real, tangible," the demon went on, apparently ignoring her thoughts now. "But the logic behind the Suffering, which is what we prefer to call them, the reasons for their presence, their purpose, is nothing you could ever hope to understand."

Out of the corner of her eye, Meaghan noticed movement, and far across the pit she saw a shadow-demon, apparently slave to the true demon, the size of an elephant. It plowed through the damned, the Suffering as the demon called them, with its huge snout. Every so often, it hung its head back, chewing—its jaws munching the bodies—and swallowing, not for a moment distracted by the shrieking and moaning all around it. The thing digested the sufferers and, as the three of them looked on, shat them out whole, covered with some kind of waste. The thing moved on, and the shit-covered sufferers shrieked insanely, knowing that it would be back for them again.

Meaghan was finally able to turn away, and she felt quite

sick in her stomach. Even though she would have found an open artery quite attractive at the moment, the shit and blood that swirled in this enormous pigpen disgusted her beyond words.

"It's a dirty job, but someone's got to do it," the demon said, and giggled, reading her mind again.

"Lazarus?" she asked when she realized he'd not spoken a word since they'd emerged from the tunnel. She turned to find him with his back to the pit, though keeping the demon in his peripheral vision. Standing there, erect and proud, his face more sad than repulsed, he gave Meaghan a sense for the first time of an innate goodness in this vampire. Though many others, herself included, tried hard, there was something in Lazarus she had not ever sensed in their kind. At that moment, he looked almost—*No.* Mcaghan stopped that line of thought. No matter what good could be found in her people, no matter what words could be used to describe them, she found it impossible to think of any of her kind as "holy."

Lazarus smiled at her then, dispelling the image. He looked as if he were about to speak, finally, but his mouth snapped shut, and they both turned their full attention back to the demon at the pit's edge. It was changing.

"Really," the creature said, "this was just for you two. I didn't want to scare you off, you know."

The demon grew then, its true form bursting through the skin facade it wore. A ripple of horns like daggers stood along its spine, and its talons hung nearly to the ground. The thing's hair burned, and the face fell down around its neck like a scarf. Its true head was cloven halfway to the snout, and flames leapt from inside the beast's skull.

It lifted its hands, and fire sprang up from the pit, singeing their faces and shooting up through the stovepipe in a terrible torrent. It lasted for several seconds, and when it ended, a shower of bodies began to fall, their flesh slapping into the pile and onto the rocks with the sound of raw meat dropped into a sizzling pan. When the demon finally turned its three eyes back on them, all the humor had fled its demeanor, and only a cruel cynicism remained. Meaghan thought it strange that she had never worried about the creature's attacking them, but Hell had been affecting their thought processes from the beginning. She promised herself that they would be more careful.

"Lord Alhazred," Lazarus said, bowing, and the demon's eyes narrowed.

"How do you know my name?" the demon-lord demanded, but Lazarus ignored the question.

"I bear the greetings of the Stranger," he said, and the demon blinked several times, surprised, and then sneered.

"Do you, now?" it said, with a voice like an echo in an empty room. "It has been a long time since we have seen the Stranger, down here," the demon said to Lazarus, though it continued to look at Meaghan.

"He is well," Lazarus said. "However, he needs your assistance."

"Does he?" Lord Alhazred said, and Meaghan noticed the demon's penchant for responding with questions.

"You are surprised?" Meaghan asked, quickly, earning a sharp look from Lazarus and a noticeable twitch in the huge horn that now protruded from between the demon's legs.

"Should I be?"

"You don't know?"

"You don't think so?"

"Should we think so?"

The demon-lord stopped then, staring at her, tired of its own game.

"What do you seek?" it asked.

"One like ourselves, Peter Octavian by name," she said, "also known as Nicephorus Dragases."

"He's a prisoner?"

"We don't know," Lazarus said, trying to regain control. "He came here a long time ago, with another named Mulkerrin. Mulkerrin has escaped, and the Stranger wishes to send him back to you, but to do so we need this Octavian."

"I remember the arrival, I admit," Alhazred said and nodded, finally giving up its game of questions. "But they weren't my responsibility."

"Can you help us?" Meaghan pushed. "Will you?"

"A request from the Stranger?" The demon-lord laughed shrilly, cynically. "Of course I'll help."

It gestured toward the tunnel from which they'd emerged, and then it disappeared. A portal appeared in its place, burning red with flame rather than silver like those they had seen before. Meaghan was immediately concerned. This demon-lord seemed malicious enough, and she suspected malevolent was closer to the truth. Could this portal be a trap?

"Oh, it's safe, foolish vampire," the mind reader said and laughed. "It would be in bad form to destroy agents of the Stranger. This is the fastest way for me to help you. Through there you'll find many more of the Suffering, but if you ask the other lords, you may find your friends' point of arrival. From there, well, you never know."

The creature turned back to its work, raising its hands so the flames leapt up again, bodies raining down in their wake.

"How do they come to be here?" Meaghan forced herself to ask.

Lord Alhazred turned around, shaking its head.

"Silly thing," it said. "The Suffering are always here, no matter where else they may be."

Lazarus grabbed her hand and pulled her toward the portal. The passage was not as painful as she had expected. And of course, nothing compared to what the Suffering endured.

Salzburg, Austria, European Union.
Wednesday, June 7, 2000, 7:11 A.M.:

Knowing.

That was the strangest thing about it. The knowing. He knew, for instance, that dozens of feet above the chamber in which he lay, the sorcerer Liam Mulkerrin worked his magic, marshaled his forces. The fortress was like a small village surrounded by stone walls, and it was nearly filled with his soldiers, living, breathing human beings whose bodies had been invaded, possessed, by the spirits of those who had once been posted to that place. The spirits themselves were not evil, but the semblance of life Mulkerrin offered them in exchange for their service was irresistible.

He knew.

Soldiers manned the open windows, though many were hundreds of feet atop sheer walls. Huge, mindless slave demons patrolled the battlements of the fortress and prowled the many halls of the lower levels even as hundreds of their kindred poured out of new passages onto the Earth plane, tearing into those who would lay siege to Mulkerrin's base.

He knew.

The battle raged all around the monolithic structure, and though the humans held their own, in the end, the battle was destined to be quite one-sided. Mulkerrin's resources were almost limitless, and yet he could feel that the once-priest did not know his own abilities well enough to use them, and what he did use took a toll on him, his grip on the magic being tenuous. The sorcerer stood in the middle of the open courtyard in the center of the fortress, his concentration complete. He was surrounded by a black, swirling mist through which he was nearly invisible, though the sun shone down on the courtyard.

And that was beginning to change. Thunderclouds pregnant with a monstrous storm, glowing with a sickly, reddish radiance which the human soldiers below deemed wholly unnatural, moved slowly in from the south, as if answering a call Mulkerrin had sent.

He knew, but it wasn't knowledge that came from experience—not from seeing, or hearing, or touching. It was a transcendant awareness which reached out from that cold, dark chamber and encircled the fortress, not yet able to envelop completely the battle, the attacking forces, but spreading. He knew Mulkerrin, then, completely and totally, the sorcerer not believing such an intrusion possible and therefore not registering the subtle penetration of his soul. Of his magic. The knowledge, the awareness, met the magic, and danced with it in the ether, becoming intertwined with the magic, intrinsic to it. Whatever Mulkerrin commanded, that joining gave him knowledge of, awareness of. And that awareness sent tendrils of anger, hatred, disgust, into the magic, not tugging or pulling, not screaming, but insinuating, tainting, whispering to it, so that it changed.

And in the glory that was his evil, Mulkerrin barely noticed.

Down in that cold, dark chamber, at the center of the awareness that enveloped the fortress, that joined with and unsettled the magic, he lay. And below the awareness, the knowing, the magic, was pain. Pain both simple in its totality and incredibly complex in its persistence.

His blood had been spreading in a large pool for many hours and was beginning to cake into many of the grooves between the stones of the floor. The gaping hole in his chest, where the bones stuck sharply out at all angles, had long since stopped sucking at the air. His eyes were open, but he did not see. He did not blink, or breathe, did not smell, or hear.

His hair was long and white, the beard and mustache the same color, and his skin was mottled, wrinkled and pale. His body was tiny, shriveled, the hands like claws, the limbs truncated. Rot had appeared in several places, especially around the ragged chest wound.

Thum-tum.

A trill went out, into the awareness and the magic, and Mulkerrin felt it, through yards of stone, like a pre-orgasmic shiver. The sorcerer merely laughed, thinking it nothing more than the rush of the magic.

Thum-tum.

This time, the awareness suppressed the trill, confined the tickle of it to a more subtle level. He reached out, with his own awareness, and smoothed out the lines of what he felt. Above the pain, within it, enveloping it and giving it birth, he knew.

Thum-tum, thum-tum, thum-tum.

He knew.

Thum-tum, thum-tum, thum-tum, thum-tum, thum-tum, thum-tum, thum-tum, thum-tum, thum-tum, thum-tum, thum-tum . . .

The newly formed, tiny, infant heart rattled along like a freight train, speeding out of control to do a job it was never meant for. It screamed at the trauma of the pain, but kept drumming as a thin film of muscle stretched across the open wound. Around the body, blood that had dried, scabbing the stone floor, was wet again, warm again. And just as it had slowly seeped from him, pooling on the floor, so now it was absorbed by his skin, through his pores, flowing back into his body like the tide rolling in. And high tide wouldn't be long.

Cody knew.

CHAPTER ✦ TEN

The American media had become far too powerful over the past few decades, and as Henry Russo, the President of the United States, prepared for his midnight address, he silently vowed to himself to research new ways to stifle their nagging, insistent voices, at least to quiet them long enough for a man to think! *Call it censorship*, he thought. *Call it whatever the hell you like*! Nevertheless, he would not be bullied by a bunch of reporters.

Or so he told himself. In reality, that was exactly what had happened in the past, and what had happened today. Doubtless, despite his best efforts, it would continue long into the future. Though there was not yet news from inside Salzburg, word from Austrian media had been pouring in all day. First about the earthquake, felt by a very few, and then about the military evacuation taking place. In addition, several people had been picked up on the outskirts of the city, apparently refugees, spinning tales of monsters rising from the earth. Of course, it didn't help that Doris Toumarkine from *The Hollywood Reporter* had called to confirm a story that Will Cody and Allison Vigeant had been in Salzburg at the time. Heaven forbid somebody not know where celebrities were vacationing!

Just fucking dandy!

Henry had held off as long as he could, but with Operation: Jericho already under way, it would do no harm to present the news of that op to the world. Certainly, it was his duty as President to be sure his own press conference was held before that of the UN secretary general. And he knew Rafael Nieto would be up at first light with a report of the battle. No matter that they fought the war together —the political skirmishing must go on. And maybe then he could get these reporters out of his hair, just for a little while.

"Henry?" Julie Graham stepped into the Oval Office, and he smiled at her, despite his mental grumbling.

"Come on in."

"Bill was a little worried about you, wanted me to check in," she said, her raised eyebrow enough to make him certain of the joke.

Ah, the joke. William Galin, the vice president, hated him more than anything else in the world. In fact, it wouldn't have surprised Henry to learn that Bill Galin wanted him dead. He had, after all, chosen Bill as his running mate essentially to keep an eye on him. Bill was an excellent politician, but to those who knew him, he was also a bigoted, classist, sexist, petty egotist who might have given Henry a terrible time down the road.

With Bill as his running mate, Henry had been assured of a certain number of ultraconservative votes, as well as almost the entire middle-of-the-road constituency. Once in office, he had put Galin under his thumb, had, in effect, banned him from the White House. The man had become more invisible than any public official since Dan Quayle. In fact, the only time the public really saw him was behind the President at the podium. But it just went back to something Henry's parents had taught him growing up: children—especially petulant children—should be seen and not heard.

"Henry, you okay?" Julie's concern wiped away the scowl Bill Galin always brought to the President's face.

"Yeah, Jules. Sit down."

"Look, I know you've got this thing scheduled for midnight," she said, taking the leather chair in front of Henry's desk she had long thought of as "hers," "but the media is going crazy. Maybe we should bump this thing up, startle them for once?"

Henry shook his head.

"What do you mean? Why are they any crazier than they were?"

"Nobody tells you anything, do they?" Julie said, eyebrows creased and without a trace of humor. "Somebody leaked word of Gallagher and Nueva's disappearance, for starters. And to top it off, the name 'Mulkerrin' is already on the wire."

"Shit."

Henry was up and out of his chair in no time. He didn't even bother to grab his jacket.

"Is Marcopoulos here?" he said as he swung the door open.

"I don't know," Julie answered, following swiftly, even as Henry's personal contingent of Secret Service jumped to attention and swarmed around them, muttering into their collarcomms as they went. Gary Williams, the agent-in-charge at the moment, flanked the President on one side, and Julie was on the other.

"Get the VP," Julie said to Williams as they hustled, the fed-up look never leaving the President's face. Williams merely lifted a finger, and two agents ran on ahead.

As they approached the conference room, George Marcopoulos stepped out of a side corridor, followed immediately by Vice President Galin and the agents Williams had dispatched.

"Henry?" Galin frowned, obviously flustered. "What's the rush?"

The agent in the lead banged open the conference room doors, throwing the press into a whirl of activity, for once taking them completely by surprise. Henry almost smiled at that, as he turned to look at Galin, who fell into step just behind him.

"I'm through playing games," he snapped, and then he was mounting the dais amid a hundred voices asking questions, camera lights popping on. Galin, Marcopoulos and Julie Graham stood behind him, as their chairs had not yet been set up. Henry tapped the mike to see if it was on, and when he discovered it was not, he simply shouted.

"Quiet!"

The room was suddenly silent, and behind him Julie Graham tried not to laugh, wondering how this would all play out in the press. She knew that was the last thing on Henry's mind, and she was glad. But beside her, Bill Galin cringed.

"Now, ladies and gentlemen of the press, a brief statement and then I'll be happy to answer any questions," the President began, rising up to his full height behind the podium and lowering his voice when the microphone suddenly snapped on. Behind him, chairs were put in place and the others sat down.

"Please be aware that what I'm about to do is almost unheard of in politics: I'm going to give you the facts. I'm tired of rumor, hearsay and outright falsehood. So here goes.

"Early this morning, Liam Mulkerrin took over the Fortress Hohensalzburg in Salzburg, Austria. Not long afterward, an earthquake reportedly took place in Salzburg. I say reportedly, because this quake did not register on the Richter scale at all. William Cody is apparently Mulkerrin's prisoner at this time. A UN Security Force operation is under way to assist Austrian troops in the evacuation of the area and the capture of Mulkerrin.

"Questions?"

The Warner Network correspondent was the first with her hand up.

"Yes?"

"Mulkerrin was reported dead after the Venice Jihad.

Why? And what involvement do Meaghan Gallagher and Alexandra Nueva have in this operation?"

The President scowled, openly, on international television. Anyone watching could easily have seen the smile that spread across Julie Graham's face then.

"Mulkerrin was *believed* dead, Marinna," the President said. "As far as Nueva and Gallagher are concerned, as you may have heard, their whereabouts are unknown."

The room exploded with new questions, but Henry pointed to Pamela Martin from CNN.

"Mr. President," she said grimly, "we've all seen the video from Venice. What of the reports of similar creatures in Salzburg, and do you know whether Allison Vigeant was taken captive with Mr. Cody?"

"I've seen the video too," Henry answered. "I hope there's no truth to that, and no, we've no word about Ms. Vigeant."

Before he could even choose another hand, the Fox correspondent spoke up.

"In light of their suspicious disappearance, could the shadows be involved with Mulkerrin's return?"

Even from behind, Julie Graham could see that the President was about to blow his stack. Barely thinking, she elbowed George Marcopoulos, who was on the same wavelength and already standing up. Marcopoulos cleared his throat, and the President turned around even as he began a stern warning to the media never to jump to such conclusions.

"Ah, it appears that Ambassador Marcopoulos has a response to your question," Henry said, and stepped from the podium to allow George to approach.

"You may be sorry," he whispered to the President as he stepped up next to him and leaned into the mike.

"I am appalled that such questions may be asked at a time like this. Human and shadow are united against a common enemy. The SJS fights side by side with the UN Security Force. Will Cody is captive, perhaps dead. If two prominent shadows have disappeared, we should be concerned for their safety, not accusing them of betrayal. As you say, you've seen the video, you know how many of their people were murdered by this madman. And you suggest they are in league with him? Like all minorities before them, like all humans in fact, there is evil to be found among the shadows. But we cannot turn on our allies because they frighten us!"

Bravo . . . A voice floated out, over the audience, seemingly soft but loud enough for everyone to hear clearly . . . *Well said, dear George, but you see, your services are no longer required.*

And then they were there, six of them, in the room where they hadn't been before. Nobody, not even the Secret Service, had seen the mist creeping along the floor, so fine as to be almost invisible. Now, for some, it was too late. Four of the creatures were in the audience, tearing the cameras from the grasp of frightened, soon-to-be-dead media personnel. The two others, a tall black male and a slick, deadly-looking Asian, were on the stage.

"Mr. President!" Agent Williams shouted, up the steps with other agents in tow. But the Asian vampire, apparently the leader, already had him.

Knocking George Marcopoulos into the vice president and the secretary of state behind him, the creature clutched the President's neck with one hand, lifting him from the ground, and grabbed the microphone with the other. Before it could speak, it was buried, along with the President, in a pile of Secret Service agents. A dozen more brought their weapons to bear on the other creature, even as agents in the audience moved in on the shadows there.

It was over quickly. The leader, buried in flesh with the President, burst into flame under the pile, sending agents screaming, rolling off the stage and into the stunned media. Two agents tried to drag the singed President away, even as the others emptied their weapons, to no avail, into the tall one. Knowing that the President was as good as dead, Gary Williams made a decision. Ignoring his orders, he grabbed the two nearest VIPs—Vice President Galin and Ambassador Marcopoulos—and shoved them through the escape panel behind the curtain, pressing the button that sealed the corridor behind them. They ought to have been safe back there, but already Williams could hear a terrible pounding on that panel. He wished he could have saved the secretary of state, but she'd been moving toward the President instead of away.

Julie Graham grabbed Henry Russo's charred hand and began to pull him toward her, ignoring the dead and dying agents surrounding her. The screaming continued from the press, and she couldn't hear a thing, but even as she made eye contact with Henry, a heavy, booted foot came down on her forearm, shattering the bones. Wailing in her agony, she looked up into the face of the once-human thing that reached down and took the President's hand from her own. It leered at her, then ground that boot back and forth on her broken bones, and mercifully, she blacked out.

The once-Asian thing, the leader of the band of assassins, stepped back to the podium. It hoisted the President by the neck once again, and those in the audience who did not turn away saw that Henry Russo was quite awake, though barely able to whimper with his throat so tightly clutched.

"Good evening," the shadow said into the microphone. "I have a message from Lord Hannibal. Humans take warning, vampires take heed."

Henry Russo, the President of the United States, screamed one last time as the creature leaned its face in and tore out a chunk of his throat with its teeth. It sank those fangs back into the wound, drinking deeply and moving its face around, purposely wetting its cheeks with the President's blood. Finally, it turned back toward the press, toward the cameras now operated by its fellow shadows.

"*This*!" it cried, blood dripping from its face onto the podium. "This is our destiny!"

Then the creature lifted the President's body above its head with both hands and brought it down across one knee. Henry Russo's corpse broke in half and was flung into the pack of media hounds he'd once considered his greatest burden. The shadow-assassin turned back to Julie Graham, who was just coming around, and smiled.

It took its time with the rape and murder of the secretary of state, and though the other vampires controlled the cameras, the broadcasters could easily have stopped the feed, chosen not to show the atrocity live on the air. None of them did. The rules changed during war, and there were, after all, ratings to consider.

"Go! Go! Go!" Agent Williams shouted, even as he shoved at the vice president's back. Williams was nearly dragging Ambassador Marcopoulos, slowed by age, down the narrow, "safe" corridor that led from the room where the press conference had been held—and where carnage now reigned—to the Oval Office, which had its own defenses. Still, the office had only so much protection, and its parameters did not really include safety from vampire attacks.

Williams had been studying the creatures since their existence had been revealed, and as far as he could tell, their abilities and weaknesses were spread across a broad spectrum. He knew from books and articles, as well as from rumors along the national security grapevine, that only a very few were still unable to bear sunlight or the presence of religious symbols. Nearly all of them had recovered from the mental programming that had been spread among them like a virus by the Catholic Church. While silver was not fatal to them, most still had a reaction to it, and science reports indicated that they did weaken in its presence, as if it were some kind of poison.

According to numerous accounts, the shapeshifting abilities of the creatures varied widely, but government studies postulated that eventually the things could learn to become almost anything. Though no one wanted to discuss it very loudly, there seemed only one sure way to destroy the creatures. They had to be dismembered, and the parts of their bodies separated, kept apart. Of course, in light of their capacity to become mist or fire, and depending on the individual vampire in question, such an act could be quite difficult, almost impossible.

And here he was, Gary Williams, with the lives of the vice president and the shadow ambassador in his hands, one big motherfucking vampire on their backs and a bunch of hypothetical bullshit as his only weapon.

They were halfway down the corridor, and not nearly far enough away, when the steel door they had used flew off its hinges and clanged fifteen feet down the hall. Williams noted that the shadow had chosen to use brute force rather than attempt to mist through the door frame, and filed that thought away. He hoped he'd get a chance to use it.

"Run!" he roared, and shoved the ambassador forward, hoping he was fast enough, knowing the vice president was a scumbag and wouldn't bother to help the poor old guy.

Williams had reached the first control junction, just after the halfway point, and with the speed that was the shadow's legacy, the black male one, who looked as if it'd grown even larger with its anger, rushed down the hall toward him. It would be only seconds before the vampire had him, and then the other two men as well. Agent Williams's handprint was enough to activate the safety program's voice control, and it ticked away three seconds as the inhuman thing bore down on him, its mouth open to reveal fangs, lengthening even as it came. A loud pinging indicated that the program was on-line, and Williams responded.

"Blast door twenty-one," he yelled, noting the number on the wall, *"down!"*

And another steel door, much stronger than the first, its seals airtight, slid into place. As the pounding began, Williams flipped on the comm at his control junction, to hear the sounds on the other side of the door more clearly, and even then, he began to run again, toward the Oval Office and his duty there.

"Garth!" a voice shouted, far away, and Williams knew it was addressing the creature who was after him.

"What?" Garth shouted back, its voice almost a howl as it continued to pound on the door.

"Mission accomplished," the first voice, obviously one of the other vampires, back in the conference room, shouted again, barely audible. "We're pulling out!"

"Not until I kill the other two," Garth wailed.

And now Williams slowed, stopped in the steel corridor, almost to the next control junction, almost to the door leading into the Oval Office. The outcome of this conversation could save lives.

"They're not a priority!" the other voice yelled down the hall. "We're leaving, but suit yourself. You can find us later."

And that was it—no more conversation, just more pounding, and though Garth couldn't have misted through, it didn't even bother to try, just continued to rely on its strength. Williams turned around and sprinted to the next control junction, the Oval Office only ten feet behind him. He thought he caught a glimpse out of the corner of his eye of the shadow ambassador lying on the floor in the office, but his priority was stopping the vampire.

The pounding continued, and Williams began to wonder whether the thing would be strong enough to break this door down. And if not, what then? Whom did it kill on its way out? Or would it leave at all? Would it try to find another route to the office? Williams couldn't let that happen.

At the control junction, he primed the voice comm, then hit the release that would open the door. It slid up, revealing a somewhat stunned vampire. The creature's eyes narrowed as it looked at Williams down the hall. Williams wondered if the vampire was at all concerned that it might be walking into a trap, but he doubted it. Vampires were nothing if not arrogant.

"Shadow containment door twenty-one," Williams said softly, "down."

The door slammed shut behind the vampire, and it spun around to look, then back to Williams, its grin widening. The creature did not notice that this door was somewhat different from the one it had been attacking moments before.

"Don't worry," the thing known as Garth said to Williams. "I won't run away from you, my friend."

"Shadow containment door twenty-two," Williams said loudly, "down."

And a foot in front of Agent Gary Williams, another door fell into place, in which there was a small window two inches by four inches, made of glass a foot thick, just like the door.

"Shadow containment measure one," Williams said, and watched through the hole as the ceiling between the doors dropped slightly, the floor rose, and the vampire, Garth, looked entirely off balance.

A second later, the vampire looked up at the tiny window and rushed, roaring, at the door to begin pounding anew. But as soon as the first blow fell, the vampire shrieked and fell back, cradling its right hand. The walls, ceiling and floor were made of silver in this part of the corridor, installed five years ago but never expected to be used. Now, Williams knew, some shadows could escape just about any containment. But most would not be able to free themselves from this one.

All surfaces were of silver, and even the glass of the window was sealed, airtight, and covered with a fine silver mesh. Had Garth been barefoot, it would have known much sooner that it was chasing its prey into a trap, and yet Williams was fairly certain now that the vampire would not have stopped. Even now, as he watched, Garth stepped forward again and, painful though it must have been, began to pound against the silver door, its rage growing with each touch.

Still, though its rage grew, its strength began to leave it. Surrounded by that much silver, it was only a matter of time before it would be incapacitated, though all evidence showed that such an effect was temporary at best.

Williams watched through the window as Garth struggled, falling to his knees. In moments it would be too late for the vampire to shapeshift, and though it had shown an aversion to it, Garth did so now. Turning to mist, it floated toward the upper edge of the door, and Williams knew that the vampire had given up its former targets and narrowed the field down to one bothersome Secret Service agent.

In the Oval Office, George Marcopoulos felt as if he were having a heart attack. He'd run all the way down that long corridor, and as soon as he'd stepped through the steel door, the pain had hit, momentarily paralyzing him with pain and fear, the agony in his chest and arms driving him to the ground, where he hit his head. He'd been unconscious for only a moment or two, but when he came around, he saw Bill Galin, the vice president, sitting behind the President's desk.

"Ah," Galin said as George began to move. "You're alive after all, what a shame."

The man looked terrified still, his eyes wild, but his mouth was split by a gleeful, maniacal grin.

"If that thing doesn't get in here," he went on, "and I'm willing to bet that it won't, that makes me the President . . . President Galin. I rather like the sound of that."

"You didn't call for help," George mumbled, his voice sounding somehow off as he tried to sit up, hand still clutching his chest.

"Too bad, so sad," Galin said in a singsong voice.

And then he was up, stepping up onto the President's desk and then dropping down from it to crouch by George on the rug. The vice president, more than likely about to become President just as he claimed, leaned in to whisper to George.

"Mr. Ambassador, your Hannibal doesn't know what he's done—"

"He's not my . . . ," George began, but Galin put a finger to his lips.

"Ah, ah, ah," he scolded, "it isn't polite to interrupt. Anyway, as I was saying, you and I know that Hannibal doesn't represent all of those monsters, but he *is* chief marshal of the SJS. With this attack attributed to him, the world will believe that the shadows have declared war on humans. It's open season on those . . . things you have befriended, and I'm now the chief hunter."

Galin smiled, and his hands slipped around George's neck and began to squeeze.

"You, Mr. Ambassador, are out of a job."

Heart pounding in his ears, George could not breathe, and Galin's hands continued to tighten.

I'm dead, George thought.

"I think not," a polite voice said, and then the hands were gone and George heard a crash.

Looking up, he saw that Galin had been thrown backward, across the desk, knocking videophone, lamp, everything, from the desk and landing in the President's chair hard enough to knock it over. Galin sprawled on the ground, and George Marcopoulos knew he hadn't gotten there by himself. Out of the corner of his eye, he saw movement, and he looked back toward the open emergency door where the Secret Service agent was still trying to destroy the vampire that had followed them.

Standing in front of it was a man he had never seen before, all in black as though he meant to be inconspicuous, but more conspicuous because of it. He was a slight man, and George couldn't imagine he had thrown Galin across the room. And then he turned around, and though George had never seen him before, he recognized the man. As a vampire.

He knew immediately that this shadow was not with the others, but he still flinched when the creature kneeled at his side.

"Dr. Marcopoulos," he said, in a respectful, almost feminine voice, "my name is Joe Boudreau. My uncle was Henri Guiscard. Meaghan Gallagher asked me to watch out for you, and I really think we ought to go now."

Guiscard! Henri Guiscard! The mind boggled. George nodded even as the shadow delicately lifted him and carried him to the window. Henri Guiscard had been the start of it all, in a sense, a Roman Catholic cardinal who had discovered *The Gospel of Shadows* accidentally, then abandoned the Church, fleeing to Boston, where he hoped to reveal the book's contents to the world. Liam Mulkerrin had followed Guiscard and killed everyone the old cardinal came into contact with, dragging Peter Octavian into the web of that mystery, a mistake that led to Mulkerrin's defeat in Venice.

Yes, George thought he remembered Peter saying something about Guiscard's nephew. He'd run the bookstore where the cardinal had hidden the *Gospel*. But he'd never heard anything of the boy becoming a shadow himself! Still, those questions were for later. They had enough to worry about just getting off the White House grounds where the new President had become homicidal and the shadows' tenuous relationship with the world had been shattered.

"Let's go," Boudreau said, dumping Bill Galin's unmoving form off the broken chair, then lifting that chair and hurling it through the bay window behind the President's desk, all with one hand while the other cradled George Marcopoulos as if he were a baby.

"Yes," George agreed. *But go where*?

The shadow known as Garth was in mist form and drifting quickly toward the door frame. Williams knew the thing could kill him in seconds, but he wasn't about to let it get that far.

"Air lock," he said, and with a double bang and the sound of hydraulics, the room was sealed.

Even as mist, the vampire couldn't find any way out of the silver-lined room, and it turned back to human form after floating around nearly every corner of the room. The ceiling was blocked off into circular tubes, and Williams experienced a moment's worry when the mist disappeared up inside them. But several seconds later, the mist emerged again, its attempts fruitless. Finally, Garth returned to human form and curled up on the floor, eyes burning into Williams's own, where he stood behind that foot-thick glass.

Eventually, there would be no more air in the room, and that on top of the silver should make Garth weaker and weaker. Williams didn't know whether vampires needed to breathe at all, or if their bodies just kept breathing out of habit. Regardless, the silver was doing its job. Garth wasn't going anywhere.

Agent Gary Williams knew what he should do. He knew what his government required him to do. He knew he ought to simply stand guard until somebody came along to help, preserve this insanely powerful creature for study by the Pentagon. He knew he should do that.

"Fuck it," he said. "Canisters."

And inside that silver room, the last phase of the never-before-used special anti-shadow security precautions activated. As Williams watched through the tiny window, the ceiling fell, hundreds of silver-plated steel cylinders with razor-sharp edges slamming into the ground with a thousand pounds of weight behind them. Garth didn't have time to move as its body was dissected into more than a hundred pieces, each trapped within a cylinder.

Almost as quickly, the floor began to slide out, into the wall, and as it fell away, the cylinders snapped down, rotating, sealing themselves so that in moments silver-lined canisters filled with the flesh of a shadow filled the inside of that room in neat rows. They could still study it, Williams figured, but now he wouldn't have to fight it anymore.

He turned, rotating his head, neck and shoulders to relieve the tension, and walked into the Oval Office. In the middle of the confrontation he'd just ended, and over the shouting and screaming of the vampire, he thought he'd heard banging and the shattering of glass from this room, but he didn't have a moment to spare. Now that he was there, in the office, he couldn't believe what had happened.

The bay window was smashed, the President's chair was gone, his desk was a wreck and the vice president, his face bruised and bloody, sat propped against one wall, cradling his left arm.

"They're in it together," he said as Williams entered the room. They were joined a moment later by a group of agents who burst through the main door of the Oval Office.

"Who is, sir?" Williams asked, wondering how badly the man was hurt.

"Marcopoulos, Hannibal, all of them. The ambassador tried to kill me!" Bill Galin snapped. "They're all in it together. This whole Mulkerrin thing is part of it too."

"Sir," Williams started, reaching to help the man up as the other agents went out the window after Marcopoulos and whoever else had gone out that way. "Mr. Vice President, do you think that's likely?"

Galin leaned against the big desk, then looked up, glaring at Williams.

"Don't ever question me again, Agent," Galin snapped. "And that's Mr. President to you."

CHAPTER ✦ ELEVEN

Hell.
Seventy-Seven Days, Twenty Hours, Forty-One Minutes
After Departure:

More than two months had passed since they had met
Lord Alhazred, and there had been other demon-lords
since. These lords were nothing like the shadows which
they had battled in Venice and which were plentiful in the
deep caverns of Hell. Those others were work beasts, slave
demons, and Meaghan thought that perhaps they were
made from the flesh of the Suffering, the damned. They
had seen many such damned beings, displayed in abject
humiliation, abused in every way imaginable, tortured and
physically, literally torn apart, only to re-form so that it
could begin again. The demon-lords they had met, including Erim, Yezidis and Azag-Thoth, were polite when Lazarus mentioned the Stranger, though he refused to tell her
why. Some, a cowardly few, looked frightened; others were
hostile but still cooperative.

Through it all, Meaghan could not forget the words of
Lord Alhazred: *The Suffering are always here, no matter
where else they may be.* She didn't truly understand it, and
though she no longer trusted him, Lazarus claimed he did
not know what it meant. Eventually, Meaghan decided it
might be better if she remained ignorant.

Since Alex had died, they had not been attacked at all.

Not by demon-lords, or their hellish slaves. They had been completely unmolested, and the more Meaghan thought about it, the more she wondered if they weren't being manipulated the entire time. Days, weeks and months had passed as they moved from one pit of Hell to the next, without a trace of Peter. All of the demons—and it seemed to her they had become progressively uglier—knew exactly what they were talking about, but couldn't tell them where they might find Octavian.

Meaghan had to think, eventually, that they were being led on a wild goose chase. She also became very concerned about the time they had been gone. Lazarus had told her that time would move much more quickly here, but how much? They had been in Hell for months. Was the battle all over in their world? Had Mulkerrin been victorious? Had their dimension become nothing more than a playground for Hell's work-beasts, freed from their masters?

On this day, which seemed like every other, she was at her wit's end. They were standing in the center of a cavern in which jackal-like creatures raped the Suffering over and over in every orifice, splashing some kind of sulphuric ejaculate all over the damned things, all over the stone floor, its acid eating through flesh and bone and stone.

"I wish I could do more for you," the demon-lord said, sitting back in its stone chair and overseeing the terrors visited upon the damned in its care. This latest lord was almost blue and seemed made of chalk. Its belly was bloated and for the most part hid the bony phallus between its legs, though the thing's testicles were the size of melons and hung low enough in their sack to rest comfortably on the ground. On its head was a crown of penises, woven with flesh ropes unmistakably made of women's labia. Its jaws were long and filled with suckers like those of an octopus. Apparently, it had no eyes.

"So do we," Lazarus said, obviously wanting to leave as much as Meaghan did.

"I can send you on to—" the thing began, but Meaghan

couldn't take it anymore. Alex was dead; she wouldn't let her world die too.

"What's your name?" she asked the thing, and it turned its head toward her, mouth open. She wondered if it would try to attack her, but then realized the thing didn't have a nose, that the suckers in its mouth were for breathing, for smelling, among other things.

"My . . . name?" it asked.

"Yes, your name. What is your name? I wouldn't have thought this a difficult question."

Lazarus whipped his head around to stare at her, jaw agape, thinking she had lost her mind. And perhaps she had.

Then, what looked like fleshy folds of skin on the demon's huge testicles parted, revealing, finally, the thing's eyes. Meaghan wanted to vomit, but she wouldn't show her disgust, or fear.

"So you *can* see," she snapped. "What I want to know is if you can hear."

Her words had the desired effect. The demon had expected her to be silenced by the opening of its eyes, and was sorely disappointed and quite angry. It rose to its feet and took a step toward them, and Meaghan thought she saw the suckers inside its mouth elongate just slightly, and when it spoke now, in anger, it had something of a lisp.

"I am Pa-Bil-Ssssag!" it yelled. "How dare you ssspeak to me in sssuch a manner?"

Before it could continue, Meaghan interrupted again.

"How dare I?" she shouted back. "Simple. I dare because I am an agent of the Stranger. We come here on the Stranger's mission, not our own, and we have been played for fools for far too long!

"Now, Pa-Bil-Sag, if your name is as you claim, then I know you, I know your power, I know your name and I know the spell of binding, taught to me by the Stranger," she lied. "I can think of several places to relocate you that you would not enjoy!"

Pa-Bil-Sag merely stared at her then, and Meaghan found it disconcerting to be looking down at its testicles when the danger of its gaping jaws was much higher and closer to her. But she would not be the first to look away. This was a staring contest, like the ones she had had with her childhood friends, but this one was for much higher stakes.

Pa-Bil-Sag's eyes closed, and it sat down. Meaghan heard an audible sigh from Lazarus behind her, but she resisted an urge to step back, to uncross her arms, to look away.

"You are strong, female," it said. "Though perhaps not as strong as you would like me to believe. We owe the Stranger no allegiance, only courtesy, and my courtesy is hard-pressed with you. Still, I have no wish to confront your master again, and this charade was purely for the amusement of my brother, not myself. As such, I see no reason to perpetuate it."

Meaghan saw Lazarus move closer, stunned to realize that they were about to receive answers, but she listened carefully, searching for the deception she had found in all demon-lords' speech.

"This Mulkerrin and the one you seek are and have been the playthings of my brother, who found them when they first arrived here," he said. "I am certain they have endured extraordinary suffering. I am also certain that my brother will be very pleased to add to his collection."

"What is your brother's name?" Lazarus asked.

"Not that it will help you any," Pa-Bil-Sag said and grinned, tentacles reaching out from inside its mouth, sucking at air, latching on to each other and to the demon's face. "My brother isss Beelzebub, but he will not be concerned with your sssmall magicksss. Beelzebub is sssecond in power only to the First Fallen and will never allow an alleviation of sssuffering for one of his toysss."

"And where is the lair of this brother of yours?"

Meaghan asked, still arrogant on the surface, but filled with sadness and dread.

"Outssside."

"And how do we get there?"

And now the demon laughed, a huge, bellowing roar. On its crown, though apparently not connected to it in any way, the penises seemed to grow erect, and Meaghan finally had to look away. A mistake, she knew, but it couldn't be helped.

"A bargain," the demon-lord said, stifling its laughter. "I will transssport you there, to the outssside, and you mussst only walk toward the fire to find my brother'sss land. For this ssservice, you will do one thing for me."

"And what might that be?" Lazarus asked, waiting for the catch.

"Tell him I sssent you," Pa-Bil-Sag said and chuckled down in some phlegm-filled throat. "Tell him I sssent you . . . as a gift."

Salzburg, Austria, European Union.
Wednesday, June 7, 2000, 7:19 A.M.:

It was madness.

Gloria Rodriguez floated out of the sky, H-K blazing. As they approached, her paratroopers unhitched, dropping the last fifteen or twenty feet to the ground, rolling over and blasting Mulkerrin's possessed "warriors" into as many pieces as they could. It was clear to them that the sorcerer was somehow controlling these people, but they would have to be listed as "casualties" in the destruction of the city. The repercussions of those civilian deaths couldn't be taken into consideration here. A war was on.

Many of the paratroopers didn't make it to the ground alive, savaged in the air by flying things, chutes destroyed, bellies torn open. But most of them did make it, and some of those who did had flamethrowers. Fire was their most effective weapon, and getting it inside the fortress was key.

As demons and weird, mind-controlled soldiers burned, the intensity of the green glow surrounding the sorcerer at the center of the fortress's courtyard seemed to dim just for a moment. One of Gloria's men fired on Mulkerrin, but the bullets seemed to pass right through, appearing on the other side to scatter among the others, wounding one shadow, who shook it off and kept going.

"Shadows!" she shouted. "The door! Let's go!"

And then they were around her, in arrow formation, as they headed for the huge door to the fortress. Here she was, in the middle of the battle, surrounded by vampires, and all Gloria could think of was the giant gate in the original *King Kong*. She forced the thought back and spun to fire at a figure rushing her from behind. A torrent of bullets cut across the body, but even before it hit the ground she knew she'd made a mistake.

Gloria Rodriguez had killed one of her own men.

"Carlos!" she shouted, but even as she considered kneeling at his side, she sensed something different about the battle in the courtyard.

Looking up, Gloria was stunned to see that, even though most of Mulkerrin's civilian warriors had been destroyed, and the main portal in the courtyard was being continuously blanketed with fire, torching everything that came through, they were not winning. In fact, they were losing.

Losing, because her troops were killing one another. She watched as Maria Santos turned and blasted her blowtorch in the faces of two of her fellow soldiers, her friends. Gloria's unit began firing at one another, bodies falling rapidly.

"What the hell?" she began to say, and then saw the movement out of the corner of her eye, where the body of Carlos, the man she'd killed, lay. From his still form, a sickly yellow cloud rose and floated toward her. A quick glance showed her that others of these clouds flitted among the soldiers in the courtyard, and she watched one disappear into one of her paratroopers, who pulled out a knife and leapt on his nearest comrade.

"God, no," she whispered to herself, and then heard a ghastly, sickening chuckle.

Mulkerrin, whose eyes had been closed as he wove his spells, protected from the fighting around him, had finally opened them, and was looking right at her. Rodriguez turned to run, and then realized she couldn't. Mulkerrin had to be stopped or all human troops would be useless.

"Go!" she shouted at the contingent of shadows around her. "Help your people get those doors open, now!"

Gloria turned back toward the sorcerer, and the ghost, or whatever it was, had come much nearer. She moved as fast as she could, and faster, obviously, than that yellow, evil mist. She dodged right past the thing, firing at Maria as she went. Thirty-five feet separated her from Mulkerrin, and she closed that gap in seconds. Gloria slung her H-K over her shoulder, knowing bullets would do no good, and pulled her knife from its hip sheath. Steel flashed in sunlight even as she passed through, into the green glow surrounding the former priest.

Reflexively she had taken a breath, and without reason she held it, though it tasted of death, the burning of stinking monsters and a bitter poison she imagined came from those tainted, ghostly things. None of that worried Gloria, but something inside her warned against inhaling whatever was causing the glow around the sorcerer. And Mulkerrin just stood there, arms wide, head hanging as if in supplication. He looked up at her, his eyelids drooping, his stare either tired or seductive. The smile remained on his lips as he spoke to her.

"Welcome, little girl," he said, and even as Gloria thrust the knife toward his belly . . .

. . . she stopped. Or something stopped her, still, paralyzed where she stood. The mad being who had once been Liam Mulkerrin reached out and passed a hand through her black hair, and Gloria opened her mouth and breathed in. The smell was awful, rotten, dying, and she wanted to throw up but could not command the muscles in her stomach to do so.

"Kneel before me," Mulkerrin said, his smile turning into a leer even as the weight of his words forced her to her knees, "and I will give you your communion."

All around the fortress, the United Nations security force was fighting on two fronts. While they tried to get over the walls of the fortress, past the demons that continued to emerge from the portals, only to be destroyed but often at the cost of lives, they also had to guard their own backs against those demons that had come up into the city and were now rampaging there, hunting down the many humans still left cowering in basements and hiding under beds. Many of the demons also attacked the troops from behind and prevented a good portion of the forces from reaching the fortress at all.

Commander Gruber's unit, having come down the river and into Mozartplatz, had been almost completely slaughtered, and even the commander himself had been killed. The majority of the shadows with Gruber had also died, though several had disappeared at the same time that Hannibal had abandoned Commander Jimenez's strike team, a couple hours earlier. In fact, each unit lost a handful of shadows at that time, and there was no trace of Hannibal or the other AWOL shadows. They were, simply, gone.

The other commanders—Locke, Surro and Thomas—all continued their attacks, and the more than one hundred fifty shadows still in action had finally been moved close enough to diminish the danger from the portals, so that the troops could concentrate on the walls themselves.

Finally, it seemed to UNSF Commander Roberto Jimenez, they were getting somewhere.

Roberto and his team were outside the gate. Including Rolf, there were thirty-five shadows with Jimenez, and though they could easily have flown over, they had to open the gate if the rest of the forces were to enter. Jimenez had attempted to blow the gate to splinters using a pair of CAMELs, easy-launch, hand-held missiles with computer-aided targeting to find the weakest structural point. They exploded before ever reaching the door. In fact, any artillery used on the gate was rebuffed, and even the strength of as many shadows as could line up in front of the gate couldn't budge it.

Though nervous, even frightened at first, Jimenez's men had warmed to the shadows immediately. Handpicked by Rolf Sechs, for the most part they were top-notch soldiers and engendered an easy camaraderie with their human counterparts. All of them, that is, except for Jimenez himself. Though he had a grudging respect for Sechs, he was glad to have the cold, sharp silver of his dagger hidden safely away in his clothing.

"Rodriguez," he snapped into his collarcomm, "what's taking your guys? We need extra strength on the gate, I said. Get those shadows out here."

Rodriguez didn't reply, but a sudden squealing shrieked from Jimenez's comm, forcing him to cover his ears, and the commander couldn't be certain his message had been received. Satellite communications were out, so they'd had to rely on primitive broadcast methods in the field. Still, they seemed to be working for the moment.

"They're here, Commander," came the computer-generated voice of Rolf Sechs behind him, and Jimenez looked up to see a bat flying above the gate, signaling the arrival of Rodriguez's shadow unit. Sechs put away his voice-pad then, and the assault on the gate began anew, joined by pulling from the other side. As Jimenez's strike force, of which forty-six men still lived, stood and watched, roughly sixty gray-clad vampires tore and dug at both sides of a magically protected gate. On the hill to their left, soldiers shot grapples into the sheer stone wall and began to scale it. Shadows with no immediate chore changed form and flew to the top of the wall with ropes, anchored them, and let them down for the human soldiers to climb.

By God, Jimenez thought, they were going to do it.

And then the gate opened and swung wide, crushing a number of shadows behind it. It was clear that it had not been their diligence that opened the door, for even now it pushed tight against the wall, attempting to destroy the vampires it had trapped. Jimenez let out a breath he hadn't been aware of holding as he saw the mist float from behind that door, signifying that the shadows were all right. He had no love for the creatures, but he needed them. And now the gate was open, though apparently by choice.

What to make of that?

"Move!" he shouted, though he needn't have. The team had passed the point of waiting for his order. Under normal circumstances, he would have felt bound to reprimand them. But now . . .

"Get the son of a bitch!" he yelled as he led the pack, screaming, up the curving path toward the courtyard, the air around him turning suddenly cold, and the sky darker than ever. Rolf Sechs ran beside him, and Roberto was pleased to see that the shadow did not shapeshift, but remained in human form. Also, though his speed was greater, Sechs stayed with him, and Roberto had to wonder whether the creature thought he was *protecting* him.

"Rolf," Roberto thought he heard somebody whisper, and then the vampire fell to the ground, writhing in pain, with his hands on his head. But Roberto Jimenez was commander and could not stop for one soldier.

He rounded the corner and came into the courtyard just behind several of his men and half a dozen shadows. The tableau that unfolded before him was grotesque. His forces had begun to come over the walls, firing into Mulkerrin's soldiers and demons and at the sorcerer himself, though none of the bullets were able to reach him. Several dozen shadows had already come over the wall, and they engaged warriors and demons alike, shrugging off the friendly fire as Jimenez had known they would. And in the center of it all, sheathed in a greenish glow, was Mulkerrin.

Kneeling before him with her head buried in his crotch was Gloria Rodriguez.

"No!" Jimenez screamed, and started toward them.

Rolf lay on the cold ground, feeling every stone and pebble that pressed into his flesh, hands holding his head as the voice boomed his name again.

Rolf, it said, but softer this time, as if it knew it had hurt him.

And then it wasn't an "it" anymore, for Rolf recognized the voice.

Cody, Rolf thought, sitting up and shaking his head.

Yes, it's me.

You're all right?

Strong enough to mind-link at least; otherwise I don't know. But never mind that. They've got to go—the humans. They've all got to go.

And then the words stopped, and the rapport that they'd always shared, the mind-link which had allowed them, as children of Karl Von Reinman, to experience events as one, to know things the other knew, to hold actual, mental conversations, told Rolf the story, everything he needed to know. In seconds, he knew Cody's pain, knew he was not yet healed, but knew that he had somehow joined his spirit to the magic flowing around the castle. And Rolf also knew why the humans had to go.

He moved more swiftly than ever before, knowing that Cody would be safe for now, knowing what he must do. In two heartbeats he had come in sight of the sorcerer, and Commander Jimenez racing toward him. Rolf had to prevent that meeting, for hovering about Mulkerrin, just outside of that vile green glow, was a spirit cloud, the ghost of a dead soldier, and it began to drift toward Jimenez.

Rolf caught up to the commander just as the ghostly mist started to waft around his head. Rather than simply knocking him out of the way, the mute shadow bent and threw the commander over his shoulder on his way to the other side of the courtyard, where there seemed to be relatively little going on.

"What the fuck are you doing?" Jimenez yelled as Rolf put him down, then turned to look back at Mulkerrin. "Gloria!"

He went to run back there, but Rolf grabbed him by the arm, shaking his head in a firm *no.* But Jimenez's eyes were wild; he wasn't paying attention. He reached inside his shirt, and in a second he brandished a silver dagger-crucifix in front of Rolf's eyes, something Rolf had seen before. In Venice. He didn't have time to wonder where the man might have got something like that. Jimenez lunged for Rolf, stabbing forward toward his belly, but when his knife and hand got there, they passed only through flame.

Jimenez cried out, briefly, in pain, then switched the knife to the other hand and, holding the burnt one gingerly away from his body, made to go after Rolf again.

"Damned thing!" he shouted, but Rolf grabbed his wrist, holding it nearly tight enough to crush it, then shoved him to the ground, the dagger clattering to the stone. By the time Jimenez had regained his feet, Rolf was searching frantically inside his jacket for his voice-pad.

Jimenez came after him again before he could pull the pad out of his jacket, but Rolf stopped the commander, with one hand this time, and then slapped him, hard, across the face. Their eyes locked, Jimenez's burning with hatred and Rolf's imploring, trying to send a message. He held up a hand and with incredible speed whipped out his voice-pad and scrawled upon it with a suddenly elongated fingernail.

"Soldier spirits possess you. Humans must leave," the electronic voice said, translating Rolf's stunted scribble.

A woman screamed, and they turned. The two warriors, shadow and human, saw it at once. Mulkerrin had thrown Rodriguez out of his sphere of influence, onto the stone floor of the courtyard, and the vile cloud was hovering over her . . . and then it disappeared inside her.

In seconds she was on her feet, H-K in her hands, and firing up at the soldiers, her own troops, coming over the wall of the fortress. Rolf glanced at Jimenez, and knew that the commander understood, that he had seen the look on his lover's face, in her eyes, and that it wasn't her anymore.

"Dear God," Jimenez said, then looked back at him. "But they can't possess *you*?"

Rolf shook his head, pocketed his voice-pad, bent down and retrieved the commander's dagger and returned it to him. Jimenez barely looked at the thing as he sheathed it. Rolf shooed him away, using both hands.

"Dear God," the commander said again, then spoke into his collarcomm. "Withdraw! Immediately! All human troops withdraw from the fortress immediately. SJS troops assist in the evacuation and keep Mulkerrin's human soldiers away from our people at all costs! Do it now, people, or we're done for! All units converge at the Nonnberg Abbey. SJS forces keep Mulkerrin contained within the fortress."

And then the comm was off, and Jimenez turned to Rolf.

"Now what the hell do we do?" he asked, knowing an answer would have to wait.

The exodus began, the shadows acting as guards, protecting the humans from their former comrades, trying not to kill those possessed, for the ghosts within them would only find new hosts. But as Rolf and Jimenez followed the outside wall, passing Mulkerrin on their left, the sorcerer laughed louder and louder, and several of the possessed soldiers turned their guns on one of their own, on Gloria Rodriguez. They kept firing until each had an empty clip, and only then could Jimenez look away, look up at the man, the thing, responsible. Rolf dragged the commander away even as Mulkerrin looked straight at them, clearly aware of his actions, enjoying himself immensely.

Outside the gate, and over the roar of gunfire, Rolf heard the cawing of birds above him. He looked up to see three eagles fly overhead, then swoop down to land, transforming into shadows he'd never seen before: a short, stout female and two young males, twins.

"Rolf Sechs," the woman said and nodded, and next to him Commander Jimenez turned toward the newcomers, obviously wondering if this were another threat. Rolf wondered as well.

"I am Martha, and these are Isaac and Jared, the sons of Lazarus," the woman went on. "We are here to assist you with the sorcerer, and you should know that reinforcements are on the way. Also, I am saddened to inform you that the disgusting Hannibal has returned."

"Hannibal!" Jimenez snapped. "Now? He's on Mulkerrin's team after all then."

"Actually, Commander Jimenez," Martha said calmly as they jogged down the path that would lead to the abbey, "he will not attack your forces, because he wants you to destroy Mulkerrin, so that he does not have to. In fact, he and his coven have eliminated a great many of the demons left behind in the city."

Rolf could sense Martha's hesitancy, and though he guessed what was coming, he was not prepared for it.

"Then what's the problem?" Jimenez asked.

"They are murdering those of the townspeople they are able to find, feeding off them."

A scream built in Roberto Jimenez's throat, but whether it was the name of his murdered lover or a damning curse, he would never know. For he swallowed it, and as the scream dropped down into his belly, it burned.

Oh, how it burned.

Salzburg, Austria, European Union.
Wednesday, June 7, 2000, 7:32 A.M.:

Liam Mulkerrin was a madman, and he knew it. More to the point, he reveled in it. Once upon a time, so long ago to him, he had been a Roman Catholic priest. But more than that, he had been a sorcerer, the most powerful in centuries, whose power led him to engineer what should have been the destruction of all "Defiant Ones," and the seed of his own eventual control over the world's most powerful church.

Indeed, it would have been so, if not for Peter Octavian and the other children of Karl Von Reinman. Octavian had become the savior of his people. Mulkerrin had been stopped, his followers killed or dispersed, his power gone, and he had been taken, body and soul, into the very Hell from which he had been calling his servants for nearly a century. Once the demons had discovered he was there, within the confines of their world, they were . . . less than charitable. He and Octavian had been there together, for what seemed like forever, among the Suffering, amid the politics of Hell.

And though they'd suffered, so had their strength grown. With pain came power, and Mulkerrin began to see his previous goals as foolishness, locked into parameters created by his human experiences. As years flew by, as Hell worked changes upon his body, and his soul, Mulkerrin grew to be something more than human, with the taint of the demonic upon him. His desires followed suit, informed by the demonic infection in his soul. Though the minds of the Suffering were easily invaded by Hell's masters, the demon-lords, Mulkerrin used his agony to blind them. Even as his body suffered, and his mind registered every excruciating moment, so did a part of it, the part he would call "soul," become more aware. He spread his spirit, his aura, as far out from his physical form as he could, searching for a sign, any sign, of a weak spot in the barrier between worlds.

And eventually, when he found that spot, the sorcerer made his escape, leaving his demon-masters in a terrible fury, for they could not come to this plane unless individually, and specifically, called.

In the forever he had spent in Hell, Mulkerrin's faith in

Heaven had only grown. And while his body and mind had been tainted by his time there, and his power, his magic, fed upon the fires of the place, he knew his soul was pure. For he had talked to God. While in Hell, the voice had come to him, and Liam Mulkerrin had experienced revelations that had humbled even him.

"Let's make a deal," God had said to him, though not in so many words. And Liam was in ecstasy. God wanted him to escape back to his birth-world to begin a new, and final, crusade. Liam was to cleanse the world of the taint of Hell, of the vampires that now lived among God's children and of all other impure souls. The world was to be subjugated to the will of a new church, with Mulkerrin as the rock upon which it would be built. He alone would judge the guilty, he would mete out their justice. The world would become purgatory for its inhabitants, and when they were judged ready by Mulkerrin himself, he would send them to their God.

And any who attempted to prevent God's word from becoming reality would be cut down by his right hand, Liam Mulkerrin, and sent to Hell. When Mulkerrin was done, when he had achieved all God had set out for him, then the Lord had promised to wipe the taint of evil from him and take the judge, the once-priest, to His bosom. And God helped Liam to rise above his suffering, to escape. God promised that if Hell sent its vile issue after him, or one of its foot soldiers, like the fiend Peter Octavian, then Liam would be given the power he needed to prevail. God told his former priest that he'd been right all along, that there was glory in pain—his own and that of others. It was this skill that made Liam the perfect tool, God told him: the ecstasy such work brought to him.

Liam Mulkerrin, madman, believed it all.

And now he stood amid the bloody warfare, his magic reaching out from the fortress he'd made his own, surveying the landscape around it, aware of the soldiers fleeing his influence, of the Defiant Ones working with them. That alone was proof that these humans must be purified, cleansed or sent to Hell if purification were impossible. As for the Defiant Ones, Mulkerrin sensed that he'd known some of these, even just one or two, before, but could not locate them just yet. But his power, his magic, still grew.

Mulkerrin was past simple spells, though they were still sometimes useful. No, now he controlled true magic, could manipulate the flow, the essence, of the world around him. But such magic was difficult. His primary concentration must go to his own protection, self-preservation. His hold on the other magics he controlled—the portals, the ghosts of dead soldiers, the weather—was much more tenuous.

Mulkerrin would rest now, though his influence would continue to grow and spread further out from the fortress. For the moment, he was content to replenish his supply of demon-slaves from the portals, and to wait for the humans to attack him again. That was their test and one he knew they would fail miserably. They could not face their own evil, and so they would fight his—God's—judgment. Fight it, yes, but not escape it.

As a priest, Liam Mulkerrin had been fond of saying that God's work was never done. But now that God had set him this task of judgment, the day would soon come when the Lord's work would finally be complete.

Judgment Day had arrived.

CHAPTER ✦ TWELVE

Inside Mount Untersberg, Austria, European Union.
Wednesday, June 7, 2000, 2:03 A.M.:

"Are you blushing?" John Courage asked with a smile.

Allison Vigeant turned away, furious at having been discovered and blushing even more. Behind them, Charlemagne and his men bathed in the underwater stream that ran through the cavern. The emperor had ordered all of his men into the water, but there was only room for perhaps a dozen at a time, so they crowded at the stream's edge, awaiting their turn. For his part, the emperor swam as best he could in the shallow stream, up and down its length, not bothered at all when one of his men would block his path. In truth, he seemed to be enjoying himself.

When they had disrobed, Allison had been more interested in their vampiric nature than in their nakedness. These shadows were different from all those she had known, even Cody and Peter Octavian. Though they were naked in her presence, not one of the men turned to leer at her. There was no bickering among them, no shoving, no posturing, only a deference to their emperor (and to Courage) and pride in themselves. And then Allison realized that there was one shadow who seemed somewhat like these soldiers, and that was Courage himself.

Pushing her thoughts aside for later examination, when she would confront John with her many questions, Allison

realized that while she had been staring into nothing, not
focusing, her eyes had been on the naked men at the
stream's edge. Now she noticed that some of them, at least,
had noticed her looking their way and seemed uncomfortable themselves. And that was what had caused her to
blush, and then to look away as John made a joke of it.

Allison's eyes came to rest on the bed carved of stone
where she had given her blood to the sleeping emperor,
and the strangeness of what had happened since came back
to her. She didn't know what she had expected, but the
surprises grew by the moment, and not the kind of surprises she had been prepared for. First, Charlemagne had
seemed ready to kneel before John Courage, but John had
stopped him. No matter what else it might indicate, it certainly proved that Courage was far older than he let on, as
he had admitted to her that Charlemagne had not been out
of the cavern in nearly twelve hundred years!

If that were not enough to think about, the emperor had
then knelt, along with Courage, and led one hundred vampire soldiers in what was apparently a prayer, at the end of
which all present made the sign of the cross! And that she
didn't understand at all. The vampires greatest enemy had
been the Church, and here they were using its symbols,
praying to its God. After the prayer, Courage had looked
at her and smiled, and Allison had wanted to slap him. He
knew what was going through her mind, the confusion she
felt, and he was enjoying it!

Charlemagne had then taken John aside, and Courage
had suggested Allison get some rest while he explained all
that had happened and tried to prepare the emperor for
what was ahead, not only in battle, but in the world outside
as a whole. They had spoken quietly in Latin as they sat
together on Charlemagne's stone bed, and the soldiers had
become silently industrious, sharpening and cleaning their
weapons and repairing worn clothing. It amused Allison
quite a bit to see these ancient warriors performing such
quiet duties. And so, though she had assumed she could

not possibly do so, Allison had fallen asleep on the cold, stone steps leading up and out of the mountain.

She had come awake a short time ago, only to be confronted by the sight of one hundred naked men. And now she sat with John Courage as Charlemagne pulled himself out of the stream, dried himself and dressed.

"Do you speak Latin?" Courage asked her, even as the former emperor approached.

"No, sorry."

"Italian?"

"Just a little bit, a few words," Allison said apologetically.

"Greek?" John suggested, but Allison only raised an eyebrow, which was answer enough.

"I do speak some Spanish, if that helps," she said, finally, as Charlemagne joined them, and Courage's face lit up.

"Spanish!" he said. "Excellent. Charles spent years fighting in Spain."

Charles?

Allison had the urge to giggle, but suppressed it as Courage turned to the other shadow and began speaking rapidly in Spanish. It was a dialect she was unfamiliar with, and she hadn't studied the language for years, but concentrating hard, she picked up enough to know that John was simply asking "Charles" to speak in Spanish when he could, as well as asking if he minded the two of them referring to him as Charles. Apparently, he did not like the name "Charlemagne" very much. In any case, he didn't seem to care, and so Charles it was.

The more he spoke, the easier it became for Allison to understand him, and once he got going, Charles spoke quite a bit. He was fascinated by her, and yet she sensed it was not because she was a woman, but rather because of her newness, her youth, her familiarity with a world nearly alien to him. Eventually, as the soldiers finished their bathing and set about drying and dressing, John Courage wandered off to leave her alone with Charles, and Allison barely realized it. She liked this old king, who smiled at her in a grandfatherly way and patted her hand when she said something that amused or concerned him. His eyes had crow's feet around them, which became quite pronounced with either emotion.

"I'm proud to know you," he said, or at least that was how she understood his Spanish. "I gave my daughters the same education as my sons and, so many centuries later, see what the world has moved on to."

"Thank you," she said, beaming herself, for his energy was infectious.

Allison knew that Cody had gotten younger after he became a vampire, and though she thought Charlemagne—Charles, rather, had been older when he died, she wondered aloud why he hadn't reverted to a more youthful appearance. She complimented him on his looks, admired his beard and mustache to soften the question, but he waved her words away.

"I am satisfied with my appearance," he told her. "It is appropriate that an emperor look somewhat older, more . . ."

And then she couldn't understand him, but she knew that he meant many things: distinguished, regal, noble, venerable. And he had all that. Yet still, he was far friendlier than she had ever imagined such a ruler could be. In school, she had always imagined historical figures to be either vicious madmen, or wise, grave, slightly curmudgeonly old men. Charles was a pleasant surprise.

And a vampire. It was so strange to think of one of the most pious of historical figures becoming such a great enemy of the Church, and yet she seemed to recall vaguely that Charlemagne had dealt harshly with those who had executed people believed to be witches. And her mother had told her she'd never do anything with a history major!

They were laughing about something, and for Allison it was not important what that something was, only that they were, indeed, laughing. And then the vampire's face grew dark, and serious, and he looked at that moment precisely as she might have pictured him.

"We must go," he said. "You are a beautiful girl, who does not belong in this thing. But I understand that women are no longer made to stay safe at home. Your lover is captive, and we will free him, so let us go, and pray to God for his assistance. With the Lord's help, we will destroy this Mulkerrin. The Irish were my subjects once, and it seems that this one needs to be reminded.

"Come," he said, and stood, offering Allison his hand and helping her to her feet.

When she looked around, she was surprised to see his soldiers, one hundred of them, prepared to depart and awaiting only his command. John Courage stood with them, but apart, and those nearest him would not even look in his direction.

Allison realized that once again she had not been able really to question John, but promised herself that she would make the time on the march. For that was what was ahead of them: a march across miles of Austrian country-side. They could have flown, sharing the burden of carrying the token human in the bunch, but Courage had said they wanted to conserve all of their energy. Certainly it would not be easy for her to keep up with the shadows, who would walk the entire way without tiring a bit, but she would make it.

For Will.

Morzg, Austria, European Union.
Wednesday, June 7, 2000, 7:17 A.M.:

A dozen ravens flew in arrow formation a mile or so to the north, and to anyone else looking up, they would have appeared to be nothing more than birds. But Allison knew that they were far more. There had been so many other things to wonder about that she'd barely considered the strange deaths of those ravens that had flown at the top of

Mount Untersberg, but she thought of them now. She watched the progress of the birds, scouting ahead as they'd been ordered, and not for the first time, she wondered what it would be like to fly, to be one of them.

Not a raven, of course. A vampire. For that is what those birds were, soldiers of Charlemagne, surveying their path, mentally communicating the images of the land around them to their emperor. And Allison had to wonder what it would be like to have wings, to glide on the wind. It wouldn't be the last time she would wonder such things, but she knew that she would always push such thoughts aside. For the pain, the sadness, the little tragedies of immortal life seemed far too terrible to her. Though her friends, even her lover (if they got through this), would live on while she grew old and died, she could never accept the "gift" that the so-called Revenant Transformation offered. She saw it as a double-edged sword at best.

She walked between John Courage and Charles, and though the two tried to engage her from time to time, they invariably lapsed into Latin, apparently discussing both the battle to come and the status of the world. She noticed more and more that Charles deferred to John, but decided to wait until they were alone to ask Courage about it.

Their exit from the mountain, or at least Allison's, had been less than graceful. A return to the cavern ledge by which she and Courage had entered led to a slope disappearing down inside the mountain. They had gone down that slope, many shifting to forms better suited for the descent, and eventually, she had ridden on the back of a bear that was actually John Courage himself. Regardless of everything else she had seen, that ride, holding so tightly to this thing that had become her friend, had unsettled her. Then she had realized that they were out of the mountain, and on the march.

Now, with the ravens at the point, they trooped along Morzgerstrasse, a wide highway, already cleared of cars in the evacuation. Twice they had been confronted by Austrian and German military roadblocks, and both times Allison had been called upon to speak for them. Though they obviously did not trust the shadows, and the German soldiers wanted to hold them back, or try at least, the Austrians wanted their nation saved, and so waved the shadows on. Allison didn't know whether to be more surprised that they had been confronted, or that they had been allowed to move forward.

"Demons," Charles said, finally, and Courage barely noted the word. Apparently the ravens had alerted their blood-father—for Allison was fairly certain that that was what Charles was to his soldiers—of the presence of Hellish creatures ahead.

Quickly, the vampires moved around Allison and John Courage, and Allison realized they were protecting her the way a herd would protect its young from predators. Courage was with her as extra insurance, but Charles was at the front of the group, preparing to confront the few demons they had come upon.

"It's a good thing we're here," John said to her. "This area is being ravaged. It looks as though most of the military is concentrating on the fortress, but these people need some help."

"And that's us, huh?" Allison asked, and her tone was such that John looked at her strangely.

"Something?" he wanted to know.

"Lots of things."

"Ah, your questions again," he said and smiled. "Well, let's hear what you've got so far, my journalist friend."

Allison just didn't know what to make of Courage. Though he seemed unwilling to speak of his origins, he was perfectly happy to have her discover them; he seemed, in fact, to want her to do so. *So be it,* she thought.

"Okay," she said, eyes narrowing. "You're at least twelve-and-a-half centuries old, and capable of metamorphosis that is beyond any other shadow I've known. Wood, metals, things the others haven't even considered. Your current appearance is not your true appearance—"

"Why do you say that?" he interrupted.

"Let me finish. You receive a deference from those familiar with you that is unlike anything I have ever seen among your kind. You pray to God, are aware of events before they take place and know things about other shadows that you should not know. And you seem to be in the right place at the right time. Also, you know a lot more about the origins of your kind than any other shadow I've known, yet you refuse to discuss them. Finally, call it a hunch, but I'd say you're blood-father to both Lazarus and Martha, as well as to our friend Charles here, and I can't even begin to imagine where that train of thought will take me."

They kept walking, Courage looking down at the road. When he raised his head and spoke, he was looking around.

"I can tell you're exhausted," he said. "Why don't we find you something with wheels on it?"

"Fine by me," she said, and meant it—she *was* exhausted. "But first let's finish our little chat here."

"You mean you aren't finished?" he said, a false innocence coming over his face.

"Don't even . . . ," she began, warning him, but she didn't need to. He was prepared to talk to her. As for how much he would tell her, that was another question.

"First, tell me a couple more things," he said. "Like why you don't think this is my true appearance, and what makes you think I'm blood-father to those you mentioned."

"When you introduced me to Martha," she began, "you told me she was Lazarus's sister, and Jared and Isaac his sons. If she was your sister as well, you would have said so. The way the three of them treated you, I got the feeling that you were in charge, and that Martha didn't need to speak to communicate with you.

"As far as Charles is concerned, that was even more of a

hunch, but it also ties in with your age and appearance. The soldiers who first met us did not recognize you immediately. You had to perform some change which you purposely—no, don't argue—purposely did not allow me to see. Only then did they know you. But even though Charles had been down there just as long as they had, and therefore had not seen you for at least twelve centuries, he knew you immediately. I guessed that this was through your mind rather than appearance. And of course, for such an emperor to defer to you, who would seem so young in the scheme of things, there could only be one answer as far as I was concerned.

"You're the boss," Allison said, and watched him for a reaction.

John Courage smiled then and gave a small clap.

"Bravo," he said, even as the noise of the slaughter of demons continued to the north. "But as you can tell, there really isn't a 'boss' per se."

"Not in general, but certainly you have a coven of your own, though its size is still a mystery to me." Allison nodded, satisfied with what she'd determined thus far, but Courage seemed deep in thought and did not reply.

So she punched him, hard, in the shoulder, the way a child might punch her younger sibling to get even for some imagined transgression. John looked at her, eyes wide, simply stunned at the action, and Allison gave an exasperated sigh and frowned. And then the corners of John's mouth began to turn up, and they couldn't stop themselves from laughing at what Allison had done. John gave her a little shove, to let her know he understood her game, and she punched him again.

"Don't mess with me," she said, in a boxing stance. "Now, give with some answers."

As John's laughter subsided, Allison wondered what she was doing, playing around with a being as old and powerful as Courage obviously was. She'd never really thought about it, but put to the question, she realized she would have expected shadows as old as John and Charles to be crinkly old wise men. And that couldn't have been further from the truth, though Charles looked the part.

"You're right on track," John said. "I've got to hand it to you, Allison, your instincts are very, very good."

"What about the praying?" she asked. "What's the story with that?"

"Charles is a pious man, as am I in my way," he answered, quite serious.

"But, the others, the younger ones . . ."

"A product of their long persecution by the Church, which you helped to end, by the way." He put a hand on her shoulder. "Thank you."

"John," she said, exasperated, *needing* to know, "what's the truth? What aren't you telling me? Will and the others are tortured because they don't know what they really are, what their origins are. If you know, you've got to tell them."

Courage said nothing.

"Do you know?" Allison pleaded. "If you're praying, does that mean vampires aren't evil by nature? But then what of Hannibal, and the others like him?"

Courage nodded, as if deciding something for himself.

"I do know," he admitted. "But it is in searching for the answers to those questions that our friends, and the rest of my kind, will create them. To you I say that we are not natural, we do have a taint of evil, but we also have a trace of the divine. Like man, we have free will with which to determine our individual destiny. I will tell some of them, to ease the burden the question lays on their souls, but only those who have already chosen which side to follow, the demonic or divine.

"And I will tell you," John said, sincerely, "but not now."

Allison's mind was spinning, hungering for the answer to a mystery the depth of which she was only just beginning to understand. She realized something else, something the existence of Hell should have tipped her off to. No matter what she'd believed in the past, here was a creature telling her that God did exist—not that he had faith that God existed, but that, in no uncertain terms, there was some kind of . . . of being that exerted an influence on Allison's world, something "divine." Something to be prayed to. And as much as she believed it, more than ever now, she didn't *know* it, the way John did.

But she wanted to. Still, he had said he would tell her the whole story, the true nature of the shadows, and she knew that there were revelations to be had in that story. And if he wasn't prepared to tell her now, it was worth waiting for.

"Just one thing," she asked. "At least tell me who you really are, your name, where you're from, how old you are."

John's smile returned, even as they started to move ahead once again. The demons had been dealt with, and she and John were shuffling forward to join Charlemagne in front of the soldiers.

"Ah," he said to Allison, almost in a whisper, "but that would give it all away."

And now she was really confused. But at least it kept her mind off Will Cody.

Just then they were passing a convoy of evacuees and were once again questioned by Austrian troops. Allison was relieved to hear that the military believed that all or nearly all civilians had been evacuated from the area, and as John and Charles spoke to the officer, a bizarre thing happened. From the backs of several troop carriers, now filled with frightened people driven from their homes, several figures rose and jumped.

A total of eleven men and women came toward them, ignoring the shouts of the soldiers, and Courage translated for her as they spoke to Charlemagne. They were offering their blood. Some were blood-cultists, others volunteers and worshippers, but at least half were merely people who wanted to see that their homes were returned to them, that their city was saved from further destruction, and Charlemagne's soldiers were the only ones they had seen heading into the city rather than away from it. Once the soldiers had given up attempting to stop the people, several of them also offered their blood.

Charlemagne accepted, and the convoy waited as each vampire in turn took only a taste of life, to bolster his strength. It was a bizarre tableau; vampire warriors lining up to share in the blood of those people whose lives they were attempting to save, but it gave Allison infinite hope for the future, and pride in humanity. Maybe they could win this thing, and share the world after all. Maybe.

Above them, the sky was blue and the sun warmed their faces, but up ahead death hung over the city of Salzburg in a terrible curtain of unnatural clouds. Allison had enjoyed smelling the early summer air, but now the wind shifted, and her nose wrinkled at the scent of something rotten that was carried south to them on the breeze.

Salzburg, Austria, European Union.
Wednesday, June 7, 2000, 7:58 A.M.:

Hannibal was no fool. He was very concerned with the apparent retreat of Roberto Jimenez's troops from Hohensalzburg Fortress. After all, if the foolish humans and their traitorous vampire allies could not be counted upon to destroy the sorcerer Mulkerrin, then Hannibal would have to sway from his plans and join the battle as well.

For the moment, however, he continued upon his original course, secure in the knowledge that his new coven could act without fear of any serious opposition.

The President of the United States was dead, and that bitch Julie Graham as well. Hannibal was upset that his blood-son, Garth, had been destroyed during the assassination, and that the vice president, and the old Greek, Marcopoulos, had escaped. He had learned as much through his psychic rapport with his blood-son Sitoshi, who had led the attack, and torn out the President's throat with his own teeth. However, in retrospect, Hannibal thought that leaving Vice President Galin, a rabid xenophobe, alive might only serve to speed his plan to fruition.

In the days before the Venice Jihad, Hannibal had set up a worldwide coven, a network consisting of more than one hundred of his own blood-sons and -daughters and their offspring. He had an international stable of human spies as well, inside nearly every nation's government, which pulled strings in human politics and carefully monitored those of shadows. Hannibal had been one of the architects behind the volunteer program, through which humans enamored with the vampiric mystery of the Defiant Ones offered their own blood, often their own lives, for a chance just to be in the presence of an immortal. He had been a power.

And then Venice, and Von Reinman's coven proved themselves to be far stronger than he had ever realized. They averted one disaster, gaining a huge following among their people, and caused, in Hannibal's eyes, another. Many of his coven had died during that final battle with the Church, and Hannibal had been confused, unsure of his support in the community. He had had no choice but to seemingly conform to the new world order that was quickly established.

But only with words.

For in action, Hannibal never changed. He rebuilt his power base, reenergized his coven, used his status as chief marshall of the SJS to draw other shadows, not his blood-sons but powerful and like-minded vampires in their own right, to his cause.

Blood.

Hannibal took pride in his savagery, his bloodlust, his skill as a hunter of men, and his coven. His people had always been the scourge of humankind, and would be again. It was their nature, their destiny, to take the blood and the lives of humans. They were predators, and humans their only prey. And now that their existence had been revealed to the world, all the better, for rather than stalking one human, Hannibal would now prey on the fears and the political weaknesses of an entire world.

The first step, of course, was to shatter the peaceful co-existence of vampires and humans, one which had been tenuous at best. It was not proving terribly difficult. Though Hannibal's plans had not been fully conceived, Mulkerrin's return had presented the perfect opportunity to execute them. There would be so many shadows in one place, at one time . . . and so many humans. His assassins had killed the President, and now he was certain that the United Nations secretary general, Rafael Nieto, was trembling in a well-guarded room somewhere. Well, let him tremble. Hannibal would get to him eventually.

And now, with the world's attention focused not only on the battle with Mulkerrin, but on the state of the UN's alliance with the shadows, he had upped the ante yet again. While his softhearted brothers and sisters fought alongside the humans above, Hannibal had gathered more than fifty of his coven to him in the north of the city, out of range of the communications-inhibiting magic of Mulkerrin. While at the fortress the UN commanders could not be told of the President's assassination, the actions of Hannibal and his men were easily recorded and transmitted around the world by media cameramen. Through that bitch Allison Vigeant, whom Octavian's clan had rescued from his cellars, the world's media had discovered the Defiant Ones. And Hannibal would use those same tactics to his own ends.

He let the cameramen live. Otherwise, it was a slaughter.

It had begun when his followers gathered and dispatched the stray demons that rampaged through that portion of the city. And yet, the vampires destroyed the demons only because they, themselves, were threatened. But once the demons were destroyed, they had gone after the police and military in the area. And once the people had no more protection, Hannibal and his coven went hunting through the streets and alleys, through crumbling homes and still intact blocks. Hunting for blood.

And now, Hannibal knew, he had drawn the attention of the combined human and vampire forces at the fortress. They had withdrawn from that battle, but he knew it was only a matter of time before they made another attack. He was right, and wrong, as it turned out. They would, of course, mount another attack, but Hannibal's assumption that they would not be able to spare troops to come after him was obviously wrong.

Even now, as he watched his blood-daughter, Pamela, feast on an adolescent boy she had dragged into the street, even as he received mental reports that at least a dozen of those SJS members he had not recruited had defected to his cause, Hannibal's first son, Hector, flew to him as a bat, changed to his true form and growled a warning.

"They approach!"

"What?!?" Hannibal was incredulous, for he had heard Jimenez issue no such orders over his collarcomm . . . but of course the commander would be smart enough to change frequencies if possible! Damn!

"A large force comes down from the fortress, and it is made up almost entirely of humans!" Hector said, obviously stunned himself that an event Hannibal had been certain would not happen was now happening.

Hannibal was confident that his coven could destroy the humans if necessary, but he was also confused. Why would they abandon their attack on Mulkerrin, a more immediate threat at least in their perception, to launch an assault on him?

"How many of the human soldiers come after us, and how many remain to battle the sorcerer?" he asked.

"They are *all* coming after us," Hector said, shaking his head in wonder. "It seems only shadows remain to launch another attack on the fortress."

Astonishing, Hannibal thought. *They're sure to lose.* It was outrageous in his mind. First, Hannibal would be forced to slaughter the human armies (which he had intended to do only after they had destroyed Mulkerrin), losing many of his own in the fight, and then he would have no choice but to use his remaining forces to help his traitorous kindred destroy Mulkerrin.

Jimenez must be insane!

As much as it hurt him to do so, Hannibal had to create an alternative possibility, a new course of events.

Stop, he commanded them mentally, *no more killing*.

And how he hated those words. As he sent his psychic orders to his blood-children, so they passed them on to members of the coven not of Hannibal's family.

Take as many of the humans as you can, he told them. *We will use them as shields in order that I may speak with the human commander. I must know why they turn away from the fortress. None of you will attack, none of you will draw the blood of the captives you now take . . . until my order. This is a minor delay, nothing more.*

Hannibal vowed to enforce that guarantee. He was furious with the unforeseen change in plans and wanted nothing better than to tear Roberto Jimenez's head from his body. And he promised himself that he would indulge that urge, as soon as Mulkerrin was out of the way.

CHAPTER ✦ THIRTEEN

Salzburg, Austria, European Union.
Wednesday, June 7, 2000, 7:49 A.M.:

"Commanders!" Jimenez barked into his collarcomm. "Set up perimeter guard and get a head count. Locke, take command of whatever's left of Gruber's troops. Anyone left from Rodriguez's paratroopers, converge on me. All shadows . . ."

Roberto shot a look at Rolf Sechs, in effect the new chief marshal of the Shadow Justice System, and got a nod in response.

". . . converge on myself and Marshal Rolf Sechs. Yesterday! All commanders report immediately after these orders are carried out."

Jimenez turned to look at Rolf again, and the mute vampire realized that, no matter what, the two of them had become partners in the outcome of this thing. They had to prevail, and therefore they had to rely on one another.

Rolf's human family had been murdered ages ago, and he had never had any other children. He had never created a blood-child, made another vampire, and he didn't think he ever would. Therefore, though it would have eased the burden of his muteness, he shared his mental rapport only with his blood-brothers and -sisters, of whom only Cody and Alexandra Nueva still lived. He knew sign language

and, when necessary, his second, Stefan, could translate it
for him. But the voice-pad was an adequate substitute.

Just in case, Rolf motioned for Stefan to come forward,
effectively promoting him to deputy marshal the way Rolf
had taken Hannibal's post. The group around Jimenez was
growing, and as they awaited word of their next move, Rolf
turned to the newcomers: Martha, the woman had called
herself, and the men were Isaac and Jared, supposedly the
sons of Lazarus. Martha had been the one to tell them of
Hannibal's actions in the city, and now she cleared her
throat to get Commander Jimenez's attention. The man
whirled, ready for trouble, and then relaxed, realizing how
high-strung the battle had made him. The female shadow
looked at Rolf then, deferring to his command, and he
nodded for her to go on.

"Chief Marshal Sechs, Commander Jimenez, on behalf
of my brother Lazarus, who apologizes for his being un-
available, we," and at that she noted Jared and Isaac, "offer our services to you. Also, it will please you to know that
reinforcements are on the way."

"What?" Jimenez asked, and Rolf knew that the commander's whole attention was on Martha now. She had his
own as well.

Rolf motioned for her to explain, and Martha went on.

"Well, it seems obvious," she said, "that the human
soldiers cannot return to the fortress. In fact, so that the
ghostly beings up there cannot find new hosts when they
are killed again, it would be best if all humans got as far
away as possible from the fortress. Therefore, it seems only
logical that the human troops move to prevent Hannibal
and his coven from committing any more murders. We
shadows must return and confront Mulkerrin on our own.
A corps of one hundred powerful vampires is on the march
here as we speak, to assist in just such an attack."

"How do you know this?" Jimenez asked, shaking his
head. "Who sent you? And who's bringing these so-called
reinforcements?"

Martha opened her mouth to speak, but Rolf held up a finger, indicating she should wait, and then pointed to Jared, lifting his hands in a sign that he should continue in her stead. Rolf thought that Martha sounded too practiced, and he wanted to hear this from the boy's perspective. Rolf knew what Jimenez was thinking—that perhaps Martha was working with Hannibal—and he couldn't help but consider the same thing.

"Me?" Jared asked.

Rolf nodded, brow furrowed in expectation.

"We are here to help," Jared said. "What's so difficult to understand? Who sent us and who's bringing the reinforcements are one and the same being, but his name will mean nothing to you."

He was lying. Rolf knew he was lying, but strangely, he didn't sense any menace or ill intent in the lie. He cocked his head slightly, allowing his doubt to show through, prompting Jared to continue.

"His name is John Courage," Jared said.

Courage! Will Cody's voice boomed in Rolf's mind.

Turn down the volume, Rolf shot back. *I didn't even know you were still with me.*

Sorry, Cody sent, from his prison within the fortress.

You know this John Courage?

Oh, yes, Cody thought, and in those thoughts, Rolf could sense the weight of not just knowledge, but secrets that Cody wanted to share.

I know him, Cody sent, *and somehow, now, I know the truth of him. Work with this Martha, Rolf, and I'll tell you the rest when I see you.*

You've recovered from your wounds? Rolf asked.

Not quite, but I will be in time to help when my help is needed. Do me one favor. Ask Martha if Allison is all right.

Rolf realized he was the center of attention. Martha had apparently continued to speak, but with Cody's voice booming in his mind, Rolf had not heard. Now she, Jared, Isaac and the commander all waited for his response.

"What's your recommendation, Marshal?" Jimenez asked, and Rolf noted that the gray at his temples seemed to have spread a bit farther since dawn.

Rolf didn't think twice. Cody was his brother, and his word was the only assurance Rolf needed. He motioned for his deputy, Stefan, to come forward, then pulled out his voice-pad and began to scrawl with a fingernail.

"Stefan, here," the electronic voice said as Rolf pointed at the vampire, "will take orders from Martha, as will the rest of the SJS agents. I will pick a dozen shadows and accompany Commander Jimenez to confront Hannibal. It is the only path open to us."

Martha nodded in approval, and Stefan stood at attention, accepting his orders, but Jimenez shook his head as he looked at Rolf.

"What are you talking about?" Roberto asked. "Secchs, we know nothing about this . . . woman. How can you . . . ?"

"I know you'll have a hard time with this request," Rolf scratched onto his voice-pad, "but you're going to have to trust me."

Jimenez was speechless, even as Rolf turned his words to Martha.

"Martha, Will Cody asks if you know the whereabouts of his lover, Allison Vigeant, last seen with John Courage?"

"Will Cody?" Jimenez snapped. "Where the hell is he?"

Rolf waved for the commander to be quiet.

"Tell Mr. Cody," Martha answered, aware of the true origin of the inquiry, "that Ms. Vigeant is safe for the moment, that she is with John and on her way here, now."

"Also," she said, smiling at Rolf, "tell him he's a lucky man."

"How can you tell him anything?" Jimenez said, exasperated, stepping closer to Rolf to get his attention, even as Jared and Isaac moved forward to block his way.

Rolf held up a hand, and the vampires stopped.

"You all misunderstand," he wrote. "The commander is

not a threat to me, or to you. He does not trust us, but we stand together."

Rolf turned to Jimenez now, writing faster.

"Vampires made by the same father can communicate mentally. I was out of communication with Cody for a time, but now, this close to the fortress, where he is a prisoner, we are in contact again."

"It couldn't be a ruse, a trick to throw us off course?" Jimenez asked, needing to understand, to be sure.

Rolf shook his head, and then Jimenez was equally silent. The man was not a fool; he was aware of the stakes. Commander Thomas appeared then, responding with the other commanders to Jimenez's earlier orders. Immediately, she and Rolf exchanged glances that communicated their mutual concern, for each other and for the situation, but professionalism and discretion allowed no greeting. Rather, Rolf nodded to all of the newly arrived commanders, even as Jimenez opened his mouth to voice his decisions.

"Commanders," he said to acknowledge them. "I admit that I have a difficult time putting any faith in shadows, but it seems we don't have much of a choice. If we attack the fortress again, all we're going to end up doing is killing each other."

Rolf nodded as Jimenez issued the only orders he could. The commanders' faces were grim.

So that's it? Cody's voice came to him again, much quieter this time. *We'll just have to wait for Courage and his "reinforcements," I suppose.*

Any ideas on that? Rolf asked. *You seem to know a lot more than you're letting on.*

The only thing I can say, Cody answered, *is trust John Courage. Even if you think he's crazy, trust him. He may be the only one we can trust.*

You "heard" about Allison? Rolf asked.

Yeah, thanks. I just wish she wasn't coming back with them. But then, I guess I wouldn't love her if she was the kind of woman who turned tail and ran home to Momma. Still . . .

There was silence a moment, around Rolf and in his head, and then he had to ask . . . *What about you, brother? There are so few of us now; what are you waiting for? If you need help to escape, let me come, let me help.*

Rolf could sense Cody's laugh, even if he didn't "hear" it.

Amazing, isn't it? Cody thought. *A few years ago you wanted me dead, and now you want to save me. It means a lot, Rolf, but no. I'll explain it all, or as much as I can, later. But I think I can be of more use to you if you leave me right here.*

As you say, Rolf sent, and then Cody was gone from his mind.

Turning his back on the gathered humans, though not without catching Elissa's eye again, he signaled for Stefan and Martha to give orders to the dozens of Shadow Justice System agents who had gathered there.

"Martha will lead the assault on the fortress," Stefan said. "However, when Will Cody finally makes his escape, he will assume command of all shadow forces there. Try not to kill the humans if possible, for their possessors will only search out new hosts. The object is Mulkerrin's death, as quickly as possible."

Rolf had put away his voice-pad, and now he scanned the vampires gathered around him. He would take twelve of them with him to help the humans against Hannibal, a paltry number, but Mulkerrin was the priority. The three newcomers, this Martha and Lazarus's two sons, certainly knew more than they were letting on, and Rolf wondered whether that might not come in handy later.

He pointed to Jared, who looked at Stefan for instruction.

"He wants you on his team," Stefan said, not needing any communication from Rolf to understand.

Rolf had expected the apparently young man, who might

have been far older than he, to look to Martha for approval of this choice, but he was pleasantly surprised when Jared only nodded and stepped forward to stand beside him.

When he had chosen eleven others, Rolf turned to face the humans again, and Commander Jimenez had just finished giving the details of the plan for their attack on Hannibal. With demons running loose down there, buildings burning and locals in the line of fire, it was not going to be easy.

This time, when Jimenez turned to meet Rolf's stare, that was all the communication which was necessary.

"Let's hit it," Jimenez said quietly. "And God bless us all."

Hell.
One Hundred Three Days, Two Hours and Twelve Minutes After Departure.

Lord Pa-Bil-Sag had been as good as his word. He had, indeed, transported them to the surface . . . a surface they had never expected to exist. And yet they'd found themselves there and so had to incorporate that into their view of this world. Hell was apparently a planet. They had discussed, at first, whether they were in a different dimension or an uncharted part of their own universe, but neither could come up with any real evidence or logic to support either question. And what was important was that they were there.

They had walked through a fiery portal conjured by Lord Pa-Bil-Sag and found themselves stepping out onto a broad, dusty plain. The darkness of the sky was cut by the light of fires shooting from the earth like geysers all around them, cinders floating away on the hot breeze that whipped past, roasting the planet. Rock formations went from familiar to incredible, and some looked as if they'd been built rather than occurring naturally. Despite the fires around them, they'd had no trouble determining which way their destination lay. Pa-Bil-Sag had referred to "the fires," and far off in the distance, flames engulfed a mountain ridge, shooting high into the air, lighting the entire horizon line as if it were dawn at that end of the world. But no sun ever rose; the dawn was perpetual, a promise, a cruel tease.

After two weeks of walking, after they had spent three months in Hell, both Meaghan and Lazarus had finally started to feel a little hungry. Though they would be able to function completely for quite some time, hunger would eventually unhinge them. They had known then that, slowed time or not, they would need to find blood eventually.

Two more weeks had passed. They had alternated between walking and flying, though Meaghan had been a bit nervous about flying when she thought about the winged creatures that had attacked her in the stovepipe. Finally, their trek had led them to a huge gate in the middle of what could only be described as a desert. In some places, the sand had been blasted with such high heat that it had turned to glass. Beyond the gate, glass spires stood tall at the foot of flaming mountains, and it was hot enough that Lazarus wondered aloud how the spires kept from melting.

"A better question is how we've kept from melting," Meaghan said, only partly joking. After all, though they could have turned to flame and ashes themselves, their human shapes would not have been able to withstand the kind of heat necessary to create glass from sand.

"It does seem," Lazarus admitted, echoing Meaghan's thoughts, "that those mountains aren't giving off as much heat as you would expect."

They stood for a moment in silent reflection. They'd been quiet through much of the month it had taken them to get here, Meaghan mostly thinking of Alex, and of what she might say to Peter if they found him. She had no idea what Lazarus was thinking, but guessed part of it was the other thing on her own mind: time. If they'd barely begun to hunger after three-and-a-half months, that meant barely more than a day had passed in their own world. How much time had passed for Peter in Hell while five years had gone by on Earth?

All of those things were on Meaghan's mind now, and she assumed on Lazarus's too. Not to mention the new questions as to Lord Pa-Bil-Sag's "brother," the glass spires beyond the gate, and the most obvious question of all.

"What now?" Lazarus asked, and Meaghan snickered, then smiled to show she meant no offense.

"No idea," she admitted. "Though I don't think the denizens of Hell take kindly to uninvited guests. I'd like to vote against flying over this thing. On the other hand . . ."

She looked at him, and knew he understood.

"We could just knock," Lazarus said, and they nodded together.

And so Meaghan stepped forward and pounded on the gate, its ringing sound making them both realize that what they had imagined was some kind of metal was actually a dark black glass. The gate, then, was hollow glass, offering no protection at all.

Meaghan shot a look at Lazarus, who merely shrugged.

"Then again," he said, "who would come here uninvited?"

They waited a long while, and each pounded on the glass several times more, but there was no answer.

"It's not as if we can come back later," Meaghan said finally. "And then again, if the place truly is empty, what better time to try to get Peter out of here?"

"If he's actually in there," Lazarus said.

"Oh, he's in there," Meaghan said, "I can feel him."

Which was true. Throughout their entire journey, she had sensed that they were going in the right direction, and as they got closer, she had known that he was there, at the fires that were their destination. She had called out to him with her mind several times each day, but what bothered Meaghan was not that she received no answer. What bothered her was that when she tried to reach out and make contact, force the connection, she was shunted aside. It disturbed her that she was forced to consider that Peter might be consciously blocking her out, shielding himself from her the way that he and Cody had shut out the rest of Von Reinman's coven for many years.

And if Peter was intentionally blocking her out, Meaghan couldn't begin to guess why. Or perhaps she could, but the path down which those thoughts led was one, at least for the moment, better left untraveled.

"That's it," she said, breaking the silence and startling Lazarus, who'd grown used to it. "We're going in."

Meaghan became a cloud of mist, spreading herself thin to be as inconspicuous as possible, and Lazarus followed suit. Floating above the black glass of the gate, their minds, ephemeral things in that state, were able to feel the place, the sprawling city of glass, the fires that burned within, and its emptiness. As they floated through the city, Meaghan reaching out her mind for Peter, they did not see anything living—not a demon, not a human, not a thousand suffering souls. Still, Meaghan focused on the mind of her blood-father, Peter Octavian, and though he tried to block her out, those efforts were almost a beacon, leading them toward him.

The city was vast, its glass buildings of widely varied styles, some imitating those of their own world, with turrets, terraces, eaves and steeples, and many of boring, square design. Others were foreign, alien, and at first glance seemed ugly because of it, though as they became more familiar, Meaghan found many of them to be strangely beautiful. And above it all, at various heights, were the spires. As if they were a trap laid for some beast that might fall from the sky, the spires stretched up throughout the city, sharp as spikes. Nearly every other building rose from its foundation, many of which were mediocre, to become, at its apex, a towering knife of glass.

Other spires simply sprang from the ground, no building for a base, no purpose other than themselves.

Meaghan thought of icicles hanging up rather than down, and was pleased with the image, or as pleased as she could be, considering how unsettling the overall picture of the city was. They neared its far border, where the black cinder mountain stood blazing in the sky, and the closer they got, the hotter it became and the more she could sense Peter.

Why are you blocking me? she asked in her mind, nearly frantic. *Can you have been here long enough to forget? To forget your people? To forget me?* And though her love for Alexandra had superseded everything that had come before, she could not suppress the sadness that that thought instilled. How long would she have to live to forget those she had loved? It was a question Meaghan never wanted to answer. And unbidden came the memory of the loss of *The Gospel of Shadows*, the fear that they might never escape from here. That they might join Peter here forever, rather than returning him to his own world.

They were close now, and she floated to the ground and returned to her human form. Lazarus followed close behind and questioned her as soon as he had changed.

"Have you found him?" he asked.

In truth, she could not say yes. She knew that Peter was very close, but so close that she was finding it difficult to choose one direction over another.

"He's near," she told Lazarus. "But we'll have to search."

Meaghan realized that the elder vampire was no longer paying attention to her. He stared past her shoulder, then turned away from her and looked around them, disgust and disbelief etched in his features.

"God, no," he muttered, and Meaghan barely caught it as she whirled . . . and understood.

Though she had sensed the buildings while in mist form, this was the first good look she'd gotten with her true eyes.

And she shared her companion's horror. The glass was not perfectly clear, but rather tinted red. There were no doors, no windows. In fact, it was easy now to see that the structures were solid glass, without any rooms or interior at all. Almost.

Lazarus walked to the nearest building, a huge thing that looked for all the world like a medieval castle, battlements and all. Meaghan watched as Lazarus stared into the glass, and reached out a hand as he bent to peer into its pinkish red depths. He laid his palm on its surface . . .

. . . and screamed in pain. Pulling back his hand, Lazarus left the first layer of skin behind, and Meaghan looked at that flesh as it blackened, charring down to nothing and sliding down the glass.

"It's impossibly hot," Lazarus snarled, and Meaghan turned to look at him just as his hand began to heal up.

She knew what he meant. If the glass all around them was that hot, why wasn't the air itself hotter, never mind the fire burning on the mountain nearby? Still, those questions paled in comparison with the others racing through her mind. Meaghan walked to Lazarus and put her hand on his shoulder, and he lifted his head to again peer into the glass. Neither spoke.

Trapped inside the glass, faces frozen in horror and pain, bodies locked into place like flies encased in amber, were this region's Suffering. They could not move, and breathing did not seem to matter. The heat of the glass seared their naked skin red, but nothing more, as if they were constantly being healed enough to withstand continued torture. They looked at one particular woman, limbs contorted wildly, legs up and out as if she'd been frozen in the midst of a terrible rape, and Meaghan had to wonder if the glass was inside her, inside all of them, as well.

"Her eyes moved," Lazarus said, almost in a whisper, and Meaghan shivered.

She had to turn away, and Lazarus turned as well, eyes closed as he walked with her, as if to deny what they'd seen. It dawned on her then that the reddish tint to the glass had to be the blood of the Suffering, and she was glad she had looked away. Beside her, Lazarus opened his eyes, and they both realized that they could not avoid seeing the Suffering here. The entire city was a Hell of glass, with no relief for the damned, or their witnesses.

"Peter's here," she said, but almost couldn't believe it. "This way, toward the mountain."

Lazarus nodded and they moved on, the fire so huge that even at this distance its roar was incredibly loud, the crackle nearly deafening. As they approached, ash fell from the sky like fine snow, and soon they realized they were walking on, and in, layers of it that had fallen over time. They had not noticed before, but now they could see that the blaze did not start at the base, but more than one hundred feet up the mountainside. There, even over the roar of the flames, they could hear another sound. That of suffering. The damned burned there, on the mountain, cried out for deliverance that never came. Yet Meaghan wondered whether they were not fortunate in comparison with those within the glass. For at least the flames varied, died down at times. For the others . . .

And Peter was probably one of them. She refused to think about it any longer.

"Where are you?!?" she screamed finally, the thought bursting from her aloud. "We need you, you son of a bitch."

"Meaghan," Lazarus said softly, and she turned to her right to see him pointing along the outskirts of the glass city, along the mountain range, to a structure they hadn't seen before. This one was closer to the mountain than any of the others. It was tinted red, or appeared to be in the flickering flame from above. Its spire climbed higher than her eyes could see.

And she knew. Lazarus had sensed it as well, the difference in this one. Its red was darker, and yet where every other structure had clearly held dozens of sufferers, their dark forms visible even from a great distance, they could see only one form in this spire. Lazarus had pointed it out because of that difference, and because it was set so close to the mountain, but as soon as she looked at it, Meaghan's focus grew sharper, into certainty.

It was Peter.

Salzburg, Austria, European Union.
Wednesday, June 7, 2000, 8:12 A.M.:

Hannibal's coven had been moving through Salzburg when his blood-son Hector brought the news that the UN security force was moving down into the city proper. He'd known immediately that they were after him, but he'd also been stunned. How could they abandon their attack on the sorcerer, a much greater and more immediate threat? And yet they *were* coming.

He had instructed his vampiric troops to take human prisoners, not to harm them, and then he had moved to find more open ground in which to face the humans. Residenzplatz, with the Salzburg Cathedral filling the south end, was large and open, offering ample space, and even as the coven moved into position around the fountain in its center, the plaza was suddenly filled with soldiers, streaming in from Mozartplatz and Kapitelplatz. They hadn't even bothered to surround him, and in a strange way, Hannibal admired them for that.

Several shots rang out, and then the warm June morning was silent. Even the birds were quiet, unless they'd been driven out by Mulkerrin. The French Commander, Surro, and the American, Elissa Thomas, brought their people in from the north, while the Brit, Locke, moved in from the south. There were several alleys and side streets leading into the plaza from the east, and hundreds more came through that way, with Commander Jimenez in the lead. Hannibal saw that his former deputy, Rolf Sechs, was with them.

Traitor, he thought, but there was little venom in it. How could they have abandoned their attack on Mulkerrin?

"Hello," he shouted, breaking the silence in the plaza, which had previously been broken only by the working of gun mechanisms and the shuffling of feet, perhaps a whimper or two from his captives.

So many hostages, so many vampires, all those guns—it was a messy picture that could get even messier, and very ugly, very fast. Hannibal could see that Commander Jimenez understood that. The human had hundreds awaiting his command, Hannibal as many, but the vampire knew the outcome. But, he chided himself, he'd also *known* that there was no chance Jimenez would break off the attack on the fortress. So perhaps the outcome was not as inevitable as he wanted to believe.

"What can we do for you, Commander?" Hannibal asked softly into his collarcomm, assuming Jimenez would be back on that channel. "What brings you down from the mountain today? I would have thought you had better things to do."

Hannibal had worldwide information networks and centuries of experience gathering such material. He hated ignorance, in himself more than anyone else. It pained him to admit he didn't know something, and it was agony to do so in front of so many enemies.

"Release your captives, vampire!" Jimenez snarled in response, loud enough for Hannibal to hear on his comm and across the plaza. "Release them now, unharmed, and surrender."

"Oh," Hannibal said and laughed, mocking him, "I think not, sir. Now you will draw back and leave us alone or these people will die."

Even from across the plaza, Hannibal could see the scowl that crossed the face of Roberto Jimenez, the look that was exchanged between Jimenez and Rolf Sechs, the way Jimenez patted his hand over his breast, as if calming his heart, or searching his pocket.

"You had planned to kill them before we arrived," Jimenez said finally. "Give them up and you will be treated accordingly. You will not escape justice for your actions, though you seek to use the sorcerer's presence to mask them!"

Silence again, as Hannibal thought.

"Why did you abandon your attack? Mulkcrrin must be destroyed before either of our futures can commence," he said, his voice dropped lower, insinuating. "I had counted on you handling that end of things for me."

"For you!?!" Jimenez sputtered into the frozen battle in the plaza, which awaited only a thaw. "The only thing I'll do for you, demon, is end your godforsaken, misbegotten life. Your kind are dangerous, and you the worst of the lot."

Hannibal smiled then, as he watched the look Rolf gave Jimenez. The big mute was unhappy with this exchange of words, but Hannibal could see that he would let it slide.

"Oh, I do hope so," Hannibal said. "For after today, my kind will be more dangerous than ever, out of necessity. I'm sure that your communications have yet to be reestablished, so I'll share the good news with you myself. A couple of hours ago, operatives of mine assassinated the President of the United States, and when I feel like it, *whenever* I feel like it, I'll have other heads of state murdered. I have that power. Your boss, Rafe Nieto, is tops on my list."

"Thomas," Jimenez said into his comm, obviously no longer speaking to Hannibal, "can you verify any of that?"

"It doesn't matter whether she can or not," Hannibal said and laughed. "It's all true. What you fail to understand, all of you, including my treacherous shadow brothers who are obviously launching a private attack on the fortress, is that this is war. War! After Venice there was a new world order, but that was just a stepping stone. My kind, the real vampires, the hunters and bloodsuckers, have been driven from hiding. That will be our freedom. The order of the world will change yet again, return to days eons past, hunter and hunted in a final war, one without end.

"And it starts . . . now!"

At Hannibal's signal, the vampires' human captives were broken, bled and gutted in three heartbeats, and seconds later, the gunfire began again and the tide of soldiers swept in to close the ranks, a small number of shadows and flamethrowers in the front line. Hannibal consoled himself with the knowledge that he had tried, albeit halfheartedly, to prevent this massacre. But now that it had started, the very thing he'd fought so hard for, the savage hunter, the predator in him, took control.

In a far corner of his mind, he wondered who would be left to battle the sorcerer, to lay siege to the fortress, when they were done. And then all such thoughts were gone, and the scent of the blood spilled all around him, the violence that slashed the air, formed a sensual symphony, to which the vampire, Hannibal, now moved in primitive sync.

CHAPTER ✦ FOURTEEN

Salzburg, Austria, European Union.
Wednesday, June 7, 2000, 8:29 A.M.:

The remnants of the Shadow Justice System, those vampires who had not been killed or betrayed their new lives in favor of Hannibal's return to savagery, were fifty-nine males and thirty-six females. With the addition of Martha, Isaac and Jared, the total number reached ninety-eight. Twelve had accompanied the human forces down into the city to attack Hannibal, which left eighty-six shadows to attack the Fortress Hohensalzburg in a second attempt to destroy Liam Mulkerrin.

Stefan bit his lip. He was worried that it wouldn't be enough. Though he would never have questioned his orders aloud, he could not help but doubt the wisdom of such an attack. Certainly the humans could not join the siege, but the shadow forces attacking Mulkerrin had no leadership. Hannibal had turned against them, Rolf was trying to protect the citizens from him, Will Cody was a prisoner, and the rest had simply disappeared.

Now Rolf had put this newcomer, Martha, in charge, though none of them knew anything about her. Sechs was lucky more of his people hadn't followed Hannibal, and Stefan knew that if not for their respect for the new chief marshal, and the overwhelming threat of Mulkerrin, many of them would have done just that. Especially since a lot of them were beginning to get *hungry*!

"Now!" Martha said next to him, and Stefan gave the order to attack.

Where before they had had to worry about getting the human troops in, this time they had no such concerns. The shadows moved as one, in many different forms, flying or floating over the walls of the fortress and engaging Mulkerrin's demons immediately. The plan was to destroy them as fast as possible, without attacking Mulkerrin directly unless he acted first. In the initial skirmish, he had seemed preoccupied enough with controlling everything around them. As horrid, and as dangerous, as the demons appeared, Rolf had schooled the shadows on the easy destruction of such creatures. And without responsibility for the human troops, they could force a much more direct and sweeping attack.

"My hope," Martha had told them only minutes ago, "is that we can clear out the current wave of Hell-creatures, and then by putting all of our pressure on Mulkerrin, force him to let the portals throughout the city close in order to protect himself. If we can get him off balance, that will be the first step."

Stefan only hoped that it worked. They were also supposed to try not to kill the human soldiers, as the warriors possessing them would only find new hosts. Martha suggested they attempt only to knock these soldiers unconscious, thinking that perhaps the ghosts would be trapped within their hosts' minds . . . Stefan had almost laughed at that. It might be a legitimate plan, but she couldn't possibly expect dozens of starving vampires in the frenetic madness of battle to treat their enemies with such tenderness. Oh, they might try, even succeed for a short time . . . but not for long.

They were on the ground now, in the courtyard of the fortress once again. Stefan reverted to human form from the hawk shape he favored while flying, and signaled for the flamethrowers to start burning the demons down. They could have transformed into fire and swept through the yard, and probably would have to eventually, but for now the throwers were less painful. Demons howled as fire leapt into the air.

Mulkerrin was safe within his protective shield of magic, and he barely looked up as the assault began. Then he called out to them in a strange voice—not loud, but somehow loud enough for all of them to hear.

"Yes, come," Mulkerrin said. "Come and be purified."

Stefan frowned. The sorcerer didn't think of them as a threat, for the moment. Stefan vowed that would change.

"Stefan!" someone shouted in warning, and he kicked one of Mulkerrin's soldiers in the chest, knocking him down and out of the way, even as he turned to respond . . . too late. Stefan was lifted from the ground by a huge crablike pincer, one of the largest demons having shambled, burning, through the firewall. His chest was being crushed, and he cried out in pain even as he transformed himself into burning cinders. Escape would be simple, but it was not the order of the day. Instead, Stefan's flames engulfed the huge, gray thing, and withdrew only when its howling form was writhing its last on the cold stone floor of the fortress.

"Stupid beast," Stefan said, and finally looked to see who had warned him. It was Isaac, allegedly the son of Lazarus, several feet away and doing his best to battle half a dozen of Mulkerrin's ghost-inhabited soldiers without killing them. It was a noble struggle, but Stefan could see that Isaac was suffering unnecessarily.

In seconds, he was by Isaac's side, his fist caving in the skull of the closest soldier. He sank his teeth into the dead man's neck, drinking deeply.

"What are you doing?" Isaac asked, annoyed, even as he threw another soldier away from him, the possessed woman's ancient armor clattering to the ground.

"Getting my strength up, and helping you, fool," Stefan

snapped, throttling the man closest to him, then twisting his head around fast enough to break his neck. "What does it look like?"

"It looks like you are killing innocents," Isaac said, huffing as he ducked out of the way of a thrusting sword, only to be slashed across the back for his trouble. "Killing them for no reason other than expediency."

"Expediency," Stefan said grimly, "is its own reward."

They met then, face to face and eye to eye, over the thrashing body of the swordsman who'd slashed Isaac's back. Isaac held him by the arms while Stefan's hands were around his neck. Isaac looked angry, and sad, and Stefan realized that the other shadow truly felt for these unfortunate humans. But it did not stop his hands from tightening around the soldier's throat.

"No!" Isaac yelled.

"By the time the warrior spirit finds a new host, and makes its way back here on foot," Stefan growled, as he twisted and they both heard the grinding snap of bone, "this battle could be over!"

Stefan wiped his hands on his pants, tossed the corpse toward several of his SJS agents who'd complained of hunger, then turned to defend himself as another soldier rushed toward him, weapon raised high. He was not in the mood, so he swiftly sidestepped the attack, grabbed the soldier and propelled him, with incredible strength, into the stone wall of the fortress. The man fell, and did not stir again. All around Stefan, an oily yellow mist was floating up from where dead men lay. Isaac was at his side, berating him still, and then Martha was there, between them, and she held up a hand to stop his protest.

"I saw it all, and heard it, nephew," Martha said to Isaac. "But Stefan is right, I'm afraid. Right now, expediency may, in fact, be mercy, but in any case is far more important in this battle. Not to mention that if our brother and sister shadows don't get their strength back, these few lives will be nothing in comparison to what Mulkerrin will do.

The needs of the many, Isaac—though God help me, I never thought I'd say it—take precedence.

"Kill them," she said, and her face showed the pain of those words.

Stefan moved off, away from them, and closer to Mulkerrin, where the shadows were beginning to converge. He was almost set upon by a dark jackal, which had escaped the others, but it was intercepted by Lisa, one of his most powerful operatives. She was lithe, pale, beautiful, with long sable hair, and he was fascinated as he watched her dispatch the thing in seconds. Still, he thought of Martha's words, and the ease with which she had uttered them.

God help me, she'd said. Stefan had thought for an eternity that his people were beyond God's help, but now, for the first time, he wondered.

Cody was nearly healed.

He sat up against the wall of the room in which Mulkerrin had ripped out his heart, and held his hand against the pink, new tissue that covered that wound. It was tender, it hurt, and he was, for the moment, still too weak to move very far. His shirt had gone somewhere, and it had taken him a while to remember that Allison had used and lost his gun during their battle outside the hotel. How long ago was that? He didn't know. He was just happy that he still had his blue jeans and his boots on. The boots were made of very soft calves' leather, and he would have hated to part with them.

He smiled to himself; already his priorities were back on track.

Cody leaned on his hands and tried to get his legs under him to stand up. It wasn't working. Thinking again, he arched his back, bracing it against the wall, and pushed with his legs, which seemed a little stronger. Slowly, he slid up the wall until he was standing, leaning against it. He couldn't support himself yet, but he was getting there.

The only problem was that as he was regaining his strength, healing, he was losing whatever it was he had gained when he'd been . . . dead. Or whatever. His mind, or soul if you wanted to believe in that kind of thing, had obviously been elsewhere, wandering around out there. He wondered if the sorcery, the power of the magic Mulkerrin was generating, had helped to heal him. He knew for certain it had enabled his spirit to . . . What had it done?

It had traveled, it had spread. It had merged with the magic somehow, and he had been aware of all the goings-on around the fortress, of many of Mulkerrin's twisted thoughts. But that wasn't all. He had become, suddenly and completely, aware of many things, including the loyalties and the hostilities of any combatant inside or outside the fortress upon whom he wished to focus his thoughts. He heard the screams of those living hosts whose bodies had been commandeered by the ghosts of dead warriors, had, in fact, nearly been drawn himself into a human host before all the humans had been forced out of the fortress. If his spirit had not been so intertwined with the magic surrounding the place, he might not have been so lucky.

And was that part of it? Mulkerrin's spell to raise the spirits of the dead warriors—had that kept his own ghost around long enough to reinhabit his naturally healing body?

It was too much. Cody took a deep breath and pushed himself away from the wall. His legs were wobbly, but he could walk now. He searched for something, a shirt or jacket, to wear, but found nothing. The healing wound felt vulnerable.

He knew that above, the shadows had returned, and that they were even now surrounding Mulkerrin, battering against the sorcerer's protective field, trying to break his concentration, wear him down at least enough to close the portals so no more demons could come through.

Cody still had some of the knowledge and awareness he'd gained when his body had been so traumatically

wounded, but it was fading fast. He remembered certain
things, or was aware that he *had* known specific things, but
with his healing, and the growing consciousness of his
brain, his body, that other awareness had slowly slipped
away.

He could barely feel the connection he'd had to the
rhythm, the life of the magic pulsing within the fortress,
but it was still there. He could barely sense Mulkerrin now,
but knew that the siege was indeed wearing on him. He still
didn't know how Mulkerrin could have not sensed his presence, his awareness lurking there in the bowels of the fortress, but he was grateful that the sorcerer had not noticed
him.

And as for the knowledge, as he steadied himself with a
hand on the wall, moving toward the steps that would take
him up, there was one thing he concentrated on, one thing
that he had learned which he struggled not to lose. In his
awareness he had examined his handful of meetings with
John Courage, the words they'd exchanged, the battle
they'd fought side by side. He'd searched the shadows out
there for knowledge of Courage, and when he'd been in
mental contact with Rolf, and the woman Martha had
brought up Courage's name, he'd been able somehow to
read her as well.

At least a little. He didn't know, really know, what Courage was. But he had a fairly wild guess. It frightened and
thrilled him all at once.

But enough of that, he had to help his brothers and
sisters. He had to help them be rid of Liam Mulkerrin once
and for all. And he thought he might know how to set the
sorcerer off balance just enough for his people to accomplish their first goal.

MULKERRIN! his mind shrieked, sending the angry,
savage, attacking thought out along the thin strand of
awareness that still connected him to the magic, a magic he
had been able to sway just a little when he was a part of it.
The final bit of influence he had retained over the magic

was used up now, as his mind slammed into Mulkerrin's brain like a bullhorn screaming into his ear.

The sorcerer recoiled as if struck with a physical blow, shook his head, and Cody felt his surprise, his shock, and his immediate awareness of what had happened, of who his attacker was. Every one of the portals to Hell Mulkerrin had opened, throughout the city, had disappeared in that moment, and with his concentration gone, the barrage of physical force, the attack by dozens of vampires on the barrier around Mulkerrin, continued. The sorcerer was off balance, and before he could attempt to retaliate, Cody cut his own connection to the magic, which was like letting go of the string on a balloon and watching it drift away, sad to see it go, but fascinated by the beauty of the thing. The last thing he felt was Mulkerrin's rage.

Cody felt better with each step he climbed. First things first, he thought. There had to be someone topside who would give him a shirt.

Salzburg, Austria, European Union.
Wednesday, June 7, 2000, 8:56 A.M.:

Hannibal wasn't winning. Unfortunately, as far as Commander Elissa Thomas was concerned anyway, he wasn't losing either. She knew from the files she'd read that some shadows had developed to the point where they were almost impossible to kill. The majority, however, had not become completely used to their abilities, or to walking around during the day, even though five years had passed. Hannibal's coven was no exception.

A constant attack might be enough to throw some of the less experienced of them off balance so that they lost control, or confidence, and began to fear the sun. If they ran, tried to find cover, they'd never make it. Likewise, concentrated gunfire, hand-held rockets, even an overwhelming hand-to-hand attack might be enough to literally tear apart one of the creatures. If the pieces of the thing could be kept from coming back together, it would be truly dead.

The problem was that the casualties among the UN security forces were as completely disproportionate to those among the vampires as their original numbers were. For every shadow they were able to destroy, dozens of human lives were lost. As far as Elissa was concerned, that was far from a fair trade, but she didn't know any other way to stop the evil bastard. She knew now, after all the moments of curiosity, of wonder, how the myths and legends of vampires got started.

And then there was Rolf. Commander Thomas did not love Rolf Sechs. She barely knew him, after all. But even in so short a time, she'd come to care about him. She knew that he was not the evil creature Hannibal was, and yet he had the same savage heart, the same talents, and that fascinated her. She had already decided she would stand by him when the shit hit the fan. And it certainly would do that. Even now Roberto Jimenez was beginning to doubt Rolf; Elissa could see it in her commanding officer's eyes.

But could she blame him? After all, it was the President of her own country who had been murdered. Life would never be the same for any of them, human or vampire, and Hannibal had changed it all, thrown it all away. And for what? Ego? Bloodlust? Power? Or was he simply lonely in his cruelty, needing others to share in his perversity?

She didn't know, and though she was curious, Elissa realized that the answers wouldn't make a bit of difference.

We're dying out here, she thought, lifting a CAMEL tube to her shoulder. She was well back from the real hand-to-hand stuff, knowing that her troops would be hard to rein in without her guidance, but she wasn't out of it. She leapt to the hood of a nearby Mercedes, the light plastic of the CAMEL no burden, then sighted down the tube. The computer-aimed system zeroed in on a number of targets, and she searched the sight for Hannibal.

She found him, cut off from his pack, surrounded by a

large group which included Rolf Sechs and Roberto Jimenez. Roberto held in his hand a dagger, obviously silver, which she realized suddenly was actually a weapon made from a crucifix. With the CAMEL, Elissa might have had a shot at destroying Hannibal, but Rolf and Jimenez were in the way. They'd have to do it themselves.

We planned this very poorly, she thought, and then reminded herself that they hadn't actually planned it at all. It had just sort of happened. In the battles to come, and she was sure there would be many such conflicts as the world, frightened by the U.S. President's assassination, began hunting the vampires, there would have to be more planning ahead. If they'd had only one-third the men and twenty times the CAMEL tubes, they would have destroyed all the shadows already, and a lot of lives would have been saved.

She sighted the CAMEL at another shadow, a female she had seen close to Hannibal and who she assumed was one of his elite. The sighting locked on target, Elissa pulled the trigger as easily as she might a pistol's, and the missile launched. She'd counted to one when the vampire erupted in a great splash of body parts. It was a messy death, Elissa decided, closing her eyes to the carnage, but it was the fastest way to kill them, merciful really.

Hannibal was surrounded. The human soldiers had slung back their firearms so as not to kill one another, and pulled out sharp knives instead. Jimenez brandished the crucifix dagger that Rolf had seen him use at the fortress, a dagger exactly like those Mulkerrin's followers had used in Venice five years ago. Rolf and Jared and two other shadows were there, closing in on the renegade.

Renegade. A strange word for a vampire, Rolf thought. There was a time, not long ago, he knew, when only kindhearted creatures like Octavian and Cody were considered renegades. Rolf had done his share of hunting, along with all the others. In the ignorance that comes from arrogance, he had believed that humanity were little better than cattle. He had never been the vicious killer that Hannibal was, enjoying murder for its own sake. Rather he'd been like a human, kind to his creatures until it was time for the slaughter, and even then, sometimes sad for them.

What a pompous fool he'd been! They did not have to kill. There was another way to live, a better way. They'd had to be forced into it, by being thrust into the public eye, but it was a good life. And now Hannibal was going to ruin everything. The American President had been killed, and if Rolf knew his former boss, the murder would have been quite a spectacle. It might already be too late to prevent the changes Hannibal intended, Rolf knew, but that did not mean he could go unpunished.

It was a silent vow: he would see Hannibal dead.

But what was Hannibal up to now? They had the renegade surrounded, but he wasn't running. He could simply transform and fly away, but instead he stood his ground against the mob around him. Certainly Hannibal knew that if he fled, Rolf and the humans would follow, but he had to know he would have a better chance of survival if he did run.

Rolf looked at the elder vampire, saw that his eyes were desperate, white hair flying wildly as he whipped his head from side to side, looking at his attackers, looking over them where he could to gauge the rest of the battle. And then Rolf understood. Hannibal was overwhelmed, trying to run the battle from where he fought, cornered. He sent orders and received information through the mind-link he shared with those of his followers who were his blood-children, and with the battle not going as well as he'd hoped, he must have been confused about his next move.

Next to Rolf, Jimenez lunged for Hannibal.

No! Rolf thought, reaching out to snag the back of the commander's jacket, even as Roberto's arm swept out, dagger slashing through the arm Hannibal held up in protection. Even as Hannibal hissed at the pain of the silver passing through his flesh, Rolf pulled Commander Jimenez back just in time to save him from retaliation, a swipe of Hannibal's talons that was meant to tear Jimenez's face off. Hannibal went after the commander, and Rolf stepped in the way.

The battle was joined.

Rolf growled, motioning to those around him to stay back, and they did.

This must be it, Rolf realized. Hannibal had not fled because he knew any clash must come to this, a one-on-one, tooth-and-claw battle with his former deputy. While working together for the SJS, the two had woven a pretense of mutual sufferance, no more. Five years of unspoken hatred, mistrust, hostility, now seethed within them both. Rolf was elated that the day of reckoning between them had finally come.

Renegade, he thought. *Killer*!

And perhaps his hatred was enough to carry the essence of his thoughts to Hannibal's mind, because the savage seemed to respond.

"Traitor!" Hannibal yelled into Rolf's face. "Coward!"

Rolf lost all sense of self, and of time. He and Hannibal were now inseparable, their transformations, metamorphoses, almost one with each other. In their hatred, their explosive bloodlust, their minds forgot the patterns of the deadly creatures they had shifted their shapes to in the past. Instead, the flesh flowed, picking and choosing among the deadliest attributes of those forms, claws lengthening, fur sprouting, snouts stretching to accommodate razor teeth. Hannibal twisted his head and tore a chunk from Rolf's face with a horn that had appeared on his head.

Blood and flesh flew around them. The gore-spattered faces of his comrades gravely looked on, but Rolf was blind to it all as he found an unguarded spot, an unprotected moment, and shoved his right hand into Hannibal's now hard and scaly belly. His claws were sharp, and his strength was enough to slide the hand in, grab a fistful of the vam-

pire's guts and pull. Even as he struggled to eviscerate
Hannibal, Rolf had left much of himself unprotected, and
the other's terrible jaws clenched on what had become his
own snout. His body reacted, changing shape again, his
flesh trying desperately to escape the many teeth of his
enemy.

Part of his face tore away even as Hannibal's intestines
spilled out, flopping on the cobblestones at their feet. In
his pain, Rolf's awareness of his surroundings returned.
Some of his comrades were moving to assist, but Commander Jimenez motioned for them to stay where they
were. Silently, Rolf thanked him. He would kill this creature, and perhaps the disaster Hannibal had planned could
still be avoided, perhaps peace was still possible for the
weary shadows.

They held each other, like lovers, like weary boxers,
though their claws were deep in each other's back, head,
neck, scoring to the bone. Hannibal's grip relaxed a bit,
and Rolf tried to look him in the eye.

But Hannibal wasn't looking at Rolf. He was looking
over Commander Jimenez's head. Rolf followed his line of
sight and saw what had drawn his attention. Commander
Elissa Thomas, Rolf's lover, stood atop a vehicle, behind
many of her troops, with a CAMEL rocket tube on her
shoulder, waiting for a clear shot.

Rolf had been winning; it was only a matter of time, and
Hannibal had to know it. Rolf was faster, stronger; Hannibal was badly wounded, weakening. But that moment of
distraction, seeing Elissa above the terrible battle that
raged around them, was an error. Hannibal used all the
strength he had within his undead frame to heave Rolf up
and away from him. Rolf slammed into a group of soldiers,
taking them down, and the vampire Jared as well.

He looked up, his face throbbing, and Hannibal was
gone. And then Rolf saw that he had changed. Weakened
by his torn belly, the vampire had not the strength to become mist, but he apparently had enough concentration

left to transform into a huge bat. In seconds, he was darting across the plaza toward Elissa's perch. Rolf swore, and gunfire spat into the air, and a number of bullets tore right through Hannibal's black form. They slowed him down, some, but didn't stop him.

Rolf and Jared changed then, almost simultaneously, and they flew after Hannibal as a wounded eagle and a raven. Around them, several bats rose into the air, but whether they were Hannibal's followers or his own, Rolf could not tell. And neither could the soldiers, as they were all fired upon. Rolf was hit twice, but ignored the small pain, the momentary lack of balance. Commander Thomas was a soldier, that was true, and as such she faced death constantly. But Rolf cared for her, and he would not be responsible for her death.

Elissa brought the CAMEL around to aim it at Hannibal, but the fiend was almost there. She didn't have the two or three seconds it took for the computer to aim, and she didn't wait. The CAMEL's missile blasted from its tube . . . and missed. The target, Hannibal, was too small and too fast, and the computer had not had enough time. Behind him, Rolf heard an explosion as the dome of the Salzburg Cathedral exploded, the missile finding a target after all.

And then it was too late. Before the debris of the dome had begun to fall, before Elissa could even drop the tube, and long before Rolf could come to her aid, Elissa was in Hannibal's arms. He spun her to face his pursuers, and she flailed behind her, striking him uselessly with her elbows and feet. But her head and upper body did not move, because Hannibal's left arm was around her neck, the crook of his elbow powerful enough to snap it at any time. His right hand was at her face, and the long talons rested on her right cheek.

Hannibal didn't have to tell Rolf to stop. Changing back into human form, the mute vampire stood twenty feet from the car atop which Hannibal prepared to kill a woman he

had so recently made love to, caressed. Rolf didn't know
what to do. He felt his loyal shadow warriors step up, behind him, and knew that Jimenez and his soldiers were
back there too, every weapon aimed at Hannibal. It also
occurred to him that Hannibal's forces must be nearly destroyed for the battle to come to such a sudden halt.

"Ah," Hannibal said, a guttural laugh showing he was
still in pain. "This woman will be the death of you, mute."

One long claw etched a red line across Elissa's right
cheek, and though she did not scream, Rolf could feel her
pain, see her teeth clenched against the cry that lodged in
her throat. She stood rigid, but no longer struggled, resigned to whatever might come. Rolf was proud of her, and
knew that he cared about her more than he ought to care
about someone he'd known for so brief a time. He considered the possibility that he might love her, and couldn't
deny it.

A new rage began to build in him, fueled by the futility
he recognized in it. For the moment, Hannibal held all the
cards. He could only watch as his enemy let the same hand
that had scarred her move down Elissa's body to cup her
breast through the cloth of her uniform.

"Yes," Hannibal said softly, and only then did Rolf realize the silence that truly had fallen on the plaza. "I can
understand your attraction, mute. I'll enjoy this woman
quite a bit."

Why didn't they fire? Rolf wondered. Why did the
soldiers do nothing? She was just another human to them,
surely. So many others of their kind had died there that
day. But he knew why they did not, could not, fire. It was
the way it had happened, the spectacle, the confrontation.
And now, in the midst of a very impersonal, faceless battle,
where death was a means to an end, a moment had arrived
that made things very personal, made death a thing to be
feared, made them all feel as vulnerable and helpless as
Elissa was.

He felt it too, and his rage burned higher, and darker.

When Hannibal's jaws opened wide, and his fangs sank tenderly into Elissa's neck, Rolf could not move. But as he looked away, wanting to see anything but the atrocity Hannibal was committing, he saw that Elissa's eyes were closed. He knew that she had wanted him to bite her the night before. She had not said it, but it had been clear just the same. Just as now, she said nothing, but Rolf could see what this meant to her, this violation, rape of a sort. She was a proud soldier, the commander of the American division of the UN security force, and a single tear ran down her cheek until it was stopped by the slash Hannibal had made there, disappearing in the bloody streaks that dripped to her chin.

Before he was aware of it, Rolf was in motion.

CHAPTER ✦ FIFTEEN

U.S. Interstate 81, New Hope, Virginia, United States of America.
Wednesday, June 7, 2000, 3:01 A.M.:

George Marcopoulos couldn't sleep. How had everything gone so wrong, so fast? The question was unanswerable, but its truth was evident in his every thought, every movement. Joe Boudreau had saved him from death at the hands of a man whom tragedy had just made the President of the United States of America. They had fled across the White House lawn, Joe not advanced enough to fly George out, and his vampiric savior had been forced to injure seriously several Secret Service agents to make that escape possible.

George had been amazed, and relieved, to discover that Boudreau had a car parked nearby. A quick drive to his D.C. apartment, so that George could retrieve those few things that mattered, and they were off, cross-country, driving for the temporary safety of Virginia highways. It wasn't long before they were headed south on Route 81, toward Tennessee.

They had spoken little during all of this, for George had a lot on his mind. Valerie, for one. His wife and family in Boston would more than likely never see him again. He didn't think he had to worry that they'd believe whatever charges Bill Galin (George had a hard time thinking of him as "the President") lodged against him. But Valerie was very sick, and their humiliation by people who wouldn't know better was a terrible thing to consider. George worried, but knew he was powerless.

He was, after all, the worldwide symbol of human cooperation with the shadows. And the whole world had just seen shadows murder the President as a declaration of war. Their ambassador, once a mild-mannered medical examiner from Boston, had disappeared, and could only be considered to be in collusion with their efforts. George had considered trying to change his appearance somehow, but hadn't come up with a plan so far.

The world was at war, and it didn't even know it yet.

In the meantime, there was Salzburg.

As they drove through Virginia, George watched with dread as events unfolded on the dash-screen cellular TV in Joe's car. Armed guards had surrounded the United Nations building, and Rafael Nieto was under 24/7 protection. In Washington, Bill Galin was sworn in as President, and immediately ordered all agencies to investigate the disappearances of Meaghan Gallagher, Alexandra Nueva and George Marcopoulos! CNN reported that its own Allison Vigeant was under investigation, though her status in Salzburg was unknown.

And an international manhunt was declared for Hannibal, the chief marshal of the Shadow Justice System. Of course, that order, made jointly by Galin and Nieto, was essentially an indictment of the SJS in its entirety, and a clear message that it was open season on all vampires.

"What do you think is going to happen?" Joe asked, finally breaking a long silence, and in his voice George heard a tremor of vulnerable, childlike fear. He knew the answer, knew it was not what the young shadow wanted to hear, but its truth was inescapable.

"Armageddon," he said.

Joe only nodded, and they were quiet again as the news anchor switched to a reporter flying above Salzburg in a

helicopter. The aerial view was bizarre, to say the least.
Where the ground rose up on one side of the river, in the
spot where the reporter insisted the Hohensalzburg Fortress was, and where he noted that half of the battle was
going on, the picture was completely out of focus, showing
only a kaleidoscope of colors.

The reporter claimed that the helicopter had been pro-
hibited from taking off until it appeared that all of the "so-
called" demons capable of flight had been destroyed, but
also noted that it wouldn't have done them any good previously, because until mere minutes earlier, none of the cameras within the main city had been able to get *any* picture
at all. With that problem solved, the reporter said, a
ground team was working its way through Salzburg, broad-
casting the carnage it found, the destruction left by the
earthquake, the fires and other, less natural disasters. The
ground team was attempting to get closer to the fighting
now taking place not at the fortress, which still proved impossible to film, but at a place called Residence Plaza,
where human and shadow forces were clashing. It was a
clear, bright, sunny morning in Austria, and the helicopter
offered a fairly good view of the battle.

It looked, to the world and to George Marcopoulos, as
though the shadows were attempting to prevent the human
troops from reaching the fortress. The reporter repeated
several times that the blacked-out area, at the fortress, was
where the shadows were battling the sorcerer Liam
Mulkerrin. But the audience couldn't see that. All they saw
was shadows and humans killing one another. And after
the President's assassination, it was exactly what they expected to see.

Joe looked at George out of the corner of his eye, the
same way he'd been watching the TV while driving.

"Meaghan knew this would happen eventually, but not
so soon," he said to George.

She never talked about it with me, he thought, but didn't
open his mouth.

"Is Meaghan the one who made you a—"

"She gave me the gift, yes," Joe said. "I asked her, begged her really. I told her I was dedicated to helping any way I could, and she said the best way I could help was by hiding out. She knew Hannibal had his agents, and I suppose I was meant to be the first of her own.

"She never expected it to happen so soon," he said again.

"Is there a plan?" George asked.

"Not really," Joe admitted. "But there is a meeting place."

George raised an eyebrow. "Are we headed there now?"

"Yeah," he said and smiled a bit. "New Orleans."

"That's a long drive."

"You sleep," Joe said kindly. "I don't need to, remember."

George thought a bit, especially about Meaghan's disappearance. He asked Joe about it, about why Meaghan disappeared.

"She contacted me, in my mind, you understand?" He looked at George, and when he saw that the old man did actually understand, he went on. "She and Alexandra and Lazarus—"

"*Lazarus*?"

"Yeah." Joe nodded. "They went after Peter Octavian."

Now George was thoroughly confused.

"But Octavian's in . . . ," George began, but he couldn't get the word out.

And all Joe said was "Yeah."

"God help us all," George said softly. Perhaps too softly, because Joe Boudreau didn't say a word in reply.

Salzburg, Austria, European Union.
Wednesday, June 7, 2000, 9:03 A.M.:

Mulkerrin had power enough to destroy them all, despite the confusion he'd begun to experience as the shadows infiltrated the fortress and slowly overwhelmed his hellish forces, his ghostly soldiers. He'd been preparing to do just that, drawing close much of his power, weaving his magic around him as a stronger protection, as well as a battering force with which to strike. This was all new to him, a new kind of power, and he was still growing comfortable with its uses, testing its limits. It seemed only to be limited by his own ability to concentrate on several things at once.

He'd been preparing to destroy the Defiant Ones when the magic itself contracted around him, a familiar voice screaming his own name, in his head, tearing at his brain from inside like something struggling to be born. And then he'd known. Will Cody was alive and had access to the magic! His magic, the power God had given him to purify the world! It was impossible, not only that Cody was capable of such a feat, but that he was alive at all. Mulkerrin had torn his heart out!

The former priest looked up, the action itself his first signal that things had gone drastically wrong. Rather than standing triumphant as his power swept over the vampires, he was on his knees, hands clamped vise-like to the sides of his head. In a moment, along the tendrils of sensation he felt through his magical influence, he knew that all of the portals were closed. The sky above was free from his control, communications would have returned, and the sun was shining down.

And his own protective aura was rapidly deteriorating as vampires slashed and raked at it, coming ever nearer to him in their many forms.

No! He had the power!

"Away!" Mulkerrin shouted, and the aura surrounding him nearly exploded with the force of his magic, obliterating several of the vampires that had come nearest to him and throwing others across the courtyard, to slam into the stone walls around them.

Even as he reached out with his mind to find Cody, to

retaliate, he was on the attack once again, more ferocious than before. And yet he was startled once again, for now he could not find Will Cody anywhere. Only moments before the vampire had been as attuned to the flow of magic around the fortress as Mulkerrin himself, and now he was nowhere to be found.

What then? Had the death of the vampire's spirit created some backlash which struck while Mulkerrin was vulnerable? No, he could not accept it; Cody was truly still alive and yet Liam was blind to him. He felt very strongly that Cody lived, yet he could not sense his location. *But enough foolishness,* he thought. It was a mystery, but if Cody no longer had access to the magic, he could not truly harm Mulkerrin no matter where he was, and the battle was far from over. He was toying with them now, really. He could destroy them all, though he might have to drop his shields to do so, to summon the concentration. That would be foolish, when taking his time was so much more . . . gratifying.

The time for play was finished. No more portals were necessary, for the moment. Later, demons would be useful to frighten the human race, to make them see exactly what their rotting lives had wrought upon the eternal scales of justice. But for now, Mulkerrin was concerned only with this shadow race of beings without any true place. Their insolence and interference, their *defiance*, was at an end.

"Attack!" shouted the shadow he knew was called Martha. "Kill him now! He is weakening!"

And the fool led the new charge against him. The scene had changed, but it was still familiar. Mulkerrin, all in black, white hair disheveled as the air around him, tinged green by magic, protected him from harm. But it was more that the reality around him was altered by the magic, than it was that the air itself had changed. The portals were gone, the demons all dead. Many of the spirits of dead soldiers he had raised had already found new human hosts and were making their way back to the fortress even now.

But once they were killed again, they would return to their rest. He had given up sustaining them.

It was now just Mulkerrin and the vampires, and his magic could protect him as long as he desired it to. But protection was not what he wished.

"Fool," Mulkerrin snarled at Martha as she rushed toward him, and she changed the course of her attack slightly as he held his hand out to her, palm up, as if he meant to hold hands with her, to walk, quietly, joined in that way like lovers. Even as Martha's hands became talons, with which she planned to tear at Mulkerrin's weird force shield, she watched a tiny cloud of smoky darkness whirl into life above the palm of his outstretched hand. The darkness sprang into being; half a second later it was as large, or larger, than she. Dozens of red embers burned within, and Martha knew they were the eyes of a sentient being, a creature from Hell, yes, but another Hell than the one from which Mulkerrin drew most of his slaves.

There was the world, the universe, and then there was Hell, but her brother Lazarus had taught her that there was much in between those poles, many other worlds, other dimensions, and many races darker and more evil than the denizens of Hell. This thing of the burning eyes and the countless mouths filled with infinite gleaming ebony teeth, this was one of those things, a *Nachzehrer*, or at least fitting the description of one.

And it was upon her even as she exploded in flame, attempting to use her natural shapeshifting ability to drive it off. But it was no more corporeal than she, and though it could not surround and douse the flames that Martha had become, it could unfortunately consume her, a bit at a time.

"*No!*" Martha heard Isaac shout, even as the thing's attack gave her some kind of psychic pain, and then he screamed as the thing fell upon him in her place.

Martha changed back to her true form, lashing out immediately at the thing of darkness. Her talons passed through it, as did the hands and arms of those who had come to her aid. Even as dozens of vampires rushed past them to attack Mulkerrin's shield, she could hear the sorcerer's laughter as her nephew, Isaac, the son of Lazarus, continued to scream. His shouts of agony, coupled with the slurping, bone-crunching sounds of the thing consuming him, emanated from within it, but he was not there. Martha could reach right through and touch Stefan, the SJS deputy, on the other side of the *Nachzehrer*.

And then the screams stopped, but the gnawing sounds, and Mulkerrin's laughter, continued.

Cody had pulled a light sweatshirt off the first corpse that looked to be about his size, a tourist who'd been possessed by one of Mulkerrin's soldiers. And now he was making his way up a long walkway toward the courtyard. The bestial sounds of attacking vampires echoed back to him, but no gunfire, no traditional sounds of war.

When the screams began, he ran toward them. At the top of the walkway, he found himself above the yard, a short stone staircase leading down into the thick of things. From up there, he saw it all; the thing of darkness, not a shadow or anything he'd ever seen before, and the vampires swarming around Mulkerrin, who laughed and laughed. And he'd seen quite enough.

"Mulkerrin!" Cody shouted, and he could almost *feel* it as the sorcerer turned his attention away from his attackers and toward the new threat.

Not almost, he realized. Cody could feel it, the magic around Mulkerrin, pouring through the castle, surrounding them all, really, ready to be bent to the sorcerer's will if he had the strength to do it. Unlike before, when Cody's spirit was in it, was a part of the magic, he could not sense anything through it, but he could feel its presence. He knew that it was there, and that Mulkerrin wielded it with violence and hatred.

Even from forty yards away, as he descended the stairs, Cody could feel Mulkerrin's power find its focus on him, could feel the anger seething, boiling into action. Cody knew an instant before that a tentacle of magic, formed from the greenish aura that surrounded Mulkerrin, would lash out at him, slamming like a battering ram into the stairs where he'd stood but a moment earlier. He knew when another of those fearsome night things was born in Mulkerrin's hand and sent rocketing toward him.

Cody went to defend himself, but in a moment, he found he did not need to. He could feel the thing's confusion and, in a flash of his own, realized that it couldn't see him. He was somehow invisible to it.

"You will die, Cody," Mulkerrin screamed as Will came closer, though the former priest did not attempt any new attack, perhaps sensing the disturbance Cody created in the magic. The aura around the sorcerer blossomed suddenly, growing in a flash from a ball surrounding his body to a dome which stretched ten feet above him and twenty feet all around. Vampires were thrown backward and to the ground. Others were borne aloft by the growth of the thing, and changed to flying creatures so they did not have to slide down the side of the shield, so they didn't have to touch it more than necessary.

Cody reached the outer edge of the dome and helped Martha to her feet.

"You know me?" she asked, seeking confirmation.

"From Rolf's mind," he answered.

"It's impossible to estimate Mulkerrin's power," she said even as the other vampires struggled around them. "Every time we think we've got it pinned down, it changes and grows a little more."

"I don't think even he knows how much power he has," Cody muttered, turning to lock eyes with the madman, twenty feet away. "But I would like to know where he got it."

Cody had known Mulkerrin was a madman, and he had
not been disappointed.

"Where did my power come from?" Liam Mulkerrin
asked, stunned that any should question such a thing.
"From God, you vile, evil thing. The Lord Himself en-
dowed me with these abilities so that I could purge the
Earth, beginning with you and your kind!"

Cody shook his head, still tired from everything he had
been through, but energized by the situation, knowing that
many others of his people would die if he were to fail.

"You tried that once already, didn't you?" he asked,
mocking, feeling Mulkerrin's hatred of his kind, but more,
of him personally. "That's the only shot you get."

And then suddenly he knew he could do it, and just as
quickly he *was* doing it. With Martha and the rest looking
on in astonishment, Cody began to wade right through
Mulkerrin's protective field, the greenish aura surrounding
him, welcoming him.

"I'm coming for you, Liam," he said with a low growl.

"No!" Mulkerrin snapped. "You cannot. My magic pro-
tects me."

"Not from me, apparently," Cody said grimly.

And he could feel it, the strain Mulkerrin put behind his
efforts, the magic that stretched out, searching for Cody,
hoping to hurt him, or at least to reject him. But it couldn't
find him, and therefore could not affect him. Mulkerrin
was vulnerable, and Cody had been taught the lesson early
in life that in a true war, you must exploit the vulnerable.
He was wading through Mulkerrin's shield when he saw
the resolve appear in his old, mad eyes.

And then those eyes closed. Mulkerrin raised his hands,
muscles straining in his neck, and the ground shook, buck-
led, cracked beneath Cody's feet. The stone floor of the
fortress, which had withstood the siege of many centuries,
opened wide and swallowed Will Cody and several others
. . . Then, with a terrible shout from Mulkerrin, it

slammed together again, tearing new cracks in the foundation of the fortress.

But Cody was no fool, and neither were his comrades. All but one of the vampires who had fallen transformed to escape—into mist, into fire, one into a sharp-clawed owl. Cody knew now that even if Mulkerrin could not attack him directly with magic, it did not mean the madman was powerless against him. On the contrary, as the fortress continued to shake, its battlements crumbling and the stairs Cody had only just descended disappearing into a crevice, he realized that the sorcerer was creating another earthquake for the entire city, not merely the fortress.

It must stop. Cody made his way toward Mulkerrin again, the sorcerer apparently ignoring his approach. But only apparently. For as Cody neared, once again at the edge of the greenish aura that surrounded the sorcerer, the entire floor beneath both of them collapsed. A hole forty feet in diameter opened up in the center of the courtyard, falling into the rooms below, and thinking to confront Mulkerrin there, Cody allowed himself to fall, did not change shape. Only when he lay there, bruised and bleeding but not feeling the quickly closing wounds, did he realize that, in fact, Mulkerrin had not fallen at all.

Above him, Mulkerrin hung suspended at the center of the glow that was his strength, his access to magic. Dozens of vampires, in flying or floating forms, hovered around that bubble-like shield, attacking it, testing its strength, but Mulkerrin ignored them. Instead, he stared down at Cody, who lay in the rubble, and his grin was a combination of hate, insanity and fear. Fear, yes, for Cody was a threat to him, an unexpected one.

"The strength of Hell is inside you!" Mulkerrin shouted, or Cody thought that was what he heard over the noise of the subsiding quake. Then, more clearly: "Your purification will set an example, the Lord Himself demands it."

And Cody wondered yet again where Mulkerrin had gotten the power to control the flow of magic, of the ether, the way he now did. Certainly it was not from "the Lord." But the maniac believed it was, and perhaps Cody could use that against him. In any case, Cody was apparently now immune to direct attack by magic, invisible to demons and other such creatures. He recognized then that he might be their only hope to destroy the sorcerer once and for all.

A new rumbling pulled Cody's attention from Mulkerrin, and even as he stood among the rubble, he turned to look in the direction the sorcerer now pointed. Cody looked up, and the wall was coming down on top of him.

Salzburg, Austria, European Union.
Wednesday, June 7, 2000, 9:11 A.M.:

Residence Plaza was a shambles, the Salzburg Cathedral destroyed and dead civilians and soldiers strewn on the cobblestones with their throats slashed or bellies torn open, their blood painting the ground in a terrible montage. Hannibal stood on the hood of a shiny Mercedes and sucked blood from the neck of Elissa Thomas as hundreds of UN soldiers and a handful of shadows looked on.

And Rolf Sechs, her lover, was in motion.

But so was the ground.

As Rolf took to the air, flashing past his own shadow troops and the UN forces led by Roberto Jimenez, the earthquake began with a gentle tremble, like a frightened shiver down the back of every being in the plaza. But by the time Rolf was closing in on Hannibal, only feet away from those green eyes that locked with his own even as the fiend licked several stray drops of blood from Elissa's neck . . . by then the plaza itself had begun to crack, nearly in half, in a direct line from the shattered cathedral, through the gathered army and to the street directly in front of the car upon which the renegade Hannibal stood triumphant, his white hair flashing in the sunlight.

Everything happened at once. The ground opened up beneath the Mercedes, tilting the car forward at a drastic

angle, dumping Hannibal and Commander Elissa Thomas
from its hood, toward the huge crack yawning open before
them. Before Hannibal could fall, Rolf slammed into him,
sending both of them flying over and behind the car. Commander Thomas landed just at the edge of the crack, and
only managed to scramble away from the crumbling street
with the help of two of her soldiers. The mercedes slid into
the gaping hole, and the ground continued to shake, making it impossible for many of the soldiers to stay on their
feet.

Behind the jutting tail end of the Mercedes, Rolf and
Hannibal faced each other once again. Finally free of the
disorientation and confusion of battle that had surrounded
them up to now, they knew the time had come. Elissa was
weak, though Hannibal had not really taken much blood
from her, and as the earthquake subsided, she signaled for
her troops to ready themselves for the outcome. She
wanted to take Hannibal down and keep him down, negat-
ing this duel, but Rolf was in the way. Her lover and his
enemy would have their final battle, it seemed.

She wanted to shout, wanted to stop it. But she also
wanted Hannibal dead, and knew that Rolf had the best
chance of achieving that feat. Her interest in him paled by
comparison to his strategic importance. She resigned herself to that. Elissa Thomas was a practical woman.

And then she heard two words coming through her collarcomm, words spoken by Roberto Jimenez, commander
of the United Nations Security Forces: "Open fire."

"No!" she said sharply, preparing to countermand that
order among her own troops. But it would not make a
difference, and she was too slow.

The rapid bursts of gunfire that filled the plaza joined
together in one terrible rumble, as if the earthquake had
come again, and Elissa could only watch as a swarm of
bullets pulverized both Hannibal and Rolf. Their bodies
danced with each wound, pushed back farther and farther
along the Alter Markt as the soldiers advanced. Elissa

heard screaming among the soldiers, as shadows, both friend and enemy, turned on the humans as one.

"Stop this!" she screamed into her comm. "Jimenez, he is our ally!"

And Commander Jimenez surprised her by bothering to reply at all.

"He is a vampire! Nothing more!"

And then Hannibal turned to mist, a pinkish cloud stained with the blood he'd shed only a single breath earlier, and the bullets merely passed through him. Rolf continued to dance under the barrage of metal, but the cloud that was Hannibal moved forward, toward the army, toward Elissa. Even as she began to back up, to stumble through the soldiers at her sides, she knew what was happening, knew it was too late to stop.

"Commander," a whisper said in her ear, "I am Hector. I'm pleased to make your acquaintance."

And her arms were seized, each by a pair of hands, and then she was rising above the broken earth, above the soldiers and Jimenez's shout of "Hold your fire!" She was surrounded by at least a dozen shadows in forms both familiar and strange. One seemed almost reptilian, though it had wings, almost like a small dragon. And the bloody mist of their master floated along with her, too close. She could feel Hannibal's fury.

In the plaza, the vampiric SJS agents continued to battle the humans who had turned on them when the bullets began to fly at Hannibal and Rolf. There were only five of them left, and Commander Jimenez didn't really want to kill them, but he didn't want them alive either. The older and smarter they became, the harder they were to kill. The American President was dead, and the world would be hunting vampires. He realized that this had to be the first move in that hunt.

"Traitor," a voice called out, over the brief bursts of gunfire and the sounds of struggle, and Jimenez turned to fol-

low it. Six, he realized as he spotted the vampire named
Jared, the son of Lazarus, or so he'd been told. He was
about to order his troops to fire on the creature, but then
Jared disappeared. One moment he was there, on open
ground just waiting to be taken out, and the next he was
gone.

"Jimenez, you are a traitor! A betrayer! Without
honor!" the voice came again, and Roberto looked up
along the Alter Mark, where Hannibal and Rolf had battled, where they'd been concentrating all their fire only a
moment ago . . . and Jared was there. In his arms, the
youthful-looking vampire held the bloody corpse of Rolf
Sechs, lifting it with ease and walking back toward the
troops.

Automatic weapons swung to bear on Jared, and in the
moment before the shooting began, Roberto felt an emotion unfamiliar to him: confusion.

"Hold your fire!" he shouted again, and even those who
hadn't listened the first time acknowledged the order now.
In seconds, the other shadows had flown to Jared's side,
and now the five vampires stood facing down hundreds of
armed humans whose mistrust and fear had turned to hatred and disgust.

It was an insane picture, those few creatures against so
many soldiers, and Jimenez could not prevent the possibility of merciless slaughter, of genocide, from entering his
mind. Just what the Church had attempted. And suddenly
he was certain that the world would complete the genocide
that Liam Mulkerrin had begun, even if the priest were
defeated once again. Though for those five short years, it
had seemed to work, humans and vampires were not meant
to live together, he knew now. Each group reminded the
other too much of itself. Roberto knew that if he let these
vampires live, he would only have to hunt them again later.
And though he hated them, he thought, *Dear God, how
much the world has changed, been redefined, in the span of
mere hours.*

"What is wrong with you?" Jared snapped, glaring at Jimenez. "We were your allies. I could feel your hate from the start, but we have goals in common, at least. Are you stupid?"

It was silent in the plaza, as if the whole scene were being played out underwater, and when Jimenez spoke, he did so quietly, knowing the vampire could hear him.

"Not stupid," he said sadly. "Efficient."

And he was somewhat sad, which told him his actions had been correct. He had begun to respect Rolf Sechs, even to like him. That was dangerous in the new, new world. Dangerous for all. It was fortunate that the mute had died.

Died? Even now, as Roberto looked on, Rolf was stirring in Jared's arms. Jimenez looked closer, saw the sadness in Jared's eyes, the set of his mouth. Jimenez nearly dropped his weapon to his side when Jared shifted and the commander could see that Rolf's mouth was locked onto Jared's bicep, drinking his blood. Even as Roberto watched, Rolf's wounds were healing.

Then Rolf's head lolled back, his eyes opened, and he looked directly at Jimenez. He motioned for Jared to put him down and began limping toward the soldiers. Weapons clicked and ratcheted as they were brought to bear on the still staggering but quickly healing German, but Jimenez shouted for them not to fire, to allow him to approach.

Rolf's gait improved as he crossed the last ten feet, until he stood immediately in front of Jimenez, who finally lowered his weapon, giving up on preventing retribution, if that's what Sechs wanted. He owed the creature that much at least. He felt rage, but no violence.

Silence reigned once again, and Rolf Sechs, a mute, ruled that world. He had apparently lost his voice-pad, for he reached out a hand, pointed a finger and tapped Commander Jimenez on the chest. The other hand pointed to the sky, in the direction Commander Thomas had been taken, then dropped to his pocket, from which the vampire drew a single British coin, which he turned so Jimenez could see each face.

And Roberto Jimenez dropped his head, for he understood the pantomime, at least its fundamental meaning.

You're no better than Hannibal, Sechs was telling him. *Two sides of the same coin.*

And then the silence was broken once again, by a new voice.

"I would translate for you," the voice said in Spanish, from across the plaza, "but I have a feeling you understood quite well."

The troops scrambled once again, running to find new cover, new positions from which to attack, as a formidable force of strangely dressed warriors, armed only with swords, lined the open street where Residenzplatz and Mozartplatz met. Jimenez fired orders into his collarcomm advising caution, as the man who had spoken, looking ancient and regal, stepped forward into the plaza.

"Your name?" the man said, once again in Spanish, and before Roberto knew it, he was answering, as if to a superior officer.

"Commander Roberto Jimenez . . . ," he started to say, and then he was angry at his compliance. "Who the hell are you?"

The man smirked in a way that was not obnoxious in someone his age, turned to a companion who was dressed in modern clothes and then looked back at Jimenez.

"I've been away too long," he said. "But many still remember the name of Charlemagne. You will accept our assistance, or surrender your weapons."

Roberto wanted to laugh, but knew that nothing here was funny.

CHAPTER ✦ SIXTEEN

Salzburg, Austria, European Union.
Wednesday, June 7, 2000, 9:22 A.M.:

Time. They'd had none of it, confronted with yet another potential enemy, another potential battle, chipping away, life by life, at the soldiers, the men and women, that Roberto Jimenez had led into Austria. It had started out ugly, but simple. It had gotten progressively uglier, and quickly became total chaos. Rather than storming one fortress, getting past hundreds of unholy monsters to sanction one, very powerful man who had already nearly destroyed the city of Salzburg and intended to continue on that path, they had been forced by Hannibal to begin a bloody confrontation on a second front. Some of the shadows fought at their sides, others tore out their throats, and every human soldier in Salzburg stood on a razor edge of suspicion and fear, of not knowing if any vampire were trustworthy.

It was an impossible situation, one in which Roberto could only lead by his gut, and where the hand of destiny pushed him. They hadn't had a choice in leaving the siege on Mulkerrin at the fortress to the vampires' forces; human soldiers would have been killed or possessed by the dead. They hadn't had a choice in descending into the city to save whatever remained of the civilian populace from Hannibal and his renegade vampires. They had failed in that effort. Roberto felt that he had failed. The civilians had died,

Hannibal had been defeated but escaped, and Roberto had nearly killed the leader of his vampiric allies in his efforts to win. To win.

But winning was a hope long since past, and he knew that now. Instead, he could only hope to accomplish his goal, to complete his mission, to destroy Liam Mulkerrin. His noble wish to save lives had disappeared. And now this newcomer, who claimed to be one of Europe's greatest leaders, and who led a shadow force of about one hundred warriors who dressed the part, had offered to help Commander Jimenez's soldiers, or destroy them.

Roberto had perhaps five hundred men and women left, and with the number of corpses littering the plaza, he couldn't be certain there were even that many. Five humans to one vampire: automatic weapons and missile launchers notwithstanding, those were terrible odds. Even if he managed to defeat the newcomers, Roberto would not have enough soldiers left to make any kind of attack on the fortress, and that was assuming the shadow force currently battling Mulkerrin had been able to destroy the ghosts, to make it safe for the human soldiers to return there at all.

He had little choice, really.

"We would welcome your assistance, sir," Jimenez said in English, then in Spanish when he realized it was possible that none of this newly arrived army spoke English.

"A wise choice," the leader said, in Spanish still, and Roberto was consciously aware for the first time that the darkness that had hung in the distance over Hohensalzburg Fortress had lifted, and now the whole city shone with the brightness of the June morning. The air smelled fresh and clean, the wind having carried away the stench of the demons they had killed, and the sky was blue and bright. But no birds sang. The morning, the beauty of the day, was a lie.

•   •   •

You must go after Hannibal now, Rolf.

The voice in Rolf's head surprised him so much he nearly fell down. He was recovering relatively quickly from the terrible wounds he'd received, thanks mainly to Jared's offering of blood, but for a moment he had to wonder whether he was hallucinating. The only blood-relatives he was aware of who still lived were Will Cody and perhaps Alexandra Nueva, wherever she was. But then . . .

You might consider me an ancestor, came the voice again, and Rolf shook off Jared's assistance, standing tall once again to scan the army brought by the creature who called himself Charlemagne.

Oh, but he is *Charlemagne*, said the voice.

Then who are you? Rolf thought, and he saw a figure separate itself from the crowd of soldiers blocking Mozart-platz. While the entire army seemed dressed from another time, with cloaks and tunics, and cloth straps wound up their legs from their shoes, this vampire wore blue jeans, brown bootlike shoes and a fashionable pullover jersey.

My name is John Courage, and Rolf knew he was looking right at the shadow who used that name, whose voice was in his head.

Then Rolf threw a glance at Jared, who gave him a small smile in return. Martha, Jared and Isaac had been sent by this man, and Cody had known of him . . . Cody. Rolf looked up at the fortress and could see from where he stood that many of the walls had crumbled, several parapets collapsing down the side of the hill.

Isaac, unfortunately, is dead, Courage told him.

Rolf began to walk forward, across the plaza, winding his way through the bodies of fallen soldiers, trying not to smell their blood as he realized that he was still in need of sustenance. The other five surviving members of his team —Sebastiano, Carlo, Annelise, young Erika and Jared— followed behind, and Jimenez motioned for all of his people to clear a path, to allow the six vampires to pass. By the time they emerged from the pack of humans, Rolf saw that there was a single female with them as well. She too was dressed in modern fashion.

And Rolf knew her.

"Rolf!" Allison Vigeant yelled, and with John Courage walking casually behind her, she rushed toward him, arms outstretched for a hug.

And he gave her one, happy as he was to see her alive. He wanted to balk at getting his blood all over her clothes, but she didn't seem to care. She began to introduce him to Courage, but Rolf waved such niceties away. He already knew the man. In the meantime, she wanted to know what had happened to her lover, Will Cody, and Rolf was happy to have Courage there to relate his thoughts to her. Through him, Rolf explained what had happened with Hannibal, and why the human troops could not approach the fortress. Through him, Rolf was able to tell Allison that Will Cody had nearly died, but that as far as he knew, he had recovered and was even now fighting Mulkerrin at the fortress.

"Well, we've got to help him," Allison declared, her matter-of-factness distracting Rolf from his obsession with Hannibal and the confrontation of only moments before with Roberto Jimenez.

"And we will," Courage said, "though first we've got to deal with these humans . . . No offense, Allison."

"None taken, John."

Who are you, really? Rolf thought suddenly, and Courage's eyes met his again. *My ancestor, from how far back*?

But this time, Courage didn't answer with his mind.

"We'll get to that, Rolf," the man said, sounding as if he meant it. "First things first, though. You've got to go after Hannibal and his new coven. Stop him now or he may become even more dangerous to us in the future."

Oh, I'm going all right, Rolf thought, *even if it takes me forever to find him. I mean either to save Elissa or avenge her.*

"Vengeance is the work of the Lord," Courage said, startling him. "Hannibal must be destroyed to protect our race.

And it won't take you forever to find him, for I suspect I know where he is headed.

"Jared," Courage said and turned to the other shadow, "go with Rolf. Help them track Hannibal, and destroy him. At any cost."

"And fast, Jared," Allison added, and Rolf felt her pain as a terrible memory clouded her eyes.

"Rolf," she said, "I was Hannibal's prisoner once. He did terrible things to me, but you freed me before the worst could happen. You've got to do the same for this woman. I know what Hannibal does to his female prey, and I've seen what he does when he's through with them."

"Hurry."

"And what of them?" Jared asked Courage, and they all turned to face the humans, who stood alert, vigilant in the morning sun. The wind carried the mutterings of Roberto Jimenez and the French commander, a woman named Surro, across the plaza, but he could not make out their words. The whole scene seemed like a Western showdown to him, but on a much larger scale, and for much higher stakes.

It was still fairly early in the morning, but already it was beginning to get unseasonably warm for June in Austria. Blood was beginning to dry, corpses to stink of death. Rolf had to wonder how long it had been since Charlemagne's troops had eaten, and what it would take to push them over the edge. They had to be quick about things, no matter which way it went.

Then, without word or thought, Charlemagne came forward to join them, and he, Courage, Rolf and Allison began to walk toward the human army. Weapons were leveled at them, but they kept walking, stopping midway between the two forces. Jimenez had said he would accept Charlemagne's assistance, but not that he would enjoy it.

"Please keep in mind," Courage said loudly, "that the woman you see here is as human as any of you. Should you fire, we vampires would survive but she would most assuredly die!"

"What a comforting thought," she mumbled to him, and Rolf couldn't hold back a smile.

Moments later, Jimenez and Surro stepped out to meet them, accompanied by several other, junior officers. Introductions were cold, and Jimenez glared at Allison as though she were a traitor.

"The American President is dead, I understand," Courage said, and Allison's mouth dropped open. Rolf put a hand on her shoulder and nodded, though he was surprised by Courage's knowledge of the fact.

"Assassinated by Hannibal's agents," Jimenez agreed.

"I'm glad you chose to phrase it that way," Courage nodded. "Still, we are at war, are we not? Vampires and humans? As of that event, have we not become the prey of human armies around the world?"

Rolf had understood, somewhat, but now the implications of what Courage was saying truly sunk in. There would be no recovery for the shadows. There would be some people, certainly, who would stand up for the idea that just as there were good and bad people, the same was true of vampires, but most of the world would be too frightened to see it. Most of the world had been, in fact, waiting for such an ugly incident, for their fears to be confirmed, their secret nightmares to take a tangible form, so that they could strike out. The dream was over. Vampires would have to hide in shadows once again.

And now he needed to leave, to be off, after Hannibal. For vengeance, no matter what Courage said, but also for the future of his people. They might survive if they disappeared into the night for a decade or two, perhaps tried again in another era, but if Hannibal were allowed to live, none of that would be possible. Hannibal wanted war and death and destruction.

"You are savages," Jimenez said bluntly, and Rolf could see that he was uncomfortable revealing these feelings.

"You are predators born to kill, and humanity must protect itself. Look at Hannibal."

"You fool!" Allison snapped at him. "Their race created Hannibal, yes, but ours created Liam Mulkerrin! I have been Hannibal's prisoner, and I would rather be that again than be in Mulkerrin's hands. Human beings are no less monsters than shadows are."

She turned to Rolf.

"Go, Rolf. Go now. Kill that bastard."

"And you," she turned back to Jimenez, "you can do whatever you want after today, hunt them if you must. But they are going to take care of their own monster, and it's your responsibility to help us take care of yours, to defend the human race against whatever Mulkerrin's become."

For a moment, nobody spoke a word, then Jimenez nodded. Charlemagne stepped forward then and said something in Spanish, which Rolf did not understand. From the look on his face, it seemed that Jimenez didn't get it either, but Allison apparently did, and she was looking at Charlemagne with eyebrows raised.

"Your silver," Courage translated, though they all knew Jimenez spoke Spanish. "You have silver on you, most likely a weapon. We will likely have a better opportunity to use it than you will."

Jimenez was obviously stunned, but so was Rolf. He had seen the dagger Roberto Jimenez carried; it had come from the ruins of the Venice Jihad, had been used by Mulkerrin's troops there, but . . .

"How did you—" Commander Jimenez began, but Courage interrupted.

"We can smell it," he said, even as he held out his hand.

Incredibly, Rolf watched. Jimenez reached inside his shirt, withdrew the knife and handed it over to John Courage. Even more incredibly, Courage did not even flinch, but rather lifted the dagger and admired it, sunlight glinting off its surface, then kissed its crucifix handle.

I don't understand, Rolf thought.

You will, my son, Courage said in Rolf's mind. *When you return, all will be explained to you.*

Then Jared was at Rolf's side again, and he saw the four other survivors of his team standing ready.

"Let's go," Jared said. "John has shown me where we must seek out Hannibal. He must be destroyed."

And moments later, they had left the plaza, the corpses and the armies behind and begun their hunt.

Allison was afraid, anxious and angry. Angry at humanity, anxious about the battle with Liam Mulkerrin, the second that she would witness in her life, and afraid of the outcome. Afraid for Will Cody, the man she loved. She thought of Will's tenderness, the sensitivity within his showman's exterior, the kindness of his heart and the way his words changed in the quiet moments they had shared over the past five years. He had, in many ways, become her life. Her professional life had become defined by his shadow race, and her private life had become one with his own.

They might as well have been husband and wife, though they'd been waiting for the world to change enough so they could be legally married. Now it looked as though that would never happen. It made no difference to Allison. In her mind and heart, Will Cody was her husband.

She didn't know what she would do without him. And she vowed she would never have to discover that. From what she could gather, Cody and the other vampires seemed to be holding their own against Mulkerrin. But Charlemagne and his warriors were different—older, stronger, more confident and much more in control of their vampiric abilities. Their arrival would make the difference; it had to. They were devoted to God, did not fear silver, though it did have a debilitating effect on them, and believed in themselves, in their goodness, in a way that none of the shadows she had known ever had.

And that only reaffirmed what she had believed all

along. She knew that the shadows were basically good, the way humans were, maybe even more so. But they could be twisted, made into something terrible, as Hannibal had been. Again, as the humans they once were.

And then there was Courage. He was the reason, she knew, that Charlemagne's men, and the vampires she had met at the monastery, Lazarus's family, were different. He was the reason—his leadership, his charisma, his words. She was not certain yet who he was, but she suspected . . . Oh, what she suspected! She might have guessed much of it earlier, but her mind wouldn't let her conceive of it. The more he told her, the more she realized how different he was, what he could do. When he told her that he could communicate with Rolf, and why . . . she could barely stand to be near him without screaming at him to be truthful, to reveal everything to her.

She needed to talk to Will, to reason it out with him. Even though she knew he would laugh at her, tell her she was out of her mind, she needed to hear him say it. And then she would convince him, somehow, and in doing so convince herself.

For Allison Vigeant truly believed that John Courage was the first vampire. The very first.

Courage smiled at her then, as if reading her mind, though she knew—was fairly sure—that he couldn't. Charlemagne and Commander Jimenez were speaking Spanish so fast she could barely understand a word here and there, and the more Jimenez apparently learned, the paler his face became.

Allison saw movement from the corner of her eye and turned back to see John holding both hands to his head, bent ever so slightly. His face showed terrible pain.

"John," she said and went to him, held his arm, "what is it?"

"Martha, Isaac, so many others gone . . . ," Courage said quietly, almost to himself. Then he met her eyes, and she was suddenly terrified for herself, for Will, for the future. She was only human, after all, and they were so much more.

Allison looked around wildly, her mind seeking some respite, perhaps somewhere to hide from the events unfolding around her. Charlemagne and Jimenez had stopped speaking, were staring at John Courage, and Courage stood up straight, the pain in his face turning to fierce determination.

"It's over up there, gentlemen," Courage said. "Mulkerrin's won."

"Is Will . . ." Allison was finally able to get the words out, but John shook his head slowly, as if he couldn't believe it himself.

"I don't know," he said.

"Let's move!" Jimenez said, and turned to signal his troops, but a gesture from John Courage stopped him.

"Don't bother," Courage said, almost cynically. "He's coming to us."

Hell.
One Hundred Sixty-Seven Days, One Minute After Departure:

It seemed as if they had been chipping away at Peter Octavian's crystal prison forever. Meaghan knew it hadn't *been* forever, but it had been weeks. Just when they might have stopped, after more than three weeks had gone by and they were prepared to give up hope, Peter had opened his eyes, looked at them, recognized them, pleaded with them, all with those eyes. Meaghan wondered why he did not communicate through the mind-link they once shared, the natural rapport she had with him as her blood-father. She told herself the only answer was that he could not, though she had no idea why.

And there was another reason she and Lazarus kept at the glass, kept working to free Peter Octavian, but one the two vampires refused to discuss: their other options. What could hear military helicopters over the city. Cody knew the choppers were returning for the cleanup, that they would try to destroy any vampire they found alive. But he also knew the city could be saved, that the nukes were not coming. Another block and they found Stefan, weeping by the white and bloodless form of the emperor Charlemagne. When Peter put a hand on his arm, Stefan looked up.

"I don't know if he'll make it," Stefan said. "I don't know if he wants to."

With Cody's help, Stefan managed to pick Charlemagne up again, and together they left.

Somewhere in the city, church bells rang, and Will realized that some of Salzburg's residents had never been evacuated, and yet had survived. He was happy for them and, though he didn't quite understand why, proud of them as well.

Allison counted aloud as the bell rang twelve times.

High noon, William F. Cody thought, but the showdown was over.

EPILOGUE

The folks were white and stricken, and each tongue seemed
      weighted with lead;
    Each heart was clutched in hollow hand of ice;
And every eye was staring at the horror of the dead,
    The pity of the men who paid the price.
They were come, were come to mock us, in the first flush of
      our peace;
    Through writhing lips their teeth were all agleam;
They were coming in their thousands—oh, would they never
      cease!
    I closed my eyes, and then—it was a dream.

There was triumph, triumph, triumph down the scarlet glit-
      tering street;
    The town was mad; a man was like a boy.
A thousand flags were flaming where the sky and city meet;
    A thousand bells were thundering the joy.
There was music, mirth and sunshine; but some eyes shone
      with regret;
    And while we stun with cheers our homing braves,
O God, in Thy great mercy, let us nevermore forget
    The graves they left behind, the bitter graves.
          —ROBERT SERVICE, *The March of the Dead*

New York City, New York, United States of America.
Monday, June 12, 2000, 2:31 P.M.:

Roberto Jimenez was grim-faced as he prepared for his new assignment. In a well-guarded office of the United Nations building, he scanned hundreds of international military files, and thousands of résumés and letters already received on-line from civilians, mostly mercenaries, who were offering their services in the hunting of vampires.

And that, Roberto knew, was his new job description, the new definition of his life. He had become, sometime in the last week, the world's most powerful vampire hunter.

Upon his return from Salzburg, Roberto had been dogged by every media personality in the world. After that first day, he had disappeared. In modern times, you weren't supposed to be able to do that, but Roberto was not Commander of the UNSF for nothing. He had gone underground, and only the secretary general, Rafael Nieto, and the new President of the United States knew where. And even that had been a mistake. The two men had spent four days playing "Berto in the middle," as each vied for his political support.

He didn't know which of them he hated more. Secretary General Nieto was a pacifist, who had made extraordinary strides toward world peace during his tenure as the most powerful man in the world. He was personally repulsed by the vampires—even he wasn't calling them shadows anymore—but he insisted that, like humans, they were a basically decent race with an inordinate number of bad apples.

President Galin, on the other hand, was a madman. Every day that passed, Roberto became more and more incredulous that the world media hadn't picked it up yet. Galin was certifiable, and Nieto certainly thought so. But on the other hand, Galin wanted to wipe vampires from the face of the Earth, and Roberto couldn't argue with that philosophy. In Roberto Jimenez's mind, the Venice Jihad and the Massacre at Salzburg would not have happened if the vampires had not existed. He couldn't help but blame them.

Though he'd sensed a certain nobility in a couple of the vampires he'd dealt with, they were too dangerous to be allowed to survive, to multiply, and Hannibal had declared war, after all. Roberto thought the creatures should be taken out like rabid dogs, and Galin was the number one proponent of that side of the issue. Problem was, Galin was rabid, too, and Roberto didn't trust him at all. Luckily, politics had forced Nieto to at least meet Galin halfway, and that's where Jimenez had come in.

His new orders were to assemble an international tracking and investigation team to find vampires, as well as a corps of one hundred 8-member strike teams, eight hundred people whose job it would be to terminate individual vampires. They had assumed that most of the vampires would go back to their old patterns, mainly hiding in plain sight, alone. But some would gather in packs, or covens, as Allison Vigeant's book about the Venice Jihad explained. In that case, the strike teams could operate in hundreds of combinations.

According to Nieto, the whole thing had been set up just to track down Hannibal's coven and eliminate it, and him. But Galin had assured Roberto, and Nieto had quietly admitted, that this was merely the beginning. Commander Roberto Jimenez was setting up a worldwide search-and-destroy mission—a mission with no time constraints, few legal parameters.

Killing vampires had now become his life's work.

London, England, European Union.
Monday, June 12, 2000, 11:59 A.M.:

Marie Wilkins was looking for a new job. She was a pretty woman, though not as smart as most people thought. With her jet-black hair and formidable figure, she stuck out in a crowd of fair, thin British women. It had definitely helped her on interviews so far. So what if she couldn't type more than thirty-five words a minute. As far as she was concerned, with her legs, that wouldn't matter.

As she walked down Tottenham Court Road, still several blocks from her next interview, Marie's mind was on Kev, the new man in her life. He smoked too much and drank too much, he liked his sex rough and tumble, and his every word to her outside the sack was sharp and biting. They'd only met a couple of nights ago, but already Marie thought she was in love.

He was a big wanker, was Kev, and she liked them big. Strong. Bullies had always been her get, and that's the way she liked it. Oh, she didn't want them to hurt her, really. Not unless she asked for it. But she wanted to know they could if they wanted to. She wanted to be with a man who was a danger to her, who could overpower her and beat her bloody anytime he wanted.

That was why she'd gone after Rolf Sechs originally, and why she'd lost interest long before the vampire disappeared. When Marie had taken the job as receptionist/secretary for the Shadow Justice System offices in London, she liked the mute right away. It didn't matter that he couldn't speak, what thrilled Marie was that he was far stronger, far more dangerous than any man she'd ever been with. The pay hadn't been great, but she'd taken the job just the same, and Rolf had been an excellent lover.

If you went for that sensitive, gentle stuff.

Sure, he could have killed her in a flash, but Marie knew there was no chance of that ever happening. She'd lost interest in Rolf pretty quickly. At the same time, the office politics between him and Hannibal had been so interesting that she'd kept sleeping with Rolf just to infuriate the old man, who clearly wanted a poke at her himself.

And that wasn't going to happen. Hannibal didn't just feel dangerous. Marie liked men to be cruel to her; it made her feel wanted, needed. She was sure that had to do with Daddy. But she didn't want to die. And look how that had turned out. Hannibal and his flunkies had been blamed for hundreds of murders in the past five days alone. Office politics had become global politics. She'd been questioned by UN investigators and just about everyone else she'd ever heard of, not to mention plenty she hadn't. Most of those people had been mean to her, but not in any intimate way.

Ah, but Kev—she'd known the moment she'd seen him in the pub. One look at the scowl on his face and she knew he'd be coming back to her place. Her friends were all uptight bitches, though she loved them still. But they couldn't understand her, in fact denied that she could truly enjoy being with men like Kev. They just didn't get it. These men were powerful, were dangerous and cruel. But when they were inside her, no matter how rough they were, no matter how she whimpered, she was in charge. They had to have her, and that was the real power.

Her girlfriends just didn't understand. In fact, some of them were ashamed of her. *Fuck 'em*, Marie thought, *I know what I like*.

The morning had started out sunny, but the clouds had rolled in almost right away, and now it had started to rain. It was just a drip drop at first, but she knew that it would be pissin' down in no time.

Heaven forbid I should take the tube!

Two blocks from the Mackeson Building, where she hoped to find a job, since they were paying better than the others, it did finally begin to pour, and now she tried to run in her heels without falling on her face. Only a block-and-a-half to go, and then she'd take a taxi home after. She put her leather bag on top of her head, trying to keep her hair as dry as possible under the circumstances. God, she was going to make a horrendous first impression, she thought. She could probably kiss the job good-bye.

Marie was dodging now, around other people who were trying to get in out of the rain. And then suddenly she couldn't dodge. There was a man in front of her and there was no way she could get around him. Instead, she plowed into the bastard and sent them both tumbling into the rain-filled gutter along the pavement.

"Uhhfff!" Marie gasped as she hit the ground, closing her eyes as the dirty water splashed into her face. She was soaked to the bone in half a second, and she shook her head to try to sort out her thoughts.

She could hear the chuckles over the clumsy scene even with the rain absorbing and replacing most of the sounds around her. Marie tried to sit up, wanting to be away from the water as quickly as possible, but she couldn't. The man she had run into, who was wearing a long raincoat, had landed with his legs across her lower torso. His hair was silver-gray—an old man, then? She worried for a moment that she might actually have hurt him. Even though she was furious about her clothes, about the interview she would now have to cancel, Marie felt guilty.

"Here, you," she said, tapping on the man's shoulder even as he pushed himself off the ground with both hands. "Are you all right, then? I didn't mean to—"

And then, rather than pulling his legs off her, the old man pushed himself over onto her, trapping her arms and legs, her body, beneath him, like so many of her lovers had done. She had enjoyed it then, but now . . .

Marie saw his face, finally, and she screamed as his teeth sank into her neck, there in the gutter, in the cold rainwater. People all around began to yell, rushing forward to punch and kick the man, but he did not move away. Marie Wilkins stared down into the ice-blue eyes of her own death, into the eyes of Hannibal. After a moment, her screaming stopped, and her eyes felt as if they were going to burst from her face as she watched the vampire drink her blood. She heard the whistle of a bobby on the way, but she knew he would come too late.

"I will never be denied again!" Hannibal told her triumphantly, the smile on his face terrible. Cruel.

He punched a clawed hand through her chest and crushed her heart.

Her brain could not understand, but her eyes still recorded the vampire's transformation to mist.

And then they were both gone.

*New Orleans, Louisiana, United States of America.
Monday, June 12, 2000, 8:37 P.M.:*

In a three-story home with terraces that hung out over Decatur Street, four blocks from Jackson Square in the French Quarter, a small group of humans and shadows crowded into their living room. They shared this home, living together, in peace, and if anyone on the streets of New Orleans knew that vampires lived on Decatur Street, they weren't saying. They were used to the presence of shadows, and not much interested in politics. As long as their sons and daughters didn't go missing in the middle of the night, they weren't about to start trouble with the neighbors.

The room was Old South, as befitted the house. Will Cody and Allison Vigeant snuggled together on the love seat. Peter Octavian looked at his reflection in the window and ran a hand through his long hair to flatten it, a familiar gesture which only reaffirmed his identity to those in the room. Erika Hunter shared the long couch with Rolf Sechs, and Joe Boudreau sat on the floor with his back against it. They all looked up as Stefan came down the stairs.

"How is he?" Peter asked, his eyebrows knitted with concern.

"Sleeping fitfully," Stefan said. "Even with the blood we've all given, his legs have barely begun to grow. I wonder . . ."

Stefan left the thought unfinished, but they all knew where he was going with it, for they had wondered as well. Charlemagne was to have been their leader now. If he had given up, if his will was not strong enough to heal him, to replace his amputated limbs, then Peter would lead them. And they all knew, as well, that Peter didn't really want the job. The mood in the house was somber.

Will, Peter and Allison had arrived only a few hours earlier, with Stefan and Charlemagne in their care. Erika and Rolf had been there a full day, and had been met by Joe Boudreau and George Marcopoulos, who had already begun to ready the house for them. It was a new beginning, set up for them by Meaghan Gallagher. Now that the others had arrived, and though George was not yet home from making a most important phone call, they finally had time to mourn, together, everything and everyone they had lost.

They mourned for Alexandra Nueva, for Meaghan Gallagher, and for Elissa Thomas. They mourned for Martha, Isaac and Jared, and for John Courage. They mourned for Lazarus, who might be dead or trapped forever in the bowels of Hell. They mourned for an old king who lived in agony, and his faithful warriors, who had been resurrected only to truly and finally die, but whose valor had been instrumental in their salvation. They mourned for Annelise and Carlo, whose last names Rolf and Erika were forced to admit they had never known. They mourned for all those nameless soldiers and civilians, humans and vampires, who had died at the hands of Hannibal and Mulkerrin and the lords of Hell. And they mourned for themselves, forced to live in a world where they would be hunted by both humans and vampires, trapped between two sides in a war, like all others, without a victor.

They rejoiced to have discovered the true nature of shadows, to know their history, to have obtained a foundation for the future. They planned for the future, together, and spoke excitedly about their proselytizing mission, to seek out shadows across the Earth and bring them to their cause, to enlighten them with the truth about themselves, to undermine Hannibal's barbaric efforts.

They worried about the new American President, his hatred for shadows, and George Marcopoulos's contention that the man was insane. They hoped that one day human-ity's leadership would have more vision, better perception, and see that for all their power, vampires—shadows—were more like humans than not like them. They wished they didn't have to hide, and secretly, sometimes, that they had remained hidden.

"If wishes were horses," Allison said when that was men-tioned, and a light chuckle filled the room.

"There's no going back," Cody added. "We move for-ward or we die."

"I'm not prepared to die again," Octavian said.

"So what then?" Joe Boudreau asked. "We just hide out, wait for the humans to hunt us down?"

"We find Hannibal," Erika said gravely, "and we kill him. That's half our problem taken care of."

"I'm not so sure—" Stefan began, but Erika cut him off. "*I'm* sure," she said.

"And then?" Allison asked, her eyes on her lover, Will Cody.

"And then, darlin'," Cody said and squeezed her hand, "we start chipping away at the world outside. But we start by taking care of each other. Our own coven, in a way, but the first made up of shadows *and* humans. We stick to-gether, and watch out for one another, and we'll be just fine."

"I wish I could believe that," Erika said, and it was Rolf, next to her on the couch, who answered in his own way. He reached out and stroked her cheek and merely nodded, as if to say, *Believe it*.

They were quiet after that.

A few minutes later, George Marcopoulos came in, ready to tell them that the UN had joined the American declaration of war against all vampires, but before he got two sentences out of his mouth, he saw Allison and Will. And Peter.

Peter Octavian, his best friend, whom he had thought dead for five long years, whose survival he had been unaware of until that very moment. He couldn't say a word as Peter crossed the room and took him in his arms. Peter was gentle, for George was getting old, but they hugged each other tight. They were like father and son, though which was which had never been certain.

"Oh, my friend," George finally whispered into the silence of the room, "I missed you. We have so much to talk about."

And so George took his place in the high-backed chair that had been left empty for him, put his feet up on the ottoman while Joe went to get him a cup of tea, and told them all that the stakes had risen higher still. And he told them of the death of his wife, Valerie, the only woman he had ever loved, who had apparently missed him too much.

Once again they mourned, they remembered, they cried. Later, they laughed and talked and dreamed. Finally, when it was far past George's bedtime and they admitted that they all needed rest, they prayed.

Together.

THE ULTIMATE IN FANTASY!

From magical tales of distant worlds to stories of those with abilities beyond the ordinary, Ace and Roc have everything you need to stretch your imagination to its limits.

Marion Zimmer Bradley/Diana L. Paxson

Guy Gavriel Kay

Dennis L. McKiernan

Patricia A. McKillip

Robin McKinley

Sharon Shinn

Katherine Kurtz

Barb and J. C. Hendee

Elizabeth Bear

T. A. Barron

Brian Jacques

Robert Asprin

penguin.com

M12G1107

Penguin Group (USA) Online

What will you be reading tomorrow?

Patricia Cornwell, Nora Roberts, Catherine Coulter,
Ken Follett, John Sandford, Clive Cussler,
Tom Clancy, Laurell K. Hamilton, Charlaine Harris,
J. R. Ward, W.E.B. Griffin, William Gibson,
Robin Cook, Brian Jacques, Stephen King,
Dean Koontz, Eric Jerome Dickey, Terry McMillan,
Sue Monk Kidd, Amy Tan, Jayne Ann Krentz,
Daniel Silva, Kate Jacobs...

You'll find them all at
penguin.com

*Read excerpts and newsletters,
find tour schedules and reading group guides,
and enter contests.*

Subscribe to Penguin Group (USA) newsletters
and get an exclusive inside look
at exciting new titles and the authors you love
long before everyone else does.

PENGUIN GROUP (USA)
penguin.com